THE KINDLY ONES

Also by Caroline Stickland

The Standing Hills
A House of Clay
The Darkness of Corn
An Ancient Hope
The Darkening Leaf

THE KINDLY ONES

Caroline Stickland

HEADLINE

Copyright © 2000 Caroline Stickland

The right of Caroline Stickland to be identified as the Author of
the Work has been asserted by her in accordance with
the Copyright, Designs and Patents Act 1988.

First published in 2000
by HEADLINE BOOK PUBLISHING

10 9 8 7 6 5 4 3 2 1

All rights reserved. No part of this publication may be
reproduced, stored in a retrieval system, or transmitted,
in any form or by any means without the prior written
permission of the publisher, nor be otherwise circulated
in any form of binding or cover other than that in which
it is published and without a similar condition being
imposed on the subsequent purchaser.

All characters in this publication are fictitious and any
resemblance to real persons, living or dead, is purely coincidental.

British Library Cataloguing in Publication Data

Stickland, Caroline, 1955–
The kindly ones
I. Title
823.9'14[F]

ISBN 0 7472 7351 0 (hardback)
ISBN 0 7472 7352 9 (trade paperback)

Typeset by Avon Dataset Ltd, Bidford-on-Avon, Warks

Printed and bound in Great Britain by
Mackays of Chatham plc, Chatham, Kent

HEADLINE BOOK PUBLISHING
A division of the Hodder Headline Group
338 Euston Road
London NW1 3BH

www.headline.co.uk
www.hodderheadline.com

To
William

NOTTINGHAMSHIRE LEISURE SERVICES	
Cypher	2.8.00
	£17.99

Prologue

1871

He was wearing mourning. It was inappropriate for a bridegroom but no one tried to persuade him to do otherwise. There were whispers, of course, and those who said that black gloves could not hide the blood on his hands.

The room was dark. A wavering gleam on the ivory brush, abandoned on the window-sill, showed that the winter sun was gaining strength but its vigour had not yet lightened the dusk within the walls.

He tilted the cheval-glass and regarded himself. A young face made older by experience looked out into the shadows where he stood. Margrave of Vauchurch; a name that merited shadows. Adjusting his cravat, he felt how melancholy his appearance was but the weight of the past was too heavy for gaiety. He was used to rumour; he almost courted it. Let people say what they would.

'Frank, are you ready? The carriage is at the gate.'

His sister came through from the connecting sitting room and, putting her prayer-book down, smoothed his already perfect hair.

'Not so severe, my love,' she said. 'This is a day for joy. Nothing need be remembered.'

'Can you forget so easily?'

'There is always death.' She picked up her book. 'There may be celebration too. This is a new beginning.'

'Oh?' He considered her words. 'Is this an end to guilt?'

'Come,' she said, and led him to the door.

PART ONE

Vengeance Begins

1855

Chapter One

He could see that all the world believed the day to be hot. It was, he had already been told three times, a perfect June morning and likely to set fair for the week. The information had been irritating enough for him to cut the third weather-prophet, the ostler who had hired him the raw-boned nag on which he rode, short in mid-sentence, adding remarks in a native dialect that would have made his servants quake at his displeasure. Dorset, however, was not Delhi and he spoke only to relieve his feelings.

Since he had set foot in England, he had fallen into the habit of deriding all things English. He was, of course, English himself, being the son of a Sussex-born nabob and the London miss his father had snapped up on a rare visit to these shores, crossing marriage off the perpetual list of matters to accomplish that had helped build so successful a trade empire. His origins did not prevent him condemning every difference from home that came under his eye. The whole of his twenty-eight years had been spent in various provinces of India. His father, brisk in all his operations, had ensured that the new Mrs Eliot had been gravid when she boarded ship for Calcutta and the infant Paul, now surveying sunlit hamstone with a scowl, had made his appearance behind the marble walls of a usurped palace.

He was used to luxury, to respect from business rivals, deference from employees and casual disdain from the civil servants and military of the East India Company, who considered their callings superior to his own. It was not a mixture that was suited to any weakness of character and it had not improved his failings. The wealth commerce had brought his family was too much a part of his being for him ever to have imagined what he would have been without it, but his lazy arrogance made him resentful that he did not have the idleness and status of a gentleman. In India, he felt the smallest slight that came his way with exaggerated sensitivity, but the power of his position gave him the confidence of a merchant prince; in England, where rank was still so rooted in land, he felt at a disadvantage. It was a comfort to be critical and tell himself, as he gazed right and left at the townspeople going about their affairs, that he could buy and sell any one of them.

This fortifying consciousness made the spavined creature ambling beneath him all the more galling. It is generally an outrage to the rich that money cannot secure them what they demand on the instant of their making their desires known, and Eliot felt it to be an insult to his dignity that no better horse than this could be provided by Sherborne's livery stable. The assurances that finer could be had by waiting until noon were no help. It did not fit his purpose to dally in the town. His host expected to receive him that evening and it was Eliot's intention to catch the household on the wrong foot by arriving before preparations had been completed. Apologies and back-stairs bustle would soothe his sensibilities.

A nursemaid was struggling to cross Cheap Street with two bumptious charges and a wheezing pug. He reined in to let her pass, holding out his whip to halt a dray that was approaching. The driver's obedience to his gesture pleased him and the young woman's grateful smile and swiftly downcast glance set his thoughts into a more entertaining train. He was a lascivious man, and the months since he had parted from the plump, adoring concubine he kept in the cool, scented privacy of his secondary residence, where peacocks dragged their tails beneath silken awnings and, beyond the gates, cranes stalked stiff-legged on white sandbanks, had come to be a tedium and torment. Recollections of evenings more carnal and satisfactory than those spent in the roast-beef atmosphere of railway hotels diverted him as he rode slowly out of the town. Relaxation stole upon him.

There were only two miles to travel before he would reach Knapp, where he was to visit another of those useful acquaintances his father had dispatched him to cultivate. He had already made himself intimate with those London merchants whose ways of thought and living corresponded with his own. Forston and, further to the west, Margrave were an unsettling variation on a theme. Two brothers of an old family, they had come by accidents of birth and inheritance to unite ancient property and position, with trade as profitable and far-reaching as that of the Eliots'. Their situation was anomalous in this country where impecunious landowners believed they were conferring favours by marrying the fabulously rich daughters of Manchester men. He could not anticipate whether they would fall on the side of fellow box-wallahs or treat him as though he were expected to enter by the back door. It was this uncertainty that was leading him to arrive early.

As the morning ripened, he began to feel the heat. The chill that had seemed to cling to his flesh since he had left the Mediterranean changed to an inclination to remove his light riding-coat. Haymakers, raking long swathes of sweet grass in the meadows beside the lane, had rolled their shirt-sleeves above their elbows, and skin that rarely saw the light of day was reddening above their hard, brown hands. Cattle stood still and somnolent in the shrinking shade of oaks.

It was as well that he had been told his way. The valley that wound towards Knapp was as deserted as if it had been abandoned by mankind. Wooded hills rose in soft undulations to each side. There was no sound but the slow rhythm of his horse's hooves. Even the birdsong had died in the sultry air.

His angry trepidation returned. Before him, high wrought-iron gates opened onto a curving avenue of limes. Stone gryphons in unlikely helmets gazed disapprovingly down upon him from a pair of pillars as they clutched eroded shields in their claws. They were the embodiment of old money, that easily-gained plum that gave its recipient so unshakeable a conviction of superiority over those whose wealth smelt of the warehouse.

He kicked his horse and entered the gates. Bees were busy amongst the limes, filling the vividly green tunnel with an all-enclosing drone. There was no reason for anxiety. Forston might come of a parchment pedigree but this manor-house, where Henry Tudor had sat cannily calculating its worth, had come to him from his mother's uncle and had required the forfeit of his surname as its due. Gerard Forston had been bought; he had considered the prize and deemed it worth the payment required. It was an action that showed how little difference there was between lineage and a balance sheet.

His plan to cause dismay came to nothing. The master was from home, the mistress at some distant point within the park and arrangements for his lodging already made. He found it did not distress him. There was no hint of contempt in the manner of manservant or maid. It was enough to instruct that Mrs Forston was not to be searched out; he would take the offered glass of wine and seek her himself. As he smoothed his hair in a room where the bed-hangings were Georgian toile-de-jouy and rose-petals floated in his washing-ewer, he felt pampered and restored to his proper place.

A footman was waiting in the hall when Eliot descended the stairs. A lad had been sent to fetch sir's luggage from the station, he said, and might he lead the way through the grounds? He might not. The drowsy atmosphere of the silent valley and quiet house was affecting Eliot strangely. A tale told him long ago of a knight cutting through a forest of briars to find a princess, a hundred years asleep, had come into his mind and charmed him. It would be amusing to indulge this fanciful mood while wandering in pursuit of the, no doubt, matronly Mrs Forston. He stepped out onto the flagstones alone.

The air had grown stifling; it shimmered above the moss-grown balustrade. Heat smelt differently here from the pungent weight of summers he had known. Scents he could not name hung above plants that showed no sign of having been without rain. He walked down the shallow steps from the terrace and through an ornate garden of intricate beds with gravel paths leading to, from and round a sundial. She was not there. He did not expect her to be. It was a day for resting in the shade.

A pergola of ripe, red roses, with heads too heavy for their stems, led on to a grassed walk between high borders of clematis and loosestrife. He could have left the path to enter an enclosure where a marble shepherd poured water everlastingly from a jug and doves murmured in their round, stone cott but she was not there.

He went on to the end of the walk and opened the gate into the wood. This was another land; no longer formal yet not quite wild. Paths were plainly kept free of leaves and encroaching branches; honeysuckle had been trained into picturesque drifts. It was welcoming. He stepped into the shade as he might have slid into a lake, feeling the dim light press against his face with a deceptive impression of being cool.

There was a sudden movement and a small, brightly-coloured bird flashed between the hazels and up into an elm. It was yellow, black and red; inappropriate, he thought, in this English setting and he could not identify it easily. The memory of a book of watercolours, studied in his youth, at last gave him 'goldfinch' but the necessity for thought reminded him that he was 'country-

8

born', contemptible to those raised amongst scenes like these, who carried ignorance of their Indian surroundings like a badge of honour. Anger against Forston flickered in him again.

He walked further into the wood. The silence of the valley had been replaced by the slumberous hum of insects and the barely-heard flow of a stream he could not see. She was not there; he must go deeper.

His quarry eluded him. The sunlight fell through the trees in pillars of midge-hazed brilliance. When he raised his face to the sky, the radiance of the leaves dazzled his sight. A butterfly wavered across the path, its wings first white, then olive as it reached the shade. He felt sweat begin against his skin.

A sound he knew but could not place drew him between hawthorns, whose writhing branches closed a hand's breadth above his head. The path turned to run beside a curved yew hedge. A Gothic archway had been clipped into the yew.

She was there. He pressed back into the dark, night-scented foliage, the stiff mass of twigs resisting his desire to watch unseen.

A young woman stood within the wide circle of the hedge. The turf was smooth beneath her feet and she was braced lightly against it as she drew the string of her bow. Her arm straightened, her fingers poised for release; there was an instant of perfect rigidity, upright yet sinuous, a promise of movement, and the arrow flew. He could not see the target but he heard again the sound he had half-recognised, the thud of a shaft entering straw. She considered what she had done, smiled at her reflection in the stone-rimmed pool by her side and walked forward out of his sight.

It was unlike him to be tentative with women. He leant against the hedge and closed his eyes. A moment more and he was himself. Stepping out of concealment, he was revealed beneath the arch. There was a hiss, a swift motion of air and an arrow passed his cheek. It struck a thick limb of yew and its immediate stillness bewildered him with its impression of having always been there. He stared at the branch whose scarred and pock-marked bark showed its familiarity with victimhood.

Her footsteps were soft and unhurried as she came towards him with no trace of embarrassment or concern disturbing her composure. She noted the shocked reverence that passed across the stranger's face and accepted it as her due.

Eliot thought of wrenching the arrow from the wood to present to her but it was so far embedded that it might merely give rise to unmanly struggles; he contented himself with removing his hat.

'You almost pierced my heart,' he said.

The vision smiled. 'It's agreeable to find that a gentleman has a heart to pierce,' she said. 'Tell me, who would I have destroyed?'

'My name is Eliot. If you are Mrs Forston, I am come to exact your hospitality before my hour.'

'Mr Eliot? You're our Indian, bringing the news and habits of exotic lands. Do you drink sherbet?'

'It has been known.'

'I offer only more familiar temptations. Let me refresh you with lemonade. Or don't you find our temperate summers hot?'

'I feel a surprising warmth.'

She turned, beckoning him to follow and he walked slightly behind in order that his view should be unimpaired. He was aware that she felt his scrutiny but it caused her no diffidence. Why should it do so? Such beauty must summon veneration in all who chanced to see it. Homage would have been paid to this face, this form, since they first flowered. If admiration had abashed her, she would have needed to live veiled and cloistered.

She led him to a pavilion set close against the yew. The rill that fed and emptied the pool at the centre of the grassy circle flowed through a basin let into the ground to add to the natural and artificial luxuries of the park. A corked bottle lay within it, the waters rippling over its amber glass. She took two porcelain cups from a fretted cupboard within the pavilion and sank down on to the turf to fill them from the bottle. The broad-brimmed hat, which had hung against her back by its ribbons whilst she took aim, covered her eyes as she poured and its shadow played over lips that opened a trifle with concentration. Her white gown spread round her in graceful folds, her green, plush quiver lay at her slender waist and emphasised the incongruousness of her warlike pastime. She was as she wished to seem.

Eleanor Forston was glad that Eliot was here. Her restlessness had been so great that morning that only the violence of archery would relieve it. She was a woman with no inner resources beyond the appreciation of her effect on others; no talent beyond the ability to fascinate by the simple fact of her presence. To say that she was beautiful was to describe the length and breadth and depth of her. It was her fortune to be the ideal image of her age, a fair angel with colour flushing and retreating from a pale, fragile

10

face, yet with this image raised and made timeless by some process of unconscious response to the longings of spectators. She could be as placidly come-hither as a bowl of cream, as voluptuous as a lily but she could not have been an actress. Thought played no part in her instinctive actions.

Vanity was all her being yet the word vain implied a sharpness in her character that did not exist. She was without rough edges and softly pursued her comfort with the smooth inevitability of the stars in their courses. Her boredom on this delightful day was immense. She believed that she too was declining from bright morning to afternoon, and the prospect of evening was repellent.

She had married Gerard Forston ten years before when she was eighteen. The match had been her choice and had been approved by her relations, who, though of a higher social rank than either the Forstons or Margraves, were inclined to entangle themselves in scandals – a circumstance that made them understand the value of solid wealth. She had never had any ambition except to be the idolised wife of a rich man, and even this ending to her maidenhood had been so confidently expected that it was as unremarkable as the ambition of ivy to wind itself about a tree. A fortune and respect for her loveliness were the tributes she demanded, but the years passed and they failed to be entirely satisfying. She was tired of her surroundings and acquaintance and, most particularly, of her husband.

Forston had been astounded that it was he, of all her suitors, who had won her hand but a decade of possessing that hand, of sitting opposite that face, had necessarily made his devotion less ardent. He had grown inclined to grumble that she could not order a good dinner if the gravy were not just so; he had been seen to chuck the coachman's sister under the chin; he had asked her to pull off his boots. She craved worship and variety with a petulant resentment that neither came unbidden.

Holding the two filled cups, she rose with a pretty, exaggerated care and carried them into the pavilion. It was a miniature Chinoiserie fancy, with scarlet lacquered dragons, that had room only for two wrought-iron seats and a table in the shape of a roofless pagoda.

Eliot sat holding the cup she had given him with a sensation of peculiar gratitude to the Fates who had brought him to be seated in this Oriental nonsense with such a creature. Was there a world outside the circle of yew? He thought not. The winding path had

11

delivered him to the Musselman's paradise and he would lounge there for ever, taking cups from the houri's hand.

'My husband will be sorry you had to make your own way here,' the ministering angel said. 'He intended to send a carriage to meet the evening train. We don't usually treat our guests so sorely.'

'It was my horse – and I use the term loosely – that treated me sorely. Knock-knees and cross-eyes were the least of it, but if you arrive unexpectedly you must take what you can get and accept that you'll frighten old ladies in the street.'

Eleanor leant back against her chair. In the shade of the pavilion, her skin was dusky. 'Perhaps,' she said, 'they thought you carried your travels with you and were riding an exotic beast.'

'I'm sorry to have brought shame to the House of Forston. I'll have four men and a palanquin hurry the poor brute away.'

She thought it did not matter what was said. An unaccustomed calm was growing in her as she sat with this man who was acting with an informality that made her at once reassured and fevered. He unbuttoned his riding jacket, stretching out his legs to cross them at the ankle. In the close air, she could smell the fine leather and wax of his boots. He threw aside his hat, running his palm over the sweep of his hair. She could smell sandalwood, rich, foreign and familiar. He reached forward to put down his cup and the motion released the moist scent of tobacco into the heat. She did not want to go from this place.

They sat until a faint bell summoned them away. The sun was at its height and they were blinded alternately by darkness and glare as they entered the wood. They chose a different path, one that he did not know and she rarely used, and made game of being lost so that it was hard to say who led and who followed.

The plateau dominated the landscape. Massive and gorse-covered, it loured over hills that were themselves precipitously steep, causing heedless travellers to underestimate the effort it would take to reach its foot. The promontory that jutted out on its seaward side had been the home of man since Iron Age tribes had raised the great earth banks that encircled its heights; obscure gods had witnessed bloody sacrifice on its slopes where the wild daffodils blew amongst the blackthorn; Romans, weary of warfare, had looked down from its summit and seen beckoning valleys where fields could be ploughed.

Scholars differ over how the first Margrave to take possession of the eyrie came to have his name upon the deeds. Records have been lost. Some say that he was fortunate in marriage; others that there were convenient deaths. What is certain is that he and his descendants had a talent for being on the winning side of whatever turmoil was disturbing the nation and, having settled at Vauchurch, they determined to remain. Prodigious avarice coupled with an eye for a bargain increased their property and thus their influence. For three centuries, they prospered and their name was feared by those who opposed their whims.

Financial twilight fell upon the Margraves in the 1700s. Unwise speculations brought disaster in their trail. The family retrenched; ancient stands of timber were hauled away, leaving bare hillsides pocked with stumps as a public pronouncement of humiliation; farms at the edges of the estate were sold in angry, astonished despair and still debts mounted. There being no prospects for him in his homeland, the younger son was despatched to India where he observed the ways of Clive and found them good. He was a natural adventurer, untroubled by conscience, and when an opportune bout of scarlet fever deprived him of both father and elder brother, he returned to be master of Vauchurch with a fortune in plunder. What was left of the Moghul empire was glad to see him go.

He was a practical man. It was his decree that there should be no resting on landowner's laurels. His own sons were brought up to trade in tea and indigo, jute, sugar and silk. The family developed a robust and unrepentant attitude to commerce which was cloaked by their old, respected name.

The two representatives of this driving tradition were presently walking along the outer bank of the earthworks towards the gardens that separated the deer-haunted park from the courtyards behind the house. An irregular chipping of stone grew louder as they approached. A slight breeze carried a salt tang from the sea that was glittering in the distance, making the day fresher than it was at Knapp.

'I can't stay much longer,' Forston said. 'I'll be hard-pressed to get home before that Eliot fella arrives as it is.'

Margrave ignored his protests, aware that his brother was in no hurry for a hot ride along sunbaked lanes.

'He's coming on the seven o'clock train,' Forston continued.

'So you said.'

'I wish him to the devil. If I'm to go to Liverpool next week, I'd prefer not to be nursemaiding a stranger.'

'Leave him to Eleanor.' Margrave waved his cheroot. 'Let her do what she's good at. You'll need to wait until Charlotte's finished her letter, anyway. We'll never hear the end of it if we prevent their gossip. Though what they can find to say...'

He shrugged and looked irritably back at the house where his wife was writing a note which, while not containing any secret matter, she would seal with the impress of her ring in the wax, thwarting untoward curiosity on the part of either brother. Of course, the men could assert their rights and open any letter, however sealed, and she acted only to prove a point.

Marrying sisters, who each had money settled upon them that was protected by lawyers used to hampering husbands, had not been as tranquil as the brothers could wish. Forston was the more contented of the two. Less restless and predatory than Margrave and having chosen the more indolent sister, he found little to annoy him in his marriage. It was true that he did sometimes marvel at Eleanor's ability to exist without any suggestion of thinking, but this was no bad thing in a woman, keeping her from inventing dissatisfactions and plaguing him for novelty. His domestic life ran smoothly onwards, the same today as yesterday, with never a hint of the suppressed struggle for supremacy that marred the peace at Vauchurch.

Charlotte had been born to wear breeches and Margrave was not the man to let her. Tyrannical by nature, he had no tenderness for women, believing them to be good only for breeding and housekeeping. The very sight of his daughters, who were not yet of an age to have embraced the useful activities of their sex, aggravated him and induced a feeling of peevish helplessness as if he were faced with animals of unknown habits that might or might not be dangerous. Finding the two girls sitting with their mother was enough to send the blood rushing to his face and make him suspect unspecified malignant schemes were being woven against him. He despised the lack of spirit of submissive women and yet resented his wife's strong character. It was a mystery to him, when he could put his finger on no diminution of his authority, that Charlotte's presence constantly provoked him into asserting that he would have mastery in his own home.

'I see you've had the pantry window reglazed,' Forston said, nodding down at the house.

Margrave had not realised that he had stopped walking as he thought of his wife's contrariness. He laughed. 'You heard about that?'

'Charlotte wrote to Eleanor of it.'

'Frank's a rare hand with a catapult,' Margrave said. 'No one could wish for a boy more ready to seize the moment. Unfortunately, his intentions and their consequences are often at variance. His aim isn't what it might be.'

'The stable cat's safe, then?'

'I think it always was.' Margrave gestured towards the kitchen-court and a thin line of smoke hung above the movement. 'He says the cat was stalking a pigeon but the Boots says the cook was just bending to examine a basket of peas and Mrs Martin has a fine, tempting rump for a target. I like a lad to be fond of sport.'

They stood and looked down at the house for a moment, remembering youthful mischief of their own it had seen. That first Margrave of Vauchurch had understood how to build a house to last. He had been adamant that he was not raising a castle, for his was not a century in which to give kings any uneasiness, but Portland stone was to be had close by and it was only prudent to erect a building that could be defended at a pinch. The house had been added to over the years, but the fundamental structure remained and the impression it gave was of formidable strength.

The cessation of the chipping that had accompanied their walk along the earth bank roused them and set Margrave to looking impatiently at his watch.

'What have they stopped for?' he said. 'This isn't an authorised time.' He closed the watch firmly, thrusting it back into his waistcoat pocket as he turned to pursue his course.

'They're probably just catching their breath,' Forston said amiably. 'It's damnably hot. There'll be no breeze where they are.'

His brother glanced at him contemptuously. 'There'd never be a day's work done if we were all as lax as you,' he said. 'I expect a sovereign's worth for a sovereign's pay.'

'Oh, come.' Forston returned his gaze wryly. 'You always prefer a guinea.'

They descended a flight of steps cut into the turf and let themselves into the formal gardens that ran in a long rectangle of paved paths and geometric flowerbeds behind the house. As they passed through the wicket, the chipping began again and it was plain that the two masons, one balanced confidently on a ladder, the other rummaging industriously in a canvas tool-bag, had not hurriedly recommenced their labours on hearing their employer.

Margrave threw the butt of his cheroot into a carved stone water-tank where it fizzled sharply, sending goldfish darting into the depths, and floated to await the silent wrath of the under-gardener. The workman who had been searching for a particular mallet became aware that the gentlemen had arrived and, tapping his companion's ankle, removed his wide-brimmed straw hat and prepared to be instructed in his craft. Waving the masons aside, Margrave contemplated their progress.

The entire garden was enclosed by a high wall of ruddy, crumbling brick, relieved at intervals by apertures giving views of the parkland that stretched away over the plateau. At the centre of each of the longest sides, grand gateways flanked by hamstone pillars opened widely to let the family ride back to the stable-yard through the elaboration of geraniums and lobelia if they chose. Seen as part of the whole scheme of fiddling carpet-bedding, the gates were discordant and somehow ridiculous, but taken alone they were magnificent and their grandeur was being increased by the addition of monumental lions, rearing skywards under the masons' chisels. The beasts filled Margrave with an appreciation of his ability to command such marvels and he stood splay-legged before them in admiration of his vision.

Forston came to stand at his side. 'Gryphons are always agreeable,' he said.

His brother's levity habitually left Margrave unsure whether Forston were more clever or more simple than appearances would suggest, and he had learnt to ignore many of his remarks. The necessity to reply to this one was removed by a distraction cantering into sight in the shape of Margrave's son and elder daughter, who emerged from behind a distant clump of beeches with crescents of dry turf flying up from their ponies' hooves. It was a vigorous scene for so warm a day and it called up all that there was of love in Margrave's soul.

Frank was sitting his robust Shetland as if every one of his six years had been spent in the saddle. His linen tunic had come adrift from his knickerbockers and ballooned out each time his mount put down its head and kicked its heels in a cheerful sideways twist, but the boy was plainly in no danger of being unseated. It was a display of valour to gladden any father's heart and, at this instant, was especially pleasing because it upheld Margrave's

16

superiority over his brother. He had an heir and Forston did not.

'Kate's become a fine girl,' Forston said.

Margrave had barely noticed her. He looked beyond Frank and the nettled boredom he expected to feel on being obliged to observe his daughter did not come. She was riding carefully behind the boy, clearly tempering her pace to his so that she was always close enough to rescue him from difficulties yet could still give him the belief that he was the leader. It was gracefully done in thought and action. Margrave was too far away to see her expression but her face under the streaming veil of her hat was continually turned to her brother in an attitude of attentive concern that increased the supple elegance of her figure. It struck him for the first time that she was not only eighteen and marriageable but that she could attract men to want to marry her. As he watched the sway of her dark skirts against her dapple-grey mare, he calculated how substantial a settlement he could ask from a husband and, what was more pertinent, what benefit there could be to himself by the prudent selection of the man. His eyes followed her approvingly as she and Frank rounded a clump of aspen and passed out of sight, scattering a herd of deer that fled lightly into the distance.

'We'd better go back to the house,' he said. 'I daresay Charlotte's finished her letter by now.'

They went through the gates, both involuntarily glancing up at the lions, and took the path that ran alongside the wall. The deer had recruited their nerves and were slowing their delicate flight, the swift bounding subsiding into a stiff-legged, head-raised jog-trot before they settled to their interrupted grazing.

Forston thought regretfully of the white hind his brother had shot the previous autumn. He was himself an enthusiastic hunter but he had a liking for female beauty that made him prefer to enjoy it in motion. The creature made an unusual trophy in its glass case in the billiard room, but it had been a finer spectacle stepping timidly out of the mist on a September morning.

Margrave became conscious that they were not alone. He turned suddenly and the favourable sensations that had risen upon viewing his elder daughter deserted him on beholding, as he expected, his younger one.

Olivia had been a disappointment and annoyance from the moment of her birth. There had been a nine-year wait between the production of the sisters, an interval of dedicated endeavour

17

on their father's part that did not even result in the miscarriage or stillbirth that could be expected in such a term. He blamed his wife, going so far as to refer to a barren field on the home-farm as 'Charlotte's Meadow', but there was little satisfaction in baiting a woman whose sarcasms were much more potent than his own. When, at last, it became certain that she was to bear another child, he had no doubt that it was to be the long-anticipated heir. It was a daughter. The news was brought to him in the wine-cellar where he and the butler were discussing which vintage was to be chosen to celebrate the continuation of his name. He ordered that the infant be thrown in the horse-pond and drank himself into oblivion in the roughest of his clarets.

His decree, naturally, was not carried out and Olivia had lived to plague him. She was staring at him with all the intensity of her startling dark eyes and thin, obsessive face. To his irritation, he saw that she had escaped the servants' clutches without her sun-bonnet and her pallor was beginning to redden so that she would need to be scrubbed with lemon-juice, but it was not this nor any simple feature that was most noticeable about her. There was a tension in her manner, composed of adoration and a readiness to take offence, that put him on edge. The adoration was for himself yet it had a quality that did not prevent him suspecting that she shared the vague, malign purpose of her mother and sister. He liked to thwart her but preferred that she put the blame on someone else.

Forston did not trouble to speak to her. The young of the species were of little interest to him, and although he had more affection for his daughter than his niece, this did not raise Hermione to the level of importance attained by his horses and dogs. The specimen of future womanhood glowering at them above its striped stockings had an air of potential danger that was quite out of keeping with flowing hair and starched petticoats.

'What're you doing in the garden without Nurse or your hat?' Margrave demanded.

Olivia did not reply, merely lowering her head while continuing to stare fixedly at him.

'I will have an answer,' he said.

She raised her chin slightly. 'Nurse is talking to Mamma about new boots for Frank,' she said.

'And you should be with them. Your mother told me she wanted you with her until tea.'

18

The child's face grew sullen and she showed no sign of moving. Both men felt an unaccountable powerlessness stealing over them. Margrave exerted himself.

'Be off with you,' he said. 'Do as Mamma says.'

The basilisk turned and walked away, not slipping silently along the grass as she had done when stalking them but grinding her heels into the gravel in a way that made her obedience seem defiant.

'Where's that pup she had trailing about after her?' Forston asked. 'I thought they couldn't be parted.'

'I had it drowned. It was yap-yap-yap all the time and tearing up the newspapers. Couldn't bear the sight of it.'

'And how did that go down?'

'Oh, I had Charlotte tell her it ran away. There were tantrums and sulking and she had to be forbidden to leave the grounds. Seems to have got over it now but we had a week of her prowling about with a mutton-chop, shouting "Bengi!" If she ever turns into a lady, I'm a Dutchman.'

The object of her father's unease had no intention of returning to the house. She felt herself too old for nursery discipline, and the constant company of her nurse was irksome. Her habit of disappearing to be alone was the bane of the servants, who were soundly blamed for her escapes despite both Margrave and Charlotte knowing that no amount of vigilance had proved successful in confining her. It was only the sound of her father's voice that had drawn Olivia out of cover. Continual rebuffs had not dented her peculiarly menacing devotion, and where he was so she would glide towards him as the alligator glides towards its prey.

She turned the corner as if she would follow the path around the walled garden and go indoors by the route Margrave and Forston had come, but as soon as she was hidden from their view she ran down the first earth bank, scrambled up the steep side of the outer rampart by grasping tussocks of grass with her hands and, after looking searchingly about her for incriminating witnesses, lay at full length to roll alarmingly, intoxicatingly to its foot. This manifestation of childishness achieved to her satisfaction, she resumed her usual self and followed the side of the hill to a rocky hollow that formed a rough amphitheatre on the edge of a further precipitous slope. Had she given the matter any thought, she would have realised that it was the romanticism of this

19

secluded place with its lichened stone, its spindle-trees that shivered their delicate leaves in the slightest breeze, its hawthorns, frozen into arthritically balletic contortions by the wind that appealed to her – but she had not analysed its attraction. It was a congenial site to settle for a stolen hour with Sir Walter Scott or a volume of Gothic tales, and it provided one particular treasure in the form of what had once been a stunted oak and had become the decayed shell of a trunk, its cavity large enough to hold a small girl and her secrets.

Olivia hoisted herself into the hole and eased into a sitting position with her knees drawn up and her shoes buried in the bracken with which she had lined her nest. Summer had dried the tree so that the soft musk of wood had none of the sharp overtones of wetter months. She leant back against the trunk, observing the deliberate scars of boring insects, the rusty spores on the wilting ferns, the brilliance of the sky where her refuge opened above her head. It was of no consequence that she would bear the marks of her shelter on her clothes. Her roll down the hill already showed her to be a hoyden and a penance would have to be paid. The rules of life were arbitrary and complicated but retribution was understandable, giving form and security to a difficult world.

However, she must not be missed long enough for a hunt to be made. She delved into the bracken and withdrew a tin box that had held sugared biscuits. Inside, wrapped in oiled cloth was the pocket-book that was one half of the letter she and her cousin exchanged whenever the opportunity arose. At Knapp, concealed beneath a floorboard was a similar book in which Hermione's private thoughts were being recorded for Olivia as Olivia's were in this. At their next meeting, they would smuggle the journals to each other, each reading the lines in the utmost, delectable stealth, adding comments in their meticulous copperplate hands before beginning anew the story of their claustrophobic, neglected lives.

Olivia picked up the pencil and continued: *Mamma told me he had run away but when a week was past the stable-boy said I should not grieve, for the pup's end was merciful and dogs do not fear drowning. He was hushed by Henderson but it was of no avail for then I knew what she had done. Nurse says it is a sin to hate, for the Lord commands that we honour our mother and father but He is a just God and all-seeing and will not punish where hatred is due.*

There were candles burning brightly all around them – in wall-sconces, on the vast stone mantel with its carven heraldic shield, in the three-branched candelabra on the white-clothed table – yet the effect was not to lighten the room but only to create fire in darkness like the line of beacons that calls a warning from hilltop to hilltop in time of war. Eleanor, Forston and Eliot sat in a panelled chamber that had resisted the heat of the day, eating charlotte russe in a pool of night softened by gleams on silver and mahogany, on Eleanor's pale shoulders and pearl-threaded hair.

Forston's ride home through hot lanes that brought him deeper and deeper into the humid, inland air had not made him want to trouble himself for a guest. He had arrived later than he intended, ready to be irritated by servants, wife and stranger but neither Eleanor nor Eliot were in the house and he learnt that the visitor's coming had been so much before its anticipated hour that he could not be expected to apologise for not being in attendance to welcome him. A cold bath, a bottle of seltzer and clean linen encouraged his hospitable instincts, and when the party was summoned to its turtle soup he was prepared to be amiable. He saw at once that Eliot admired Eleanor. This was nothing new and gave him no concern. All men coveted his wife to one degree or another but, so far as he was aware, no vulgar overtures had ever been made to her and he did not fear that they would. He, himself, lusted to possess a certain thoroughbred mare that his friend, Cranton, owned but would never translate that eagerness into theft. Cranton knew of his longing and felt his ownership more keenly for it. A treasure is more precious for other men's envy. He watched Eliot's careful rationing of the attention he paid to Eleanor, the veiled expression in his eyes that gave away what it meant to conceal, and the amused pride that was Forston's usual reaction carried him smoothly through the evening.

Eleanor, too, noticed every glance from Eliot. She sat passively, radiating a satin-swathed beauty, responding when remarks were addressed to her, giving no sign of her bewilderment. She found herself conscious of her body not as an object to be adorned to receive homage but as a thing of flesh and heat connected to her thoughts in a manner foreign to her before. It puzzled her. She felt the blood moving in her veins; she was aware of the depth of each breath she drew. What was this?

She had no experience of desire. The affection that made her marry had been stunted without reaching the lowest ground of passion. Her daughter had been conceived before she had risen

21

from the bridal bed and suddenly she, who expected physical perfection, was thrust into a world of ugliness, bloodshed and the threat of death.

Pregnancy and birth had horrified her. In the years since, she had not resisted Forston's demands because she knew her duty, but she showed no pleasure and he had never believed it necessary that she should. It was only tonight as she looked at her husband's auburn head bent over his dish and at the stranger's quick, dark gaze that she wondered of what she had no words to describe.

Forston let the footman clear his place and took a handful of almonds.

'Margrave's in high feather over those lions,' he said. 'You'd think he was self-made, the way he preens himself about them.'

A stiffness passed over Eliot's face and Forston interpreted it as a lack of understanding.

'My brother's having his masons provide him with a pair of extraordinary beasts to guard his gate-posts in the flower-garden,' he explained, cracking shells with a sharp, explosive force. 'As inappropriate a sight amongst the geraniums as you could wish to see, but you'd think he was a counter-jumper renting his first villa to hear him. Why they should have taken his fancy so, I can't imagine but there – we all have our whims.'

He brushed splinters of shell from the cloth at his elbow and raised one finger to have his glass refilled.

'I daresay you've any amount of queer carvings at your place at home,' he went on. 'Some of the gewgaws we've had shipped over would give you the shivers.'

'I hardly know which house to call home, I'm obliged to travel so much overseeing our estates.'

Eliot was reaching out for a peach as he spoke. His eyes were on Forston as his fingers touched the velvet of the fruit and slid forward over its curve to meet smaller, softer fingertips. The other hand recoiled. He saw Eleanor draw back her arm and her white neck flex as she drew a long breath. They stared at one another before she looked fearfully at her husband, who had been sampling the new bottle of wine and had seen nothing.

Forston put down his glass and noticed Eliot gazing at the epergne.

'Will you try some fruit, sir?' he invited. 'The figs and peaches are from our hot-houses and are quite fine. Or you, my dear,' he turned to Eleanor, 'you're flushed, I think. Some grapes would cool you.'

She was holding her napkin as tightly as a snake.

'I am too warm,' she said. 'If Mr Eliot would excuse me, I'll retire.'

The gentlemen stood up. As she passed Forston, he brushed her arm briefly and nodded. She hesitated, inclined her head and glided on towards the door. Eliot understood. He had seen this reluctant acquiescence in his own women. It was the obedience of one who would submit without argument or enthusiasm and his anger taught him more of himself than he had known that morning. He sat down again with Forston, and Eleanor moved slowly through dim passageways, gazing into mirrors where confusion was all that she saw.

Chapter Two

The Mansion House Hotel
MANCHESTER
16th June, 1855

My dear Leopold,
I left Liverpool this forenoon after high words with Wilkins
and Son. Neither of the brigs they wished to sell us was fit for
a mill-pond. Had we scraped the barnacles from their hulks,
we could have looked down through the hatches straight into
Neptune's Bower. I wonder that they thought they could
deceive us but Wilkins has become but a poor body since this
week twelve-month. He has run to flesh and his wits wander.
'And Son' is master in all matters and cannot grasp that trust
is worth twenty shillings in the pound. We must look elsewhere. You were right to suspect that there is much amiss
here. My unexpected arrival at the mill caused consternation
in certain quarters and a jovial effort to keep me from the
counting-house. I have begun my examination of the books
and have them under lock and key. It appears that my stay
will be longer than I had anticipated.
Your wearied brother,
Gerard Forston

The weather had held at Knapp. In the meadows around the
park, hay was stooked to dry beneath the rampant sun and farmers
slept soundly in their beds never needing to check the sky. Children
singling turnips drooped in the heat, the ridged earth crumbling
under hard, bare soles in sudden dusty slides. Pike lay below
green rafts of water-lily, champing their overreaching jaws in cow-
like contemplation. Day followed balmy day and the last of the
winter-bournes became trickles, then parched streambeds awaiting
autumn rain.

Eliot was still in residence. No date had been set for him to move on to Vauchurch and Forston would have thought himself unmannerly to chase away a guest who had come so far. The sunlit hours passed and Forston found Eliot easy to entertain. They rode together, smoked, played billiards in the cool of the evening, talked of trade in the desultory fashion of men who wish to gain information without giving too much of their own away and if they did not become close, they drifted through the idleness of summer in acceptable harmony or so Forston believed.

Forston's leisure had a limit. He was obliged to travel north and he left his visitor in Eleanor's care, confident that she would, as Margrave had put it, do what she was good at. Her abilities as a hostess made him sure that Eliot would barely notice his absence and he had departed with his mind entirely occupied with tonnage and the sea-worthiness of copper-bottomed oak.

And so Eliot and Eleanor were alone. They lived in a household of serving-men and maids, of gardeners, a governess and, of course, one solitary, vigilant child but neither saw this multitude as company. They were alone with Eliot's certainty and Eleanor's puzzlement and their world contracted like a bud that closes as the first harbinger of night.

They were alone and Eliot played upon their solitude. He was insulted by Forston trusting him with such a wife and though this trust handed him the opportunity to seduce, still he saw it as one of the slights that had been offered him throughout his stay. Forston's easy assurance was a constant grievance. The antiquity of Forston's name and property seemed to Eliot to be thrust in his face with every stroll through the grounds or anecdote of local happenings. It was as if a chorus of genealogists stood at Forston's shoulder, hissing sibilant repetitions of the Eliots' humble origins. Eleanor's virtue was a trophy to be taken to bite his thumb at Forston.

There was more than this to his intentions; more than he could yet admit to himself. The sheer voluptuous pleasure of her future surrender should have been enough to sate his imagination but it was not. His reaction on that first evening, when he had wanted to strike Forston for signalling to his wife that he would be coming to her room, had told him that this was a novel situation. It was not only that he had been jealous of Forston's place in her bed but that he had felt an unaccustomed, protective tenderness at the sight of her reluctance. He did not only want to sample her himself, he wanted to prevent her being forced to do what she disliked. The sensation was new and entirely startling. He turned his face resolutely from what it could mean.

Today he was riding beside her on one of Forston's hunters, whose powerful, shining flanks rippled with every pent-up pace. Eleanor was leading the way along green lanes where hedgerows frothed with guelder rose and the heavy, lace heads of elderflower. The lanes had trapped and magnified the heat but she seemed cool in her flawless, cream linen habit. There was no sweet disorder in her dress, no strand escaped from her coiled hair. When she looked ahead at the route she was taking, up at the kingfisher sky, at her mare's flicking ears, at the blossom to each side, she appeared to be serene but when she looked at him, he saw the disquiet in her eyes.

They left the track and descended into a valley. Their horses' hooves were muffled on the close-cropped turf. No house or labourer was to be seen. The hills rose in smooth, steep slopes to left and right, the coombe narrowing where it curved towards the east. A lark hung high above them, a distant fleck against the sun, pouring its song into the languid afternoon. They followed the path of the valley, deeper and deeper into a silence broken only by the chink of a bit as the mare shook her head. There was a spinney before them, an island of pines, isolated between the grand sweep of the treeless hills, where the red earth was exposed and scarred by excavations of dens.

Eliot raised his whip and pointed. A fox was slinking along the hillside above; a dog-fox, sleek and bold. It turned towards them, returning stare for stare, and Eleanor dropped her reins, covering her face with her hands.

'It's wild,' she cried. 'Oh God, it is so wild!' and tears sprang to run down to her wrists.

The senior Mr Ebenezer Benford sat at a table in the back room of his jeweller's shop in Sherborne, cleaning pearls with potato-flour. He was wearing an embroidered smoking-cap with a jaunty tassel on his thin, white hair and gold-rimmed spectacles from which he kept wiping the flour with the edge of his apron. The heavily-barred window was open and he could hear the canary his daughter-in-law kept in a brass cage in the parlour above trilling arpeggios in the gladness of its pampered heart. His own lips kept pursing to whistle a descant only for him to remember the murmur of voices behind the door that told him that his son was tending to a customer's protracted needs.

Sunlight had found its way to the rear of the building and was illuminating two-thirds of the room, making the strong-boxes and polished cabinets that lined the walls gleam. Mr Benford, already cheered by the thought of boiled fowl and an evening stroll down to the river to put his grandson's hobby-horse through its paces, was further enlivened by having seen the junior Ebenezer bustle in to seize their most expensive ladies' ornaments whilst twisting his features into a grimace indicating that he had serious hopes of a sale. He paused in his gentle rubbing and gazed out into the overcrowded garden, his soft cloth letting fall a drift of fine powder that settled on his right knee.

The shop-bell jangled and his son, a pear-shaped man of forty who had difficulty maintaining the gravity needed for receiving large sums of money spent on carefully chosen nonsense, opened the connecting door with his elbow and came through carrying a tray piled with plush presentation-cases. His face, reddened by wearing a frock-coat unsuited to the weather, was abandoning its grave professional expression and breaking out into the gaiety inherited from his father.

He plumped the tray onto the table with an air of triumph. 'The diamond locket with the sapphire bow,' he said.

Mr Benford leant back against his chair and removed his spectacles, the better to demonstrate his awe. 'Have we been visited by a duke?' he asked.

'A Rajah,' Ebenezer said, reaching into his pocket, 'and, behold, we don't need to send in our account.' He emptied a drawstring bag onto the tablecloth and a heap of sovereigns formed itself into a pool of glinting gold.

'Mercy on us!' Mr Benford exclaimed, remembering a lifetime of sending politely-worded reminders. 'Yes, he must be a foreigner. And with very pretty ways.'

'Pretty in the result but none so pleasing making a decision. Nothing was good enough for him. Every piece cast aside and criticised. Said he could find finer workmanship in a Delhi bazaar but that he must have a trinket to take home to his sister and the locket would do.'

'Sister, indeed!' Ebenezer's wife came into the room with her light tread and stood smiling at the gratifying addition to their financial security.

'Now, Sarah,' her husband said, 'you don't even know who was here.'

'It was that Mr Eliot who's staying at Knapp. I saw him from the front window and I say again – sister, indeed! Shall I take one of these to pay the fish?'

The lock of the corner cupboard in the housekeeper's sitting room at Knapp needed a particular lift and twist of its key to persuade it to give up its resistance, and Mrs Richards's long familiarity with its vagaries let her accomplish in a moment what would have caused another to retreat in despair. She opened the door and took out a bottle of her own sloe gin, made the previous year with fruit from the Home Farm hedgerows and the best Hollands. Glasses already stood on the table where Mulvey, the butler, and Ward, Eleanor's lady's maid, were settling into their chairs. A substantial dinner had recently been disposed of in the servants' hall and the three friends were preparing to spend a convivial hour with nothing more to sustain them than an uncut caraway cake, the excellent results of Mrs Richards's prowess in the stillroom, and speculations upon whether the master would have been wiser to take Mr Eliot with him on his trip to the north.

Mrs Richards poured three measures of the spirit and sat down with a satisfied sigh that said her work for the day was over and had been done well. It was not yet quite dark but she had pulled the curtains across the window, with its view of the enclosure where the laundry dried, because she found dusk melancholy.

Mulvey held his glass so that a candle-flame shone through its damson-coloured richness and took the first sip, as he always did, with a meditative air.

'Never better, Mrs Richards,' he said, with a slight inclination of his head towards her, 'and never to be bettered.'

She shifted in her chair, comfortable and content. Mulvey and Ward would both need to return to their duties – he to enquire whether more wine was to be brought to the drawing room, she to help her mistress undress and brush her hair – but there was this peaceful interval to enjoy and enjoy it they would. All three understood what being habitués of this private sanctum said about their status in the teeming household and took pride in their rise through the various ranks of service. During the years of their association, a camaraderie had grown between them that was an outlet for the affection that would have been bestowed on their families had they married.

Knapp was not a world where the servants spared any warmth for their master and mistress. None was asked of them. Neither Forston nor Eleanor considered their employees as creatures of the same stamp as themselves, fashioned by the same Creator, troubled by the same hopes and disillusionments. Servants were hired to fulfil certain practical functions and because it does not do to buy a good horse and then let him break his feet by going unshod, they were adequately fed, housed and dosed by a worthy apothecary to keep them to their mark. Eleanor gave Ward many of her cast-off gowns; this was what a woman of her position did for her personal maid and Eleanor had always been too idle to stray from convention, but there was no fondness in the gifts.

This lack of any tie except the giving or receiving of wages let the three friends, and all their underlings, speculate upon the relations between Eleanor and Eliot without the concern they would have felt if they had cared that the players might be hurt. They had no loyalty to Forston that would drive them to warn him that his lady might be faithless, no sympathy for Eleanor that would make them try to protect her from shame, no fellowship with the probable lovers that would fill them with the horror of sin that would have come had the coachman's wife been discovered in adultery. Nor were they sure that Eleanor had left the haven of respectability to which there can never be a return. The possibility was still a game and old scores were being paid off in rumour and gossip.

Mrs Richards cut the cake with a bone-handled knife that had been her mother's. Its blade was worn to a thinness that she would not have tolerated for the house but here it was another sign that she was on her own territory. She placed slices on fluted plates and passed them to left and right.

'Is there still no word from Manchester, Mr Mulvey?' she said. 'Will we see himself home again? What could be keeping him amongst those heathen cotton-spinners?'

Mulvey, aware that nothing would shake her conviction that the manufacturing districts were entirely in the grip of the starving Irish, scheming to make them Papal States, and that his own descent was from kings and bards, let her comment pass.

'We can expect him by noon on Friday,' he said, watching the interest flicker in his listeners' eyes. 'Mrs F. had a letter by the late post. She asked to have his room put in readiness.'

'As if it wasn't always.' Mrs Richards bridled and crumbled her cake between her fingers.

'Were you there when the letter came?' Ward asked. 'How did she take the news?'

'Like the lily and the rose. Pale and blush, pale and blush. First the one and then the other, turn and turn about.'

Ward brushed her mouth with her lace-edged handkerchief. Her jet earrings swayed with the slight movement, glittering as they caught the candlelight. She was in her early thirties, handsome enough to look well in Eleanor's discarded clothes without matching her mistress's beauty, and had been in her situation long enough to begin thinking, Why she and not me? If I had been born to a different station . . .

'So there are four more days,' she said.

She took a mouthful of the dark gin and let it slide slowly over her tongue. Its flavour, more than its undoubted intoxicating effects, gave her solace. She was a sensual, possessive woman whose needs had to be satisfied at one remove. Men, honourable and dishonourable, had made offers to her according to their lights but those who would marry her did not have the income to give her the life she craved and she had too much prudence to succumb to those of Forston's friends who had promised every boon except their name. She had no physical intimacy with anyone but Eleanor. When she held the towel she had heated at the hearth to wrap about Eleanor as she rose dripping from her bath, when she knelt to fit a stocking over Eleanor's foot and smooth it up her leg, when she fastened a necklace about Eleanor's throat and saw that perfection of face and form arrayed in the finest silks and jewels, it was not for her mistress's glory but her own. She had a proprietary interest in Eleanor's body; she knew every blue vein on her white breasts, how every coil of hair would fall when she drew out the combs and it was as if she lived within an automaton that went into the world at her bidding. She felt Eliot's gaze when it rested on Eleanor as if fire lapped at her own skin and her nights had grown long and sleepless.

'We can only hope . . .' she said softly, but she did not finish her sentence.

Hermione was alone in the schoolroom. It was mid-afternoon and the house lay hushed beneath the unrelenting sun. Outside, the heat pressed down on parched earth and quiet pools that shrank away from their banks. Inside, the rooms within the thick stone walls were cool, even here in the attics where the solitary child sat strapped to her backboard while her governess slept restlessly on the floor below.

Her isolation in this dreamlike hour did not trouble her. She was a thoughtful, observant girl and would have suffered more from too much company than too little. It was her nature to have a calming influence on her surroundings and a Dutch artist, chancing to see her patient, loving face, her small hands clasped upon her lap as she sat peacefully in this high, sunlit interior, would have painted her with an appreciation not shared by those who ordered her existence.

Hermione was loved by no one except her tormented young cousin at Vauchurch and Olivia, striking straight through to the strength of love that was Hermione's core, both gave and received a blessing through her recognition. Hermione's sweet, reflective presence went almost unnoticed by the relations and servants who formed her world at Knapp, but if she had been taken from them, there would have been an emptiness that they could not explain.

Obstructed by the wooden board that held her rigid, she reached into her pocket with two fingers and pulled out a twist of paper that rasped gratifyingly against her broderie anglaise skirt. Miss Armstrong, the governess, should have been a man, able to satisfy her scholarly talents at a university before entering a profession that would use her quick wits to the full but, things being what they were, she had settled for the only occupation open to the daughter of an impoverished clergyman. She had no aptitude with children and suffered from debilitating headaches yet she was conscientiously kind and, on Thursday mornings, always walked her charge into the village to buy her a few pennyworth of sweets.

Her benevolence was rewarded by Hermione's relish of the entire treat. It was rare that anything was done for no other reason than to give the girl pleasure and she extracted the last ounce of enjoyment from the anticipatory walk to the cottage where the old woman, who boiled great pans of sugar-syrup on her range, had converted her parlour into a shop, from scratching the ears of the immense, marmalade cat that curled on the counter amongst the dishes of candied cherries and almond comfits, and from the rattle of the chosen sweetmeats on the scales.

Today, she had a quarter-pound of fragile violet lozenges that could be crunched to a perfumed powder or left to dissolve slowly on the tongue, leaving an agreeable purple stain. She put one in her mouth and began to suck as she listened to the gentle cooing of the doves preening themselves on the roof-tiles.

The tranquillity that had been interrupted by the rustle of paper sank onto the room again. She was thinking of her father's return. No one had thought to tell her that he was to be back the next day but she had overheard the maids turning out his room and had stopped in the doorway to listen openly. It had been a strange, sly, half-whispered conversation that she did not understand and it had changed its tone, amidst head-shakings and meaningful looks, as soon as the women noticed her. They had repeated brightly that the master was to be expected the following afternoon and declared he was certain-sure to bring her a present, yet their voices were false and one called her a 'poor lamb' when she had passed on her way.

It was puzzling. There had never been this excited, furtive atmosphere in the house before. She could not ask her mother what was afoot. Eleanor was repelled by the daughter whose intelligence and sympathies were foreign to her, and had not encouraged intimacy. Hermione was aware from her mother's unguarded remarks that Eleanor was angry that a child of hers could be plain, and was still too young to realise that this vain, shallow woman was also relieved that the girl's face would not rival her own. Hermione knew only that she was a disappointment and encumbrance, and could not run to her mother to have mysteries unravelled.

The sound of voices and hooves scraping on stone came up from below. She could not hear what was being said. Perhaps Papa had returned early. Rising stiffly from the stool, she crossed to the window with the rod at her back giving her movements a queer formality. By leaning out of the casement, she could see down into the stable-yard.

It was not Forston. Eliot and Eleanor were waiting to mount for another of the rides they took daily despite the exhausting, sultry heat. A stable-lad was adjusting the girth on Eleanor's mare, who twitched her fine ears against the flies and rested her gleaming flank on the boy's shoulder.

From the height of the attic window, the scene looked . . .

33

Hermione could not say quite how it looked. As though it were on a stage or, shimmering and fluctuating as it was in the haze rising from the flagstones, underwater. It was only their usual ride. Why was she alarmed? Her mother was being helped into the saddle, gathering the reins, setting the folds of her trailing skirt. It was only their usual ride.

The ledge was hot beneath her tightening hands. Eliot put his foot into the stirrup and swung over to sit easily, confidently. Hermione pressed forward. The jutting edge of her backboard rapped the casement, sending the doves careering into the air in a sudden flurry of piercingly white wings. Eliot looked up at the tumult and met Hermione's eyes. He stared at her without interest and kicked his horse on. Eleanor followed him, not turning her head. They rode out beneath the stable-arch as Hermione called, 'Mamma!' in a voice too quiet to be heard.

Chapter Three

Margrave could hear his wife's firm footsteps approaching across the Great Hall. He was in the estate-room, ostensibly considering his land-agent's proposals for draining the lower meadows on two of the most westerly farms, but actually pondering on what news he had received so far about the nefarious doings Forston had uncovered in Manchester. His brother was to come to Vauchurch tomorrow for a fuller explanation and, the subtly achieved syphoning of profits into the pockets of the chief clerk and manager having been discovered and the culprits being now in the tender care of turnkeys until the next Assize session, there should have been little to disturb him.

Money had been lost but it was possible that it might be retrieved and, even if it were not, it was too little to damage the financial security of the family. Margrave was never comforted by such thoughts. He needed to be powerful, and every successful act of betrayal, however small, every bargain missed, every opportunity grasped by his competitors diminished him in his own eyes and caused him to use his authority to give an equivalent amount of pain to his subordinates. Even Forston's detection of the fraud and its perpetrators was slightly unsatisfactory because it was not he, Margrave, in person, who had whipped away the cloth to show the crime.

He was rich, he had dominion over many lives, but the fear that lay coiled in the depths of his being would not let him rest with what he had. Always, he must have more.

The door opened and Charlotte Margrave came in. When she entered a room, she became its focal point. All available space was suddenly, extinguishingly, filled by her presence. She was a dark, seductive, strikingly handsome woman with none of her sister's soft attraction. Her gaze gave its victims the impression of having been speared to the wall and there were men who would travel far to be so pierced.

Her husband was not amongst them. He had, like many another before him, married an extraordinary woman for her unusual qualities and then grown disgruntled because she was not tame. Tending to his welfare should have been enough for her; she should have bowed her head to his command. Law and tradition were on his side and he maintained a tentative mastery but it was his perpetual suspicion that she would break out into some nameless violence or treachery.

She crossed towards him, holding out a letter. 'It has Gerard's seal,' she said. 'I took it from a messenger who's ridden here post-haste. Something must be wrong at Knapp.'

Margrave took the proffered note and slid a paper-knife under the wax. 'It'll only be his account of the theft,' he said. 'There's no need for you to stay.'

'He's already told you of that and you're seeing him tomorrow. Something's wrong.'

He looked at her standing upright and immoveable and shrugged. The letter unfolded to show lines that were blotted and scrawled; Forston's writing but not his style.

'Well?'

He found that he had been staring at the words without taking in their meaning.

'Leopold!'

His face was white when he raised it to hers. 'Eleanor's bolted. Eliot's absconded with her.' His colour rose again as a rufous anger took the place of shock. He turned from side to side, unable to find a direction for his rage. 'They went yesterday – went out riding and didn't return. She left a note on her pincushion.'

Charlotte clasped her hands, the knuckles whitening as her grip strengthened.

'Did you know of this?' he demanded.

'How can you think so? Do you imagine I'm a friend to adultery?'

'Your family—. There's no trusting any of you.'

She moved over to the window. The sunlight falling through the stained-glass of the upper panes laid imprecise images of hinds fleeing through emerald foliage on her iridescent silks, her heavy gold earrings, her splendid, ferocious face.

'You must find them before this is known,' she said. 'Bring her back at once and some story can be concocted.'

'Perhaps Gerard won't want her back. A whore in his house.'

She gave an impatient laugh. 'He'll want to avoid scandal as much as you do,' she said. 'Entertain yourself with accusations when she's found. In the meantime, begin the search.'

He raised his arms, gesturing widely. 'Where?' he asked. 'All the wide world?'

'I'll order the carriage to take us to Knapp.' She pulled the bell that rang in the servants' hall. 'You'll send men to prevent them taking ship from Portsmouth or Bristol and we will go on to London. For pity's sake, must I wear the breeches for you?'

Ward was weeping. She stood in Eleanor's bedroom, her arms full of an evening gown she had been given to mend three nights before, with her breath coming in harsh gasps and tears falling on the heavy folds of satin, where they lay complete and glistening on the inviolate surface. It was touch that broke their tension and let grief seep into the weave. She pressed her thumb onto a tear and a dark stain spread outwards to meet another.

She had been given the gown because Eleanor had caught her heel in the hem and it must be stitched back. This had been her life. She followed where others walked.

The room was not yet empty of Eleanor. Its air still smelt of her light scent; there was no feeling of desertion except within the woman who wept for the emptiness of her years. Adultery was not a game any more, a delicious, piquant rumour; it was the sharp steel of rejection.

She laid the gown carefully on the bed where she had laid others for a decade. Her mistress had left and with her had gone the illusion of being necessary to another living creature. Every waking hour of her days had been given to the tending of one who had never used her Christian name, who had not been embarrassed by the most intimate attention because she had not considered a servant capable of causing such a sensation. When Eleanor leant forward in her bath to let her back be washed, the sponge and the hand that held it had both been humdrum domestic objects to her.

It need not have been so. Ward had met many a lady's maid who had been entirely in her mistress's confidence, who would have heard the first fervent confessions as a late fire lit their disrobing, who would have carried messages, sweet and secret, to the lover and been given gratitude for her excited loyalty. She saw herself packing a portmanteau to be smuggled out of the house, choosing its contents for the best advantage of Eleanor's comfort and beauty; she saw her own escape, slipping away to meet the guilty pair, their flight, her vigilance against pursuers, her insistence at hotels that her lady should receive the greatest care.

Nothing had been asked of her. She shuddered and covered her face with her hands. Her body felt hollow; neither it nor her life had substance. If her mistress were not caught and compelled to return, all that was in this room would be removed and shut away, and when that was done, she too would be discarded. Where would she go? The house that had never been a home was suddenly a refuge as she faced its loss. Oh God, to be needed and loved.

She lifted the gown again, laying her face against it, and with one convulsive wrench she rent what should have covered a heart.

Forston woke abruptly, his heart beating with the rapidity of the train that had brought him to the city. He lay staring up into the darkness, his nightshirt sodden with the sweat of his restless night. He did not know where he was. Grief filled him but, for a moment, he could not remember why. Misery and uncertainty gave the unseen room a menace he had not experienced since those first nights at school before he had learnt to be vicious.

'Eleanor.'

Memory came as the word was spoken. Eleanor; the beloved name. He turned his head as if he expected to see her fair hair uncoiled upon the pillow. They had never shared a room but when he had come to her bed, he had stayed until dawn and he knew the passive contours of her sleeping face, the abandon of an outflung arm, white upon the counterpane. He did not need light to know she was not there. Their midnight hours had always been pungent with their congress and he thought now that they would have had a greater intimacy if he had ever slept at her side wanting nothing but her company.

He had been agitated in his fitful, longing dreams. His nightshirt had twisted about his body and the stifling feather mattress had moulded itself into lumps of spiked malignity whose barbs protruded through both ticking and sheet. Rolling onto his side, lifting his hip into the air to let him release himself from the grasp of his garment, he reached out for where he must have left his matches, found and struck one, and lit the candle he had blown out a short, heated interval before.

Sitting on the edge of the bed, the recalcitrant nightgear leaving his legs bare from the thigh down, he pushed his feet into slippers embroidered by the daughter who knelt awake and fearful at a disgraced Knapp, and yearned for Eleanor.

He had not realised he loved her. She had been a trophy he had won in a game that had no definite rules yet conferred merit upon him for being the victor. When once the novelty of being her possessor had passed, she had simply been present in his house, an ornament and the means of raising other men's envy, no more. Tonight, staring into the shadowed corners of the hotel bedroom, he yearned to see her trick of rubbing her chin with her forefinger when she was engaged in what passed for thinking, to hear her sing the gay, old-fashioned songs he liked when he was tired, to feel her warm, compliant form in his arms.

A pain that was more than physical pierced his chest and he laughed aloud. He had suffered shock, confusion and outrage. Since he had ridden back to a home where blanched faces had lowered their eyes from his, he had been angry and despairing, but until this instant he had not felt the obvious implications of his wife's flight to be real.

He stood up, wrapped himself in his dressing-gown as if the night had suddenly grown chill, and paced back and forth, kicking away the boots he had forgotten to put outside his door. The candle flickered in the draught of his passing, calling a faint gleam from his cigar-case on the wash-stand. He stopped to light a cheroot, drawing the first smoke into his lungs with the same harsh gasps that had racked Ward as she wept. This was the worst that he had known; this was jealousy, raw, primitive, with savagery in its strike. Where was she now? He need not ask. She lay beneath the guest he had welcomed to his house; she lay with Eliot, lascivious, treacherous, lost in a debauchery that took from him what was his. If she were here, he would close his hands about her throat and choke the last breath from her faithless lips. She was his. What man would blame him? And Eliot? He gripped the bed-hangings, crushing the damask in his fist. Another revelation, another new desire.

He wanted to kill.

'Are there any letters for Margrave?'

The young man with the discreet manner and particularly starched cuffs, who was guarding the desk in the lobby of the hotel, consulted the interior of a drawer and apologised for the dearth of correspondence. Charlotte, ignoring his assurance that a boy would be dispatched to her directly any epistle was received, announced that she would take tea. A commanding gesture from the young man summoned a waiter to bow her across the thick, violently floral carpet into the invigorating chink of china.

Tea at the Wallingford was enjoyed in what, because of a locked Gothic bookcase filled with impenetrable sermons, was known as the reading-room but which was devoted entirely to the refreshment of the body and spirit with the inspired fancies of a volatile French pastry-cook. The confections being disposed of by ladies robustly wiping away whipped cream moustaches were too frivolous to be suitable for those who had come to town in pursuit of errant wives and sisters. Charlotte, however, was hungry and wanted to consider what they had learnt so far. She allowed herself to be ushered to an alcove looking across the murmurous room to the conservatory and waited as the appurtenances of tea were brought.

The owner of the establishment had married an enterprising woman, who had been governess to the children of a Russian count. She had brought her years in St Petersburg home with her in the shape of a love of extravagant indoor arrangements of living foliage and Charlotte sat at her white-clothed table embowered by leaves. Ivy rioted out of tin boxes on the floor, up trellises on three sides of her enclosure and over an arch above her head. Her view was of similar bosky retreats, larger tables hedged about by exuberant jardinières, glass doors flung wide upon a rampant conservatory, that made travelling to explore the Dark Continent a pointless exercise, and thence to the gardens.

It was all singularly at variance with her mood but its jaunty air served only to emphasise the handsome nature of her serious face, and the man watching her from a wicker chair amongst the conservatory palms thought her no whit less lovely than she had been as a girl.

She hardly noticed her surroundings. Crumbling her *puits d'amour* with her fork, she took stock of what had been achieved since the news of Eleanor's flight had reached Vauchurch, and considered both what should be their next moves and her own reaction to the matter.

Much activity had been crushed into the hours since Margrave had opened the note. Forston had been roused from a state of stunned rage that paralysed his thinking without appearing to wake him to a true sense of the enormity of the desertion, bags had been packed by agitated housemaids, a journey to London by the late train had been undertaken after the attempt to leave herself to comfort Hermione was foiled, private enquiry agents had been hired and the shipping offices quizzed for an unexpected couple taking berths for the East. Forston, alive with a cold belligerence she had never known in him before, and Margrave were now closeted in their lawyer's chambers in Lincoln's Inn taking advice on the capture of the lovers and the subsequent financial ruin of Eliot by the damages the injured husband intended to extract.

Stirring her second cup of Indian tea, Charlotte brooded on the possibility that either the Margraves or Eliots might own the very hillsides where this infusion had begun its progress towards the Wallingford reading-room. If neither were the possessors of the ground, they may yet have caused their buyers to choose it, their ships to carry it, their warehousemen to walk between dim towers of its scented crates. The anticipation of the men's varied lusts giving rise to a trade war excited her. It was, she was sure, a reprehensible sensation, coming as it did not from a righteous wish to punish wrongdoers but from a primitive urge for aggression and jealousy of Eleanor's escape into carnality.

Charlotte had never been a religious woman. Her determination to bring her sister back to her duty before her reputation was lost had been entirely practical. Aware that libertines cast off their conquests when the novelty of each had passed, she wanted to save Eleanor from the misery of the isolation she must face when Eliot abandoned her and she found the doors of Knapp and all respectable houses closed against her. Eleanor was not a woman with the mental resources to support her in such a condition; she would be deceived by the sympathy of the next voluptuary who chose to comfort her, passing from him to the next and next. There was genuine concern in her hunt for Eleanor but she could not disguise from herself that the pulse that beat within her resolve was impure.

It had been no lie when she told Margrave that she was not a friend to adultery. There were scandals in her family's past that had caused deep unhappiness and social ruin to those wretches whose infidelities had not been conducted with the discretion that let spectators pretend to be blind. She had no inclination to become one of their number. If she were to keep her rank in life,

41

secondary as it was to the husband whose wit and daring were inferior to her own, she must bind herself with iron to do so. She had never considered jeopardising her position by leaving Margrave, but she had burned for a man to match her, and Eleanor's wickedness stirred her hunger.

'Charlotte.'

She looked up and the colour drained from her face, returning twofold in an instant. The man standing at her table read the change with satisfaction and smiled with that same sideways lift that had weakened her twenty years before.

'Quinn,' she said in a voice too soft for Margrave to have recognised.

'You didn't see me. I came from the conservatory and you didn't raise your head from that unfortunate tart.'

She pushed flakes of puff pastry with the fork that had been their destruction. 'I didn't think to meet you here,' she said.

'It's where we Margraves always come.'

There was a drawl in his words that was not merely sarcasm. She liked it.

'May I sit down?'

'Of course.'

He slid into her retreat, waving away the waiter who had begun an approach.

'What was concerning you so nearly that you didn't notice me?'

'Eleanor. We've come to Town to seek her. She's run from Forston with an India merchant.'

He leant back and laughed. 'By God,' he said, 'I'd never have put Nell down as a bolter. Where did she find the energy?'

'It seems her seducer has enough for two.'

'And he's more wealthy than Forston?'

'I couldn't say.'

'Oh, I think he must be. What else would have made her fly? I can't believe Forston beat her. I would have.'

She looked into his eyes. 'Would you have beaten me?'

'Not you, Lotta. Never you.' He smiled again. 'You wouldn't have let me. And how is the illustrious Margrave? Has he proved the loving and protective husband your father thought he'd be?'

'I doubt Papa believed anything of the kind. He saw a large estate and allied himself to it.'

In the room, waitresses moved smoothly to and fro, fancies were lifted from silver trays with tongs, young men urged blushing girls to take the last strawberry and, in one arbour, desire and its consequences seemed less prohibited than they had done the night before.

'Margrave must be beside himself at this,' Quinn said. 'And he with such a keen sense of family honour.'

The injustice of Leopold's taunt about her relations gave Charlotte a pang of anger peculiarly mixed with the amusement her companion found in the situation. Scandal had struck the Margraves more forcibly than her own ancestors, but it was a forbidden subject in their household and had come to be a story that was somehow apart from them.

This man, who had been the cause of frost settling upon her heart, had once been called Margrave. For six hot weeks, when green silk blinds hung at the windows to soften light falling on infant faces, three sons had lain in the nursery at Vauchurch. Three boys, born within as many years to two different mothers, the delight of their father in the pride of his dynastic ambitions. Leopold, Gerard and Quinn. Leopold just old enough to miss the mamma who had died at Forston's birth; just old enough to resent the attention his father paid to the latest arrival and the strange young woman whose entrance to the house had come with pomp and circumstance before the first wife's funeral wreaths had withered.

There had been scandal in the speed with which Henry Margrave had wooed and won the lovely Maria – it was said behind fans and in smoke-fogged billiard-rooms that the wooing had been done whilst Eliza Margrave still moved heavily about Vauchurch, fearing another confinement so soon – but worse scandal was to come.

Henry had a brother. Jack Margrave was dissolute, charming and bitter about his inheritance. He had been left handsomely provided for as a younger son but, true to his family, he wanted more. Henry believed Jack to have been given too much. The brothers studiously maintained a veneer of civility; the intercourse between their households was as constant as if their goodwill had been genuine and each sought relentlessly for secret harm to do the other.

Maria was only a girl, beautiful and weak-willed, longing foolishly for the romance and passion the husband she had married for his position had no intention of giving her. Jack discovered her weeping in a summerhouse a fortnight after her wedding and saw his opportunity. He had never taken such satisfaction in a seduction; he revelled in the haunted expression that grew on her face as her belly increased, sure that she would never be so witless as to confess. Quinn was born and there was private and public jubilation in the house.

And then guilt became too much for the young wife. Frail and distraught, she threw herself upon her husband's mercy and found that no mercy existed. Perhaps Quinn was his child, perhaps his brother's; Henry chose to believe that he saw sin in the small features. He turned Maria from his door and she, who had always ridden in carriages and had her burdens carried by servants, walked to the cold welcome of her lover with Quinn in her arms.

Henry's vengeance did not confine itself to the weak. He charged his brother with criminal conversation, suing him for damages that sent Jack to a dank and venomous stay in debtors' prison. The price of adultery was indeed high. Maria, disgraced, unwanted and in fear of both men, drank the opium-laden sedative her apothecary had meant to last a week in one desperate draught and passed from a world that had been too much for her.

Her destroyers did not mourn her going. She had been no more than a tool to either man and had warmed neither as did their hatred for each other. An inheritance from a second cousin as wicked as himself restored Jack to liberty and plenty, and he took Quinn to his depraved bosom, openly acknowledging the boy as his son.

It was an affront that soured the lives of the legitimate Margraves. Quinn was always there in the county, not received by respectable families yet constantly to be encountered as he grew older, a standing slur upon the family and bearing the name of the creature who should have had no memorial. Leopold believed that it was the shame that shortened his father's life. In this he was wrong, for Henry's indulgences, whether in port, malice or rich sauces were all of a nature to beckon apoplexy and could not be separated one from another.

And what of Quinn, standing aside from the flow of life that should have been his, absorbing the education and manners of a gentleman while bearing the mark of Cain upon his brow? He was capable, clever and quick, as aware of his talents as he was of the faces turned away, the confidential whispers behind his back, the excuses made not to invite him to friends' homes. Any surmountable obstacle set in his path would have been nothing to him, but with this he was helpless. He could not undo the past. There never was such bitterness within a Margrave heart as was nurtured in his.

His father's health failed and, in the summer when Quinn was twenty and the woman now sitting beside him in her magnificent maturity was seventeen, he travelled to Baden Baden, a filial companion to a tremulous husk wrapped in tartan shawls. Charlotte had been there with her aunt and a sincere love between the two young people had burgeoned and flourished amongst the fountains and sprightly military bands.

Charlotte's father would have none of it. He swept down upon the spa in the righteous rage of one whose bastards were not recognised and dragged his daughter across the Channel if not by the hair then by the bonds of duty and authority she would shortly learn to despise. A marriage was arranged, a union of two powerful bank-accounts, and the distraught girl was delivered over to the Margraves, a sacrifice whose spirit was hardening even as she stood at the altar.

'Did anyone ever tell Margrave about us?' Quinn asked.

'No. When I learnt how things were between you, I wondered whether you would, but—'

He pushed the handle of a knife a little to one side. 'I'd do a great deal to hurt him,' he said. 'Grind him beneath my chariot-wheels – but not if it would harm you.'

Charlotte could not recall the last time anyone had spoken to her tenderly. Four women rose from a table close to theirs, bending for parcels, reaching to touch each others' hands, and their blues and violets and reds were a blur across her sight.

'Do you know?' she said. 'I believe I wish Eleanor a fair wind across the seas.'

The air in the smoke-divan was so laden with the fumes of the cigars it had seen that day that the movement of Forston's foot as he crossed his legs drew a line through the hovering layers that languidly filled with grey fog once more. He raised his palm and made a sharp, upward thrust. Smoke lifted, eddied and curled downwards in slow, elegant spirals.

Margrave lay at full length on a leather sofa. They were alone in the room, drawing breath after their hours of investigations and discussions, of wharves, shipping-offices and cabs edging through crowded streets. Outside, they could hear the rumble of a dray rolling ponderously over the wooden paving-tiles and the urgent cry of an optimist trying to sell pickled eels to a hurrying throng not yet ready to dine.

Both men held lighted Havanas. Forston's rested untasted between his fingers, a soft mould of ash leaning outwards from its sullen glow. Margrave drew on his with long, thoughtful intakes, letting the smoke out through pursed lips as he brooded over what they had learnt and consolidated the plans they had made.

Eliot had set a trap for them and they had fallen into it, but he had had no notion of the consequences that would come of his false scent. He had taken berths on the merchantman *Margaret Hine* that had sailed for Suez on the night tide, sending aboard a couple who would pass for Eleanor and himself when described to questioners at the docks. It was his intention to meander across Europe, delighting in his conquest, while any pursuit followed the decoy vessel into the East. He was not given to long-term plans nor, until he succumbed to Eleanor, to driving obsessions and imagined that, the first chase failing, Forston would accept defeat. Who would want to retrieve a woman whose reputation was so utterly destroyed? He did not know his men.

The room was still except for the wraith-like drifting of smoke but it was alive with an enmity that caused a barrister stepping over its threshold, cheroot in hand, to retreat and consider, as he took his seat in another room, whether he would be defending one of the hard-eyed occupants before the year was out.

Forston's violence had not diminished. Civilisation had sloughed from him as if he were a cobra shedding a dullened skin. Blood-lust was upon him. There was no corner of the earth that was too distant or too secret for him to hunt down his quarry if they took refuge there. The shock of realising that he loved kept him from hating Eleanor – she was too precious and too foolish to be worth his malice – but the set lines of his cold face hid a ferocity that was to be relentless and sated only by a savage vengeance against Eliot's crime.

His brother's malevolence pleased Margrave. His own anger was less personal – it was not he who was the cuckold – yet his family honour, painfully built up after the routing of his adulterous stepmother and her byblow, had been tarnished in a manner that also threw doubt on the business judgement of Forston and himself. They had invited this traitor into their midst in the hope of advantage, and had been duped. Eliot and Eleanor had set sail.

46

Public humiliation was inevitable and would come on top of a court-case revealing that the profits of their mill had been bled by fraudsters. It was unendurable. Revenge must be absolute.

He blew a stream of pale smoke upwards. If there was one activity that he relished more than another, it was forcing a man into bankruptcy and taking over his trade in triumph. He had long wished to increase his enterprise in India and here was the trumpet-call. Forston, in his new hostility, would be a worthy ally. Together they would see their empire increase and the Eliots brought down into the dust, sorrowing for the day they had invaded a Margrave possession. But how was it to be done? Plans for blocking Eliot commerce, undercutting their prices, damming the flow of their supplies leapt to his mind with exhilarated rapidity. It could be done; he could have mastery but it would be a hard war to win unless he gained confederates with strategic powers to do his rivals harm.

Knocking his ash into a brass urn at his side, he placed one arm behind his head and luxuriated in his abilities. He was almost grateful to Eleanor for having raised him to such a pitch of astuteness. Smoke hung, obscuring his vision, and he lay, motionless as a lizard, seeing a Dorset hillside and a girl, young, lithe and dutiful.

Chapter Four

The heat had not lessened. At Vauchurch, it lay upon the land, oppressive and menacing, its sultry presence like a stranger whose brooding silence has grown to suggest dread. A walker on the ramparts could look up to the dull, metallic skies or out over the steep, parched slopes to meadows far below where long-horned sheep, angular and vulnerable since shearing, snuffed apprehensively at the thunderous air.

Kate Margrave, taking the winding path that led to the chapel, felt sweat bloom beneath her arms and between her breasts and longed for the cool sanctuary that awaited her. The thought made her guilty. She was seeking the calm silence of the family's private chapel to pray for the safe return of her Aunt Eleanor and she reproved herself for her lack of concentration. Allowing her own comfort to intrude upon her intentions seemed to detract from their sincerity.

She was aware of what had happened. Eleanor's defection had been flung at her by Margrave in a terse, accusatory statement that seemed to include her in the shame. As of course, she reflected, it did. How could she not be touched by it? Are we not members each of another? It had been pitiful to see her proud father suffer such agitation at their disgrace and yet his state did him more credit than her mother's cold, businesslike preparations for departure. Pausing in the shade of an elder – a shade barely noticeable in the uniformly grey humidity of the afternoon – she took herself to task again. Perhaps her mother had reasons for her briskness. She could not tell. Aunt Eleanor was Mamma's sister, after all; perhaps the degradation was too painful to allow the slightest sign to show for fear of giving way completely.

The heat weighed more heavily when she was still. There would be a storm tonight and she would need to take Frank into her bed if he was to sleep. He did not lack courage and would lie awake as the thunder crashed, gripping the edge of his sheets, without complaint, but his sensitivity would make him pay ten-fold for the spirit that he summoned. She would tell him that she was afraid to be alone and he would curl securely against her back, content with the belief that he was protecting her.

And all the while, Olivia would scorn to be in bed and kneel at the window, letting the lightning glare on her upturned face, laughing aloud with wide, excited eyes as the sky turned livid.

Putting up her hands to ease her chignon away from her neck, where tendrils of fine hair had escaped the braid net to cling to her damp skin, Kate walked on. The chapel, a squat, grey edifice as old as the house, stood on the edge of the plateau facing east over a descent that somehow had a more vertiginous effect when viewed from inside the building than from the turf outside. Despite the solidity of the walls, the suddenness of the slope gave a feeling of insecurity and impermanence, as if the chapel and the centuries of Christianity it contained were on the brink of falling to destruction. The antiquarian, Julian Dameroy, claimed that it was raised upon the foundations of a temple of an older religion, unspecified but more terrible. Kate, unlike Olivia, did not have the temperament to see blood when there was wine in the chalice and she did not hear the cries of old gods when she sought forgiveness there.

It was cool in the chapel. The whitewashed walls were a relief from the tired, grey sheen of the day. She had often been here at dawn, slipping out of the house with a scarf thrown about her head, and had witnessed the sun rising behind the altar, shining in a crimson glory through the one window of rippling clear glass, flooding the space with jubilant light, causing the crucifix to be ringed with fire. It filled her with exultation and the belief that love – love other than what she felt for her brother and sister – love must exist.

She took her usual seat in an old box pew and tried to compose herself. Later, she would kneel and pray conscientiously for her aunt but the heat had sapped her strength and she needed to rest. She suffered from strange surges of energy and inexplicable tiredness and, though she had correctly diagnosed her symptoms as signs of a malaise of the soul, she had wrongly decided that her own fundamental flaw was the cause. Nightly, she laid her failings before God, pleading for the power to overcome her dissatisfactions and nameless yearnings and submit joyfully to a life that seemed to have no purpose.

The heavy door swung open with the two-toned creak with which she was so familiar. Startled and faintly, shamefully irritated by the thought of having company in her haven, Kate turned to see who had come.

Margrave stood in the doorway. He was wearing black instead of the pale grey frock-coat he favoured in summer, and his sombre appearance made her afraid. Laying his hat aside, he came down the aisle towards her and she moved further to the wall to give him room to sit down. His eyes increased her fear. They held hers with an intensity she could not place and had never seen in them before. She was reminded of Olivia. He was not a tender father and she was used to seeing boredom, exasperation and dislike when he looked at her, but this ferocity of concentration was altogether new. Or rather, new in her own kind. She had witnessed it before. Running to free a snared hare, she had come upon a stoat poised to rend the helpless creature. The shrill scream that had summoned her had died as the hare, red from the wire that was lacerating its flesh, stared at its inevitable death. Girl, victim and killer were motionless, frozen in the moment of sacrifice. The stoat darted, its teeth slashed, the hare's hind-legs drummed, twitched, were still. She had turned away and told no one of what had been done. Margrave was the hunter but she could not guess what wire was at her throat.

'Have you had news of my aunt, sir?' she asked.

'Yes, my dear, I'm sorry to say I have.'

A tremor made her shift a little on the pew. Endearments were foreign to his nature and though he spoke of sorrow there was none in his voice, only determination and suppressed excitement.

'Is she dead?' She knew her words were foolish even as she said them. They did not accord with his condition and seemed to give him greater power.

'It would be better if she were. She's dragged our names through the mire, brought disgrace upon herself and shame – perhaps ruin – upon our family.' He spoke voluptuously and she felt nausea twist beneath her clasped hands.

'I don't understand you,' she said.

'Of course you don't. If you did, I would have raised you wrongly. This is no business for a woman.'

He turned his head and his hard gaze passed through the eastern window as if he could call another ocean and continent to view. When he looked back to her there was an instant of trance in his eyes before the harshness returned.

'But a woman began this,' he said, 'and a woman may save us.'

Fear had grown to fill her body as heat had filled it in the sickly air.

'I've never troubled you with details of our trade,' he said. 'We are merchants and your brother must learn to bear the burden of providing for our House when I'm gone – but that's a man's part and no concern of your sex.'

She was mute, feeling again an unnamed accusation.

'Your aunt has taken ship for India with her paramour. Yes, you may well blush. It does you credit. And there are circumstances too difficult to explain to a mind untutored in these matters that have made her flight financially disastrous for our family. We face bankruptcy. Your uncle and I must follow her to India to save what we can.'

There was a tightness beneath her skull that was preventing her from thinking clearly. She could not comprehend how Eleanor's defection had brought them to ruin but it must be so. Perhaps Eliot had committed a more successful fraud than the unfortunate men in Manchester had done. Realising she had thought them unfortunate, she trembled and put her hand to her mouth.

'Are we truly in such straits?'

'Do you doubt my word?' His lips drew back as he spoke. White teeth slashed the hare's throat.

'No, sir.'

He had brought the threatened storm into the church. The air was heavy; she laboured to breathe. A fly, drugged by failure, rose to beat hysterically against the glass, and fell defeated.

'Providence has favoured you,' he said. 'You were always a good, obedient girl and now, as you enter womanhood, you're to be rewarded. Your future happiness and our prosperity may be secured by one action on your part.'

'What – what would that be?'

'That which is the highest destiny a woman can attain. You are to marry. Unsworth has offered for your hand.'

The light had changed within the white walls. It lay thickly on stone and wood calling out no answering gleam.

'I danced with him,' she whispered. She heard Margrave's intake of breath.

'At the Dunstons' ball,' he said.

'I barely know him.'

52

'He's certain of you. And his – his family's wealth, his foreign interests, are to be put at our disposal. We may retrieve our fortunes and good name. You have only to say yes.'

'I barely know him. I had no thoughts—'

'He sails for Bombay this day week. With his bride, if she can accept her father's guidance for her good.'

'A week? Papa, no.'

He stood before her. She did not need to look into his face.

'I'll leave you to pray upon it,' he said. 'Pray to be shown where your duty lies.'

They left Vauchurch before dawn in a covered carriage. There had been two jagged forks of lightning but the storm had not broken and the horses, sweating with dread of coming thunder, tried to shy at the flares that lined the winding, precipitous drive down to the valley. As they passed out of the great gates that divided park from pasture, Kate lowered the window, and clutching the leather strap in her gloved hand, leant out to see the last of her home but the points of yellow flame, diminishing as they coiled towards the plateau, led only to darkness.

She felt Margrave watching her with contempt and, though she was pained by her submission gaining her so short a reprieve from his disapproval, an embryonic rebellion shocked her with its seductive murmur of his waning authority over her actions. Another man was to take his place. There was little doubt that she had been sold to suit her father's purposes, just as he might have sacrificed one field to save a farm, one bale to save a cargo. She was going willingly to her immolation for the sake of Frank and Olivia, Eleanor and Hermione, for the preservation of their House yet she was sore and heartsick that she could be torn from them and sent across the world, in the possession of a near-stranger, without a soft word to ease her fears.

A gust of honeysuckle, cloying in the heated night, pressed its velvet presence against her upraised face. Her lips opened as if she would cry out. She knew this scent as she knew each sight and smell and sound within the familiar boundaries of her eighteen years. The carriage-lamps, swaying with the slow rhythm of a careful pace, drew a wraithlike glimmer over hedgerows that slid back into obscurity. It was here amongst this tangle of honied flowers surging over a decaying ash-stump that she had found a wren's nest just at the level of her eye when she was on her pony

53

a decade before. She had brought cake crumbs for the fledglings and had lifted Olivia to gaze with her queer concentration through the leaves.

She yearned for the children. They were to follow their elders to London for the wedding, then she would sail and who could say when they would meet again. These dear ones who had taken all her love. Perhaps she would have a child of her own. A shudder shook her at the thought and she could not tell whether there was more of pleasure or apprehension in it. The memory of Nat Unsworth and his kindly smile as they waltzed beneath the ivy wreaths at the Dunstons' Christmas ball returned to her, bringing a shy and tantalising warmth. She had not expected him to remember her.

The light fled over a pale form. Wings stretched, beat and the owl drifted upward, its sorrowful face turned to hers. The ache within her breast tightened as the wire had tightened about her hare. She did not want to be used this way. She looked up towards the soaring of the owl. Dawn was breaking; a crimson sky between the louring clouds. She would not weep before her father; from this day, she would not weep before him.

He could hear the click of wood on ivory as the footman led him towards the billiard-room. Playing seemed too casual an occupation in the maelstrom of intrigue and revenge that had become his world and he wondered how Unsworth could pass his time so frivolously. He felt the documents he carried in his inner pocket press against his chest and resolutely set his mind against the guilt that tried to invade it.

The footman opened a door and stood aside to let Forston pass through.

Nat Unsworth was standing with his billiard-cue resting on the floor, watching his uncle take a considered shot. Seeing Forston, he leant the cue against the oak panelling behind him and came forward smiling to shake hands. His open, pleasant face showed a welcome that Forston wished he could accept wholeheartedly. That part of him that was the injured husband was prepared to use anyone for his ends, but that part that was the uncle, lazy and lukewarm though it was, knew the cruelty in hurling Kate so abruptly into adulthood. But she is a woman, he thought as he exchanged greetings with Nat and shook his chalky hand. Marriage is her portion in life. What does it really matter whether she misses a few weeks of cooing in conservatories? She's a docile child; she'll adapt.

The elder Unsworth finished his shot and watched its successful conclusion before acknowledging their guest. He was a spare man in his sixties and as great a contrast to his nephew in his general aspect as could be imagined. Nat had benevolence written over all his features; Bryce had devoted five decades to unscrupulous and downright wicked commercial pursuits that showed themselves plainly in his gaunt and cunning face. His sinister intelligence had made Nat heir to a wealth so great that even if his conscience, when the time came, obliged him to cast off the trade in opium and whores, he would still be rich beyond counting. An alliance with this family would give the Margraves remarkable mercantile leverage and, in particular, would completely hedge in the Eliots' Assam plantations with Margrave and Unsworth land, closing all routes out to their markets.

Bryce walked over to join Nat and Forston. He was wearing a long, loose silk damask dressing-gown of exuberant flowers and leaves over his shirt and trousers, and slippers with pointed, Turkish vamps – and was looking every inch the nabob.

'Good day, sir,' he said. 'No doubt you've brought the contract?'

Nat laughed. 'You're too hasty, Uncle. Can't we ask after the lady first? Ask after Kate? There's more to this matter than signing at the bottom of the page.'

'If the lady were indisposed,' Bryce said, looking wryly at Forston, 'we would have been told. It would change the dowry.'

'Uncle,' Nat laughed again but less comfortably, 'you will have your jest.'

'Aye, lad, so I will. Now, Forston, romance is for the young. Shall we leave this mooncalf and see what the lawyers have to say?'

He led Forston back into the passage and across the hall to his study. It was a room with the same exotic air as its master. Swathes of dark green satin embroidered with golden stars had been pleated up from the walls to the centre of the ceiling, forming a flamboyant and claustrophobic tent. Brassware gleamed in sunlight falling through a barred window and the marble mantelshelf sported erotic carvings wholly unsuited to its austere Georgian lines. There was a stale, sickly tang to the atmosphere that told Forston Bryce had been sampling his own wares.

The two men seated themselves at the desk. Bryce was watching

Forston with amusement. He had seen his visitor recognise the smell of the drug and smother an instant revulsion.

'As a rule, I prefer brandy,' Bryce said. 'I've never been one to like a pacifying effect but now and then it's sweet to look upon Xanadu, wouldn't you say?'

Forston had not come to be teased. He took the marriage settlement from his pocket and set it beside the inkstand.

'You'll find it's as we agreed,' he said coldly. 'Pass your eye over it and summon your legal man.'

Bryce tapped his long nails on the ribbon tied about the document. 'That young fool's my only male relative,' he said. 'As tender in his ways as a maid. I'd as soon leave my money to the Foundling Hospital as to such a milksop, but there it is. Perhaps your girl will make the next generation stronger meat.'

'Will you read it? Time is pressing.'

Bryce began unfolding the heavy paper. 'I knew your father,' he said. 'He wasn't one to cross, as your pretty little stepmother found out. I like a man who can hate his brother and teach his wife her place. I wish you joy of your voyage. I believe, after all, you are your father's son.'

Quinn walked softly over the grass beside the gravel path. He was never afraid to draw attention to his actions but he had discovered, rather to his surprise, that there was one person in existence whose well-being was as important to him as his own and, though he would not hide his going to meet her, he would not advertise his presence with crunching footsteps.

Darkness had fallen and the hotel garden was criss-crossed by the shadows of laurels, sundials and plane-trees illuminated by multi-coloured lanterns. In the centre of the lawn, where an abandoned croquet-mallet had not yet been gathered up by the staff, a fountain involving a convolution of dolphins was splashing softly into a bowl lit by emerald flares. Beyond the high, spike-encrusted walls, the constant noise of city life was gaining its peculiar late-night qualities of stealth and excitement. He could hear streets thronged with carriages, omnibuses and riders, with returning diners and theatregoers, with hungry, blank-eyed girls and men sauntering forth for beckoning company, but he could see a verdant stillness and smell the green dampness of a watered garden.

She was already waiting in the summer-house. Her gown rustled as he approached. He passed the great ceramic jars of lilies, with their warm intoxicating scent, that stood at the entrance to the retreat and she half-rose to meet him, subsiding again before he could take her hand. The wrought-iron, fern-swirled seat, the lilies, a moth that drifted towards them and back into the dusk, all were white in the enveloping shade. He sat beside her and heard her indrawn breath.

'Charlotte,' he said, and ran one finger down the curve of her neck.

She lifted her head, her heavy earring swaying against the skin he had touched, and stifled a shuddering sigh. This was why Eleanor had given up her name. This and this. She moaned aloud.

Quinn held her, regardless of who might look in upon their tryst, and thought of the lost years since he had first loved this woman. He had not been faithful to her memory. His heart had indeed been broken but his body had been whole and a source of predatory pleasure. He had been a libertine yet the only passion he had felt had been then, when she was the girl who was to be his, and now, when, at last, he would take her for his own.

It would be affectation for him to pretend to himself that the life he had led without her had been a wasteland. Success and self-indulgence had crowded his days. For a year after she had been wrenched from him, he had tended to his father's health. They had been as close as two essentially depraved characters could be, and though there remained uncertainty about his parentage, Quinn willingly accepted Jack Margrave's claim to have sired him, deviating from this acquiescence only when he wanted to tease his 'cousins'. Jack's death grieved him but the sudden accession to wealth, rebuilt by rack-rents and suspicious good fortune at card-tables, did not. His ambiguous social position made England less attractive than it was to those born on the right side of the blanket and, for some time, he devoted himself to travel. There was much to enjoy in such a life. His money gave him entrance to the most luxurious of European resorts, where there were too many strangers for his history to be well-known, and his bold, vigorous nature took him to Eastern deserts, to African plains and, finally, westward to America.

The strange and poisoned society of the Southern states, where an apparently cultured elegance disguised a deep barbarity, appealed to him. He was at home with savagery that wore a graceful face. Its hypocrisy amused him and the way of living it gave the rich was flattering and convenient. There was nothing to tie him to his mother country; he bought a plantation in Georgia, with its complement of slaves who came to curse his name, and acquired the trace of a slow drawl that ravished Charlotte.

Still, there was a restlessness in him that made him long for change and new boundaries to cross. A certain difficulty over a duel had brought him back across the Atlantic. He had been respected, by his kind, as a hard master but in the eyes of a Southern gentleman the killing of an uppity black with a laconic lift of a pistol was one thing, spilling the blood of a rich white quite another. The duel had been a matter of honour, a lady's name had been abused, and yet, and yet . . . He had no wish to fall with a bullet in his back. It had been politic to leave.

'When does the ship sail?' he said.

Charlotte tried to drag herself back to rational thought. She, who took pride in her coldness, had fallen into a delirium that clouded her sharp mind. The love she had felt for this man, the love that had never died but merely been walled up within her most secret being, had burst forth, an obsession that filled each moment of her day. The passion that had driven her resentment and hatred, her fierce repression of her sensuous nature, was flowing into the need for Quinn. She pressed against him and laughed shortly at the effort it was to speak.

'Kate's or Leo's?' she asked.

'What's Kate to me? I want to know when your husband leaves.'

'In three weeks.'

'And his brother?'

'Goes with him.'

'They were always fools.'

They both laughed, husky with cruel anticipation, as wolves might laugh as they set forth for their prey.

'But I must go soon,' she said. 'He'll be back and wonder where I am.'

'A moment more.'

She leant against his shoulder and looked out across the garden with its dim scarlet, blue and amber lanterns to the brilliant lighting of the hotel where her eldest daughter lay sleepless and afraid. Kate was the only one of her children who had roused Charlotte's maternal affections. In the bitterness of her regret for having obeyed her father and let him marry her to Margrave, she had waited for her first child with a hungry hope that it would fill her emptiness. Perhaps if Kate had been outwardly ardent and rebellious, she could have channelled her devotion into motherhood but the girl's anxious docility reminded her too much of her own disastrous, dutiful mistake and there had been no lasting attachment.

She knew that Margrave had always intended to make dynastic marriages for their children. He made no bones about the Unsworth alliance being arranged by him for the sake of its usefulness in their present situation. If another man were to have been the bridegroom, she would have fought to thwart Margrave's stark use of their daughter, but she had noticed Kate's liking for Nat and the resurgence of her own desire made her unusually eager for her girl to have the happiness that could have been hers if she had not been torn from Quinn. When Providence offered a union that would content both father and daughter, it was foolish to say it nay.

A sensation so unfamiliar to her that she hardly recognised it as guilt did disturb what little of her consciousness was not centred on Quinn. The hurry with which Kate was being despatched to another's care in a foreign land was uncomfortable. Its haste made the true nature of Margrave's purpose too plain; a few weeks of courtship and fittings for a trousseau would have covered the arrangement in a decent mask of conventional pretence. But the Unsworths' ship was sailing; if Nat had gone ahead to meet his Indian obligations, sending for Kate to follow him, the bride would have had a lonely, daunting voyage without a protector, and so a special licence had been obtained and weary seamstresses must work through the night that the wedding-gown might be delivered for a ceremony two mornings hence. Resolutely, she closed her mind to the inner whisper that Nat was no secretary to be summoned back to his desk, that he could have delayed his departure a trifle if he chose; it was better to remember the blushing softness on her daughter's face when she had waltzed with him.

A gust of song hung in the scented air as three men, trying to recall the glee they had heard the night before, stepped out of the conservatory onto the terrace. They stood together, lighting cigars and singing snatches of the refrain between the sucking breaths that drew a dull red glow into the tobacco. Outlined against the bright windows in their evening dress, they were a puppet-show of innocent companionship as they shared matches and recollections of how this singer and that had struck a pose to emphasise their sentiments. By degrees, pausing on each step to break into the others' speech, they came down onto the path and wandered towards the arbour.

Quinn raised Charlotte's hand and kissed it. He slipped out of their refuge, strolling confidently back towards the hotel, exchanging pleasantries with the smokers as he passed, his easy manner rousing no suspicion of an illicit meeting.

He did not enter by the conservatory, where more decorous lovers lounged amongst the palms, languorously waving fans like the slow beat of the moth's wings as it had turned in the dusk, gazing at the beloved with shadowed, ardent eyes. His thoughts were occupied as he went into the hall that led to the rear of the reception lobby, intending to go to his room for his hat and cloak. He was too stirred to rest and would go out to walk the lively, sinister streets in search of diversion. Night had much to offer an interested observer.

He had reached the desk and was about to cross to the staircase when he became conscious of a hostile glare. Such aggression was being directed towards him that he was immediately as alert as if he expected an assault. In the instant before he recognised what was afoot, his mind jumped to an encounter with an aggrieved citizen of Georgia.

Margrave was standing before him with a belligerent self-assurance that had grown during the years since they had last met. Quinn could see that here was a man unused to being opposed by anyone except his wife and the sight entertained him.

'Good evening, Cousin,' he said.

Margrave stiffened. 'Do you dare to use that word to me, sir?'

'You'd rather I claimed a closer kinship?'

He smiled and Margrave, who harmed men by guile and commerce, was consumed by an unfamiliar desire to strike a blow. The need was powerful and disturbing, and though he did not so much as clench a fist, he noticed eyes being drawn to him amongst the passers-by and conversations grew hushed. He turned abruptly to the alarmed young man behind the desk.

'I was under the impression,' he said, 'that this was a respectable hotel.'

'Now, Leo,' Quinn said amiably, 'is this any way to greet me after my absence and when we're to be parted again so soon?'

Margrave exerted himself to master his rage. The exhilaration and successful strategy of the past days had given him a belief in his invincibility that was damaged by this living embodiment of family failings. A superstitious dread of Quinn as an evil omen slid into his thoughts, destroying the complacent anticipation in which he had been luxuriating. Guilt for the sacrifice of his daughter flooded through the breach in his conviction but his arrogance was too strong for doubt to last. He waved a hand dismissively at the reception clerk, who was murmuring about the manager.

'The absence was too short,' he said. 'I'd like to forget everything about you.'

'Would you?' Quinn was urbane. 'There we must differ. I hope to make myself intensely memorable.'

Kate sat beside Margrave in the carriage holding a stiff, round bouquet on her lap. She was trying to quell the trembling that made its lace fringe rasp against the garlands of orange blossom sewn to the wide satin skirts of her wedding-gown. Since she had been brought to London a day and a half before, there had been little activity except fittings for this glossily white confection and the hurried trousseau that had been bought, altered and packed in trunks bearing the name *Unsworth* and the direction of the ship that would carry her away from all she loved.

She suspected that there had been more bustle than was necessary in order to keep her from a moment's quiet in which to dwell on the enormity of what was being done, but she did not know. Her head ached and the inability to think clearly that had descended on her in the chapel had not dispelled. She tried to believe that her marriage was for her good as well as the family's and that her parents would not hurt her, but she was tired and scared and there had been no one to encourage her trust. Her mother seemed distant and she had barely seen Forston or her father. She would have liked to have met Nat. He had brought a letter to the hotel, telling her of her new home and signed prettily *Your Impatient Betrothed*, accompanied by a handsome set of a pearl and ruby necklace, earrings, bracelets and pendant – the trophies of a rich man's wife – but she had been out at the dressmaker's and he could not wait.

Putting a hand to the simple cross she wore around her throat, she closed her eyes. A stranger looking into the carriage at the delicate face lapped by the veil that fell to her feet, would have said she was calm. She had grown accustomed to hiding the

61

strength of her emotions and it would be useless to give way at this late hour when Margrave, she was certain, would show no pity for her fears.

Behind the shelter of her lowered eyelids, she took herself away from the crowded city street with its hawkers and horse-dung, its shouting of wares and constant movement. She went back to the sweep of the hills as they curved from Vauchurch to the sea, to the cold, brown peace of the winter landscape, the pale glitter of moonlight on grey waves. Her desire for her home, for the heights and valleys that were lush and bleak in their beauty as season followed season made her feel more like a Margrave than she had ever done. She shared none of her father's fierce elation at her departure, nor could she wrest satisfaction from knowing that fulfilling her duty would save their name. What was that to her in this loneliness? She was an outcast. Tonight she must lie with a man who was a memory of a smile, and tomorrow and all the days after, she must be obedient to him as she was now to her father.

She touched the finger that was to wear the ring and strove to recover her hope of love. There was no need to shrink from her husband; he was a good man, but this was not how she had dreamt her wedding would be. Tears welled behind her closed lids. The carriage was too hot, too close. It was hard not to scream for release. Still, she sat motionless except for the tremor of her bouquet.

They drew to a halt. A footman jumped down and opened the door. She stepped out and stood giddy and bewildered as she waited for her father. The tumult of the street was worse without the protective shell of the carriage. She did not hear the compliments of onlookers nor see the gardenia an old Colonel took from his lapel to throw at her feet.

Margrave came to her side and gave her his arm. She walked forward through the Gothic arch of the porch into the church, over flagstones and the memorial slabs of a past age. Darkness and cold, a chill that settled into her blood, dim, wavering candlelight that swam in her tear-filled vision. A long walk through empty pews. Her mother, her brother and sister standing watching her trance-like progress. A blur of white before her; the vicar. Two men moving to their stations; Nat and his uncle. She was delivered to them; she turned to her groom, to Bryce. *To Bryce.*

The ceremony began. Charlotte remained standing, clutching her prayer-book so tightly with shock that her nails pierced her gloves. She could almost have laughed at her stupidity. Searching back through every word that Margrave had said about the marriage, she saw that he had never named which Unsworth was to be favoured. When she had spoken of Nat, he had not answered her directly. There had been a smooth evasion in everything he said. And of course it would be Bryce. Only a roué with no regard for a young girl's heart would have expected Kate to be given to him in such a manner. She looked at Bryce as he stood beside her daughter, his vile face alive with lascivious anticipation, and her own young misery ached within her awakened breast.

The vicar was speaking: '. . . To which holy estate these two persons present come now to be joined. Therefore if any man can show any just cause, why they may not lawfully be joined together, let him now speak, or else hereafter for ever hold his peace.'

'I object.'

Her mouth was dry but the words were firm. Silence fell as suddenly as an axe. In the stillness, Charlotte was aware of the high, cold reaches of the church, the emptiness that should have been filled by a divinity she suspected none within these walls, except her daughter, knew.

Kate turned, lifting her face to her mother and there was a depth of beseeching love in her eyes that made Charlotte yearn to retrace the years and begin afresh. Then there was movement. The vicar, Margrave and Bryce were all drawn to take a step towards Charlotte as if there must be action in this crisis, and the malevolence she felt from the latter two returned her to her old self.

'There's been a deception,' Charlotte said. 'My daughter and I were led to believe that another was to have been the bridegroom.'

'My name is on the licence.' Bryce spoke directly to the clergyman. 'Bryce Sebastian Unsworth. Is that not so?'

'It is, sir. It is.'

'Then let us continue. There is no impediment.'

'My daughter does not wish to proceed.' Charlotte clutched Frank's shoulder. 'She's been imposed upon.'

Margrave took Kate's elbow and pulled her slightly so that he was between her and Charlotte. He stared into her eyes and the appeal they contained called forth no mercy.

'Remember the family,' he said. 'Would you shame me?'

A lifetime of submission to his authority overwhelmed her but she said nothing.

63

'You prayed for guidance,' he said. 'You have already pledged yourself before God.'

She was again the trapped hare, mesmerised by dread. He tightened his grip on her arm.

'Will you marry this man?'

'I will.'

She walked from the church like one whose spirit had died. Her face was blanched and her breathing shallow. The ring was heavy on her hand. She stepped into the Unsworth barouche with its white ribbons on the coachman's whip and sat as if she were a waxen image of a bride. As the horses began to move, she roused and turned her head but Bryce spoke sharply and she did not look back again.

Chapter Five

A wind that warned of autumn blew in from the sea, rustling leaves in tired woods, whining through coombes where shepherds feared a hard winter, rattling dry stands of oats. On the ramparts at Vauchurch, Charlotte stood alone, feeling its chill touch on her closed face. Darkness had fallen. The last of a bloody sunset spread a crimson stain low towards the west. All else was black but for the cold glint of Venus piercing the engulfing night.

She was heavy with sorrow. A letter from Quinn was folded in her breast but she did not think of it. News had reached her that day that Kate's ship had foundered, wrecked in a sudden storm off the Arabian coast. There had been no survivors.

Her first-born was dead; the loving child who had turned to her for rescue. Her gentle girl was dead, drifting beneath rough waters, turning with the turning of the tide.

This was too high a price to pay for fortune. Honour was a mockery and sham. She stood like stone as the wind died and dew fell; she stood with hatred and vengeance in her heart.

PART TWO

Darkness Falls

1860

Chapter Six

They stepped softly into the shrouded room. As they pulled the door to behind them, closing it with deliberate care, the darkness that had been faded by the lamp in the passage, bloomed about their candle-flame with doleful, velvet menace. There was no present threat within the shadowed walls; the hurt was old, a stale betrayal, a melancholy, corroding selfishness that had left a house desolate, a child forlorn.

The flame burned unwaveringly in Hermione's steady hand, a wisp of smoke rising towards the high ceiling. Olivia and Frank pressed close to her. This was the first time that Eleanor's room had been unlocked while the Margrave children were at Knapp. It was open only because the housekeeper, engaged in answering questions about preserving the hangings from damp, had neglected to secure it after Charlotte's inspection. They should not have been there. The consciousness of sin – their own and that of others – subdued their venturesome spirit and kept them huddled between the cold depravity of the tainted chamber and the indignation that would greet them if their leaving it were seen.

It was a haunted room; they knew that but they were not yet old enough to understand its phantoms were rumour and the envious lusts of those who fed their own night-hours with eager imaginings of what had been done there. They had their own ghosts.

Hermione moved the candle slowly, letting the light fall on the ornate bed, the button-backed chairs, the great fireplace with its carved swags, the dressing-table with its tortoiseshell brushes and combs, its cut-glass jars of dried and cracked pomade, its beaded pincushion where Eleanor had left the farewell note that had made Forston cry out like a wounded deer.

She had no tender memories of this room. When she had woken in the dark, her heart beating with the fear that her nightmares were real and waiting to clutch her beneath the sheets, she had not fled to be gathered into the safety of her mother's arms. This coverlet had never been flung back to let her into a warm, protective hollow as Eleanor moved over with loving, slumberous concern. She had never sat on the ottoman watching admiringly as beauty was dressed in satins and gold. It was a room glimpsed longingly as the door was closed or entered on tiptoe at the skirts of a maid.

The flame quivered as she raised her hand, glimmering on the edge of a cheval-glass and Olivia's white face leapt onto the tarnished silver backing, seeming to hang alone, vehement and pained, in a haze of dark reflections. Frank drew in a breath sharply and Hermione touched his arm.

'I'll open the shutters,' she said.

She crossed to the nearest window and lifted the catch. As she folded back the panels, the dim December afternoon flowed into the room, its bleak light transforming a place of myth and dread into one that was sombre but ordinary. Leaving the candlestick on a cabinet, she went from window to window, letting the pale day wash over wardrobes, rugs and portraits. Perhaps the uncovered casements would be noticed by someone outside the house but it was better to be scolded than leave Frank with an impression of having been faint-hearted. He was a boy who needed all the courage of his eleven years to endure the normal trials of life. A shameful remembrance of trembling at his sister's image or, worse, a superstitious fear of what might have lurked within the unseen corners of the room would have woken him, sweating, in the night, longing for his dead Kate to comfort him.

As she opened the last shutter and turned to watch her cousins, Hermione saw that the tension she knew had been tightening Frank's temples had already eased and he was prowling silently about, clearly enjoying being in forbidden territory. He had grown several inches whilst away for the last school-term and was wearing a new, loose jacket, fastened at the neck, that was not yet part of him. With a touching, childish pride, he had earlier lifted his waistcoat to show that his stout trousers were moored to him by braces lovingly embroidered by Olivia. Improbable foliage rioted up towards his shoulders and she had been glad to think of Olivia taking time from her obsessions to stitch patiently and affectionately at such a gift.

Olivia had moved closer to the mirror and was staring earnestly at herself and the reflected room. It was typical of her to prefer to see through a glass darkly and Hermione, always moved by compassion for a tormented soul, went to stand next to her.

They made an arresting picture; they were plain and yet striking. Both drew the eye – Olivia by her intensity, Hermione by her generous, serene warmth. They had escaped the gawkiness that afflicts fourteen-year-olds and, though their hair still lay down their backs and their skirts were ankle-length, they were clearly on the edge of womanhood.

Olivia was wearing black. She had worn mourning since Kate was drowned and, when pressed, would claim she clung to it for her sister's sake but that was not the truth. Privately, she had sworn an oath to wear no colours until Margrave returned. She had told no one except Hermione, and her obstinate embracing of grief made family and servants alike believe that the strange girl was growing stranger. Had Margrave known of her peculiar offering to him, his exasperation would have driven him to avoid her more assiduously than ever when they were both at Vauchurch once more, but she would not have been discouraged. She did not lose interest in the sun because it fled into the west each day and her father's irritated manoeuvrings, now romanticised by his absence, had no dampening effect on her devotion.

The severity of Olivia's dress made the quiet Hermione in her Prussian blue gown, with its flash of magenta petticoats, look almost flamboyant. The pair gazed into the looking-glass, neither seeing themselves, as Frank roved back and forth.

'I wonder what Aunt Eleanor felt when she stood here,' Olivia said. 'She would have seen something that was – that appeared to be – perfect. What would that mean?'

'I don't think Mamma needed meanings.' Hermione's voice was tranquil. She had taught herself not to hope where hope was pointless and found the lesson liberating. Realistic expectations kept her from much disappointment and left her free to appreciate the goodness that did exist in those around her. 'If she'd under-stood more than the effects of her face, she could never have left.'

'She could have lived long and been revered.'

'You talk of her as if she were dead.'

'There's no life without honour.'

'Yes, there is.' Hermione put her arm about Olivia's waist. 'The name of Forston has been shamed, people whisper about my mother before I'm out of earshot but I still look forward to riding my pony, a cup of chocolate is as sweet as if my mother was

71

virtuous, and I'm glad to be going to Vauchurch for Christmas with you.'

'But that – that's just making do.'

'I'm no philosopher or theologian, love, but I think we can go mad if we don't find chocolate sweet.'

'I prefer mine bitter.'

Dusk began to infiltrate the room, giving it a stillness that would soon bring back the ghosts.

'Twilight's coming,' Hermione said. 'They'll be asking where we are.'

She went to the far window and began closing the shutters. Behind her, Frank opened a wardrobe and a faint scent of old celebrations eddied about him and was gone. Sumptuous evening-gowns lay folded on the broad shelves, waiting for a woman who would never contemplate wearing last year's fashions. Dried heads of grey-blue lavender, the same shade as the half-darkness that was in the room, were scattered amongst the figured silks and gauzes, the handmade lace and stiff, boned bodices. These were gowns that had been clasped by dance-partners and hungered for as they glided from shimmering dining-tables, and it seemed to Frank that he had found a living thing in the desert of the discarded room, that a melancholy ache for their past rose from the abandoned clothes and would cause them to slither from the shelves and envelop him as the light failed.

Hermione closed another shutter and the inside of the wardrobe became hidden and immense. Frank locked its door and turned back towards his cousin. He watched her fastening the catches with her deft movements, so capable and graceful, as night seeped in, following at her heels.

Shadows obscured a watercolour of Eleanor in her youth that Olivia had been examining and she too turned to Hermione.

'Where's the – oh. The candle's gone out.'

All three looked at the candlestick. For the Margraves, the absolute blackness that would engulf them as the last shutter closed was sinister and, to Olivia, queerly fascinating.

'It has a winding-sheet,' she said.

Hermione reached out and smoothed the curl of melted wax that had smothered the wick. 'I should have remembered to snuff it,' she said. 'You two go out and I'll finish this.'

Olivia went to the door, listened for anyone passing and, hearing nothing, opened it. The lamp burning further up the passage let only the faintest light into the room. Frank hesitated.

'I'll stay with you,' he said.

Hermione heard the quiver in his voice. The emptiness that had always been in this room had taught her endurance.

'Keep guard for me in the corridor,' she said. 'It's a long while since I was afraid of the dark.'

In the Twelve-Acre, the sun was setting behind the hills to the west. The leafless woods covering the ridge were silhouetted against a dull red sphere, streaked with russet, that seemed too large and swollen to be the same feeble body that had hung small and pallid in the pale sky. The air was cold. It had a crisp sharpness that said the morning's frost, still lingering in ditches and at the foot of the north-facing walls, would return in force before the dawn.

Except for these traces of ice and the scarlet hawthorn berries, the world was brown. Charlotte, standing on the hard furrows of the newly-ploughed field, looked with satisfaction at the turned earth, the intricate weaving of the plashed hedges, the bare boughs of the oak that grew alone in the centre and the ranks of timber on the hills. She was not a painter but she thought that if she were, she would try to capture the elusive beauty of this muted scene, knowing that she could never portray the particular quality of quiescence that was its attraction. Dormancy used to make her impatient but now she saw the potential for triumphant growth it hid and felt the strength beneath the slumbering land.

'It's getting colder, ma'am.'

'I believe it is.' She lowered the scarf she had thrown across her face and blew slowly. A white mist was suspended before her. 'The temperature must be dropping as we speak,' she said.

' 'Twill be a cruel night.'

'Come, I'll say a word to the ploughmen before we go.'

She set off across the field, stepping firmly from furrow to furrow, the bailiff in her wake. The slowest of the ploughmen reached the end of his final stetch as she approached and a weary murmur of content passed from one man to another as they waited on the headland to see the completion of their work.

Four teams had been ploughing the field for three days, an acre a man between first light and dusk, walking eleven miles behind the curve of the soil as it laid itself down before them. Gulls settled on the exposed earth, plunging downward with raised wings and harsh cries, and rooks wheeled suddenly up from the copse at the eastern corner, screaming raucous defiance at any alien bird that flew too near their ungainly nests. Every hour, the horses were stopped to draw their breath and the men flexed their fingers, beating their arms across their chests as they made wry comments about each other's work and watched the sky for snow.

Now there was nothing left to plough but the strip of stubble around the edge where they circled at the end of each furrow. When that was done the next morning, all ploughing would have been brought to an end before Christmas, as custom decreed, and they could look forward to the festivities with easy minds.

Charlotte approved of their expertise and of the way they grew more formal and respectful as she came near. They took off their hats and she let them stand bareheaded despite the increasing chill. Passing down the line of ploughmen, she complimented them on their labours, addressing each by name and asking after their families. Cornelius Vane, a wizened man, notable for controlling his geldings with whistles as if they were sheep-dogs, told her his wife was in bed with the rheumatics and she promised to send soup and wine.

When she had spoken to the last man, she put out her gloved hand to his horses. Vane had compact, thick-necked Suffolks but these, looming above her, clinking their bits and breathing sweet, moist scents of hay, were, like the other two teams, Shires. The closest lowered his great head and nudged her, stamping a heavy hoof on the iron ground. She smoothed his flicking ears and cupped her palm on his soft muzzle, aware of the nervousness of the men who watched her.

The horses were tired and did not know her well; impatience at being kept from their stable could make them do her an unheeding injury with their massive strength but she was not afraid. She loved their power, as she loved all power that she could bend to her will and some that she could not. It pleased her to keep the ploughmen standing, afraid to warn her of her risk, just as it pleased her to oversee Knapp's lands.

She had been master of the estates since Margrave and Forston had left. In their haste to cross the world and triumph over the man who had insulted them, they had not left clear orders for the running of their households and farms. Neither had played an essential part in the cultivation of their acres, accepting rents and profits as their due, demanding deference from farmers and

74

labourers alike but rarely overriding the decisions of their agents. The provision of their domestic comforts had called for no more than their bored or infuriated reading of the accounts.

Left alone in England, Charlotte had seized the reins of Vauchurch and Knapp. She was bold, imperious and knowledgeable. No one dared to question openly her right to govern and though there were sullen murmurings about her sex and the need for her husband to return, these were only from men who did not want to change cherished and impractical ways. Her shrewdness, her habit of raising the cost of a lease to goad tenants into squeezing the last half-penny from the earth and her ruthless dealing with late payment made her feared, hated and obeyed.

She had wondered whether her success would be enough to persuade Margrave into letting her remain in charge or whether jealousy would make him send her back to the distaff, and had worded her letters to him cautiously, sure that others would not dare criticise her too strongly, believing her position to be sanctioned by him.

Absorbed in a vindictive trade-war that used his rancorous talents to the full, Margrave gave himself up to the pursuit of vengeance and did not search beneath the surface of her correspondence. She felt herself almost secure in her sovereignty, the receding danger of his interference only serving as a spur to the tightening of her grip on their lands.

And then all India was aflame. The peculiar possession of a continent, achieved through centuries of commerce, exploitation and treachery on every side, and held by a thinly-spread and riven army, was challenged by sudden, blood-soaked mutiny. Charlotte was not one to care about a sepoy's grievances, but the chance that Margrave might not return revealed the strength of her longing to retain her independence, and privately she revelled in the slaughter. Ah, God, how she had thirsted for Margrave's death; a death as charged with terror and vain strugglings as her dear girl's must have been when the Arabian waters closed about her face.

She had read the papers avidly, scrutinising each fresh account of an atrocity and list of casualties as if the pressure of her fingers on the broadsheets could bring her heart's desire. There was no mention of Margrave or Forston. She received no message and her hopes rose. Months passed; district by district, the mutineers were put down with a savagery equal to their own and word came.

Margrave and Forston were unharmed; Eliot was dead. She did not believe she had been told the truth of it. Margrave had sent her a queer tale – queer in its plainness, its matter-of-fact detail that was unassailable and yet unconvincing – of having tracked their quarry to Eliot's residence on the banks of the Jumna, of seeing him die at the hands of his syce and of snatching Eleanor to reconciliation with Forston in the cool safety of Simla. It was, she thought, exactly like Eleanor to slip comfortably from the protection of one man to another but her sister's easy summoning of forgiveness was all that did not make her look sceptically at the closely-written pages announcing life and triumph with careful, uncharacteristic sobriety.

Chaos and the ensuing eagerness for order offer abundant opportunities to men ready to grasp them. Margrave and Forston stayed to increase their wealth and Eleanor to write languidly to Charlotte, praising the luxuries of Calcutta and decrying the attention paid to women who had suffered more than she. In the aftermath of her own selfish zeal for the Mutiny, Charlotte could still marvel at Eleanor's ability to see the carnage as an irritating affront to herself.

So for five years, while Eleanor held court in pierced pavilions, lay in splendid idleness by tiled carp-pools, was rowed slowly through the crush of lilies on moonlit lakes, Charlotte ruled without restraint. She flourished. Her handsomeness increased with her fulfilment and she gloried in her tyranny like the queen of a barbaric country.

Night had fallen with silent ferocity, touching the weathered skin of the ploughmen with a metallic cold like the stroke of a knife-blade. Her breath caught on the veil that was clinging to her cheek, where it had been pressed before she lowered her scarf, and hung between the lines of black silk net.

Splinters of light were piercing the deep, clear purple of the cloudless sky. Margrave was on his voyage home. If the winds were favourable, his ship would reach Portsmouth within the week. Her husband would return.

A Suffolk stretched its short neck downward, raising its docked tail, and shook itself like a dog, setting its harness jangling. Its horseman laid a quietening hand on the bristles of its hogged mane and murmured reassurances in its weary ear.

Charlotte could not make out the features of the men who stood waiting for their release. Dark shapes in the gathered darkness, each had a history she had made it her business to learn, each moved more stiffly when she was near, conscious of her calculating eyes. These were her men, her fields, her woods; it was at her bidding that the earth was ploughed and the crop that it raised would be hers.

'I've put your sealskin cape to warm by the fire. You'll need it, I'm sure. The Dear knows how cold it'll be before we reach Vauchurch. And John Footman will have your handwarmer filled with hot charcoal to give to you as you step out of the door.'

Hermione looked over her shoulder at Ward and had her head pushed firmly back into its previous position.

'Now, Miss Hermione,' Ward said, 'I can't braid your hair for travelling if you shift about.' She tied a vivid emerald ribbon about the loose ends and, lifting the heavy plait, brushed it softly against the girl's face. 'Your lovely hair,' she said tenderly. 'Draw your shawl over your head when you're in the carriage.'

'Cloak and shawl *and* bonnet, Wardy?' Hermione asked.

'There's to be a terrible freeze tonight. Why we can't stay until tomorrow, I don't know but there – no doubt your aunt has her reasons.'

She patted Hermione on the shoulder and went to put the brush into the square leather case that was holding the odds and ends needed since the more serious box of clothes had been locked and carried down to be packed into the servants' coach. Every article in box and case was as it should be, cleaned and folded to perfection with nothing forgotten. Ward slid the brush between the pair of bronze kid shoes Hermione had been wearing before she changed for the journey and a tasselled pouch of ivory spillikins. She shut the case with a satisfied snap, content that nothing was wanting and that both she and her young lady had only to be wrapped in their outdoor layers to be ready well before time.

In the years that had passed since she had stood in Eleanor's room weeping for having been deserted, Ward's face had softened. The somewhat haughty handsomeness, that had made her look piquant in Eleanor's cast-off gowns and caused Forston's friends to suggest indiscreet alliances, had been mellowed by a wholly unexpected and absorbing love.

As the first anguish at being discarded had ebbed, it had been supplanted by the terror of having no place in the world. Her

77

employment had vanished with her mistress. How could she find another situation as a lady's maid? Who would believe that she had played no part in the elopement? Through no wrongdoing of her own, her moral character had become questionable. Perhaps she could accept that most painful demotion in the hierarchy of the servants' hall and take a position in a kitchen or as a housemaid, but she was trained for neither and the problem of explanation remained. And Knapp was her home. She had no family; Knapp was her home.

A soft, firm voice had sent for her. She had gone to the schoolroom with red-rimmed eyes and gazed into the drawn face of one who had looked about her for kindness and affection throughout nine years and finding little had set herself to cultivating what she had found.

Hermione had recognised the yearning Ward had suffered for Eleanor's notice. It was a forlorn craving that child and woman had shared, each hoping for some slight sign that their existence mattered to the beauty who moved through life sealed within an impregnable self-indulgence. Hermione had been too young to analyse what she was doing or to disguise the simplicity of her good intentions with complicated speeches. She had asked gravely that Ward be her personal maid and tend to her as she had tended to her mother. In the disturbance of the house, no one thought it strange that a thin, abandoned girl should take it upon herself to make this arrangement and Charlotte, arriving in state to take command, had not overruled it. Charlotte believed in the proper respect being paid to rank and was aching with bitterness for the treatment her own daughter had received. It seemed to her fitting that Hermione, as the only Forston left at Knapp, should have her blood acknowledged by this mark of distinction.

Ward had agreed to Hermione's request with profound relief. She had seized her chance to remain in the company of those who had become her family; it was a precarious security that could be shattered in an instant by dismissal but treasured all the more for its light and warmth on the darkling plain. Her new task was to be done with the utmost efficiency in order to preserve her foothold at Knapp; it was a job and nothing more.

She had not expected to like the child. Living as Eleanor's shadow had focused her thoughts on the sensual and trifling pleasures of the mature and shallow. She had not known where to begin with so young a girl. Reasoning that Hermione was, after

78

all, her mother's daughter, she had offered to make her a gown in the latest mode. The polite lack of interest in this treat puzzled her. It was of the first importance to keep Hermione's favour and she studied her charge, striving to discover what would captivate a child who was at the head of the house yet did not drum her heels to be pampered.

Inspiration came to her. Hermione dearly loved to play a harpsichord, ousted from the drawing room by the pianoforte to languish in one of the anonymous chambers on the attic-floor, but could not be as sprightly as she wished on the yellowing ivory keys because the conventional cut of her sleeves curbed the freedom of her small arms.

Ward opened seams, let in panels of cloth and suddenly the astounded, grateful girl had clothes in which she could move and play. It was a revelation to Hermione, both in the discovery that a restriction she had accepted as an unavoidable handicap could simply be flung aside and in the realisation that someone had taken the trouble to wonder what she would like. Neither Ward nor Hermione had heard of the movement for rational dress; they knew only that a practical idea had far-reaching physical and emotional implications.

Hermione's amazed thankfulness entered Ward's heart like the sea breaking into a desolate cavern. The voluptuous pleasure of appreciation turned the starving woman's efficiency into care. Her possessive nature wrapped itself about the girl whose calm strength could reciprocate all the love shown it. Ward took to going into Hermione's room at night to smooth the ruffled sheets; she remembered lullabies and part-songs lost to her memory years before; she developed a jealousy of the hapless governess and had to be gently chided by Hermione, who would not have Miss Armstrong's diligent, uninspired kindness scorned; she was chaffed by the frequenters of the housekeeper's room for her motherliness and received the teasing in bashful good part. As Charlotte flourished in her new-found liberty, so Ward bloomed in the loss of hers.

Olivia and Frank came into the room, bringing cold air with them. They had been out to the stables to measure Frank against the mark where he had stood last June, straining upwards, for the groom to notch the feed-room door. Their faces were flushed with the chill of the evening and the triumph of Frank's spurt of growth.

Frank perched on the padded fender, holding his hands to the fire. Olivia, looking like a crow in a snow-field, sat on the edge of Hermione's white bed, huddling her mourning round her and watching Ward with suspicion and envy.

'You should take your cape off, Miss Olivia,' Ward said. 'Or you won't feel the good of it outside.'

Olivia gave her a dismissive glare but the tips of her fingers appeared from inside the folds of broadcloth to toy with the fastening. She could not decide whether she wanted her share of Ward's dedicated attention or would rather be wholly self-sufficient. It was an indecision that led to much brooding and glowering in Ward's presence.

'We have to go now,' Frank said, winding his feet around the rails of the fender. 'Mamma's in the hall giving her last instructions to Mulvey and she said to tell you to come.'

Ward lifted Hermione's cloak from the stool where she had spread it. Hermione rose and stood obediently still as Ward arranged the heavy garments, moving only to raise her chin to have her bonnet-strings tied.

Watching her apparently being prepared for Alaskan exploration, Frank drew a bulky pair of bear-skin gloves from the pockets of his overcoat, where they had been forming ungainly bulges at his hips.

'The coachman says the roads will be slippery as a hatful of eels,' he said, 'and if we get back without being overturned, he's the Pope of Rome.' He plunged his hands into their respective paws and admired the result.

Ward, who was hooking her own cloak, cast an apprehensive glance at her chick as the disfigurement and lingering deaths of many an unlucky heroine of a ballad-sheet flitted through her mind. Simultaneously, she was certain of the safe arrival of the Margraves, luggage and herself and the imminent destruction of her tender girl.

'Will it be so?' Olivia said, her eyes brilliant. 'Will we overturn?'

'No.' Hermione looked at her with a grave smile. 'No, we'll be perfectly secure together. Come, we mustn't keep my aunt waiting.'

She walked out onto the landing and Ward, Olivia and Frank followed in her wake.

There was coldness lying in the air near the door. It had slid in from the passage when the maid had been sent away and the flames burning like spears of crimson lilies had swayed against the grate at its ingress. Charlotte pushed the bolt home. She would not be disturbed; the servants knew better than to do that.

Going slowly back to her toilet-table, she sat down on its elaborate stool and, leaning her elbows amongst the gilded brushes, pots and hair-pins, rested her chin on her clasped hands. A pastille was glowing in a ball of filigree silver and its wisp of musky smoke eddied in the draught of her movement and the change of air, drifting between her and the oval looking-glass into which she gazed.

Her reverie was mellow and expectant. It was past midnight and her day had been full but she felt no tiredness. As she sat before her reflection, the velvet swathes of her evening-gown surrounding her with luxuriant folds, her body was vibrant with anticipation. It was not that she felt young. Her youth had contained little joy and no fulfilment. This was the lavish, devouring energy of a woman who had come into her deserts in the prime of her talent and desire, after long years of frustration had taught her their power and worth.

She arched her back, putting her hands to her cinched waist as she turned her head from side to side, revelling in her readiness. Her pulse was beating strongly; she could almost feel the surging of the blood in her veins. Stretching out one arm, she traced the blue lines of its soft, inner side. He liked the whiteness of her skin.

The familiar sound of the latch lifting made the breath shudder in her throat. She twisted on the stool to see the ancient oak door set into the far wall open and Quinn enter beneath its pointed arch. There were few candles burning in the great chamber and he was in shadow until he had crossed half the room towards her. He had discarded the tail-coat he had worn as they dined and when he came up behind her, smoothing her shoulders and bending to kiss her raised mouth, the seals on the watch-chain strung across his waistcoat pressed into her back, leaving the imprint of a scarab and hawk on her flesh above the rigid edge of her gown.

'Your coachman must have cursed you,' he said.

'What do I care? I would have made him rue it if he'd kept me from you.'

They had eaten together, as they did on most evenings but, aware that the servants offering fricassés and Bavarian creams with such decorum, had ears, they talked only as the master's wife

81

might talk to his cousin. It was a form that they knew fooled no one yet they persisted, the illusion of respectability amusing them and increasing the vehemence of their more solitary pleasures.

The night-journey from Knapp had been for this moment; the bitter drive through freezing lanes, the horses' rough-filed shoes seeking a grip beneath the painful sky, the ice cracking under the carriage-wheels, the children slumped within their layers of clothes, neither waking nor sleeping, had been for this precious freedom, this freedom that must soon be lost.

'Are you warm at last after your journey?' he asked.

'Can't you feel that I am?'

He lifted the heavy garnet pendant from where it hung between her breasts, cupping the jewels in the palm of one hand as he stroked her lightly with a fingertip. The looking-glass gave back the smoke-glazed image of her parted lips. He had given her this necklace as dawn broke the morning after Margrave had sailed for India. They had been too impatient for each other to care about the risks of discovery in a hotel and Quinn was not a man subject to fears. In the grey-green light of daybreak, as they lay amongst the twisted sheets, their eyes large with sleeplessness, clutching one moment more before he must leave, he had reached down below the bed where he had hidden it and passed her the box that held this gift; the first token of love he had ever given and the first she had received. She had wept a little as he clasped it round her neck and the fierce tears had fallen on the cabochons, glistening amongst diamond-drops, that twined about the carbuncles, as if they were meant to be there.

He remembered the tears as he touched the lesser stone, a coulant that slipped smoothly up and down the chain. They had been welcome to him as the sign of her fervour but he had not wanted to see them twice. Unlike Margrave, he was not afraid of her strength. He had watched the ripening of her ruthlessness and resolution with pride; he would not retreat and let her be crushed back into a wife; he would not have her weep for misery. The red gem gleamed within his grasp; the pastille flared into sudden brilliance and the jagged flame burning behind his hand made the blood glow beneath his skin, staining his fingers with the same translucence that gave the stone its life.

'So few more nights,' he said. 'Ah, love, so few.'

Chapter Seven

The swell lifted the deck beneath Margrave's feet in long, regular surges that made him stand with his legs apart, flexing his knees with the movement. The heaving rhythm of the ship as it held its course through the night answered a need within him for more purpose, more achievement, and the sensation of flying through darkness into port was mesmerically satisfying.

He held the rail at the ship's side, ignoring the spray that hit his face beneath his wide-brimmed hat with startling coldness and the dank smell of brine. The black sky was tempered only with sharp stars; the black sea only with far-flung leaps of foam. All was obscurity and motion, the creak of straining wood, the rigorous force of wind.

England was summoning him with a power he had not expected. The barbarous success of his years in India had fed his covetous appetites as his homeland had never done. He was returning because he had a son who must not be left under petticoat government. It was his duty to raise a Margrave worthy of the name. He had torn himself from his belligerent, mercantile world for Frank's sake and had resented time lost from gorging upon a defeated continent, but as he neared the shore of the small and potent island, that sent out such as he to subdue the world with fanatical confidence, he felt a tightening of his heart as he thought of its green wooded hills, its familiar customs, its dialects spoken without the belief that shouting would make them understood. He yearned for Vauchurch and its massive solidity. It was not his way to interpret symbols yet he had a half-formed consciousness that the ancient walls that had seen his birth, as they had seen those of a myriad cruel generations, called to his blood and would make him complete as India could not.

'We're to have a squall, sir. Best to go below.'

Margrave turned to the seaman, already dressed in oilskins, who had addressed him. He disliked any directing of his behaviour and a harsh retort was almost at his lips when he suppressed it. If heavy weather were in the offing, the captain would naturally want the decks clear of passengers, just as he himself preferred to negotiate without his victim's family flitting in and out of the office.

He walked carefully across the sloping gangway to the head of the staircase that led down to the cabins. His sea-legs were good; they had been since the first day of sailing and it was one of his vanities to despise those unfortunate souls who staggered, grabbing at handholds, with the skittering runs and queer, exaggerated bendings of ice-skaters. He had never lost his footing or felt the slightest queasiness, regarding pale sufferers, whispering of mal-de-mer from behind cologne-scented handkerchiefs or tumblers of brandy-and-champagne, as having brought their sorrows on themselves from weakness of spirit.

Opening the door to the saloon, he stepped inside and stood on one of the Turkey carpets, shaking salt drips from his hat. The curious mix of vessel and opulent drawing room had struck him with its oddity when he had boarded but he no longer noticed it. He waited, letting his eyes adjust to the increase in light. Few of the lamps were lit but as they swung on their chains, they called up gleams on the many mirrors ranged between the cabin doors, on the gilded frames of vigorous portrayals of racing clippers, on polished mahogany and on their own burnished brass oil-chambers. The effect of shifting brilliance and dusk served to magnify the rise and fall of the ship and Margrave rocked back on his heels, regaining his balance without needing to steady himself against the screwed-down plant-stand at his side.

He did not want company and was glad to see that most of his fellow passengers had retired to their berths. Four men – a spice-merchant, a gentleman-botanist, a muscular chaplain bound for a northern bishop's palace and a lieutenant wasted by fever – were sprawling at the long central table, desultorily playing mah-jong on a baize board. Margrave watched them throwing their squares. The clack of the ivory pieces and the tap of an overturned sherry-glass rolling in a perpetual semi-circle onto the retaining rim of the table-top were drowned in the groan of planking and the ravaging roar of the sea. Ever and again, the dragons and winds slid from their places and were replaced by the long yellow fingers of the lieutenant.

Margrave passed the length of the saloon, nodding to the

84

players, who acknowledged him with drowsy, meditative bows. As he walked, he noticed the tip of a soft, kid shoe protruding from an edge of satin skirts where a revolving bookcase with corded shelves formed a small bay. The young woman seated on the plush sofa in this slight privacy did not raise her head from the volume she held as he drew closer. He could not believe she was reading but was unsurprised by her pose. She wore a long, glimmering shawl, shot with gold thread, wrapped about her gown in an oriental manner and was resting its silken fringe against her handsome, melancholy face as she gazed unseeingly at the open pages. In her brooding reverie, she did not seem aware of her surroundings.

He left her undisturbed and went on with his firm gait through the wavering maze of lustre and shadow until he reached his cabin. The steward had lit his lamp and the soft radiance from its green glass shade gave an effect of welcoming intimacy that was lost on one of Margrave's temperament. He had never needed a haven and moved about the swaying room, taking off his outer clothes, his frock-coat and cravat with his mind on the invigorating, unforgiving savagery of the sea.

The ocean brooked no mistakes; no quarter was given by its vehement waves to the frailty of the men who set sail upon it. The depth of its power appealed to him and the same instinct that was drawing him to Vauchurch tempted him to see the wrath of God in the fury of the cold, chastising waters.

Opening the top drawer of the chest beside his bunk, he laid his watch and chain amongst his neck-cloths, where he could reach it in the night without having it slide irritatingly back and forth. As he turned away, unbuttoning his waistcoat, the lamp lurched with an unexpected roll of the ship and sent a flash of searing light onto the long smear of blood on the cabin wall.

He was instantly alert, poised for determined, forceful action. His hand reached for the pistol he had worn habitually during the most turbulent of his Indian years but, before he could be alarmed by its absence, the trick of light faded, leaving him staring at the thick strap of the red leather letter-pouch he had hung from one of the brass hooks. He stood, letting his heartbeat slow and his breathing ease.

The strap must have caught on a lower hook as it swung with the ship. Its crooked outline mimicked the macabre stain he had seen on the demurely flower-sprigged wallpaper in a bungalow shaded by jacaranda trees in a deserted cantonment.

A cantonment deserted by the living. Beneath the rusty streak, a young Englishwoman lay slumped, her throat cut, her unborn child ripped untimely from the womb and placed at her breast. Her limbs had swollen in the stifling heat. The stench hung as heavily in the fly-pocked air as the lace curtains that still covered the dusty windows. He had looked out, across the neat entrance hall with its bamboo stand for parasols and its dish for cartes-de-visite, over the verandah where a single severed hand pointed grotesquely towards the gate, to the overturned pony-carriage where vultures squatted with bulky indifference around what had been a subaltern, too sated by their gruesome holiday to flee from the set-faced men prodding them with rifles.

Margrave remembered how he had stood in that charnel house and, seeing one distended bird finally make waddling hops backwards with an indignant glare above its bristling ruff, had been reminded of the outraged evasive shufflings made by a stout, be-feathered dowager, sprayed by the wheels of a curricle in Mayfair twenty years before. He had laughed then at the splattered satin and he laughed again, mirthlessly, in the reeking drawing room as he took the cloth from a table and spread it over the desecrated form.

The Mutiny had suited him. All the repressed violence in his nature had leapt forth in naked brutality. He was a warlike man and the opportunity to plan and execute strategies to defeat the enemy with no limit put upon the barbarity of his deeds unleashed his capacity for conscienceless cruelty as his previous life had never done.

Tactics fascinated him. He had none of the cold relish for killing that made Forston feared. It was the game that interested him, manoeuvring and outwitting, and if this particular demonstration of superior cunning ended in screaming and gore – well, then? What of it? There were innocent wives cut down in their homes to be avenged, there was the well at Cawnpore, choked with the bodies of mothers and children and, to left and right, in the tainted night-winds and the pestilence-bearing rivers, there were the pathetic signs of those who had sought an escape and found none.

His anger over the atrocities was real and undiluted by questioning what had caused them, but his disgust did not weaken his bellicose pleasure in conflict nor did he lose sight of his original aim. In those bleak months, when every man who could fire a gun was of use, he had campaigned with soldiers without being restrained by the discipline of the Army and as the tide turned, he and Forston, with their company of guards loyal to the Margrave name, had a freedom not dreamt of in England since their piratical ancestor had raised Vauchurch.

It was impossible to embrace such ferocity and be unchanged. As he swayed in the cabin, gazing at the line of red that had taken him back to the sultry horror that had liberated his malice, he knew himself for a different man from the one who went East. What little softness there had been in his nature had been pared away. The wife of a corporal in Kurnaul, a Highland woman who prided herself on having the 'sight', had called after him as he rode by that he would have a darker shadow when he returned to his home. The image pleased him.

He would need his severity to curb his wife. It seemed a small matter compared to what he had achieved yet, as he grew closer to home, she and her antagonism loomed larger in his mind, rousing the old, familiar irritation. He had not thought of her as a woman since they had parted in London. Even the accusatory letter she had sent, laying Kate's drowning at his door, had not touched his feelings as a husband or father. She had never behaved in what he considered a maternal manner and he dismissed her grief as affectation. It had interested him to find that he suffered no sorrow for the daughter whose obedience had served his purpose and he could not believe that Charlotte, who despised passivity, sincerely mourned the girl.

For five years, his dedication to destroying the Eliots' commercial empire and expanding his own had prevented him dwelling on the part Charlotte was playing in England. In his more honest moments, he admitted that he had always known that she had taken charge as soon as his back was turned, but she had not trumpeted her suzerainty and he had turned a blind eye. There would be no comfortable blindness for either of them when he crossed his threshold. He would discover every invasive tendril of her influence and sever it; she would see who was master in his house.

In the kitchen of the King's Arms, the scullery-maid opened the oven-door, releasing a bloom of hot air into the already over-heated, beef-scented room and receiving a sharp tap of a wooden spoon on her saucily-capped head.

'Not that one,' the cook said. 'How many times must you be told?'

'Sorry, Mrs Morgan.'

The victim closed the door upon the cooling pies within and shuffled on her knees to a smaller opening on the far side of the range. Mrs Morgan turned to the lady's maid sitting companionably on the settle.

'Frills a-top her ears,' she said, 'and nothing in between.'

'Nothing but her young man, eh, Mary?' said the ostler who was sitting at the far end of the long deal table, chopping turnips to add to the horses' feed. 'Nothing but lovely Ned with his kerchief oh-so-gay?'

Mary, with a simper on her dumpling face, coloured up to her unsuitable goffering and continued to take hot bricks from the oven, wrap them in flannel and pack them into a small, straw-lined hamper.

'Your mistress will be feeling the cold, poor soul,' Mrs Morgan said, by way of inviting conversation. 'And yourself, no doubt.'

Greaves crossed one smartly-booted ankle over the other and looked down at her equally smart grey silk skirts complacently. She was enjoying both the warm, ordered commotion of the kitchen, with its constant turmoil of the many servants needed to run a flourishing inn, and the interested deference being paid to her as a traveller, a survivor of the Mutiny and the handmaiden of a lady, whose silence and escort were already causing speculation. The eagerness to be friendly that was exhibited by everyone, from the sleek girl straining soup through a cloth to the ancient, one-legged man seated on a stool on the corner, scouring a pot with sand, his peg-leg wedged into a groove in the flag-stones for support, amused her. She was perfectly aware that they were agog for blood-curdling tales of her experiences and she had no objection to returning when her duties were over to oblige. It did not trouble her that the stirring adventures she would recount were not her own. She had long since grown lax in her disapproval of deviations from strict morality and she found it answered very well.

'Dorchester isn't such a shock to me, Mrs Morgan,' she said, 'for all its frosts. I left Norwich to go out to Calcutta as maid to the late Mrs Edward Singer and I know what it is to break the ice in your pitcher of a morning. My lady, now, was born and bred in

India and never set foot in England till yesterday noon. And cold! She sits shivering like she was the King of Russia.'

'India be a powerful hot country,' said the peg-leg, plying his sand in slower circles.

'It is, sir, it is.'

A head appeared round the door from the passage, called, 'Two mutton chops for Number Five,' and retreated.

'Will you take a cup of tea later, Mrs Greaves,' Mrs Morgan asked, 'when your mistress is resting? Or a glass of something hot to keep out the chill?'

'I will, sure enough.' She stood up. 'There's the bricks ready, I see. I must put them in the bed as quick as maybe.'

The boot-boy seized the hamper and she followed him out of the kitchen towards the stairs. She was glad to have an appreciative audience to look forward to for, although she was preserving a confident front, she was worried by the equivocal situation that she and her lady must enter. It was not what either of them had expected. They had thought a separate, discreet establishment . . .

Following the boy into a bedroom of dark draperies and sombre, gargantuan furniture, she snubbed his hope of a penny and, shooing him onto the landing, placed the bricks between the sheets of the four-poster. The fire had been built up while she was away and was crackling zealously with hissing spurts of clear, blue flame. Greaves took the poker and struck the piled coals, reducing them to a more demure candescence. Her mistress could not bear the sound of burning.

She went to the window, intending to check that no draught could slide past the curtains and was tempted into parting them to look out into the street. It was a dozen years since she had stared up into an English winter sky. Last night, she had been too hurried and harassed to find a moment for stillness and thought. Her face grew lines and character as she raised it to the stars. She had known cold and the brittle thrust of starlight in the Himalayas. Why should it be different here? She did not recognise constellations or the changing patterns that delight a sailor's soul; she saw only the hopes that had died since these skies had flared above her and the readiness to make the best of what was at hand that had replaced them.

How fortunate she was. She had an hour of merry company ahead of her with a glass or two of grog and it was enough to make her cheerful. And thank God for the same. If she had had her lady's temperament, she would have been defeated by her disappointments. Her breath had misted the glass and with her fore-finger she drew a childlike picture of a ship onto the pane – the *Bountiful Oak* – the ship that had carried her, sharp with anticipation, to the far side of the world. All had gone well. Mrs Singer had her faults – not least her inability to keep her lace out of the mulligatawny – but she was generous and willing, in her slothful good nature, to be directed by her maid. Dysentery had brought the poor creature to a squalid end and, in a rash moment of sentimentality, Greaves had succumbed to the proposal of marriage from the wine-waiter at the ornate, palm-ridden hotel in Simla where they had been staying. Hard times had come upon her. Few of her husband's wages had reached her pocket and she had been obliged to take in dressmaking to placate the tradesmen. Then, to her joy, Mr Greaves, weaving his way home after his ritual finishing of the heel-taps, had tripped over a pariah dog and contrived to drown himself in two inches of stagnant water. She believed his death had come about through his unfamiliarity with that particular liquid but kept her opinion to herself.

She had much to be grateful for, as she was aware. Not only had Providence removed her marital burden, it had shown her this mercy in a town whose only excitement during the Mutiny had been intemperate threats of throat-cutting by a milkwoman accused of watering her wares and the audacious twirling of an Indian moustache at an agitated memsahib.

It was while she was strolling through the town in her widow's weeds, pondering on her prospects, that she learnt that a lady of good family but now under the protection of a wealthy Englishman was in need of a personal maid. Having suffered from her own respectable but disastrous mistake, Greaves was less impressed by a fall from grace than by the depth of the purse that might pay her wages. She applied for the post, was accepted and found herself in the twilit world of as unlikely a fille de joie as could be imagined.

Hearing the door from the private sitting room open, she stepped back from the window and drew the curtains together, pressing the overlapping edges with long strokes of her hand.

'That should keep the night air out, ma'am,' she said.

The young woman who had not raised her head to Margrave in the ship's saloon walked over to the fire and stood gazing into it with her sorrowful eyes.

90

'The nearer we get to his home, the colder it becomes,' she said.

'I've put the hot bricks in your bed.' Greaves pointed to the humps beneath the quilt. 'That should get rid of the damp.'

Celia Eliot stared at the high bed as if she were seeing another time and place. 'He'll come to me again tonight, I think,' she said. 'After so long a separation on board ship, yesterday won't have sated him.'

'Perhaps he'll stay away, miss. We're too close to his home for him to want a scandal.'

'He isn't afraid of scandal; he's too powerful here for anyone to complain. Who would dare to lose his custom? It was the captain's right to punish indecency that kept him from my cabin. He can't bear another man's authority.'

The two women stood lost in their dread of the coming night and its unendurable morning. 'Did he send to Vauchurch, ma'am? His wife may come to meet him.'

'His message said to expect him late tomorrow afternoon. She doesn't know we're to lie close to her; she doesn't know that you and I are part of his baggage-train.'

'God save and protect us.'

'Are you sure the good Lord will trouble Himself? When has He before?'

Greaves turned away and began taking the few remaining items from the small travelling trunk to cover her discomfort. She was far from being a devout woman but Celia's openly-expressed loss of faith always made her feel that she was about to be summoned before a severe master to account for a lifetime's unadmitted guilts.

Celia sat in the elbow-chair before the hearth and contemplated the glowing coals. Fire had come to fascinate her. It was true that she could not suffer the sound of crackling, spitting flames and would back from them, rigid and white in her remembrance of charring flesh and the bright writhing of smouldering hair, but to look into their ardent heat both repelled and drew her. It was a beguilement born of the violence of the years that had taken her from a girlhood, in which she was cosseted yet scorned for her quick mind by her family and their down-to-earth, mercantile friends, to these bleak days when she was the trophy of a man who prized her submission because she was the last Eliot left for him to degrade.

She had never believed that there was a role for her in the world. Her mother had not lived to see her out of long-clothes; her father had been the kind of man who would have enjoyed the company of a butterfly-girl, flitting lightly amongst the luxuries his riches could command, quivering upon his finger to display the splendour of her wings. He could make nothing of this grave, observant creature, silently watching fantastical dusks. He said she was not natural and would be better for a whipping. An unsatisfactory daughter was aggravating but of little account in the life of a busy man and he found it easy to ignore her, accepting that he would find her at table when he dined at home and leaving her to play her futile part in a social round that offered no comfort to one who was of its tribe and yet not quite –.

Her cleverness and ability to see the consequences of actions made people wary of her. She had warned her brother that flaunting his possession of Eleanor Forston would bring tragedy, that the Margraves were not men to stomach an insult to their name. He had laughed at her, taunting her for a sour spinster. She had feared a native uprising and been sneered at for lack of patriotism until she learnt to keep her mouth shut. Her thoughts were swift but she had no enterprise and her circumstances made her passive.

'Shall I undo your hair, ma'am?'

Celia turned her head and saw that Greaves had placed a stool next to her.

'Yes,' she said with a sigh. 'Yes, you may as well.'

She rose, grasping her skirts and settled onto the unevenly padded stool. Greaves began drawing long, silver pins from Celia's coiled hair, spreading and lifting the heavy tresses as they slithered downward. When it was all hanging like a cloak about her shoulders, Celia felt the first slow brushstroke and closed her eyes.

'I thought I'd have to have it cut off after Lucknow,' she said. 'It had grown foul. There was so little water for washing.'

It was rare that her mistress mentioned the siege and Greaves did not know how to reply. Making a soothing sound as if she were grooming an unpredictable mare, she continued to brush.

'That would have been a shame,' she ventured. 'A terrible loss.'

'A greater loss would have been better.'

Nothing was said for a moment, then Celia flexed her neck and held out her hands to the fire.

'You couldn't wash the lice out,' she said. 'We called them the light infantry. Yes, a greater loss would have been better.'

She stared into the grate. The red coals had been sculpted by their pulsing heat into the domed and turreted vision that was Lucknow. It scorched the tender skin of her palms. She had been staying with the family of what passed for friends in their house outside the Residency compound in that unlucky city when the Mutiny broke upon them. Their roof had been fired and fire had followed her throughout the months of heat, disease and death. Two thousand people had sheltered within the ravaged buildings of the compound, under constant bombardment from the rebels; two thirds did not live to see their relief. She could not fight or flee. Patiently, without hope and, gradually, without interest, she had endured the days in which she could do no more than exist. She waited as her companions died about her; she waited as hunger thinned her cheeks and rumours of rescue came and went. She watched as the young wife of an army surgeon was struck in the breast by a bullet as they sat at a scratch dinner, falling back in her chair with pursed lips, then forward into the spirit lamp and a sudden rise of flame; she watched as the palaces were sacked and the orange groves were bright with sepoys wrapped in fire.

Escape passed her to her father and she watched him, weakened by recurrent fever and broken by the death of his son, let himself be outwitted, undercut and harried by the men who had retrieved Eleanor and still were not content. When news came that he had been found hanging from the barred window of his empty counting-house and that the very walls that kept her from the sun belonged to Margrave, she could not feel surprise or grief. She waited in the hushed house, making no plans, having no expectations, until Margrave came to claim her as his booty. In her strange, tortured helplessness, she did not question his right and entered concubinage with submission, puzzled that Eleanor had embraced it with joy. Margrave consumed her. Hatred and dependency roused an obsession that took the place of love. She lay beneath him alive with rage at her own pleasure and slept beside him tormented by memory and fear.

The fire smouldered in the quiet winter night, frost settled, and she waited for lust and dreams of burning towers.

Chapter Eight

'Aldibirondifosdiforniosdikos.'
  'Six!'
'Aldibirondifosdiforniosdikos.'
  'Seven!'
'Aldibirondifosdiforniosdikos.'
  'Eight!'
'Aldibirondifosdiforniosdikos.'
  'Nine! Huzza!'

Hermione stepped down from the stool with relief and triumph, executing a curtsey that was not without the sin of pride as the others clapped.

She, Olivia, Frank, Ward and Nurse, whose stoutness and dropsical ankles had given her the right to sit while the others romped, were in the nursery summoning the spirit of Christmas by playing Snappen-tongs. The curtains had been drawn against the severe night and a brisk, resin-laden fire was burning with a strong, outdoor scent of pine-cones. Vauchurch did not lend itself to a cheerful aspect but this room, with its unusual abundance of lamps and candles and evidence of a young visitor, had risen above the solitary brooding of its black-clad possessor and emerged full of gaiety and excitement as a welcoming meeting-place for youth and vivacity.

The four whose figures let them, began circling the three chairs in the centre of the floor. They started slowly, still catching their breath from the last time but, with every turn, they could not help an unreasonable fear of being odd-man-out seizing them and an imperceptible increase in speed had them quicken and quicken their pace until they were running round and around, their hearts beating with delighted terror. Nurse snapped the tongs together and the players flung themselves at the chairs, shrieking and clutching at each other as they jostled and rocked.

Frank was on the floor. It could not be denied despite his

protest that Olivia had slid beneath him onto the seat in an outrageous display of low cunning.

'Forfeit, forfeit,' they cried, leaning together in an ungainly, panting heap.

Olivia bent and whisked a gaudy silk handkerchief from Frank's pocket. She brandished it above her head in all its indiscreet splendour.

'Here's a thing and a very pretty thing,' she chanted. 'What must the owner do to redeem it again?'

' "Old ox",' Ward said, her fingers spread over the rapid rise and fall of her chest.

'Yes, yes,' Olivia cried. ' "Old ox".'

'There's no mercy amongst women,' Frank said and took his place on the stool. He clenched his fists in the manner of a younger boy being forced to give a recitation, looked up at the ceiling with its play of shadow, then began:

> 'One old ox opening oysters,
> Two toads totally tired trying to trot to Tewkesbury;
> Three tame tigers taking tea;
> Four . . .'

He paused, grimacing for inspiration and Olivia shook the handkerchief tantalisingly. There was a croak from Hermione and Olivia turned on her.

'You're helping him,' she accused.

'I was clearing my throat,' Hermione said, all innocence.

'Four fat friars fishing for frogs,' Frank declaimed. 'Five – oh!' Another pause and arms outstretched in frustration. 'Five . . . Five . . .'

'Can't you finish?' Olivia asked.

'Five . . . No, I can't.'

'I can.' Hermione got up from her chair. 'Hark!

> 'Five fairies finding fire-flies;
> 'Six soldiers shooting snipe;
> Seven salmon sailing – sailing in Solway;
> Eight elegant engineers eating excellent eggs;
> Nine nimble noblemen nibbling non-pareils;
> Ten tall tinkers tasting tamarinds;
> Eleven electors eating early endive;

Mine, I think,' she said, taking the handkerchief from Olivia and knotting it about her neck.

'Oh, Hermione.' Frank was pained. 'That's new. It cost me four-and-sixpence.'

'Jack-a-dandies must learn their lessons and then their finery won't be taken from them. Snappen-tongs!'

They circled again, faster and faster about the chairs. The tongs snapped and Olivia was alone, whirling for a security that could not be found.

'Forfeit, forfeit.'

Frank darted to the chest at the foot of Olivia's bed. Lifting the lid, he slid his hand inside while looking back over his shoulder at his victim, gave a startled gasp and withdrew a sprig of holly.

'Here's a thing and a very pretty thing,' he said, crossing back to the others. 'What must the owner—'

The disapproving silence stopped him. He put the pin-prick of blood on his thumb to his mouth as he watched Nurse rise from her seat and stand over a sullen and abashed Olivia.

'For shame, Miss Olivia,' Nurse said. 'What are you thinking of, to be bringing trimmings into the house before Christmas Eve? And your father still at sea.'

'He is not at sea,' Olivia said defiantly. 'He's on land. Mamma had a message today that he'll be here tomorrow.'

'God willing – with you bringing ill luck upon the house.'

'She meant no harm,' Hermione said. 'And it was out of sight, not really being used.'

'It was inside the walls,' Ward said. 'It's tempting Fate to call up misfortune.'

'Oh, Wardy, that's superstition.'

'Sometimes old heads know best, my dear.'

'What else do you have?' Nurse opened the chest and brought out a tangle of ivy and mistletoe. 'Mercy on us – if the next year's not as black as judgement for us all.' She shook her head and placed the inauspicious vegetation in Olivia's arms. 'Take all this into the garden and don't bring a leaf of it back until the proper hour.'

The three young people knew that it would be of no use to argue. This was not a consideration that had ever stopped Olivia, but she had been unnaturally good-humoured for several hours and was prepared to let the women have their way with nothing worse than glowering resentment.

'Shall I help you carry them?' Hermione asked.

'No.' Olivia crushed the trailing stems into a more manageable load. 'There's no reason for two of us to be frozen for the sake of old wives' tales.'

She left the room and began to walk slowly along the passage. It was far cooler between the unpanelled stone walls than it had been in the nursery and the solitude, the chill touch of serpentine draughts and the dim light from infrequent sconces brought her quickly to her usual state of mind. There was no sentimental attachment between herself and Nurse but, although she would not admit it in this case, they shared a fascination with myth, symbolism and the occult attraction of superstitious lore. Nurse believed in the power of magpies and crossed knives because she was too lazy-minded to question accepted wisdom or wonder why she must live without a name; Olivia verged upon belief because her passionate, neglected heart longed for meaning and order in a world that had failed her.

A girl of Olivia's intensity should have had an ardent, intelligent companion, strong-willed and concerned enough to refuse to be dominated by her charge's emotional hunger and scorn. Instead, the fragile governess, who had left the household when Kate was betrothed, had never been replaced. On Tuesdays and Thursdays, a drawing-master, having spent two hopeful years in Paris and five resigned and wine-filled years in Rome, attempted to tame her artistic imagination and bring her to the watercolour meekness suitable for drawing rooms whilst improving her languages. The curate, whose luxuriant side-whiskers had quivered with virtuous excitement at the sight of Kate's earnest devotions, had approached Olivia with a tract on the duty of submission in women and now found it necessary to be elsewhere if he saw her coming.

These were the only efforts made to occupy her thoughts. She did not protest, choosing to embrace her isolation as a novice might embrace the austerity of the cloister. Her life was dedicated to grief and yearning. She had not been offered a room fitted for her age and she lay alone in the long nursery, brooding upon her observations of Charlotte and Quinn, raging against their brazen flaunting of their guilt. In these past months, since she had learnt that Margrave was returning, a fevered expectation had consumed

98

her. She prowled Vauchurch, laying her hands on stone and oak as if the ancient structure were a sentient vessel waiting to be filled by the master and his power. Her touch recognised a shared anticipation and was not intended to soothe. She stroked rock and ramparts as she would have stroked a thoroughbred straining for the race.

Quinn's presence had always been gall and wormwood to her. During the first part of her father's absence she had not understood what was afoot. This sardonic stranger who, she could not deny, reminded her of Margrave, was a cousin of her father. He had returned from America and bought a small estate within easy riding distance of Vauchurch. It was natural that he should often visit – but so often? So often that he should have his own bedchamber in the tower? So often that his brand of cigar was kept in the box where Margrave's had been; that the periodicals he favoured were sent to Vauchurch, not his home? She could see that Charlotte was obsessed by him as she herself was with her father and, with stealthy, fearful dread, she was aware that if she did not hold fast to her hatred of Quinn, she would adore him but still she did not understand.

She grew older. Dictionary in hand, she read the Latin verse on the higher shelves in the library; she questioned the most forthright of the farm-girls at lambing-time; she overheard the badinage when the stallion-man came walking his snorting, hot-eyed Shire through the lanes on lascivious May mornings.

Knowledge came to her. The inner vision that was her mirror on the world shifted, tilted and gave a new interpretation that was wholly abhorrent. She had thrust aside the leaves to look directly at the apple. The physical nature of the carnal act did not trouble her. She saw straight through the mesmerising lure of the body to its inevitable connection to the spirit. Her verdict was harsh. She made no allowance for the frailty of the creatures in the grip of desire, she gave no credence to love nor considered what hurts had led to such treachery. The magnitude of the betrayal of Margrave was uncovered and Charlotte was an abomination in her eyes.

Turning a corner of the passage, she came upon a narrow flight of steps, its slabs worn concave by the centuries, that curved round upon itself as it rose to the floor above. A house of this age and grandeur did not follow regular patterns with level layers of precisely-characterised rooms and logical routes of access. There was a randomness in its design that had offended the Georgian mind.

She stopped. The main stairs were ahead of her in the distance and she had intended to go down them and so out into the crisping garden. Crushing the foliage to her chest, she inhaled its green scent, lowering her face to brush against the stiff edge of an ivy leaf as she thought. Being the bearer of ill omens appealed to her. There was a deep attraction to being sent alone into the night to avert evil but it was a pity to let malevolence miss its aim.

This twisting flight of steps would take her to a little used passage that, in its turn, revealed another, more hidden, spiral and on, by back ways where servants were unlikely to accost her for bearing curses in her arms, to the tower-room where Quinn slept.

She speculated upon the outcome of a change of plan. Only a small part of her believed that she was carrying misfortune but that part whispered that she should help Fate punish the wrong-doer if she could. Her rational mind urged that Christmas was the time for mischief and that the discovery of these unlucky offerings in the usurper's room would add its beckoning shade to the legends and portents recounted in the firelight when work was done. She would pretend that she had found the bean in the pease-pudding and been made Queen of Misrule.

There were fewer candles burning on the floor above. For a long stretch of wide corridor, there was no light whatever and she walked with one elbow extended to graze the wall for fear that she would lose her direction in the darkness. She was conscious of the empty rooms to each side. Kate and she had played hopscotch here on wet days and been given no supper for forgetting to rub away their chalk lines. They and Frank had run in and out of these rooms, including them in their games. For all of one winter, the blue chamber with its squat four-poster and antique hangings had been a Crusader's castle, the bare, wedge-shaped room beside it was the desert that must be crossed to reach Jerusalem and the great closet where mattresses were stored was the divan where the wicked sultan plotted the downfall of Christendom and sliced silk scarves in two with a sweep of his scimitar. Now, Kate was no longer a princess who would never renounce her faith and the wind entered through the unused chimneys to curl desolately where no girls played.

She was walking softly as she turned into a gallery where eighteenth-century Margraves posed as Greek deities in swathes

100

of satin and ornately-carved frames. The main staircase, which had dwindled from its robust magnificence, joined this coterie of Danaës and Persephones at its far end and proceeded up into the tower.

Frost was forming on the narrow windows in the tower walls. Already, it was a dense, fragile fur on the ledges and lead divisions of the panes and a harsh, splintered pattern of ferns and arabesques on the glass. Her breath bloomed whitely about her and condensed like dew on the pearls of mistletoe. The yearning for Margrave that had heated her blood for weeks past suddenly rose into an ache of longing that made her pause between steps as it racked her. He was near; he was near. He was a few short miles away and would be among them tomorrow. She had been faithful; she had been true. There would be no more loneliness for her when Vauchurch had its master again.

A cold sweat was on her brow as she climbed on. The tower was not high; its square eminence was a statement of strength, not a necessary vantage point. The ache had subsided enough to let her regain some of her more pleasurable excitement. She momentarily pitied Hermione for her calm acceptance of her parents' absence. Forston and Eleanor were lingering in Egypt, preferring to gaze upon the Sphinx than their equally enigmatic offspring. Her pity was soon gone. It was wasted upon one as quietly certain of her values as was Hermione.

She had reached the landing before Quinn's room. The door was ajar and a stream of saffron light spread across the floor and was lost in the dusk. He could not be still here; he would return to Vauchurch, no doubt, when Margrave was enthroned, claiming to be a harmless relation wishing to heal old and mysterious wounds. Surely, even his audacity would not keep him in the house on the eve of the injured husband's recovery of his own. Walking boldly to the light, she looked beyond the door.

Charlotte was in the room. She was standing upright and regal, her hands clenched against her heart, her eyes closed, ferocity plain upon her face. Her reverie made her moan aloud. She put out one arm and clutched the bed-post, curving her body against it as if she were in pain. Behind her, the panels that swung back to reveal the secret staircase to her chamber lay open and forlorn.

Olivia had not known that there was anything of her mother in her. She watched, aware that this was too intimate for a daughter to see. The thorned holly pressed into her flesh as she crushed it to her, piercing the tender skin of her wrists. Silently, she stepped back into the darkness. Her lips moved without a sound.

'My father is come home,' she said. 'There are forfeits to be paid.'

A lantern burned in the stables, shedding a mellow glow over the gleaming rumps of the cosseted horses that stood in the row of stalls. The air was warm and pungent with the sweet scent of hay, the comforting musk of the beasts and the tang of harness. One of Charlotte's pair of matched bays stirred the straw as he shifted position, the grey mare Kate had ridden tugged another mouthful from her manger and chewed with slow, crunching determination, the Shetland pony Frank had outgrown wheezed gently as she slept.

Two men entered, bringing a coldness with them that trailed from their clothes as they moved down the line. Ears flicked and heads were lifted. It was the weather for hot bran mash with treacle and there was a drowsy anticipation that sank into the previous tranquillity as snuffing nostrils caught no such alluring smell.

'When he wants something done, he d'want it done afore he's asked,' one of the men was complaining.

'Now, Lemual,' said the other, 'that ent fair. You can't rightly say he asks.'

They laughed softly and stopped at the stall where Quinn's black hunter stood like an embodiment of night. He was a horseman's animal, fine-boned yet powerful, afraid of nothing and zealous for his master's approbation.

'No more warm stable for you, my lovely,' Lemual said, going into the stall and unhooking the halter-strap from the iron ring on the wall. ' 'Tis out into the freeze and himself as grim as February.'

The gelding rubbed his brow on the man's shoulder. Lemual scratched him beneath the forelock and received an affectionate buffet that knocked him against the partition between the stalls.

'Lord save us,' his companion said. 'Do you want him in amongst us? Stop playing silly-adders.'

'What is it about him that makes these beauties eat out of his hand, eh? This'n and the mistress both. Would they do it for I if I had his suit of clothing?'

'That they would and the Queen of Sheba with them. Now let's get this tack on.'

They led the hunter towards the door and fastened on his saddle and bridle. Both worked deftly at the familiar task but with an excited expectancy that communicated itself to the horse, making him stir as if he could hear the hounds. The whole houschold was moved by more than the usual sensations of the season. The news that Margrave would return tomorrow had raised a hectic apprehension that was pleasurable, vexatious or alarming according to the degree of giddiness in the character of the hearer. None could believe that Charlotte would renounce her lover and bow her head to the marital yoke nor that adultery conducted with so imprudent and shameless an openness would remain concealed for long. There would be a hint here, a remark there and then someone would feel it his duty to unburden himself of a secret that had been troubling his conscience.

The laundry-maids, with their red arms and flushed faces, giggled over the ructions there would be, as they boiled and starched and ironed in their world of steam. The footmen and stable-lads made knowing, leering comments in low voices that they would not repeat to the women. The cook and her great friend, the head gardener's wife, fretted that the house would be shut up and the staff turned off or put on board wages. The lady's maid and housekeeper and all who could see that real blood is shed when those whose lives are a sideshow for others are scourged, grieved for the pain that was to come and gave the children gentle greetings when they encountered them.

Iron-shod hooves rang in the brick-paved yard and Quinn emerged from the harness-room where he had roused out the men. He mounted easily and nodded at them as, silent now and wary of his displeasure, they spread the skirts of his great-coat evenly over his legs and the hindquarters of the horse.

Quinn looked up at the clear, dark sky, his breath pluming about him. 'A cold journey,' he said.

'Yes, sir.'

Quinn stared at the one who had spoken. 'Oh, yes,' he said, 'cold, indeed.' He slid his hand into his coat-front and took two sovereigns from an inner pocket to toss to the men. 'Here's to keep Christmas and to bring success.'

'Good fortune to you, sir.'

He rode out of the stable-yard and turned down the precipitous carriage-drive, following its sweeping course with confidence. The Margraves had always needed horses of unfailing strength to draw their coaches, phaetons and landaus up this merciless slope, and many an unprepared visitor had been forced to abandon his own transport to approach the house, humbled and gasping, on foot. Quinn did not know whether he would prefer the way to be kinder.

His horse walked carefully, placing his hooves with delicacy on a road that was already slippery with a crackling skin of ice. When they had reached the gates and more level ground, he stepped out smartly, unworried by the night or the frigid air that closed about them with its intimate, piercing touch.

Vauchurch above them was a black presence against the black sky. Quinn was interested to discover that there was an ache in his breast as he rode. He suffered a sense that he was betraying the woman who kept vigil in the stronghold he had left. It intrigued him that Charlotte was the only being who had ever caused irrational thoughts to intrude upon his judgement. There was no abandonment nor was there any weakness in her that made a need for his protection yet still he felt that he was deserting her.

He put this nonsense from him. Their decision had been made.

The lanes were still and hushed. A sliver of moon had risen amongst the stars and its faint light fell on hedgerows that were stiff and spectral with frost. Woods loomed motionless and dense, their fantastic tracery of branches glimmering with a mild and faery sheen. As the rime deepened, the world became lustrous. Each icy crystal that cloaked twig, stone and blade of grass reflected a dim radiance into the bitter air, making the frozen land hazily luminous.

Quinn's face tightened in the cold. There was much to occupy his mind and he rode unhurriedly, observing the transformation of the hills without wonder. He felt a readiness for action that made him alert and vigorous. Had the road been safer, he would have set his horse to a gallop. As it was, he contained his energies, luxuriating in the mastery it gave him. A grave elation beat in his blood.

He thought of Margrave. The wish to avenge himself upon this man who might be his brother had not contributed to his taking Charlotte for his lover but it added zest to his indulgence of desire. It was a satisfaction Charlotte shared. As she unfolded into the voluptuous freedom of a woman loved as an equal, they had spoken, in the tangled haste of urgent unlacings and the heavy, sloe-eyed languor of gratified exhaustion, of the anguish that would strike the prideful Margrave should he learn who had taken possession of his property. It pleased them.

The horse moved through the white lanes and his rider remembered the past. It was not necessary for Quinn to know whether Margrave was brother or cousin. They were bound so closely together by hatred and injustice that the degree of their kinship no longer mattered. The penalties of his illegitimacy had hurt him sorely in his youth but they had released a malevolence that had stood him in good stead and saved him from the restraints of morality. If he had grown to maturity at Vauchurch, acknowledged as a legally-begotten child, he would have been the youngest son, always two steps behind Margrave, always reliant upon a wealth controlled by the first-born. He would have reached manhood with less rancour but also less enterprise and independence than was bred of the slurs he suffered. Every insult he had received from the Vauchurch Margraves, every private sneer and public cut, lay in his memory waiting for vengeance and he would not fail them. Life had taught him to fear nothing.

The narrow road was rising from the valley. This was a lonely place of winding, aimless tracks and deep coombes where deer flitted through shivering stands of hazel and sallows fringing marsh-pools. His house was to the west, over these hills and into the fertile meadows the Margraves had sold before India restored their riches. He had bought a four-square manor-house with enough land to give him the status he required but it had not been his home. It was an address and an excuse for his attendance at Vauchurch; he lived with his love.

His hands were stiffening with cold inside his gloves. He flexed his fingers and thrust first one hand, then the other inside his coat until they were supple again. The lane had climbed to a plateau that fell away steeply at his side. If the moon had been brighter, he could have looked far out over blanched fields and spinneys to the sea. The quiet illumination of the night gave him only the brittle perfection of the frost within yards of where he rode.

Iron Age man had come to this height and seen the security it could give. Ditches had been dug and ramparts raised. The fortress did not have the majesty of Vauchurch; it did not tower above hill and lowland with the brooding menace so dear to the Margrave heart. Trees had invaded it. Ancient oaks spread wind-twisted boughs over hollows where bluebells and campions bloomed before their time. Ice had turned it to a wood of glass. Withered glass leaves still clung to glacial glass branches. White upon white in the darkness.

Quinn listened to the silence beyond his hoof-beats. The peace seemed at one with the cold; bleak, beautiful and threatening. There was beguilement in it; an invitation to be still and rest in its welcome until snow covered you and breath did not come.

He would have none of it; he urged his horse on. A sudden rustle, a movement in the copse, a slithering leap, the cry of a deer. The horse threw up his head, his ears back. Quinn stared into the thicket. If there were poachers, he would see them swing. He was not yet on his own estate, but his or Margrave's – what difference was there now?

He slid from the horse, casting the reins around an elder, and moved stealthily into the wood. His anger was as cold as the night. The hunger of the poor was nothing to him. What was his remained his. The sound of thrashing led him through crossed shadows to the edge of the fortress. From the ridge, he could look down into the trench.

A stag lay in the litter of last year's leaves. It leant against the earth panting, a fore-leg hideously askew. A stump it had trusted for its flight had proved treacherous and its fall carved a raw wound in the immaculate frost of the slope.

Cautiously, Quinn descended into the trough. He stood over the deer. Its eyes were wide and its nostrils gaped; its lips were drawn back over its teeth as it wrenched air into its cavernous mouth. There was fear in the heaving of its stricken body but it did not struggle to rise. He put his hand on antlers that arched into points that gleamed in the moonlight and it dropped its head, accepting what had come. Quinn knelt at its side. The animal smell was rank in the sharp scent of ice. It kicked once, its snapped bone grating, and shuddered in its pain.

Quinn unclasped his knife. There was power in the quiet night and lonely sacrifice. He set the point of the steel against the trembling spine and bore his weight down upon the blade.

Chapter Nine

There being no one in the carriage to disapprove of their intimacy, the two men sat side by side on the box sharing the horse-blanket that enveloped their knees. Both wore caped overcoats in the Margrave livery but the cold had not eased, despite the progress of the white sun in the grey sky, and mid-morning was no warmer than dawn. The blanket was necessary.

'Did they put the rugs in the back?'

'A two-three bearskins.'

The men returned to their companionable silence. They had been dispatched by a grim Charlotte to bring their master from Dorchester and did not look forward to renewing their acquaintance with him. Neither they, the horses nor conveyance could have been brought to a greater pitch of smartness but Margrave was one who found fault to prove his dominance and punished where he found fault. Rattling through the iron countryside, the red curve of their ears showing above their collars, watching the bays' sweet breath trailing like smoke behind them, was preferable to reaching their journey's end. They snugged down into their layers of broadcloth and savoured their peacefulness.

The coachman sucked on an empty pipe as he handled the reins. Ice still lay, rigid and treacherous, in the ruts and a less steady hand would have had the horses jinking this way and that in search of the best route. Symonds knew better. He had no intention of setting the carriage rocking until he lost its balance and overturned them all into a ditch, and kept his pair to a moderate pace that let their winter, nail-studded shoes grip the slippery road.

'Roughed up the soles of your boots, 'ave ee?' he asked.

'Give 'em a good scraping afore we set out.' Lemual flexed an ankle under the blanket. 'Still, I fair dread coming home. That footplate'll be slippery as a parcel of sprats. If I don't freeze to a stone, I'll be jounced off and break my neck.'

'Maybe he'll let you sit up along of I.'

' 'Twould be twitching a lion by the ears to ask a favour. Best take my chances.'

They drove through the white, frost-bound landscape alternately apprehensive, curious and lost in wondering whether they would have time to dart amongst the shops and street-stalls fulfilling domestic obligations. Each had a heavy purse of the other servants' money and Symonds, who could read as well as a parson and had written many a homesick maid's letters, had an interminable list of last-moment Christmas requests tucked into his waistcoat.

There was little of the seasonal spirit about them, however. Margrave was a rock onto which frail, hopeful vessels of jollity and celebration could smash to their destruction. He had never brought merriment to Vauchurch when Charlotte was a sarcastic but dutiful wife, and neither man anticipated reconciliation and welcome now that she had taken a paramour. The signs of Quinn that had so angered Olivia – the cigars, his chosen port, his whip beside the door to the stable-yard – had been removed, but his was too pressing a presence to be displaced by such simple measures. The house remained full of his forceful spirit. No one believed that he had been banished and the varied apprehensions of the household had begun to draw into a sense of foreboding. There could be no happy resolution of the circumstances and the threat of what might come hung over the festive preparations as if, Cook said, they were readying for a funeral before the corpse was dead.

The oldest of the washerwomen, who came up from the valley to help on hurried occasions, reported that Miss Kate had been heard wailing on the ramparts, crying against her father and, though the soothsayer was advised to take more water with her gin, her hearers shook their heads and blessed themselves, passing on the tale with sighs and added detail.

The carriage-wheels slithered over a spread of ice, causing the body of the coach to pull to the left. Symonds called to the bays in the soft, commanding voice of a true horseman and they leant into their harness, trusting his directions, until all was righted again.

A fox tiptoeing across the powdered ridges of a ploughed field, froze with one paw raised to gaze at the carriage. Lemual saw it decide there was no hunt and slip unconcernedly through the hedge, its brush gaudy against the rime.

'Miss Olivia had a blue sash to her gown this morning,' he said.

'I saw. She d'come out to give her pony a carrot and there 'twas.'

They thought of the sight. Had a raven been seen in a scarlet neck-ribbon, it could not have looked more startling or incongruous.

'Two daughters,' Symonds said, checking the near horse, who was roguishly trying to bite his partner's neck, 'one of them gone and t'other Miss Olivia.'

' 'Er's a powerful queer maid.'

It was Symonds's habit to think of people in terms of the animals he tended. He had long ago decided that if Olivia had been a mare, he would let a child ride her but that no one she had seen use a whip would be safe within her reach; he admired and pitied her for it.

'She must put away childish things,' he said. 'The Lord preserve and keep her from harm.'

'I can't chide you for doing nothing – you do it so well.' Margrave stood in the hotel bedroom, looking down at Celia as she lay amongst the tousled sheets.

'They haven't brought my hot water yet,' she said. 'Greaves is seeing to it.'

'You should have sent for it long ago. We must be away. What were you doing lying in bed till all hours?'

'I couldn't sleep.'

He put his head back and laughed. 'I remember,' he said.

She half-closed her eyes. 'I couldn't sleep after you left.' She drew a hand from beneath the covers and put her fingers to her temple. 'I took some drops and, later, I dreamed.'

'What do you expect? Soak yourself in laudanum and you will dream.'

She did not reply. Her face took on the remote expression that both aggravated and aroused him. He would not have wanted her had she been eager for his attentions. Her indolent, reluctant acquiescence, her withdrawal into cool regions of passivity made her submission delectable; her angry, unwilling descent into pleasure quickened his lust as a ready fervour could never have done. When she had cried out in her impure desire, she would lie beside him, staring upward as she retreated to her cold sanctuary, weeping silent, scornful tears and his own drumming heart would slow with another satisfaction. She was his prize, the representation of all that he had conquered and the dominance that was to come.

Vauchurch awaited him and, with it, Charlotte. He would not tell her that he had brought a concubine until she asked. Let her look upon this younger woman, docile in her hostility, and be humbled.

Greaves entered carrying a large jug. Her face, veiled in steam, wore the bland expression she always adopted in Margrave's presence. An obedient servant with no indication of personality in voice or manner was invisible to him.

'Dress yourself, Idleness,' he said. 'The carriage will be here for us shortly.'

Left alone with Greaves, Celia showed no sign of moving. Her clothes had already been laid out for her and she lay gazing at them absently. The act of raising herself from the bed to wash, be brushed and plaited, laced and hooked into the many layers needed to defeat the English weather seemed impossible. If she simply continued to lie motionless, perhaps time would stop and she would not have to live through this day. There would be no final journey to a house that filled her mind with dread; she would not stand before Charlotte, knowing herself a captive, the disgraced, despised sister of the man who had lured Eleanor from her family and brought destruction on his own.

Fear so great that it almost paralysed her overtook her thoughts. She was grateful for the numbness that kept hysteria at bay. Margrave approached his return to wife and home with belligerent arrogance, confident that Charlotte would accept private humiliation rather than expose herself to the opprobrium visited upon a woman who left her husband. Not that Margrave would let her leave. He was not one to have his property slip through his fingers and he had grown too fond of making people tremble to let Charlotte go because her role caused her misery. Other wives had accommodated themselves to the company of a mistress and Margrave would brook no disobedience on Charlotte's part when he ordered her to do the same.

Celia could not believe that matters would be resolved so simply. Desultory, heat-laden conversations with Eleanor, through drowsy afternoons caught in nets of latticed shadow, had shown her a portrait of Charlotte that was more formidable than the younger,

110

languorous sister realised. It seemed to Celia that a strong-willed lady, who had become used to independence, would not turn meek at a word from Margrave. Her dreams of riven, blood-soaked India shaded into portents of evil yet to come and her nights were haunted by unformed terrors that cried like jackals in the darkness beyond the city walls.

'Come now, my lady. It must be done.' Greaves was standing anxiously at the bedside. 'He'll lose his good temper if you tarry,' she said. 'And that won't do today of all days.'

Perhaps I should just stay here, Celia thought. I should let the carriage go without me and set myself up as a seamstress or day-governess. The idea of being so enterprising and industrious, so stripped of fateful mystery, amused her enough to raise a smile. She pushed back the covers and lowered her feet to the floor.

'Anoint and wreath me, then,' she said. 'Prepare me for the sacrifice.'

When Greaves's work was done, Celia looked as gentle as a lamb but there was nothing else sacrificial about her. The worth of her gown, her astrakhan-trimmed cloak and muff, her velvet bonnet with its curtain of black Chantilly lace, her gloves of Swedish kid, the gleams of gold at throat and wrist proclaimed her above receiving impertinence from those who would challenge her coarsely if she were not plainly a rich man's toy. She understood what it was to be under Margrave's protection. For as long as she interested him, she would be shielded from her helplessness in this harsh world and could walk down to a carriage, through a hotel in which no one would still be ignorant of her standing, without insult from anyone below her lover's rank. Life had proved hollow and precarious; the needs of a man who could offer the illusion of safety were a shelter worthy of their high price.

Or so it appeared during those rare hours when there seemed to be a point to being alive. Most of her days were spent drifting in a spectral, desolate landscape of lost hopes and remembered terrors; a Gothic kingdom in which no one existed but herself. She saw no future beyond entering Vauchurch. There was darkness at its door. She would follow Margrave but there was no path for her to take.

Though Carew Sherren was a sincerely devout young man and felt the mystical significance of his Christmas duties as a curate to

111

a degree that made his vicar smile tenderly at his conscientious eagerness, he was equally drawn to the worldly delights of the season. On this grey December morning, he was happily engaged in painting scarlet waistcoats onto the sketches of plump Robin Redbreasts passed to him by their artist, Delia, the eldest daughter of the Reverend Mr Speerling. She was executing her whimsical talents on cards whose edges had been carved and pierced to a fair representation of lace by the mother-of-pearl scissors of Eliza, the middle sister. Harriet, the youngest girl, was carefully propping the finished paintings near the fire to dry and composing an ever-increasing list of friends to whom they must be sent.

This convivial industry was taking place at the circular table in the florid and well-cushioned Rectory in Bridport where Sherren was spending an agreeable two days as a pampered guest. This was not his parish. His own 'master', as Sherren called him in racy moments, was Mr Garstin, the incumbent at Vauchurch Marling. Garstin, a cool and level-headed man, able to tread the line between offending the Margraves and being subservient, was inclined to think his curate took life too seriously and pitied him for the anxiety that consorting with the family at the Great House engendered. Christmas with its necessities of a service in Vauchurch's private chapel and a dinner to be eaten in the presence of whatever Margraves were at home caused Sherren acute distress and Garstin had dispatched him to dally with the cheerful, conventional Speerlings to recruit his strength. Garstin was one of the old school of clergy, dispensing coals and shillings to the poor in his domain without troubling them for more in the way of doctrine than a brisk trot through the catechism and sleepy attendance at morning church. He had instructed Sherren that when sin is screened by wealth, a blind eye must be turned until the last possible moment, but he was aware that deeply felt principles made the young man come out in a rash after an evening of forced conversation with Mrs Margrave and her cousin-by-marriage, Quinn Holman.

It was unfortunate that Sherren had found himself undertaking his curacy in the shadow of Vauchurch. He was a kind and earnest fellow, neither stupid nor overly intelligent, who would mature into a sensible and worthy man, but his innocent virtue and youthful nervousness unfitted him for contact with the self-confident depravity of the Margraves. Garstin, watching his protégé flinch, often sighed and wished he had been sent one of

112

the tedious muscular Christians, who were all too prevalent these days. A creature of this dull breed, unable to see beyond the next cold bath or hearty game of rugby, would have been far better able to endure the cross-winds of desire and hatred that seared the thin skin of the alarmed Sherren whenever he was within Vauchurch.

It was a sign of Sherren's growing resilience that he had relaxed so completely in the short time he had spent at the Rectory. He was such a frequent visitor and favourite of the house that when the pudding to be eaten on Christmas Day had been made six weeks before, he had joined the members of the family in stirring the aromatic mixture for luck and had been given the spoon to lick by Cook, who thought he needed building up. If there had been any way he could have been persuaded that he was needed more by Speerling than Garstin during the festival's services, the older men would have united to deceive him into staying in Bridport, but they knew that his thorny sense of duty would reveal their machinations. He must return to Garstin's side by evening and the spectres of the brazen adulterers on their promontory at Vauchurch were already sending delicate shivers of dread over his back as if they were drawing a net of apprehension about his warm and comfortable body. When he had sat down to his task, he had been perfectly content and his hand steady; an hour nearer to his departure and he was inclined to let the scarlet spread beyond the proscribed lines.

The door opened with the rush of air that indicated that the tradesmen's door was also open – a peculiarity of the building that had led to much ineffectual discussion between Mr and Mrs Speerling, Mr Speerling and the carpenter, and the carpenter and his comrades in the snug at the George – and Mr Speerling entered to see his daughters and Sherren all arms as they tried to prevent their handiwork fluttering to the floor.

'Oh, Papa!' the girls cried.

'Oh, Papa, indeed.' Mr Speerling parted the skirts of his frock-coat and stood firmly in front of the fire. 'That gale is a force of nature as you are well aware and I can't fairly be blamed.'

'Did you order the oranges?' Harriet asked.

'I did, pusskin, and was told roundly by the overwrought assistant that I was the third member of this household to do so – your mamma and Cook both having done the same on their separate occasions.'

'Oranges, sugar and brandy,' Harriet sighed happily.

'Of course,' Mr Speerling said, flapping his coat-tails behind him so that they narrowly missed the flames, 'I neither receive nor expect sympathy from daughters who take my errand-running for granted but I am more than the seeker of fruit. I bear tidings.'

There was a general downing of tools by his listeners. Gratified, he looked from one to the next.

'I met Plowden outside the Scientific Institute,' he said. 'He was in Dorchester yesterday and who did he see going into the King's Arms? Margrave himself! Plowden went in later to have a bite before he rode back and the tale was being talked up and down how Margrave was back from India and travelling on to Vauchurch tomorrow – today, I should say.'

His news had the effect on the girls that he had hoped for and intended. They were, at once, alive with ignorant curiosity as they speculated upon what Margrave had been about in foreign parts for five years, how he had survived the Mutiny, whether he was tanned as brown as a tobacco pouch, how his wife, who had mentally donned breeches as his ship sailed out of port would welcome him and would there be a ball to exult in his homecoming.

Their curiosity was the natural interest of amicable beings, who had lived all their short lives in the same town and well understood the social implications of the arrival of the grandest landowner in their small world. Their ignorance lay in having no notion of the real implications of Margrave's return or, indeed, in the meaning of the word 'adultery'. Despite ranging in age from sixteen to twenty, they had been kept from all knowledge of carnal matters and, not having Olivia's enquiring, suspicious mind nor labouring girls' exposure to the indecencies of the farmyard, they had no inkling of the surprises the future had in store.

Mr Speerling, gazing at faces undarkened by comprehension of the corruption that polluted Vauchurch and Knapp, was proud of their unsullied maidenhood. In his eyes it was to their credit that they moved through life misinterpreting a large proportion of the motives and activities of their acquaintance. They had shown a proper outrage on hearing that Eleanor Forston had fled her husband's home with Eliot, but their scorn had been for the breaking of the spiritual tie that united man and wife and this, too, had gladdened their father's heart.

Sherren wished he shared their innocence. As he sat in the

114

cheerful drawing room amongst the clutter of paper and paint, he felt surrounded and oppressed by Vauchurch. His usual apprehension deepened into foreboding at the sound of Margrave's name. A crisis must come. There was no submission in the character of Charlotte, Margrave or Quinn that would lead to an easy resolution of their treacheries. He did not want to leave his haven. Looking up from the cloth on which he was wiping the soft bristles of his brush, he caught Speerling's eye and, with it, an instant of conspiratorial male consciousness. He was being included in the number of the wise and those who used their wisdom to protect the weak. It strengthened him.

'Is he alone?' he asked. 'Did Mr and Mrs Forston travel with him?'

Eliza made a *moue* at Eleanor's name and Harriet became aloof. Sherren blushed slightly but Mr Speerling did not seem to consider his question out of place.

'It seems they're still abroad,' he said, 'climbing the pyramids, but Margrave is not alone. We must do him honour for a sample of Christian charity I, for one, would not have expected of him. He brings with him a Miss Eliot, the sister of the rogue who caused Mrs Forston to forget her duty.'

'Mercy on us,' Delia said. 'What can she be doing here?'

'Mercy is the appropriate word, my love.' Mr Speerling was grave. 'With her father and brother dead and their fortune lost, she is unprotected. It's an act of great kindness for Margrave to bring her into the shelter of his family after what has occurred. Such forgiveness is all too rare.'

His words were entirely sincere and Sherren felt isolated and troubled. It might have been that Plowden had withheld all coarse comment upon the strange travelling companions for the sake of his vicar's cloth, but surely this would not have prevented Speerling perceiving the wickedness for himself? With the familiar pain, Sherren remembered Kate, good and gentle beyond her years, the example to her sex, who had been sacrificed to the interests of the man being commended for his benevolence. Plainly, it was beyond Speerling's experience to imagine Margrave flaunting a mistress before his wife. It is not beyond mine, he thought. It is well within my experience to accept vice in all its disguises and thus I am defiled. You cannot touch pitch . . . And the young woman – did she embrace guilt willingly as her brother had done, or was she as defenceless as these dear girls, unable to guard her

115

chastity because she did not know in what it lay?

The fire burnt brightly behind Speerling's firmly-planted legs, the robins dried to a benign flamboyance but the fortress was not as secure as it had been and unexpected assailants could be seen from its walls.

They had made a later start from Dorchester than he had intended and had been longer on the road. Margrave gazed out of the carriage-window at the bleak landscape, suffering a potent and perplexing sense of lost opportunities. He was not used to feeling less than satisfied with himself and the suspicion of some wrong turning having been taken in life disturbed him.

Condensation from their breath was forming on the glass. Freeing the curtain from its restraining loop, he used it to wipe the pane. Celia sat beside him as if carved from marble.

It was early afternoon but the day had darkened so that it appeared to be nearer evening. By nightfall, all would be whiteness and glitter again; at this moment earth, sky and distant sea were grey, the grey of iron, of doves, of slate, a desolate shading in the melancholy sweep of downland. The road followed the ridge of the long roll of hills from Winterbourne Abbas to Bridport and he could see far out over the sudden fall of the escarpment into the sombre haze of the slow valley and the half-deciphered form of cliffs above the suggestion of cold, marauding waters.

The absence of the garish colour and shimmering heat of India became restful. He did not want to narrow his eyes against the spear-like sun. This slumbering, dolorous land was his proper place and would wake, verdant and fertile, to a richness of long-grassed meadow and heavy-leafed wood that beckoned him with the sweet ache of memory. Yearning for the past was as alien to him as dissatisfaction with himself and he turned it this way and that in his mind as he would a business speculation, searching for the greatest advantage.

He believed that he had found its cause. The last time he had driven in this carriage, he had been taking Kate on the first stage of the journeys that led her to a strange extinction and him to another continent, a brutal glory and back, in triumph, to his beginnings. He had reached a completion in his affairs and had not yet begun the task of moulding his son into his own image. This day was a pause and a transition; it did not suit his active nature but, seen as the commencement of his raising Frank to be

116

a true Margrave, it was exhilarating. Confidence and zest for the future returned and he leant back, watching the familiar scenes pass with relish.

They drove over the bridge into Bridport and along East Street, turning through the archway into the yard of the Bull. Although legal matters concerning trade were dealt with by sleek and punctilious lawyers in London, Margrave continued the long-established habit of his forefathers and had estate concerns attended to by Frenton & Lamford – or, as it was now, Frenton, Lamford & Frenton – in their redbrick Georgian offices where lamps had burnt throughout this dimly-illumined day. Before continuing to Vauchurch, he intended to pay a call upon the elder Mr Frenton to hear what had passed since he last received a report. It was not the action of a man eager to see his family after a long absence, but no one who had heard of his plan was surprised.

The horses drew to a halt, shaking their heads at the warm scent of stables and blowing streams of moist white air into the confines of the yard.

'I sent ahead to reserve a sitting room for you,' Margrave said. 'I expect to be an hour or so.'

'Greaves is not here.'

'Good God, they'll pour out your tea. You can raise it to your lips by yourself, can't you?'

Celia did not reply. Her gloved fingers tightened about each other inside her muff. It would be useless to tell Margrave that she was afraid and the presence of her woman would be comforting. He would understand neither part of her statement and despise both.

The door was opened by the servant who had ridden tiger on the back of the carriage. His face was red and rigid with cold and the attempt not to be noticed by his master. Margrave climbed down and turned to hand Celia out.

'Lemual will see you to your room,' he said, 'and I'll return to collect you when my business is over. Symonds,' he addressed the coachman, who was standing attentively at the horses' heads, 'be ready. Have the lamps lit.'

Symonds's eyes, watering from long exposure to the freezing day, held no expression as he touched his hat. Celia drew no strength from Margrave's ability to crush all trace of individuality in those around him. These horsemen were too practised in their bearing for it to have been resumed today after a lapse of five years. The subjugation of inferiors must also be demanded by Margrave's wife.

She followed Lemual to the side-door of the inn where she was met by the confident, curtseying mistress of the establishment and let herself be taken, amid exclamations over the bleakness of the afternoon and the chilling through of bones, past the snug bar-parlour with its wafts of hot cider and venison pasties, up the stairs and into a room furnished with a welcoming fire and a tea-table set with sprigged china and thinly-cut bread and butter. Refusing offers of more substantial refreshment, she stood alone in the room, holding her cup in both hands so that its steam rose in an aromatic cloud to her stiff face. Her head ached with a heavy, persistent pressure that made her temples feel they were glass that was about to shatter. It would be unendurable to sit here with nothing to occupy her thoughts but dread of the night. She went to the window and looked through the condensation on its panes to the wide Georgian street below. There were enough people passing to make her inconspicuous if she went out, but not so many that she would be jostled or crowded. She would go walking to clear her head. Perhaps exercise and air were all that were needed to ease her pain.

She settled her cloak about her shoulders. It was unusual for her to do even this small service for herself but Greaves was travelling in their luggage-coach and could not give the folds and their wearer a final, approving pat.

The coldness in the street made her catch her breath. Dusk was gathering. Lamps had been lit in shops laden for Christmas and, as she glanced at the piles of merchandise, she felt that the white-aproned assistants were weighing her in their scales and finding her wanting. She needed more solitude. Her desolation had no place amongst these promises of domestic joy.

She turned down an alley hardly wider than her skirts and so along a lane to a quieter street that held no mercy. In the long row of tall Georgian houses, of substantial homes and narrow cottages, she saw a world from which she was banished. Virtuous women spread starched cloths over tables and kept their infants from the fire, they sat working nets, anxiously measuring their twine and calculating how much of their payment could be spared for the festivities. She could not cross these doorsteps for fear of her sin corrupting the innocence within. Her skull was being pressed inward and her breath was shallow. The light of day, however dim, showed that she was lost and night brought terror and memory. She walked on in search of sanctuary as the raw sea-chill slid up from the bay and blinds were lowered against its coming.

A wraith-like haze of mist hung above the river. Ice edged the banks, holding the dead reeds upright in an embrace that had snapped the most brittle stems. When the thaw released them, the bleached spears would topple into the winter-swollen water and be carried, singly and in cross-hatched mats, down and down, catching on outcrops of the meadows between town and harbour, swirling again into the current, past melancholy sheep on the close-cropped grass and ships loading rope for Newfoundland and out into the stern, seal-haunted ocean.

Sherren followed the river-path wishing that he, too, could be drawn on a flood to escape and knowing himself held in the frigid grip of duty and convention. He had bidden the rector's family goodbye and was making his way to the church for a moment's prayer in an atmosphere free of the complications induced by Margraves before taking his seat in the dog-cart that was to transport him to Vauchurch Marling.

His heart was heavy. The realisation that he alone that morning had understood the evil in Margrave's association with Paul Eliot's sister continued to make him feel separate and tainted. A small voice had begun to say that seeing the world clearly did not diminish him, but it was not yet loud enough to be convincing. A sliver had been shaved from his pleasure in the company of the merry, ignorant Speerlings. If good humour arises from blindness, can it be valued? He wrapped his thick, clerical cloak about him, bunching the cloth in his fists, holding the warmth to him as twilight sank upon his path.

When he reached the churchyard, he found the mist had spread. It hung between the yews, softening the angles of gravestones and railings, clinging in a myriad drops to the austere branches of a hawthorn, brushing his cheeks with a fragile, retreating touch. He heard a trap being drawn up the street behind a smartly-stepping horse, and somewhere to his right someone shovelled coals with a gritty scrape and rattle into the scuttle, but the sounds seemed to be made distant by the stillness contained within the boundary walls.

A lantern had been set by the church door. Its light caused the mist about it to gleam with a beckoning spectral radiance. He was so mesmerised by this lustre and his consuming thoughts that he was almost upon the woman resting against a tomb before he noticed her. She raised herself as he stopped but kept one hand on the lichened stone as if she could not trust her strength to stand unaided. Her face was pale and held such a depth of sorrow in its eyes that his own troubles faded and he took a step towards the man he was to be.

'Are you unwell?' he asked gently. 'May I help you?'

'No one can.'

Her voice was low with a suggestion of an accent he could not place. It had a strange, seductive quality that made him feel an instant of anger against her and then against himself. There was a melancholy beauty in her form and tone but he could not justify the leaping of the word 'temptress' to his mind. He was ashamed.

'The evening is cold,' he said, 'and the damp air can do you no good. Will you come into the church?'

She turned her head towards the looming building and its glowing light. 'No,' she said. 'I used to find refuge there. I won't enter now.'

'Will you let me help you? I'm a clergyman. A curate of All Souls.'

'All Souls? Ah, God, not of mine.'

He was silent. Desperation was not in his experience and he did not know what to say.

'Is this your church?' she asked.

'No. Mine's a more isolated parish. Vauchurch Marling.'

She caught her breath and leant back against the tomb; a flowing movement that was again arousing. She laughed painfully.

'Then we are neighbours,' she said. 'My name is Eliot. Has my fame gone before me? Are any of my family known?'

He hesitated. 'Your brother . . .'

'Oh, yes, my brother.'

She stared past him into the enveloping mist. His shame did not lessen. He was in the presence of a harlot but he could not look upon the tormented creature and condemn her. A solitary, bereaved girl could not withstand the weight of Margrave's iniquity. How could he say, 'Go thou and sin no more,' knowing that she was being taken to the nest of vipers that was Vauchurch, knowing that he had no courage when confronted by Charlotte and Quinn. He saw her hopelessness and was afraid.

120

'I must go back to the carriage,' she said. 'I'm to be driven to the house. I'm to be the – guest of the Margraves, husband and wife. How shall I be received, I wonder? With rejoicing?'

'Is there nowhere else that you can go?'

She turned to him again. 'So,' she said, 'it will be as I fear.'

Shall I take her to the Speerlings, he thought, and ask them to shelter her? The plea would be fruitless. They would cast out such desolation; they do not speak its language. I am alone but in my loneliness I stand closer to the despised and wretched. She must be warned.

'I think,' he said, 'there'll be a time of trouble in the family. Duties have been forgotten on both sides. Margrave's wife . . .'

'Ah,' her sigh was stifled. 'You can't say it. There's no need. Who would know better than I what these Margraves, these Forstons do in their pride? What they will do to keep what they covet? You and your kind say the Lord is merciful. Ask Him, then, why He has forsaken me.'

'What little I can do—'

'There'll be no necessity.'

She left him, moving slowly out of his sight through the monumental trees and chill obscurity. The river-mist had spread into the quiet road and she drifted through its encroaching vapour into the sharper cold of the main street.

Margrave came up behind her as she turned towards the inn. His walk was brisk and confident. He took her chin in his firm grasp and raised her white face. She stared at the wide fur-collar of his overcoat.

'If you were taking the air to improve your health,' he said, 'you've done a poor job.'

Her dread pleased him. For all her haunted withdrawal from life, she was his, the potent symbol of his conquest of the Eliots. He had returned in triumph and Charlotte would be made to recognise his power.

Darkness overtook them as they drove from the town. In the coombes and spinneys, where the mist did not reach, the cold settled. Ice that had not melted, thickened. Hoar-frost resumed its crystalline perfection. Celia sat, unseeing, rocking with the movement of the carriage, crazed with loss that had been and was to come. His wife and her lover. The horses strained. The wheels slowed, slewed, rolled forward again. The steep climb to Vauchurch.

121

Lights all about her. Lanterns in the courtyard, torches flaring to each side of the great door. Lamps within. She stepped down in Margrave's train. Faces, servants. She was across the threshold. Margrave beside her. His wife approaching. A crimson gown against blood-red hangings.

She covered her eyes and there was nothing in her world but her scream.

Chapter Ten

The pool that was always known as 'the lake' lay on the edge of the plateau as far from the great house of Vauchurch as could be without descending the slope. It was an artificial contrivance, excavated and lined with clay and stone in the early 1700s, shortly before financial calamity had put such conceits out of the family's reach, and had been designed as an agreeable end to a ride across the park. Ladies, who had taken this exercise, could refresh themselves with cordials amongst the Ionian columns of a summer-house whilst admiring the view out over the escarpment to the distant arc of remote hills or, for those who suffered from vertigo, the gentle plashing of a fountain into the cloud-reflecting lake.

It had been the bane of many a gardener's life, having to be kept filled in summer by pumps from below, and was the source of constant argument and long-running feuds over whether its water supply was the responsibility of farm or garden. The fountain at its centre was of some undefined allegorical or mythological significance involving two unclothed nymphs and a youth horribly entwined with a stout and bearded snake. The snake brandished a trident in the last curl of its forked tail. No amount of additional lead piping or sarcastic remarks from the Margrave of the day to his artisans could make this monstrosity work with anything other than sudden, disconcerting spurts or a mumpish dribble, and its usefulness was mainly confined to acting as a clothes-horse for skaters. On the morning before Christmas Eve, one nymph was wearing Hermione's tartan shawl as a comforter while the youth had Frank's hat tipped over one eye.

The three young people had been expending their energy on the frozen pond for an hour and were all cheerfully heated and bright-eyed. Even Olivia was flushed with her own peculiar brand of joy as she whirled determinedly back and forth in the bitter air, her cape flying behind her like the remnants of the night. She was still dressed principally in mourning, having realised, as she discarded out-grown garments, that she had made no provision for being taller when she returned to colours, but the blue sash remarked upon by the coachmen was again in evidence and a linen-maid was stitching away at a bolt of emerald silk so that the enraptured daughter could appear on Christmas Day in glory.

'Come and try this,' Frank called. 'Knock at the cobbler's door!'

He ran a few ungainly steps on his skates and launched himself on a slide he had been industriously polishing on the ice with a square of old horse-blanket. Arms outstretched, he hurtled past Olivia, who had swung round to watch him, on one foot, rapping the glistening surface at intervals with the other.

In the summer-house, Ward half-rose to see him swoop to a floundering and triumphant halt. Judging him to be as safe as a venturesome boy could be, she sat down again by the brazier that was keeping her and Holland, Charlotte's lady's maid, in reasonable comfort. The original open temple had been found neither to throw enough shade in August nor afford protection from the wind in most other months. Plastered walls with lozenge-shaped windows had been constructed between the columns and the combination of this shelter and the glowing charcoal gave a creditable illusion of warmth.

'The poor, mad girl,' Holland said.

Ward unwound a flask from a thick piece of flannel in the basket at her feet and poured more tea into their cups. 'She's an opium-eater,' she said, screwing the top back onto the flask. 'Those two giddy maids who do her room found any amount of it in her trunks when they were unpacking. I wouldn't have believed it but your housekeeper was there to oversee them and she says the same.'

'As I heard, it was laudanum – bottles of syrup such as any one of us might buy at our physician's direction. I had it myself for the toothache three years since.'

'Bottles,' Ward nodded meaningfully, 'not bottle. What does she have that ails her to that extent?'

Holland laughed dryly. 'Come now,' she said. 'We know what ails her. Wouldn't you take drops too?'

Outside, beneath a muffled, ivory sky, Olivia and Hermione were clutching Frank's arms as they skated to each side of his slide, propelling him forward at a dangerous, shrieking speed. They passed out of sight of the women and a hubbub of spirited

124

mutual accusation of having been the first to stop testified to their deliverance.

Ward drew breath to assert that she would never be such a hussy and thought better of it. Holland's pragmatic, acerbic company had the effect of making her think more than was always comfortable. She remembered offers made to her by Forston's friends and knew she would have accepted them, had they come when she had no work. That was the way life was; virtue did not survive poverty.

'Her screams fair chilled my blood,' she said. 'I was up in the corridor to the nursery. The children were going to go down as soon as Mrs Margrave had greeted her husband. They were all in their best, all brushed and neat. I heard the screaming as if she stood next to me.'

'It was the best thing she could have done.' Holland swirled the dregs of her tea. 'Not that it was deliberate, poor creature, but it diverted everyone wonderfully. There was no thought of why she was there until she was shut up in her room.'

'What does Mrs Margrave say?'

'Madam doesn't confide in me, as you know. I don't have to tell you what those sisters are like.'

Ward looked out at Hermione, who was gliding alone in slow, flowing curves. An icicle, touched by the wavering heat of the brazier, dripped from the lintel to the step.

'Miss Forston's becoming graceful,' Holland said. 'She has greater grace than her mother in more ways than one. No beauty, though.'

'She's very comely.'

Holland patted her friend's shoulder. 'As you wish, Mamma,' she said. 'If Frank left any of those jumbles, I believe I could eat one.'

Ward rummaged in the basket and handed Holland a slightly crushed biscuit that smelt delicately, warmly of rose-water. As Holland bit into it, holding her cupped palm beneath her chin to catch the crumbs, she thought of June, of weaving clusters of Charles de Mills into her mistress's hair, of summer nights and heavy, entrancing afternoons.

'Did you know,' she asked, 'that it was here, in this temple to profane gods, that Mr Holman had his being?'

Ward blushed, startled. She was aware of Quinn's history, of the adulterous trysts between the foolish, young wife and her husband's brother that had banished the infant from his Vauchurch cradle and baptismal name, but had never translated family lore into practical when and how. The naming of this folly, where they sat guarding the most innocent of the Margraves, as the place of betrayal, gave life to the perpetrator and victim of a seduction whose consequences had not reached their end. A sighing breath whispered in her ear and she shivered before recognising the soft hiss of Hermione's dance. She watched her girl skim over the frozen pool between the white light of sky and ice, and the image of a young swan that had once rested on the shallow water of the lake came to her mind. It brought with it fears of traps and nets, of the fragile hart shot by Margrave for the purity of its blanched hide, of goodness crushed and defiled, but a swan has strength not apparent in the quiet fold of its wings and she comforted herself.

'I wonder that it wasn't torn down,' she said, gazing about at the cupola and weathered walls that had sheltered the guilty couple. 'To have such a reminder . . .'

'If they tore down parts of Vauchurch that had witnessed corruption, where would it end? We'd all be cowering beneath a hedge.'

The children had linked hands and were skating in a wide circle, leaning into their strides with a powerful, youthful vigour that sprayed powdered ice from their blades. 'And then,' Holland went on, 'there was a greater reminder – never far away and now closer still.'

'Amongst us.'

'Indeed.'

They thought of Quinn and the years that had passed since his mother had lain in this temple, believing words that were sweet, possessing and false.

'Will he be here again?' Ward asked. 'Will the master discover what's been done?'

Holland stared out into the frost. 'How the children play,' she said. 'You would think there was no tomorrow.'

The shadow of horns stretched across the wall, lengthening and retracting as it passed from the faint light shed by one flickering lamp to the next. The passage was always cold. Deep within Vauchurch, its stonework held a grim ability to leach heat from the living as if they were immured within the unhewn rock from which the blocks had come. The house was heavy here; unsoftened by ornament, its massive presence pressed down on the unwary, crushing them into awe and the suspicion that they had strayed into a labyrinth.

The bull roared. Its bellow filled the tunnel, expanding and echoing down long corridors, up hidden, twisting stairs, through chains of dank unfrequented rooms. Olivia, watching from behind a half-closed door, shuddered with delicious excitement, a breathless alarm that whitened her knuckles as she gripped the latch.

There was the sound of hurrying feet and two servant-girls ran by, clutching each other as they glanced, wide-eyed and panting, at what followed. The roar was louder. The horned shadow swayed against the wall; it gored to right and left, advancing with menace and deliberation. One of the girls tripped on her gown and screamed, stifling the cry with her hands as her companion pulled her on.

In the hush as the roar died, something dragged rhythmically on the flagstones, a relentless surge of sea on shore. The shadow grew, a dusky bulk beneath the horns. Olivia held the door tightly.

The Ooser passed. The great mask towered above the shoulders that bore it. Its ferocious wooden features were carved into the likeness of a primitive, vengeful god. Long, ragged hair hung about the bearded face and cow-hide swathed the form within, sweeping the ground with a heavy, regular motion. A bull's horns reared from its brow.

The jaw lowered and the roar flooded the passage and the chamber where Olivia stood. Nothing human remained in the Ooser's guise. The years fell back at its approach and Vauchurch was again the earth fortress where blood was spilt and flesh burnt to appease the powers of night. Let there be sacrifice and the sun would rise.

There was a terrible joy in Olivia's heart. Her father was home and wrongs would be put right. She had seen nothing of him beyond a moment's audience to make her curtsey with Hermione while he had been distracted by his guest falling ill. The young woman he had brought had been overcome as she entered the house. Her screams had reached the nursery group as they stood in well-groomed, fidgeting silence, waiting for their turn to be presented. It had been shocking, invigorating. They had inched forward, clustering by the banisters, peering down at the tableau beneath – the stricken figure on her knees, her veil and cloak spread in black folds about her, the anxious, enthralled servants bending to minister to the afflicted girl, Margrave and Charlotte, standing apart, meeting each other's eyes.

Ward had drawn them back against the wall as Charlotte led the party bearing the invalid – quiet now, her head hanging loosely in a swoon – up the first flight of stairs. Charlotte had turned towards the passage leading to the guest rooms most used by female visitors, but Margrave had given an order and the footmen had paused, shifting their burden as they changed direction. Olivia had seen a rage flare within her mother and be instantly subdued. It had unnerved her, giving the same uneasy recognition that she and Charlotte were alike as she had felt in the tower, and then Margrave was before the children as he walked behind the unknown woman and there was no room in her thoughts for any but him. He had nodded at the girls as they sank down before him and had laid his hand, with the Margrave seal in gold upon his finger, on Frank's head. The hand moved to hold up Frank's chin, withdrew, their father was gone and Olivia's eyes dazzled.

She could no longer see the Ooser. A shrieking merriment echoed down the passage and was swallowed by the bull's sonorous bellow as the winter beast routed more worshippers from their hiding place. Her own pulse was beating rapidly. She wished she could join more fully in the hunt, slipping through the corridors from one concealment to the next, putting herself almost within reach of the threatening horns, but this was a diversion for the servants and her presence would change its meaning for them.

Stepping softly out into the wake of the creature, she stared towards the corner it had turned. The receding shouts and footsteps left an emptiness behind. She stood still, holding the ends of her sash.

The sharp, dry scent of a cheroot curled through the musty air. She turned. Margrave was standing at the curve of the passage, watching her. He filled the sombre space between the oppressive walls as the Ooser had done. She could not see him clearly for love.

He approached her as a sudden swell in the distant cries reverberated through the maze. Once, he had lain in wait through a humid, creeper-shaded day by a forest river-bank, where monkeys chattered with bare-toothed glee and snakes dripped from branch to branch. At dusk, a tigress, his quarry, had come with her young to drink. The tender ferocity of her eyes as she looked at her cubs stayed with him after her death and was in Olivia's intense, white face as he came near.

He did not choose to be unsettled by his daughters. Kate's death had never troubled him. She had always been a milk-and-water thing, of no interest to such as he, and her going had been worthwhile. Nat Unsworth, whom she had thought in her foolish innocence she was to marry, had remained in London when she and her husband sailed and, in his shocked grief and new riches, had smoothed the path of Margrave's revenge upon the Eliots as his uncle would have done.

Kate had not been a thorn in his paternal flesh but this queer girl, in her mourning with the flash of brilliant colour he had already been told was for him, was different. It was necessary, as it had always been, to make the choice not to be disturbed by her. He pointed past her with the hand that held the glowing cheroot.

'They bow down before idols,' he said. 'What do you make of that?'

'It's harmless, sir.'

'You say so? A Christian child like yourself?'

'It is a Christmas game, no more.'

'I think you know that not to be true.'

She felt the glory of having been understood flood through her body. He had noticed her and spoken without being pursued. With parted lips, she gazed at him and he had to force himself not to take a step back. It was irritating that she produced the same discomfort and annoyance that she had done before he went away. There had been no apparent softening of her character during these five years. Quite the opposite – looking at the uncalled-for flush on her face and the strange ardency of her eyes, he suspected that her peculiarities had grown more entrenched. Just as before, he preferred to send her elsewhere.

He took a small silver phial from his pocket. 'I find I have Miss Eliot's smelling-salts in my pocket,' he said. 'She may need them. Will you take them to her?'

'I will.' Olivia clasped the phial in both her cold hands and drew it to her breast as if she were guarding a fragile, fluttering bird.

'Her room is the Green Chamber – next to mine,' he said.

She nodded, not releasing him from her unrelenting stare. Ash fell from his cheroot and he crushed it with a brisk movement of his foot.

'Be gone then,' he said.

'Yes, sir.' She went slowly past him, gliding as she had done on the lake, and paused, half-turning towards him.

'Yes, Papa,' she said.

If she stood at the deep-set window, Celia could look up to an endless, monotonous pearl-grey sky or down upon a frost-bound landscape of white hills and valleys broken by black stands of leafless trees. In ploughed fields at the foot of the promontory, white and black mingled where ridges of dark earth protruded through the rime but further from the heights, the land was white and white again until it merged with the white-grey sea.

A fire was burning in the grate with sharp spittings and crackles of resin in the pine-cones scattered on the coals. She supposed the room was warm – she had been told that it was by the maid who had come to take her tray – but the cold slid through the unshuttered window and spread its bitterness a yard beyond the lancet before it was tempered by the fire.

She was standing in this chill, wrapped in a Kashmiri shawl that had the patchouli scent of home, moving her head an inch this way and that. The glass of the leaded panes was old and uneven. In places, it was thick and opaque with swirls and waves within its diamond shapes. When she looked here, the view was distinct and she saw the world in all its unrelieved bleakness. Move her head a fraction and look there – woods and hills and meadows, sea, sky and stone merged and melted together in rippling distortions of form.

Opening her shawl into great wings by stretching her arms as she held its edges, she pulled it more closely about her and went back to the hearth. The flames sent a flickering, jagged reflection of their red light playing across the lustrous surface of her gown and she beat at her skirts, letting the shawl drop, before she realised that the silk was cold. Sitting tiredly down in the low chair beside the grate, she gathered the many folds of kashmir onto her lap and stroked the familiar buta pattern as she waited for her panic to subside.

All her hours were spent waiting. Her dread of what was to come had not lessened but she had reached a numb acceptance of hopelessness that was some protection against the hysteria that had struck as she saw Charlotte. She was glad to be shut up alone and given the title of invalid to excuse her from joining the family.

130

The room gave the illusion of security. Its solid antiquity, its oak panelling and Jacobean bed with bulbous, carven posts and green brocade hangings, its tapestries of stiff, courtly ladies dallying with unicorns in flower-sprigged glades, its time-spotted silver mirror appealed to her with its air of being untouched by the change of centuries. It was a room in which she could fade into invisibility and be forgotten.

A knock renewed her connection with the present and with fear. Margrave would come in unannounced through the connecting door from his dressing-room. It was not the maid's knock. She rose to her feet, quailing at the thought of Charlotte. Another rap. It could not be Charlotte. She would knock once for ceremony's sake and then enter before she was bidden.

'Yes,' she said and again, louder: 'Yes.'

The door opened. A girl, whose face made Celia think of the austere, white land beyond the window, walked purposefully in. Her hair was still down and swayed against her black dress as she turned to close the door behind her. She was neither child nor woman and looked out of eyes that could see into Celia's tormented world.

'You are Olivia,' Celia said. 'Your father has told me of you.'

The vehement face softened and was momentarily lit with joyful pride. Celia regretted having spoken. It had been done from kindness but perhaps it was cruel to give her the wrong impression. Margrave had indeed spoken of his daughter in terms that led Celia to recognise the girl and every word had been both descriptive and derogatory. Olivia had no value to him and it went to Celia's heart to see another love spurned as hers for her father had been. Loneliness and neglect were moulding this girl's spirit and would bring her to a place of darkness.

'He asked me to bring this to you,' Olivia said, holding out the phial. 'He thought you might need it.'

Celia took the crystal bottle from the outstretched hand. She knew without asking what had occurred. Margrave did not have the kind of concern for her that would prompt him to think of her health when she was not near. He had encountered his daughter and, finding her devotion not to his taste, had rid himself of her with an errand.

'It was good of you to bring it,' she said.

'Papa asked me.'

'And it pleases you to please him. You do what he decrees. So do we all.'

There was a sadness and an edge of venom in Celia's voice that appealed to Olivia. Margrave's naming of their strange guest had confirmed the rumour enlivening the nursery that this was Paul Eliot's sister. To Olivia, Celia's frenzy as she entered Vauchurch and her secluded melancholy were appropriate for the survivor of a family that had brought destruction on itself. She was attracted by a loss of reason that was at once suitable and dramatic.

Celia went to the cabinet that served as a dressing-table and put the phial into a drawer. Her movements were languid and sensuous. She touched the inlaid wood as if it possessed a living warmth. Her gown rustled with a peculiarly enticing susurration and, when she bent to reach in, the silk disposed itself in elegant folds.

The cabinet stood next to the door that led into Margrave's private apartments and there was no key on this side. Olivia looked from the woman's vulnerable beauty to the door and understood. She could have laughed in triumph. Margrave had been betrayed. It was his right to take this compensation. He had gathered this dolorous comfort to his bosom and would not suffer as he might have done.

She revelled in the meaning of her mother's expression the day before. Charlotte had not needed to wait for a revelation to see the connection between her husband and one younger and more lovely than she. How it must have stung. Where had been the enjoyment of her sin then? With her powerlessness cast into her face and her paramour banished by the rightful master's return?

Rising from shutting the drawer, Celia was shaken by the unholy passion that was plain upon the girl. She was used to hearing herself described as crazed and was reluctant to condemn another with the term but it was the only appropriate conclusion.

'You're my father's mistress,' Olivia said.

'Oh, poor child. You're not of an age that should know such things.'

'Don't be afraid that I'll tell Mamma.' The savagery had left Olivia's eyes and been replaced by a yearning tenderness that filled Celia with pity.

'We both know that your mamma will already be aware of what I am. But I thank you for your discretion. Sometimes good intentions are the most we can expect from life.'

'Papa will protect you.'

Celia felt the exhaustion of despair stealing over her. She wanted to be alone again, waiting for whatever oblivion was drawing near. Perhaps she should take the time to explain the complications of the world to this partisan girl, who judged father and mother by different laws. Leaving her with too harsh a view of Charlotte and too much love for Margrave could only lead to harm but she was tired to death and could not endure the hurt she would cause. Though it was wrong, it was easier to pander to Olivia's obsession and lie a little to give her temporary happiness.

'I have a gift here for you from your papa,' she said. 'I was supposed to keep them until Christmas morning. This must be our secret.'

She went to the red Morocco jewel-case that lay on the table by her bed and lifted its lid. From an inner compartment, she took a small, velvet box and put it in the tremulous, outstretched hands. Olivia, unmanned by this unexpected token of affection, gazed at earrings of tear-drop pearls with diamonds at their points. She lifted one out. It quivered in her fingers, ice and snow. Celia watched the rapt eyes and knew she had done wrong.

'Wear them when I am gone,' she said, 'and have mercy on my guilt.'

'When you are gone?' Olivia looked from the mesmeric pearls.

'Yes.' Celia spoke softly as if she dreamed. 'I will soon leave this place and will have much need of forgiveness.'

At Moule Court, ice had frozen within a crack in the sundial and forced the yielding sandstone apart. Quinn, walking in his moonlit garden, noticed the widening of one side of the pedestal and supposed that now nights would forever be longer. He had no objection to the change.

The day had passed slowly, each hour lengthened by his impatience, and his mind had always been at Vauchurch. He felt no humiliation nor lack of confidence over the outcome of Margrave's return. The sense of abandoning his love that had afflicted him as he had ridden away from Charlotte had died as he crossed the piercing hills. He did not fear it would trouble him again. The readiness to play his part exposed the thought as the sentimental weakness it had been. It was of interest as a curiosity in a life singularly free of such frailties, nothing more, and he

133

observed it with amusement as he might regard a Calvinist who wore violets on his lapel.

He had achieved the urgent calm of a soldier before battle but his need for action would not let him be still. The silent, radiant land gave him a lesson in tranquillity. A wind had risen briefly late in the afternoon and driven the cloud-cover, in torn pennants, out to sea. It had shivered the fragile branches in the woods and sent scurries of glistening, powdered frost in streaming veils across the rigid earth. Peace fell back upon the valleys and the moon had no covering to impede her light.

The garden was a fantasy of stark forms made crystalline and faerie by deep winter. He prowled down yew walks, his footsteps crushing the brittle grass as he passed between square-cut hedges and ornamental cones shrouded in their chill perfection. This glacial composure was, he knew, a deception. Though each leaf and stem was motionless, sheathed in its white crust of ice, the sap was waiting to rise. The sun would strengthen and the blind lust of nature would seize this passive place and hurl it to luxuriance. Opportunity was all.

Cold had begun to infiltrate the thick layers of the riding-coat he wore. He turned onto a lawn and, glancing once in the direction of Vauchurch, began climbing a flight of wide, flagstoned steps back to the house. A faint, lilting melody reached him as he neared the terrace; a fiddle played sweetly to a sweeter voice. He stood and listened as the lovelorn air, strangely affecting in the gleaming night, came to its close. A polka struck up and he let himself into the drawing room. The servants were keeping Christmas in the kitchen. He was allowing them the usual liberty of the season. There was to be nothing to make men whisper, 'Holman was acting differently that day.'

A hearty fire was lapping at the chimney. He threw his coat onto a chair and stood before the flames, warming his hands and grimacing as the heat brought blood back to his face. This house had been useful to him. He had bought it with its contents from a bankrupt and it could not have been more convenient for his purpose but it had never been to his taste. The more hideous pieces of the previous owner's Sinhalese furniture, designed to give a medieval atmosphere, had been consigned to the lumber-rooms and a few finer articles introduced. There had seemed no point in going to the trouble of a complete overhaul when his time was spent elsewhere. He had not decided whether he would sell.

134

Pouring a glass of brandy, he sat in a wing-chair with his feet on the fender. The fur of frost that had collected on his boots had already softened and dropped to melt upon the hearth. Another hour must be endured, another and another but tomorrow would come. Each minute ended in its turn. He had only to wait.

His thoughts were interrupted by the entry of a flushed maid.

'Mrs Margrave's woman's here, sir,' she said. ' 'Er's come for to choose the gowns for the dressing-up.'

No such intention had been told him. A warning was being sent.

'Which does she want?' he asked. 'Did she bring a note?'

'I did, sir.' Holland spoke from behind the maid.

'Come here, then, and give it to me.'

Quinn waved his girl away and she hurried back to the merry-making. Holland's cold hand emerged from her cloak and gave Quinn a letter with Charlotte's seal in the wax.

'You've had a harsh journey,' he said. 'Warm yourself by the fire.'

She stood looking into the coals as he had done. The drive from Vauchurch had frozen her to the marrow but it had not been unwelcome. She was as aware as Quinn that her orders to select costumes for Olivia and Hermione from the chest of antique silks at Moule was merely a pretext for sending a note which said something quite other. As she had told Ward, her mistress did not confide in her but her use as a messenger showed that she was trusted. It was as great a sign of respect as could be expected from one of that family and it pleased her. She could have gone to Margrave, sure that she held incriminating words but, flattered and intrigued, she had given her allegiance to Charlotte, conscious as she did so that knowledge could not be proved against her; should disgrace arise, she could still claim innocence.

Her audacity did not extend to watching Quinn as he read. She heard the seal broken and the paper unfolded. A flame cracked once sharply, flaring upward and retracting. Quinn rose and stood beside her. She glanced sideways without moving her head. His face was white and set.

'Your master did not come alone,' he said.

'No, sir.'

'You have seen the lady?'

'She keeps to her room.' Holland could not breathe easily. 'She wishes to be separate from the household.'

'Does she? Ah, does she?' Quinn held the folded note to the fire. The end brightened; red ran towards his fingers, the paper blackened, curled and flaked.

'Well,' he said, 'perhaps she will have her wish.'

Chapter Eleven

There was nowhere left to hide. In a house as vast as Vauchurch, the game had to have boundaries. She had been foolish to scorn the many chances of concealment she had passed and let herself be out in the open when Frank would be beginning his search.

Olivia ran lightly down the passageway, touching doors with her fingertips while she fled as if this would bring inspiration about what lay beyond, but no hiding-place that came to mind satisfied her. She could not say she really liked hide-and-seek. It was not that she had grown too old for it. She always agreed eagerly when such play was suggested but it caused a queer anxiety. Her desire to be well-hidden was acute, and fear of discovery as the seeker moved tentatively towards her in a darkened room had the intensity and distortion of nightmare. It did not matter that she knew it was Frank or Hermione who would tap her shoulder; the reaching hand filled her with terror.

For this game, they were using only the ground floor and, an eerie rendition of 'The Mistletoe Bough' the previous evening having both begun an exchange of dreadful possibilities and whetted their appetites for the sport, there was to be no climbing into chests or closets that could not be opened from inside.

She thought she heard a step and whirled round as she ran. No one. There had been no one throughout the game except when the players were together. It was always thus at Christmas. Hours of oppressive society were interspersed with periods when guests and family were resting and the servants snatching the time for their private amusements. One such interlude was upon them now. The house seemed deserted. The mummers had come to kill the King and were performing their robust act in the servants' hall to an audience that prompted them with raucous zeal whenever they paused for effect. They would stride forth again in their flamboyant rags and helmets to defeat and restore their enemies before the Margraves. Old Father Christmas would be astounded that a hundred-guinea potion could bring his wife back from the dead and all would be well. Mummers had always postured and struck each other with wooden swords as those of the family who had dined in grandeur sat over their almonds and port and the children, herded down from the nursery, sat on the tiger-skin before the fire. It was one of the ceremonies, Olivia believed, that was not enjoyable in itself but was necessary to make the crops grow.

She must become invisible. Hermione had hidden long ago, darting into the library, where swathes of ivy hung from the brass chandelier, and vanishing amongst the racks of calf-skin. Olivia had thought that too simple but Frank would have uncovered his eyes by now and be on her trail. Where could she go?

Softly opening a door, she slid into the summer drawing room and stood still, waiting for her sight to adjust. The darkness was almost complete. Shutters covered windows that let in the honey-light of June and the uncertain drone of fatly-wavering bees. Curtains shrouded the far wall. A sliver of grey stretching across the floorboards showed where the moreen folds did not quite meet. Dust-sheeted furniture had been pushed to one side for the carpet to be rolled up. There was a sensation of damp that did not accord with the season.

Olivia crossed the room with her hands outstretched. Widening the crack in the curtains, she slipped through and pulled them closed behind. There was heat where she stood between the thickly draped cloth and the glass door she pressed against. Was it unlocked? She tried the handle. It yielded and she stepped over the threshold.

The iron frame of the conservatory arched overhead. Humid air lay heavily amid palms and giant ferns pungent with the deep green scent of leaf-mould and moist, velvet moss. A camellia, in a porcelain pot embellished with writhing dragons, lifted stiff buds towards the sky. A single flower, coaxed by the artificial warmth, had unfurled into a rosette of petals that had no colour in the dusk. Moonlight fell upon the tangle of exotic foliage so that fronds and creepers were silhouetted against the sky like the etching of a traveller who could not recall on which continent he had seen which plant.

Olivia went forward into the jungle on a path of earthenware tiles. Leaves drooped from curving stems and fibrous trunks barring her way. It was necessary to weave between obstructions as if she were, indeed, in the tropics, trying not to be lost in the forest. When she reached the centre, where a great stone bowl held water-lilies, she left the path, balancing on exposed tree-roots so that she made no tell-tale footprints in the earth. Settling herself on a horizontal branch, she began her wait. She had found the concealment she wanted. Her view through the thicket was clear but, unless a searcher knew that she was there, she would not be noticed.

She looked up to the ridged roof. Condensation was dripping from the glass and, cool from its contact with the outside world, it splashed on leaf and tile. It is Christmas Eve, she thought, and I am too hot. She preferred frost to this sultry atmosphere of forced summer. India would not have suited her but she would have borne the debilitating heat for Margrave as Miss Eliot was enduring the cold. Thoughts of Celia filled her with a devotion that was more tender than her idolatry of her father. She felt herself within reach of love. If her mother would leave with Quinn, she and this mournful woman, who had crossed the world for Margrave, could be one in their veneration and perhaps – perhaps – he would spare some love for her.

Water dropped into her lap in two quivering beads and lay reflecting the meagre light until they sank into the cloth. Her fingers went to her breast where the earrings were pinned inside her gown. Her yearning for affection startled her. She had not realised that anything was lacking in her infatuation. Asking nothing from Margrave, she had not found it strange to receive the same but his unexpected gift had exposed his fondness for her and she was seduced into a craving to have him smile when she approached.

Her breath caught in her throat and her back straightened. The door from the drawing room had been opened. She was alert with apprehension. These last moments of the chase were the worst. It was all she could do not to cry out as the hunter drew closer, knowing the quarry was near but not yet having uncovered the hiding-place.

Frank did not come far into the conservatory. He could not be seen from her fastness and she could hear only small sounds she could not place. The wind drove a cloud fleetingly over the moon; darkness descended and rose. Outside, the bare stems of a weeping pear whipped back and forth; inside, stillness.

Footsteps came towards her. There was the drag of heavy silk along the tiles. Her heart beat more strongly and she tightened her grip on the branch.

Charlotte put aside a tendril of creeper and walked firmly through the dimness to the stone bowl of lilies. She was carrying a small bunch of camellia buds and the chamois-leather gloves she wore for cutting flowers. Laying the twigs on the rim of the bowl, she stared before her. Olivia, watching from her cover, noticed how the moonlight fell through the serrated fronds of a palm and gleamed on the camellia leaves, the quiet water and the blade of Charlotte's knife. She had feared Frank's part in their game. Here was her mother, gathering a posy; it was as innocent a pursuit as Frank's and more terrible. I have wished her gone, Olivia thought, and guilt makes me distressed in her presence. I should not wear earrings. They make me sentimental and distort my judgement. Mamma would not care to have me sentimental.

The silk rustled as if the wind had entered from the night. Charlotte moved to the far side of the bowl. By leaning a little to the side, Olivia could still see her clearly. Charlotte was drawing on her gloves, flexing her fingers and fastening buttons carefully at the wrist. Taking her knife, she carved sprays of oleander from the evergreen springing beside an iron pillar, choosing her cuttings from the rear of the shrub. She brought her collection back to where she had left the buds and bound the two sets of sprigs into one.

It was a badly designed bouquet; the outer circle of camellias hid the shorter core of oleander entirely but though Olivia delighted in scorning all her mother's actions, it was not this sign of Charlotte's shortcomings that made her breathe more quickly. She had the advantage of a neglected education. The social graces and piano-playing imposed upon other girls of her class were foreign to her but long days secluded in the library, curled in her father's chair with a pocketful of apples, had made her well-read. She knew how quick and vile a death oleander could provide. Accomplished girls might finger its blossoms and think ignorant thoughts of sketch-books but not she. A touch could be deadly; honey from its pollen could kill.

She watched her mother gather the knife and tied stems and move towards the door. A word would warn her. A single word and Charlotte would not take her burden of poison to her room, would not remove her gloves and handle the slender leaves, weaving them into a wreath for her hair whilst her maid was occupied with mummers.

Charlotte passed along the path and Olivia did not move. She went from her daughter's sight. The door opened and closed. Olivia was motionless. Stealth had always been her refuge. She stared unseeing into obscurity and silence settled all around.

> 'Tremble, thou tyrant, for all thy sin that's past,
> Tremble to think that this night will be thy last.'

St George brandished his sword and beat it against the cauldron-lid that was acting as his shield.

> 'Thy conquering arms shall quickly by thee lay alone,
> And send thee passing to eternal doom.'

He advanced upon the equally bellicose Gracious King and two young kitchenmaids, arms aching from pushing soup through a tammy-cloth for almost two hours, clutched each other with glee. The clash of wooden swords resounded through the servants' hall as the audience loudly urged its hero on.

All the staff were there – housemaids, laundry- and stillroom maids, stable-lads, gardeners and footmen, the carpenter, blacksmith and butler. No one was expected to be about his duty when the mummers came. The long deal tables, scrubbed into ridges, where the multitude had their meals, had been carried to the walls and the benches placed in lines to face the play. This was only a short break in a season of extra work but there was an air of excited holiday in the crowded room and the actors, freed for one evening from the care of their stock, rose to match the enthusiasm of their watchers.

The scandal of Margrave's return with an Indian concubine in his baggage had spread through the countryside like water running downhill. Apprehension added its razor-edge to the turbulence of the festivities. The expectation of fear was abroad.

Holland sat on one end of the second bench. As Charlotte's personal maid, her status entitled her to the front row, but she was occupied by her thoughts and preferred a position where she was neither compelled by politeness to respond vivaciously to the playing nor, as sometimes happened, have a dying Saracen precipitated into her lap.

It had been late when she returned from Quinn's house with the costumes for the girls. Her day had already been long and a cold drive through icy lanes at its close might not have seemed rewarding but her errand had a meaning that had grown in importance while she slept and warmed her when she woke. She had never yearned for Charlotte's interest and affection as Ward had yearned for Eleanor's. Her character was less tender than her friend's. What she had wanted was recognition of her worth as more than the clever manipulator of hair and dress and the efficient provider of the necessary comforts of a rich lady. It was not enough to be complimented on the dextrous plaiting of a five-strand braid or never to be reprimanded for forgetfulness in the care of the fortune in jewels that passed through her hands. She had abilities that had lain fallow and, though she had enough intelligence to see that this was so for much of the world, she wished to have them praised. It was no sin in her eyes to rise above her station.

St George and the King were bounding back and forth, belabouring each other with blows that would result in applications of wintergreen ointment and caustic comments from their wives about their intake of free cider. The Yule log burned in the vast open hearth, gleaming on the burnished copper fish-kettles and jelly-moulds that lined high oak shelves. The evocative smell of spiced beef mingled with the rich, treacly scent of the gingerbread being passed on wooden trenchers up and down the rows.

'I'll have thee this night beware.'

The beribboned warriors grappled mightily.

'See what bloody works thou'st made.'

St George drew back his sword and plunged it beneath his opponent's arm. The Gracious King groaned and lay twitching on the floor to the hooting of the stable-boys.

'He was no match for me, he quickly fell.'

The victorious knight turned his attention to a new challenger, who was prancing up on a hobby-horse with a cockade of pheasants' feathers fastened to his helmet. Holland gazed at the vanquished form of the King, saw it rise and tiptoe limpingly into the pantry where whispered directions and odd jinglings could be heard between St George's threats.

There were too many players on the stage at Vauchurch. They must divide into opposing forces and fight for power. As she stood at Quinn's fire, waiting for him to read the note that said more than she had been told, Holland had consoled herself with her innocence of what the true message was but she was no longer practising this deceit. No physical obstacle prevented her, even now, from going to Margrave and saying, 'Last night, I carried a letter from your wife to her lover. They are not cowed by your return. Beware.' She had only to rise from the bench and slip away from the gaudy spectacle of repetitive violence and warning could be given. It was impossible. There was no safety. To alert one side to treachery was to jeopardise the other. She had taken pride in Charlotte's trust and her allegiance had been given.

The hobby-horse fell to the flagstones with a clatter as its rider was struck down. Flushed faces cheered as the Irish Doctor strode on to cure the dead with one sly dose of his Jerusalem balsam. Soon old Father Christmas would knock his wife on the head for refusing to fry a dry Jack hare and would pay a hundred guineas to have her life restored. Winter had come and with it the enduring cycle of vengeance and sorrow. Nothing was necessary but to look on.

The air was thick with steam. Margrave lay in his bath with his eyes shut, wallowing in heat that had turned his skin red. Before the mummers had begun, a procession of footmen and maids had borne canisters of newly-boiled water along the passage from the kitchens, up the stairs and into the master's dressing-room where they filled the copper hip-bath, with its high sloping back, and its outer casing of painted zinc. Sheets were draped inside the bath to soften the touch of the metal and over the wardrobe and chests-of-drawers. A small furnace that stood on a square of marble at the head of the bath was connected to the casing by pipes and, once lit, caused its water to circulate, perpetually reheating itself if the furnace was kept stoked.

Before he had left for India, Margrave had been content with this contrivance. Now it no longer seemed as satisfying. The fumes from the furnace were disagreeable even when sweet herbs were scattered on the charcoal to improve the smell. And then there was the inevitable infiltration of moisture into his stored clothes despite the protective coverings. He had grown used to a degree of luxury in usurped palaces that made this homely arrangement feel primitive. He would have a room set aside solely for bathing. There were gratifications that commanded close attention.

He bent one leg, easing his thigh off the clinging sheet. Warmth eddied round him as the water moved. He had been away too long. The severity of the cold had shocked him. He was not weakened by it, as Celia appeared to be, but he was aware of its enmity as he had never been before.

Nor was the harsh frost his only foe. His certainty that he could crush Charlotte to his will had not diminished but now it rested only on his determination to have his way. Absence had made him forget her strength. She had said nothing amiss yet. There had been no objection to Celia nor any sign of suspicion that the young woman was more than an ordinary guest. Words had not been needed. Charlotte's awareness of what she confronted was plain in her silence and did not suggest submission. It was unnerving. He must summon a greater show of authority – but could not tell how to suppress rebellion that had no outward display of its existence. It was as if he had approached an enemy encampment in battle array and found, instead, a cliff-face with no path to its deserted summit.

Well, the hostilities could wait. He reached down for the glass of brandy on the low table beside the bath, added water from the carafe, and drank slowly, thinking of Celia. She was near. He could feel her strange presence in the next room. Her hysteria as she entered Vauchurch was excuse enough for her seclusion. It delayed the coming conflict with Charlotte and added to the mystery and sensation within the house. He was alive to the scandal he had caused. There was not a servant within these walls who did not recognise Celia for what she was. Half-glances of shock, dismay and admiration met his eye at every turn and were veiled by the blank docility he demanded. No one dared speak of Miss Eliot with a disapproving tone in his hearing. His presence in his house with a mistress at his heel had decreed the acceptance of an abominable flouting of society's rules. No greater humiliation could have been inflicted on his wife but who would dare censure him to his face? He had mastery of all beneath his roof and there was such pleasure in it.

The steam had thinned and was hanging in spectral drifts that wavered between the heat of furnace and hearth and the chill pressing in from the window. There was no sound from Celia's room. She would be curled in the bed, with its sea-green hangings, as still as a snake. Her face would have no expression he could read. She would be waiting while he bathed and dined, while he sat at the head of his table letting the season's pageantry unfold before him; she would be waiting when night had deepened and ice glittered beneath the cruel stars; she would be waiting when he came to her.

Charlotte set her hand on the key that secured the door between her room and Margrave's. The iron filled her palm. It was a key almost as old as the house and was of the massive construction common in those violent days when Vauchurch was young. Before Margrave had left for India, the key had been on his side and the door had not been locked. This was the way he had taken throughout the years when he had used her in his craving to sire a son. There would be no indication of his intention for the night, no tender word that evening, no touch, no playful reference to past intimacy. They had never been lovers; there had been no love between them to let joy flower. She had soon understood that any sign of reluctance only increased his satisfaction. Indifference became her weapon in their couplings. Her boredom enraged and baffled him. She had yawned once as he was most vigorous and, thwarted, he had withdrawn, defeated, cursing her for an unnatural jade. It was the only time she could remember laughing when he was in her bed.

She had endured the begetting of her children in this room and had brought them to life here as he waited below for news of their sex. Twice, he had entered, as she lay white and exhausted, to berate her with vicious contempt for the damp-haired infants swaddled in the cradle at her side. They had been small, defence-less objects for his derision. Kate had never learnt to protect herself.

This young woman Margrave had brought as his doxy was of Kate's age. Celia Eliot. Had he searched the plains of India for her, knowing the sister of Eleanor's seducer would be a more exquisite insult to his wife than a common whore? How they must revel in her supposed helplessness as they lay together. Or perhaps he had simply happened upon the girl. She was prepared to accept the Fates had thrown an Eliot in his path to entertain the gods. The little she had seen of Celia told her that the tormented vulnerability contained within the young, delectable body would be irresistible to one of Margrave's tyrannical temperament. What a victory it would have been to ruin the last of the Eliots and humiliate the wife he had always resented with one loosening of his trouser-buttons. She knew him but he had never known her. Did he imagine she would not despise him for his petty, carnal triumph?

She turned the key and went into his room. A fire was banked high in the hearth. Its flames leapt and swayed, lapping at the soot-blackened stone, filling the chamber with a juddering, tawny light. He's grown soft, she thought. He misses an alien sun and must have unnatural heat. Well and good.

There was no sign in the room that a traveller had just returned. His trunks had been emptied and stored elsewhere, their contents had been put away. No souvenirs of foreign ports sat incongruously on tables, no pile of ribbon-bound gifts revealed a sentimental yearning for his family. And why? she asked as she crossed the floor with slow, deliberate steps. Because this is the master's domain and he has given orders that it should be so. I could say, 'Let his linen be aired before folding it in drawers,' and he could countermand me. The master is home and my word is the rustle of dead leaves. I was master in house and field and now I'm to walk behind his wench.

As she opened the door into Margrave's dressing-room, steam enfolded her, glistening on her gown, beading the coils of her hair, clinging to her lashes like unshed tears. Fumes of charcoal, lavender and thyme assailed her.

'Come in, if you're coming,' he said.

She shut the door, noting how close a fit it must be to let no moisture or scents into the room beyond. Turning back towards the bath, she saw the redness of Margrave's skin beneath the hot water and its fading into white where his chest emerged. She was able to observe his nakedness dispassionately. He had aged little in the five years they had been apart. His face and hands had darkened and he was, if anything, a trifle more muscular. There was no loose flesh nor effects of idle living. It amused her that he began to raise one leg to hide his lolling genitals before restraining himself.

Lifting her gaze to his eyes, she concealed all disdain and

maintained the coldness she had worn since Celia's screams had echoed from walls that already knew woe.

'I didn't expect you,' he said.

'Don't I always see to your needs when the servants are with the mummers?'

'You do, but—' He took another mouthful of brandy and water. The bed at the King's Arms must have been damp or he had grown unused to English food. He was feeling liverish and needed to sweat out any ague if he were to keep command.

'Are you warm enough?' she said. 'I daresay you find our winter trying after what you're used to.'

'You could throw some more charcoal in the box.'

'Perhaps there's a draught.' She went to the window to check that it was closed, then pulled the curtains together, overlapping them so that no invading air could insinuate its frigid breath into the room. There was a scuttle of sea-coal beside the hearth. Taking the tongs, she lifted two lumps, dewed with steam, onto the fire where they sputtered and emitted thin jets of smoke.

'And why say "our winter" as if I'm a foreigner?' he said tetchily. 'You're forgetting this is my home.'

'How could I forget that?' Charlotte directed her reserved gaze at the door to the Green Chamber, where Celia lay dreaming in her opium-laden lethargy, and looked back to Margrave with her eyebrows slightly raised. This was the nearest she had come to expressing her feelings since he had returned and he found its restraint unnerving.

'I'll do as I please in my own house,' he said. A sudden, griping pain in his belly made him wince and he sipped again at his brandy.

'This isn't the time to talk of it.' Charlotte held out her hand for his glass and refilled it from the bottle and carafe. 'Put yourself in a good humour for Christmas. We must keep up appearances.'

He rested the edge of the glass on his chest. Much as he disliked approving of his wife, he could not help admiring the way she was accepting the situation without womanish fuss.

She passed behind him to add more fuel to the furnace. As she bent to gather the herbs to sweeten the fumes from the charcoal, she quietly locked Celia's door and slid the key into the watch-pocket at her waist. Gathering the sprays of leaves from their box, she placed them carefully inside the furnace. Seeing their edges blacken and glow, she went back towards Margrave's bedroom. As

147

she stood in the doorway regarding him, Margrave thought her dignified and inconveniently regal. There was a grandeur in her manner that had always lessened his belief in his power.

'I must accept your will,' she said. 'After all, what else can I do?'

In her own room, a gown that Charlotte knew she would not wear that evening had been laid out on the bed by Holland before the mummers came. Charlotte stared at it, seeing the continuation of an orthodox life it represented. Perhaps she would use it again but she would not sit down in it tonight to watch Margrave carve venison at the head of their table.

She did not know what to do while she waited. An energy was welling in her, drawing her upright with muscles tensed in readiness for action. It was necessary to be still, to maintain a composure, clear-headedness. She must be patient while the very stones that enclosed her pulsed with vibrant, intolerant expectation.

A familiar sound made her turn from the bed, alert and poised like a deer that hears the snap of bracken. The door from the tower opened and Quinn came through, striding towards her as if completing a journey undertaken with confidence in achieving his purpose. He gathered her to him, pressing against her so that she could not tell whether it was her heart beating so strongly or his. The smell of night was in his clothes; the fresh cold of frost and brittle woods. She raised her face and he kissed her with the ardour of a lover who has not yet slaked his first appetites.

'Were you noticed?' she asked.

He leant back, holding her about the waist. 'No one saw me here,' he said. 'They're all occupied. Did you give instructions for a place to be set for me at dinner?'

'I ordered another place. I didn't say for whom.'

'Very good.' He kissed her again to each side of her neck. 'We have only to be resolute.'

'Will you have a glass of wine to warm you?'

'I will.'

She slid from his grasp. Catching a fold of her skirt, he let the silk flow through his fingers as she pulled away. As she poured Madeira, he went to the hearth and stood before it as he had stood before his own when her maid had brought him the letter telling of Celia. He had hardly felt the rawness of the wind as he rode to Vauchurch. His thoughts had been focused upon what he was to do. The past five years had been a time of lotus-eating; now measures must be taken to protect his love and wrest his rightful place from the Margraves. He had not hesitated to form his plans; he would not hesitate to carry out the deeds.

The heart from the fire began to penetrate his breeches. He had set out, as guests who came by horse usually did, in riding-clothes with his evening-dress in a saddle-bag. When he reached the farm closest to the promontory, he had dismounted, loosened one of his mare's shoes and led her into the barton, asking for her to be stabled until she could be shod. The farmer was all concern, wishing to offend neither the man who had been all but master since the flight to India nor Margrave, whose dining must not be delayed by the late arrival of his cousin. Quinn had smilingly refused the loan of a sturdy, workaday cob or a boy to light his way and had climbed the escarpment on foot by a side-path, circling unseen to the rear of the seemingly deserted house. No loud hoof-beats announced his presence. He entered Vauchurch discreetly but openly and walked without incident or challenge through the empty passageways and flights of hidden stairs to his tower-room, where he placed the immaculate suit of black-and-white that would bear no mark that might be left by what he must do.

He took the filled glass from Charlotte, noticing that her hand was steady.

'I'm safe with wine, am I?' he said. 'Had I better not ask for water?'

She caught her breath, then let it out in a laugh that was like a snarl. Quinn ran a finger down the curve of her cheek.

'Was he drinking his usual mixture?' He raised his glass. 'You have been in to do your duty?'

'Oh, yes. I went to see to his needs, just as on every other Christmas Eve. He was surprised but he approved of the way I was adapting to circumstances. Most of the carafe was gone.'

'And the opium-eater?'

'No sight or sound of her. She'll be holding communion with her drops, no doubt. I locked the door to her room. He can't get through that way – nor the other.'

'My Amazon.'

He had been proud of her from the first. The recognition, during their unexpected encounter in the London hotel, of the depth of her contempt for Margrave had been a stimulant as great

149

as the simple awakening of his dormant love. Her marriage had never been a betrayal in his eyes. The disparagement he had suffered for his supposed illegitimacy had taught him the strength of social and family bonds; he would not despise a girl for being unable to assert her will against the oppressive force that was her father. Sitting next to the woman who had been that captive girl, in the ivy-wrapped arbour of the hotel dining room, a malevolent gladness had filled his soul as he realised that he had not wasted his devotion on one who was not worthy of it. She had grown to be passionate, strong and unscrupulous. When her husband's deception over Kate's marriage had been revealed, her bitterness could not have been more sharp. They had waited like crouching tigers for Margrave and Forston to sail and then, glorious in her rage and freedom, she had welcomed him to her heart and bed without wearisome doubts and conscience. He had seen her hatred of Margrave flare at the news of Kate's death and descend into a darkness where savagery could reign. A capacity for the sinister suited him well.

'Have you had any problems?' he asked.

'None. I cut twigs of oleander yesterday while he was busy with his trollop and soaked them in the water overnight as you said.'

'Hidden?'

'Locked in my cabinet.' She touched her pocket. 'I'm a perfect repository of keys.'

'And the smoke?'

'I fetched more sprays this evening – when the mummers had begun – and put them amongst the herbs for his furnace while I was in the dressing-room filling his carafe. I heard him come in just after I left. I believe I've a talent for this. It was exhilarating.'

'Were you careful to breathe nothing poisonous yourself?'

'Yes. It was a risk having to add them to the box before he was in the bath but I couldn't have him see me burning something I'd brought in. I buried them under the lavender and thyme. They hadn't been used. He wasn't suspicious when I stoked the furnace and I left at once.' She spoke proudly with an edge of lascivious cruelty to her voice.

'Ah, Lotta,' he said. 'You should have been with me in Georgia. How we would have flourished.' Drawing his watch from his waistcoat by its chain, he opened its case. 'What do we have? The mummers and then the servants' dinner. Another hour. Time enough.'

He felt the weight of Vauchurch around him with its serpentine history of secret guilts, its emptiness and isolated enclaves of slighted lives. The blood that had built these walls beat in his veins and was unafraid of power. A man, who might be his brother, was dying at this moment and at his instigation. The house was no stranger to treachery and death. It would accept its heir.

'Stay here,' he said.

She handed him two keys and he went into Margrave's room. The coals crumbled as he passed, their hollowed forms rustling into ash, but he did not turn his head. Leaning close to the far door, he listened for sounds that would say he was too soon. Silence pressed towards him.

Untying his neck-cloth, he bound it over his nose and mouth. Thrusting open the door, he saw that murder had been done. It gaped at him, brutal and sure. Holding his breath, he went swiftly to the curtains, dragged them back and pushed the window wide, leaning out to draw air into his aching lungs. The wind flowed round him, drawing ice and moonlight into the heated, noxious atmosphere. What was left of the steam swayed and folded quietly onto the carnage that was present amongst the trappings of domestic comfort.

Quinn returned to Margrave's bedroom and opened the windows there. Cold pressed through the warmth with the certainty of a glacier, crushing the weak defences of fires in its monumental progress. His face against a mullion, breathing the fresh night, Quinn looked again at his watch. He could only guess how long it would be before the poisoned fumes had been driven out. He could not wait. Leaving his neck-cloth hanging loosely on his chest, he ventured back into the room. The air tasted of frost and sea.

Once inside the dressing-room, he looked more closely at what he had caused to be done. Margrave lay back in the bath with eyes that were open but saw nothing. Vomit clung to his chin and was splattered across the overturned table, the floor and the carafe, that had rolled to drain its last dregs onto a red velvet slipper, as if he had tried to climb out as he retched. His glass floated heavily in water that was thick with bloody faeces. Death had come quickly but it had brought pain and indignity. It was as Quinn had wished.

He allowed himself a moment to savour his triumph. In this, as in other pleasures, satisfaction was more acute if there was no haste. He had killed before – in Persia where his encampment had

151

been attacked by bandits who did not yet know their trade, on his plantation where the lazy destruction of black lives caused no troublesome ripples on the law, in a fever-glade where the consequence of a duel had brought him back to England. All had excited him, all had brought grim triumph, but none had been like this. This had been the death he had yearned for, anticipated and planned throughout the years, caressing details in his fancy as a woman would fondle her lap-dog.

There was more to do. His dear, fierce love had been insulted by the presence of a whore in her house. Such women were of little account. He moved towards Celia's door.

In the Green Chamber, Celia lay in the ancient bed with its hangings pulled closely together so that firelight did not penetrate her seclusion. She had not wanted to see the flames. Greaves had undressed her early, recognising the signs that her tormented mistress would suffer the affliction of memory that night. The women had wanted to stay together – one from dread of solitude, one from pity – but Margrave had entered, gloatingly, callously possessive, and sent Greaves away, telling her not to come back until morning.

Alone in the room that had become her darkened world, listening to the faint sounds of water being brought for Margrave to bathe, Celia unsealed a full bottle of laudanum and measured more than her usual dose into a glass. The drops slid down her throat promising forgetfulness and ease. She clasped the wine-glass in both hands as she drank, eager for its contents as she was eager for nothing else in life. Oblivion was necessary tonight. Fear was with her in her hopelessness; she heard it in the winds that whined about the house. No barrier could keep it from its prey. It flowed through stone; it slipped beneath her door; it stirred the tapestry in the far corner of the room; it patted the bed-hangings with cold, white hands seeking here and there for a way in.

She laid her head on the pillow and drew the coverings tightly about her as she waited for release to take her in its arms. Her limbs became heavy, her heart slowed, her drowned spirit sank towards the torpor she craved. Time had no meaning, anguish failed. Perhaps there was distress nearby. She could not tell. Was her name called? She rested upon snow that blew in emerald drifts beneath a granite sky.

Quinn parted the curtains and looked at the woman. She could not raise herself and gazed at him, accepting what had come. He saw the small, black flecks that were her pupils, heard the labouring of her breath and smiled. Taking the bottle from her table, he opened her mouth and poured the rest of the drug over the back of her tongue. She choked but it did not matter; his purpose was served.

He put aside the sheet and lifted her gently from the bed. She was not yet a dead weight. Carrying her to the dressing-room, he laid her on the floor beside the bath, her nightgown trailing in the stinking slops. Her eyes did not follow him and she gave no sign of having seen Margrave. He reached over to the wash-stand, innocently set with toiletries, and opened a razor. Kneeling beside her, he wrapped her right hand about the ivory handle and drove the blade into her left wrist. Steel sliced through skin, flesh and artery. Bright blood sprang out, pulsing with less vigour than from an untouched heart but strongly enough.

He stepped back to watch the red stain growing and when it had ceased, he turned and walked away.

Chapter Twelve

Olivia ran down the corridor, her feet making no sound on the thick carpet. Empty guest-rooms lay to each side; rooms that had been filled with visitors at other Christmastides. She should have gone to her own room long ago to be dressed in the viridescent silk that was to honour her father. It had been agreed that the search was to be given up after half an hour if the seeker had not been successful and those in hiding could emerge smug and, in Olivia's case, sarcastic. Hermione and Frank would be wondering where she was. Ward would be brushing her cherished girl's hair, making unflattering comparisons between the cousins, and Hermione would be chiding her gently in her softly resolute voice. The servants would have just finished their dinner and be moving stolidly back to their duties, sleepy with beef and plum-pudding. Someone would be dispatched to call for her.

She had not intended to lose track of time. The conservatory had held her until the tightness at her temples had lessened. Clouds had fled across the moon, darkening the dusk, and she had crouched in the dank earth-scents of the artificial forest, breathing its humid musk in shallow gasps. Her mother would be weaving an oleander wreath with fingers that teased and pinched and stroked the death that was their just retribution. Poison would be seeping through her skin and into her veins. Punishment would come to the adulteress and grief to her paramour. Margrave would not mourn such a wife. Celia Eliot would recognise a kindred soul in the daughter of her lover.

To leave the secrecy of palm fronds and forced blooms to return to her chamber for the primping and chatter of the hour before the festivities began was beyond her self-control. How could she conceal what she had done? How could she disguise that she was Nemesis? She wandered through Vauchurch, down passages where she knew no one would be, lingering in brocaded boudoirs and shrouded salons, keeping to the shadows that had

155

always been her home. Margraves, long turned to dust, whispered their pride as she passed. She had upheld their name.

She had been leaning in a deep window embrasure, watching the wind scourge the bitter night, when the screams began. Shrill and despairing, they pierced the stillness of the desolate house. She was as upright as a hare, alert and poised for flight. Death had come and she found she had not truly expected it. If she ran now, if she reached her mother before the maid's first shock had ended, perhaps life would still be there.

Out of her retreat and down the long corridor towards the lamp at the head of the main stairs. Across the broad landing, her hand pressed beneath her ribs where a sharp pain drove its thin blade into her flesh. The screams were louder here, more regular and sustained as if the one who gave them voice dare not pause for fear that she must then deal with the terror that she faced. Other cries before and behind. Other hurrying steps. On towards her mother's room, twisting around maids and men as a stream twists around the rocks that litter its bed. On towards her mother's room but it was not Holland whose screams were dying into long, wailing sobs. Greaves was being held by two footmen as shocked women tried to calm her. Greaves was struggling convulsively to enter Celia's open door.

A thick, sweet stench of sickness and blood came from the room. There was a dark stain on the hem of Greaves's gown where her skirt had dragged in the gore she had found. Olivia pushed between two parlourmaids to go into the crowded chamber. One turned to speak but, seeing who had come, kept silent. Olivia heard a murmur at her shoulder, 'She should be kept out, she's too young,' but no one tried to block her path.

The door to her father's dressing-room had been flung to the wall. The foul smell was strengthening. She pulled a stable-man aside by his coat-tail and stepped over the threshold. In the passage, Greaves was quietening, exhaustion diminishing her outcry into low, keening moans. Her lament made the hush within seem absolute but it was broken by the small, suppressed sounds of shock, of breaths drawn harshly, of sudden, bitten-off whimpers that would become weeping, of the rustle of dress as those who had been frozen in place changed their stance.

There were familiar backs before her; the room seemed composed of the rigid backs of people who should be elsewhere. She went forward into horror.

The melancholy woman who was to be her salvation lay like a lily in a crimson wash of blood. The dead face, the lips that had been a sweet scarlet, the hands that had held pearls, the small feet protruding from the white nightgown were blanched and inhuman in their lack of colour. There was colour enough, to be sure. The tumbling hair, that Greaves had loved to brush, straggled in viscous red locks, red sopped the lower folds of the muslin gown, it covered the blade and ivory handle of the razor that had fallen from the dying grasp, it drenched the lace that half-covered a wrist severed down to the bone.

And beyond this, beyond this carnage that seemed to still her own blood, Olivia saw her father. Her breath left her in a sigh. She was weary; she could have lain down amidst this slaughter and closed her eyes, sleeping like the dead to dream that none of this was so. Celia had looked on this sight, had seen her lifeless love and followed him.

' "Intreat me not to leave thee, or to return from following after thee: for whither thou goest, I will go . . . Where thou diest, will I die, and there will I be buried: the Lord do so to me, and more also, if ought but death part thee and me." '

She sensed a change in the silence around her. What she believed to be her thoughts had been spoken aloud. Those who had been gazing, stricken, at the bodies glanced upward at Charlotte. The implications of Olivia's words were clear. They should not have been said at this time and place. In their shock, those gathered there could not endure the truth. Sentiment and superstition made them unwilling to speak ill of the dead. That this woman had been Margrave's mistress and had killed herself for grief, breaking the laws of God and man, was plain to all but there was a craven reluctance to have it said. The corpse was not yet cold; the injured wife, her own sins briefly forgiven, was barely a widow.

Olivia stared at Charlotte. In her distress, she had not noticed her mother yet Charlotte's presence was hardly less overwhelming than the butchery itself.

Kneeling at her husband's side, Charlotte had reached to cradle him against her breast. The loose sleeves of the wrap she had thrown on as the screams were heard were immersed in the scum of vomit and excrement that floated upon the water. Her face was a mask of tragic nobility. She might have been born for this moment.

There was a stir behind Olivia. The watchers were parting, allowing someone to pass. Olivia turned. Quinn had entered. He was wearing evening-dress and gave no sign of haste or agitation.

At the sight of him, Charlotte's rigid restraint gave way as if her powers had ebbed on finding a strength on which to lean. She clutched Margrave more closely to her.

'He's dead,' she cried. 'Oh, God!'

Quinn looked angrily from one pale-faced servant to another. 'What are you about?' he said. 'Help Mrs Margrave to her room. Has a physician been sent for? The constables? A clergyman?'

Movement began as if a key had been turned. Holland and a maid, who was shaking in staccato shudders, tried to lift Charlotte from her knees but she would not rise. Quinn gave orders for those he had named to be fetched then crossed to where Charlotte was resisting the women.

'My dear,' he said gently, 'you must let him go now. You must let Holland take you to lie down.'

He took each of her hands, pulling them from the corpse, easing Margrave from her arms. As he rested the awkward weight of the dead man back against the bath, the water rocked and slopped over the rim onto the pristine whiteness of the nightgown that had rucked on Celia's thigh. A young kitchen-girl, known for her soft heart, began to retch and was led out. The housekeeper, an extreme pallor upon her own face, stepped forward to address Quinn.

'Should we lay them out decently, sir?' she said. 'The master and Miss Eliot? This is no way for them to be seen.'

Quinn had succeeded in raising Charlotte to her feet and was steadying her as Holland became her support.

'Your intentions do you credit,' he said, 'but no. They died suddenly and there must be an inquest. It's better that the doctor views them as they are.'

Olivia felt a tear run down her cheek, pause and run again to catch at the corner of her mouth. Her tongue touched the salt warmth of the unfamiliar droplet. She could not remember ever having cried except in anger. Turning slowly, wanting neither to go nor stay, she walked from the dressing-room to the Green Chamber, where Celia had given her the earrings Margrave had chosen for her, and out into the corridor. Greaves and her comforters were no longer there but servants stood in anxious groups exchanging speculations and generating rumour in low

158

voices. Hermione and Frank had not come down. They would have been in the old nursery, too far away behind oak doors for the screaming to have seemed anything other than part of the mummers' horseplay, and Ward, if she had discovered the truth, would have been formidable in preventing her chick and Frank from running to the scene of destruction. Olivia rubbed the flat of her palm against the centre of her chest where a swelling ache was rising into permanence. No, if the truth were known, it was Hermione who would have held Frank back. Hermione would protect her cousins at all costs but was shading your eyes from the hard glare of reality the most worthy protection?

Alone amongst many, Olivia stood in the passage and considered her tears. Her heart was numb. Misery would take her but shock had not yet released its deadening grip to let sorrow surge in. I have never wept except in anger, she thought, and I am weeping now. Why is my mother unharmed and where is the poison that she cut from the bush with her own hands? Poison that kills with a bloody flux. I watched her put on gloves to cut the sprigs and my desires let me believe she was not aware of the death she gathered. And Quinn is here.

A sickness greater than she had suffered amid the stench and terror in the dressing-room rolled in her bowels. If she had set aside her own vile longings, if she had stepped from her concealment and revealed herself to her mother, warning of the danger couched within the leaves perhaps her father would be alive, bathed and hungry, fastening his watch-chain across his evening waistcoat to go down to dinner. Throughout her fourteen years, the lonely, tormented girl had yearned, unknowingly, for the ordinary but never more than when she stood in her solitary desolation, conjuring the image of a smiling Margrave calling for the mumming to begin as if the passion of her need could undo the past.

It was still possible that she was wrong. The bouquet of camellia and oleander might be innocently displayed in her mother's room, waiting in a vase or woven into a wreath. Let it be so; let it be so.

She made abruptly for Charlotte's door and entered without knocking. The bedroom was as little a haven for her as Eleanor's was for Hermione. She had never been welcomed here and since Quinn had become its unspoken occupant, she had not set foot inside. The thought of the sin committed within this luxurious seclusion, within the great bed that should have held no man but

159

Margrave brought a scorn for her childish hopes and the wretched certainty that murder had been done.

From her position, hesitating on the Turkey carpet, unable to force herself to search for what she knew would not be there, she could see into Margrave's bedroom. Her mother had sunk onto a chair and was having eau-de-cologne rubbed into her temples by Holland. The natural weakness of a woman who has found her husband dead was exhibited in the slump of her normally upright figure and the bewildered exhaustion on her handsome, arrogant face.

It brought the bile to Olivia's throat. The perfect apeing of grief was a profane mockery of wifehood that made her realise her helplessness in the face of the evil that stalked the house. The artful wickedness that had contrived Margrave's death was not a sudden manifestation of depravity that saw and took its chance but a sustained malevolence that could plan with cold-blooded cunning. Celia had understood and fled a world that offered only corruption and that would condemn her for her escape.

Perhaps there was comfort in it; the sour consolation that warning of the poison would not have saved her father. His death had been determined and he could not have evaded the hunters' snare. If not one trap, then another. The weariness that had consumed her as she looked upon the dead held her limbs as if winter had slid into her veins and ice stilled her heart.

Charlotte had risen, leaning awkwardly on Holland, and was approaching her room as if she had aged twenty years. She entered the place of her adultery, where she and he had spoken in grim whispers of the intricate care that would rid them of her duty, and let herself be lowered onto the bed. Seated on the coverlet, the edge of the abandoned gown spread ready for the night's entertainment caught beneath her, she raised her eyes to her pale, accusatory daughter.

'Come here to me,' she said.

If I show fear, Olivia thought, I will always be fearful. She walked forward stiffly until Charlotte could reach out and take her hand. Olivia stared at their clasped fingers, unable to remember seeing such a sight before.

'I was in the conservatory earlier this evening,' she said.

The tightening of Charlotte's hold was barely perceptible.

'Holland.' She turned to the maid. 'I believe Olivia and I would both be better for a cup of white wine whey. Will you see to it?'

When Holland had left, Charlotte dropped Olivia's hand and folded her own in her lap. 'You were in the conservatory,' she said. 'What of it?'

'I was in hiding from Frank.'

'Curious.'

'I saw you cut branches of oleander.'

'And so I did.' Charlotte was unflinching. 'Though hardly branches. A few fragments for my hair but they didn't suit. I threw them on the fire.'

'The smoke is poisonous.'

'Then it's as well my chimney draws so strongly. Smoke never drifts into the room.'

Olivia felt herself being tempted towards admiration. Had she had cause to kill, this is how she would have acted, shameless and unafraid. Just as when she had seen Charlotte laying open the nakedness of her love in Quinn's tower-room, she knew herself to be her mother's daughter and the revelation was unendurable.

'Oh, God,' she cried. 'Papa! What have you done?'

'What have I done?' Charlotte's voice was cold. 'I've found my husband dead at the side of his mistress and now, in my trouble, I must calm a daughter who has ever been strange. So strange that her wits may have been sent astray by what she's seen. She may make imputations in her sad disorder that have her shut away for her own safety. Or were you asking your Papa what he had done? Ask Kate of that. Ask Miss Eliot?'

'Miss Eliot is free of you.' Olivia felt her eyes brim again and this time there was a painful triumph in her anger. 'You can do her no more harm. She must have foreseen this – what you would do in your spite for his preference. She told me she would soon leave this place and asked me to have mercy on her guilt. Poor lady – to come here and say she'd have much need of forgiveness. To come to this house and hope for pity.'

Mr Moore, having had his great-coat removed by a footman, was shown into the drawing room and noted that, though it was only two days after Christmas, all signs of joyful celebration had been removed and Vauchurch was a temple of mourning. It was nine o'clock but the heavy curtains were shut against the bleak rising of the sun, as was proper from respect for the dead, and the artificial darkness was alleviated by a myriad candles, whose bright points reflected in their silver sticks, in the high polish of Honduras

161

mahogany and the massive gilded looking-glasses gave the effect of failed gaiety to the solemn gathering.

The last of the jurors for the inquest had arrived just ahead of Moore and were warming themselves at the hearth as they accepted glasses of wine. The double-doors into the dining room had been left open and they were able to see another fire burning briskly for their sakes and a table laid generously for their later refreshment. They stood in a murmuring cluster, one lifting himself repeatedly onto his toes to relieve feet stiffened by cold during the drive, another, an auctioneer, gazing about as he made an admiring mental inventory, all torn between reluctance for the task before them and a ghoulish fascination with the scandal.

It was plain to Moore, as he accepted his Madeira from the proffered tray, that they were unsure whether he, the coroner, could be included in their stilted conversation or should be separate from them until the business was in hand. He had not enjoyed his journey through the frozen, rutted lanes and was content to remain alone, staring at a blazing candelabra, until flames were imprinted on his retina and flowered like sudden crocus blooms on everything at which he looked. The case these uneasy men were to decide was deplorable but he did not anticipate any difficulty in reaching a satisfactory conclusion. He had been summoned late on Christmas Eve to examine the bodies and had read the doctor's report with the cautious attention that had earned him the title 'the Stickler' from officials of the courts. It seemed clear that Margrave had been carried off by the worsening of an Indian fever, with its concomitant digestive embarrassments, that had caused his wife anxiety from the moment of his return. The woman, a degraded wretch, unsound in mind and a slave to opiates, so lost to morality that she brazenly took residence in Mrs Margrave's home, had feloniously ended her existence on finding her protector gone. An insult to God and man in both her living and her dying.

He disliked the sordid. It was unfortunate for one in his profession that he should have a fastidious revulsion for impropriety as indecency and coarseness in life so often led to the need of his services in death. His wife did not ask for details of his days and he approved of her lack of prurient curiosity. The female sex was designed by divine wisdom to be the pillar of virtue on which men, wearied by going forth in the wicked world, could rest to strengthen their rectitude. A woman who had abandoned her

162

proper delicacy was a reef on which many a good soul had been wrecked. As poor Margrave discovered, Moore thought sadly as he watched the yellow flames quiver, for what but the wiles of a Jezebel could have made him forget his dignity and let her enter his house?

The facts were plain and verdicts of accidental death and suicide must surely be reached with little discussion and tedious delay. Commonsense found it unnecessary to have dragged gentlemen from their homes at this season and tradesmen from their business to serve as a jury. He could easily have pronounced on the case alone but the law was the law and must be followed. His only concern was that the squeamish amongst those assembled for the unsavoury purpose might be overcome when taken up to view the bodies.

'Mr Moore?'

Interrupted in his meditations, he turned to the speaker and saw, for an instant, darts of fire within Quinn's eyes. It unnerved him, putting him at a disadvantage as he considered what an insult his first thought had been to one who had acted with punctilious good sense when faced with his cousin's remains and a household in turmoil. He blinked several times, causing the imprint of the flames to flash onto the red-black of his eyelids but releasing Quinn from demonic interpretation.

Quinn, who already had no fear of the inquest, saw the coroner's abashed discomfiture and smiled inwardly. He was like a man stretching his limbs after resting, feeling the vigour rise out of somnolence. His plans had followed their course with no awkwardness but the inopportune presence of Olivia in the conservatory – and who would believe the accusations of a tiresome, eccentric girl, now locked in her nursery, when Charlotte could give a calm account of her attempt at wreath-making and distressing particulars of the persistence of the bowel complaint so usefully mentioned in one of Margrave's rare letters home?

'Mr Holman.' Moore put his empty glass down and assumed an expression that was an unhappy union of deference and authority.

'Sir,' Quinn said, 'the library has been arranged as the courtroom just as you suggested. Would you care to look over it to make sure it's as you wish?'

'I will, sir, thank you, though,' Moore inclined his head graciously, 'I feel certain that all is as it should be.' He opened his

163

watch. 'And, if we're to begin on the hour, perhaps the jurymen could be taken upstairs?'

'I'll attend to it. Mr Garstin is speaking with Mrs Margrave at this moment but will accompany them.' He beckoned to a manservant and sent him like an urbane sheepdog to collect the jury. The men, apprehensive but dutiful, allowed themselves to be ushered into the hall.

Charlotte was standing at the foot of the stairs, talking to Garstin. She was dressed in deep mourning and her face was startlingly white against the black crape and the heavy jet cross at her throat. Seeing the men, she bowed slightly and passed silently into the room where the witnesses were gathered. Her dignity as a wronged widow was magnificent and descended upon the assembly like a veil. A sombre concentration replaced the scatter of comments that had been masking disquiet. The majesty and squalor of death awaited them. A florid-faced brewer stared at Garstin's clerical collar as if, as indeed he believed, it could ward off evil. A scholarly gentleman rubbed the seal that hung on his waistcoat again and again with his thumb.

Later, when Frederick Collier had returned to his comfortable house, with its leafless shrubbery and the rose-trees he loved swaddled in sack-cloth, and was having tea poured for him by his sister, he would not tell her everything he saw. His innocent world of lazy pursuits, of a little study to keep up his Greek, of shooting, sailing, writing to old friends, of hearing the maids laughing amongst the raspberry-canes on summer evenings seemed fragile and threatened by corruption. There was a cruelty at the heart of Vauchurch that he had not encountered before and it made him feel that he had opened the gate in his garden-wall to find himself in a wild and savage land, where he must wander lost and powerless.

He thought of his sister as he shook out his napkin and spread it over his lap at the dining-table that had been awaiting the end of the jurymen's efforts. Amy would not understand if he tried to explain the depravity he believed to reside in this house. Or, he should say, had resided. Of course, he was aware that many supposed gentlemen were libertines. It was possible both to turn a blind eye to the discreet keeping of a mistress and to accept that her keeper might be respectable in all except his rakish desires. Such tolerance could not be extended to one who brought his

164

whore into the home that sheltered his wife and daughter. There was a brutal disregard for the protection of the innocent in the act, an abuse of authority, that could not be forgiven and revealed a love of vice that could only have infected Margrave's whole being.

Leaning back in his chair to let broth be ladled into his dish, Collier remembered the division there had been in the jury as they decided their verdict. They had been as one in their certainty that Margrave's death was accidental and the woman had killed herself in her drugged despair, but they had quarrelled vehemently over the degree of guilt each of the deceased should bear for their flouting of decency. It was a point that had no relevance to the court but was a matter of heated interest in the jury-room. The majority held that Eve had been a temptress and her lust had spread down the generations, bringing men to their ruin. The besieged minority, of which he was one, had not been convinced that the Margraves of this world required much tempting. The idea that men prefer a monkish existence and are dragged from it by the fallen sisterhood did not, they felt, stand up to examination.

Lifting the first spoonful of soup, Collier thought of the contrast between this return to the routine occupations of the day with the ghastly duty they had performed by looking on the dead. For a mercy, the bodies had been moved to lie clothed and straight-limbed in their chambers. He did not know how he could have borne it otherwise. The woman, a Celia Eliot, seemed no more than a girl. Impossible that she should have schemed to lead Margrave astray. She lay, white upon white, on linen sheets. The gory tendrils of her hair rippled over shoulders as white as her gown. White upon white. The curve of her breast and hip was the curve of a snowdrift carved by Arctic winds.

Bloodless. And in the dressing-room, her blood. A swathe across the floor. Dried to a gleaming black, formed into queer, broken stacks as if a mass of ebony tiles had been cast into the room. Her mother would have shed blood at her birth, thrusting a sinless infant into the stream of time that led to such an end. Blood upon the floor. The auctioneer, a man who could value nothing that did not require the strike of his mallet, had made a coarse remark during their deliberations, smacking his lips over the weakening effect of voluptuous women on men of Margrave's years. He would not tell his sister everything when he got home.

'Sir?'

Collier collected himself and turned to the brewer who had set his trust on Garstin's collar.

'May I trouble you for the salt?' the brewer asked.

'With pleasure.' Collier passed the silver cellar and his companion shovelled salt onto his plate with the blade of his knife.

'Jupe,' said the brewer.

Divining this to be a name rather than an esoteric observation upon the soup, Collier replied with his own.

'I could do with this,' Jupe said, 'and a drop of rum-and-hot to go with it. Damnably exhausting morning.'

'Indeed.'

'Never saw the like as that business upstairs. Turned my liver right over. I'll be having one of my spasms by morning if I don't get my feet in a mustard-bath directly I'm through my own door. See if I don't.'

Rather at a loss, Collier contented himself with a 'Dear me!' and found it well received.

'You look a bit peaked yourself,' Jupe went on. 'Take my advice and nip the shivers in the bud. You want to have your spine rubbed up and down with goose-grease.'

'Do I?'

'Oh, yes. Do you a mort of good.' Jupe sucked in his soup appreciatively. 'Can't have been much of a Christmas here, eh? With two dead 'ens up aloft and the womenfolk in hysterics.'

'I don't imagine Mrs Margrave lost her composure. She appeared a most stoical and restrained lady.'

'Restrained? Devilish fine on the eye, I give you that, but – what's this?' He paused to watch a succession of servants enter and place steaming dishes on the sideboard. 'Kidney pudding and very ripe haunches of venison. She knows how to keep a table. Just right for a cold day.'

Collier took his opportunity to turn slightly away, hoping to engage his other neighbour in conversation and so spare himself any further medicinal hints, but the gentleman was already denouncing the price of corn and did not notice.

There was a general relaxation taking place. Amongst most of the men, the laughter was a little louder and the camaraderie a little warmer than would have been normal in other circumstances. They had been strangers or slight acquaintances a few hours before; now they were initiated into a knowledge of horror that would make them hold each other's gaze with a furtive familiarity

166

whenever they met. Islands of solemn resistance to the growing conviviality did exist. The scholarly man, who had rubbed his seal, sat neither speaking nor eating. Mr Moore, seated, Collier observed, in the absence of both master and mistress, at the head of the table, was talking soberly to Quinn Holman at his left. It was a delicate compliment to one who had performed Moore's onerous duties to give him the position that would naturally be taken by Margrave's cousin. From what Collier had seen of Quinn as a witness, his quiet, reserved confidence was too great for him to need the forms of social position yet it was generous to take a lower chair. How fortunate for Mrs Margrave that she had her cousin-in-law to lean upon in this crisis.

Feeling hot, moist breath on his neck, he gave a start and discovered Jupe leaning conspiratorially towards him.

'I see you're looking at Holman,' Jupe whispered, soup gleaming on his mouth.

'I was.'

'I'll wager this is the first time he hasn't been where Margrave should be since the ship set sail for India, eh?'

As Jupe had every appearance of being about to elbow him in the ribs, Collier shifted in his seat. The soup-dishes were being removed and tureens of boiled potatoes were being offered. To Collier's disappointment, the delay caused by the filling of plates did not deter the eager brewer, who poured on gravy until it seemed he must call for the return of his spoon and then again stationed his lips within an inch of his companion's shrinking ear.

'Not that I blame him. Not I. That Mrs Margrave's as handsome a piece as you could meet – go where you will. Now I know your fancy was taken by that pretty petticoat-tail a-lying upstairs – and I won't quarrel with you, I won't say she wasn't ornamental – but give me a more mature vintage and I won't ask for change from ninepence.'

'Your aspersions are foul, sir,' Collier said coldly. 'Who have you not insulted in that speech?'

'Speech, is it?' Jupe's already florid face purpled. 'Foul, is it? Well, well, you're young yet and your heart went out to the poor, dead creature. I don't suppose you can imagine that a lady as proud as Mrs Margrave could play the strumpet. You should listen to the tales my draymen tell when they've brought the kitchen ale here. That high and mighty Holman's been fishing his cousin's pond these five years. Cousin or brother.'

167

Collier stared down the table to where Quinn, assured and dominant, was softly flattering Moore.

'There are children in this house,' he said and breathed again the rank air of a barbarous land.

When Frank was alone in his room, positive that no one would return to bank up his fire, he had opened his curtains. He had lain awake for hours watching the moon climb across the sky. Ice had formed on the window-panes, causing the wan disc to soften at its rim so that the pale light that mingled with the glow of coals seemed to be dissolving from a pearl.

He believed that all Vauchurch slept and the isolation of his wakeful state made him yearn for day. Kindling his lamp would be an admission of cowardice he could not endure but allowing moonlight to bring its dim radiance into the room said nothing disparaging of his character. Night was less threatening beyond these walls than within. In his earlier years, when thunder rolled across the plateau or the wind had the voice of a banshee, Kate would come to his bed, claiming that she was afraid and needed his company. She would slide between his sheets to hold him fast in loving arms, murmuring of summer rides and the trout waiting in deep, green pools, and he would cling fast to the hands that enfolded him, stronger for giving her his protection. She had gone away to drown in warm, Arabian seas, where the sun was as merciless as life, and he lay in solitude, trying to remember her face.

He wanted Hermione. The confidence of her sure spirit brought a peace and cheerfulness that Olivia and he could not conjure when she was not present. It was she who had held Olivia when she had run into the nursery and stood beating her fists against the wall, wailing like a fox in a snare because their father was dead. Ward had gone to find whether the news was true, locking the door behind her so that they could not follow, and returned, her face harrowed, unable to do more than sit staring at Hermione as if she expected to see death come for another to join its dance. It was Hermione who had talked softly, meaninglessly, to Olivia, as one might soothe a horse, until her agony had quietened, turning inward to intensify the queer, still-faced passion that was her nature. It was Hermione who had held him, as Kate had held him, rocking him in the ageless gesture of love that is our only hope in the valley of the shadow. It was Hermione who was sent

168

away early the next morning, ordered into the carriage with the tremulous Ward, bidding her aunt goodbye with expressionless eyes, unsure yet whether to believe the hissed accusations of the fevered Olivia but certain that Charlotte and Eleanor were sisters in all their ways.

There was always loss. Loss and absence. Kate was lost. His father was lost and found and lost. Hermione was at Knapp, forgotten by those who should have cherished her. More absence than loss at Vauchurch and at Knapp.

Frank gazed about the room, counting off the talismen whose connection to another existence reassured a mind struggling not to think of the still forms within the house. The narrow cricket-bat leaning in the corner by the wardrobe, the fishing-basket with the tin of ingeniously tied flies, the box of chipped lead soldiers put to the back of a drawer because he was too old to play with them, the shell of a tortoise that plump Bingham's uncle had brought back from the grey-leaved hills of Delphi, traded at school for an uninhibited half-hour at the pastry-cook's.

The fire was burning low. He saw his treasures by the cool, impersonal wash of moonlight. Lying straight and rigid in the bed, low in the hollow of the feather mattress, numb from lack of movement, he prayed, Let me go, let me be at school with Philip asleep in his iron bedstead to one side of mine and Armitage to the other, let me look across the dormitory to the line of wash-stands and the ewer where Brownlow left the newts that made the slavey scream.

He closed his eyes tightly, wishing to be gone. His head was swimming with a tiredness that had no trace of sleep. Anyone might stand beside his bed if he could not see. Raising his heavy eyelids again, he found he had been holding his breath. He lowered the sheet from his mouth, letting the pent air from his lungs in a plume of white mist that showed night had gripped the room.

The latch of his door rasped as it was lifted; a small sound that sprang like a panther into the silence, making his heart jolt and an inner voice cry, 'Kate! Kate!' A figure slipped into the room and drifted, soft-footed, to the bed. He should have been reassured that it was Olivia; he made himself be so.

Olivia sat beside him. Even in the dim light he could see the depth of possessive tenderness in her eyes; tenderness within a face fierce with grief.

'You were locked in,' he whispered.

'It isn't necessary now the men are gone,' she said. 'I can't make mischief and so I am freed.'

'Mischief? Were you going to?'

'No.' She smoothed the sheet beneath his chin, tucking it around him in a gesture that was alarming with its unfamiliar protectiveness.

No adult, who was not paid for the purpose, had ever showed her care except the two whose lives had been wrenched from them. She raised her hand and touched one of the pearls she wore despite her night-clothes, feeling it tremble at her ear, seeing again the loveliness of sorrow in the giver. In her anguish, she had told Hermione what she had seen but she knew the world well enough to believe that a girl with murder on her lips would meet with scorn from those whose judgement was mature. There was no present help. Time would pass and people would talk more recklessly of Charlotte and Quinn. Sly jokes would be spoken in field and tap-room, rumour would spread, a slow poison of distrust and condemnation would curl its debilitating vapour about the adulterers; the truth would be known and not known. Vengeance would wait in sullen majesty for justice to be done.

'Olivia?'

She raised her head.

'Do you want to come under the covers?' Frank asked, his voice that of a younger child.

'No,' she said again. 'I want you to get up and put on your dressing-gown.'

'Why?'

'For you to come with me.'

'But why?'

'Because,' she smiled a little, 'I must make you strong.'

He did not want to go with her. He was still of an age that feels a warm bed to be a shield against the terrors of the night. Put out one foot and the witches have you.

'Come,' she said, standing and pulling back the sheet she had tucked about him.

He rolled out of the hollow and stood adjusting to the subtle difference in balance of an exhausted body. The floor did not seem steady beneath his feet. Olivia held his dressing-gown open and he put in his arms reluctantly. His new nightshirt was too full in the sleeves and there was a moment of sisterly pulling and tugging to unbunch the linen that made him think of Kate. When

170

he was wrapped to her satisfaction, Olivia took his hand and started towards the door. He did not follow and, arm outstretched, she turned back.

'We have no light,' he said.

'We don't need one. I know the way.'

'It's dark,' he insisted.

She heard the hint of tears and drew her fingers softly down his cheek; another unfamiliar touch.

'It's safer this way, dear,' she said. 'Everything I do tonight is for your safety.'

He went with her then, needing to trust someone closer to him than Hermione and more afraid of fear than of what might be beyond his door.

The passageway was entirely black. He could distinguish neither walls nor ceiling nor floor but let himself be towed by the firm handclasp in a dream-like disorientation, expecting at every step to fall over some obstacle. Out of reach of his dying fire, the cold was intense. It was as if he had plunged into an underground river and was being swept through sunless caverns in glacial waters that slowed and chilled his blood.

A faint shading into grey showed ahead and they were on the landing of the great stairs, looking below to the hall where Celia had fallen screaming as she foresaw her end. The stained-glass in the high windows showed no colour in the moonlight but a tracery of pale illumination gave shape to balustrades and steps, lying on the oak in oblongs and lozenges of burnished lead.

Silence rose from the depths of the house to engulf them. Frank could no longer hear their careful footsteps nor the breathing that had seemed so loud. Olivia moved forward and they descended towards rooms that were empty of all except those who no longer needed light or warmth. He thought he heard Celia shriek, then sound returned and the creak of the stairs called down their coming to whatever waited in the shadows.

'Olivia,' he whispered, 'let's go back.'

The moon gleamed upon her face and he saw an expression that had love but no mercy. She did not reply and he went with her meekly, reaching the hall, passing again into the sable darkness of corridors whose windows were shuttered against the kindly night. At the music-room, she stopped. Frank felt the pressure of her grip increase on his hand. A dread of what was within overtook him but he could not bear the shame of turning to flee.

171

She opened the door, drawing him inside. He raised his eyes to the friendly glow of candles. Their radiance was meagre, hardly spreading to the edges of the room, but it was dazzling after the darkness that was Vauchurch. One moment of relief gave him courage. This was the worst of sights to see and he would endure it; he would not falter in front of Olivia.

The flames were yellow spears on the twined, three-branched, funerary candles that stood at the head and foot of a coffin, resplendent in scarlet velvet, that rested on a bier draped in a black silk pall. Their light gleamed on the rows of gilt bronze nails, on the lion-mask grips, on the elaborate depositum plate adorning the coffin-lid that lay on stools beyond the bier.

Frank walked forward without being bidden and looked upon his father.

Margrave wore a cashmere shroud, belted with a twisted cord, that gave him a forlorn asceticism he had never had in life. The cold had preserved his corpse. His features had relaxed, smoothing away the years, but there was no other sign of decay.

Olivia caressed the dead face with a hand bruised by the violence of her agony. A strange exultation was keeping her from grief. She put her arm about Frank's shoulder.

'Listen,' she said, 'and I will tell you who to hate.'

Margrave was interred in the family vault in the grounds of the chapel where Kate had sought sanctuary. Breaking the tradition of no women being present, Charlotte, heavily veiled, led the procession of sombre men who had come to pay their respects to name and wealth. Frank watched his mother as she leant on Quinn and he did not weep.

Celia, whose body had lain in an outhouse, was buried, as was fitting for a suicide, without ceremony beyond the churchyard wall in Vauchurch Marling. When Olivia went down into the valley to scatter rosemary on the grave, she found the curate she had scorned, privately and defiantly reading the service for the dead.

Chapter Thirteen

On the morning before Twelfth Night, the cold eased a little. The thaw began imperceptibly, so that people stepping out from the shelter of warm hearths to hurry to the woodpile sensed that there was a change without being able to say whether it was for good or ill.

A west wind began to blow gently over the iron land, bringing the remembrance of past springs. Slowly, icicles grew less brittle; their barbs became sheathed in an indecisive liquefaction that clung, hesitated and dripped suddenly onto the softening earth, leaving slender spines of transparency to melt from bough and roof. Ditches began to fill. Frost remained beneath walls and hedges, in the depth of furrows, on the north-facing bark of pine-trees; where the white sun reached it, the delicate, crystalline crust gleamed, crumpled and sank into a glistening on newly-revealed stone and branch. Water seeped into rivulets that ran in lively braids across fields that could not yet suck them down to quicken the seed, giving welcome movement where all had been still.

The ploughmen gathering in the Five-Acre on Home Farm looked up at Vauchurch as they blew on their hands and murmured coaxingly to horses stabled too long. Their sympathy for the beasts was heartfelt. It was the first Monday after the Twelfth and, for all the thaw, the weather was harsh enough to make the men hanker for the days spent in kitchens and haylofts during their time of rest. Margrave was their master's master, and his death had meant that official festivities had been curtailed but the farmer had winked at private celebrations and much cider had added a comfort to the interval when they had nothing more to do than feed and cosset their horses.

Such idleness had ended, as it always did, with reluctant, sore-headed industry. Harness and ploughs had been mended, oiled and brought to a pitch of perfection that could only be appreciated by those whose idea of beauty was closely bound to the practical. Once the first shying away from their normal labours had been overcome, the men had set to with a will for it was a mark of pride to turn out their teams in prime condition to be blessed on Plough Monday.

They stood in a row on the damp soil, each at the flank of their lead horse, waiting for the Margraves to descend from the plateau. All were wearing a token of mourning. Black neck-cloths were worn with brushed and threadbare frock-coats, black scarves were tied about billycock hats and the combination of spruce and shabby Sunday best and the symbols of death gave a funereal air to an occasion that was usually serious but enlivening. There would be no luck with the harvest if the ploughs were not blessed. The parson must bring the power down upon them and the Corn King woven from the last sheaf to be scythed must be given back to the earth to keep hunger from their doors next winter. Margrave, as the head of his House, should have cast the corn beneath the blade. His son must take the duty on his young self.

No one envied Frank his position. The deaths of Margrave and his fancy-piece had been a strange business. Margrave had been ailing, as anyone might be coming half across the world from a heathen land, and tales of the woman being kept confined after falling into a frenzy made her end seem natural – poor, distracted creature. Murder had not been spoken of, and yet . . . and yet . . . They would not want their own sons reared within walls where a man could flaunt a demented mistress before his wife, nor where the wife was a harlot herself. There was no blame put on Celia. The violence of her dying had wiped away what small censure there had been. They were born to poverty and knew that an unprotected woman must survive as she can; they knew the despair that could end in the sin of a razor letting out a wretched life. Their silent contempt was for those they feared, for Margrave, Charlotte and Quinn, Eleanor and Forston, the unthinking rich who held the defenceless in the palms of their hands and did not care how many fell. Master Frank must look to himself if he was not to grow up like his kin.

Rooks flew across the colourless sky, screaming their raucous, discordant caws. A wind caught them, scattering their flight like the upward rush of cinders from a fire. Stiff-winged, they swooped back to their formation and their cries faded into the distance.

One man touched his hat and the others looked round abruptly.

174

Mr Garstin and his curate, in their full clerical regalia, had entered the field while the watchers' eyes followed the rooks.

'Good morning to you,' Garstin said.

'Good morning, sir.'

'A fine day for the ploughing. Last week, the share could not have cut the furrow.'

'Aye, sir.'

Garstin turned towards Vauchurch. Far up, at the top of the winding drive, two carriages could be seen beginning the steep descent.

'They'll soon be here,' he said to Sherren.

He was concerned for the curate. As so often, he wished he could teach his assistant to be more worldly. The lesson of turning a blind eye was growing old-fashioned in this time of evangelicals and enthusiasts but acting on it made the days pass comfortably for everyone. He was aware that Sherren's conscience was troubling him. The unfortunate Miss Eliot had impressed him with her tragic melancholy when he had encountered her moping in the churchyard. The romance of a mist-wreathed meeting was unhealthy fuel for the imagination for one as susceptible as Sherren. He, himself, took the lady's troubles with a pinch of salt. Why could she not become a governess? Or the companion to an irascible dowager? The world was full of women in reduced circumstances walking the spoilt pugs of their elderly employers or demonstrating the use of globes to stolid girls who would never, unprompted, seek the whereabouts of Timbuktu. It was not necessary to become a concubine. And self-slaughter on the death of a lover was mere histrionics.

He had not expounded these views to his curate. There had been no discussion between them on the subject, beyond his mild refusal to consider burying a suicide within the churchyard. Protracted argument and the eventual firm assertion of authority would only have encouraged a sensation of martyrdom with all its potential for indecorous religious zeal as well as fixing an image of sorrowful beauty more firmly in a sentimental head.

That head was now bent over the table where, on a cloth as white as the frost had been, the intricately-woven corn-doll lay between the earthenware pitcher and cups and the decanter and glasses awaiting the refreshment of ploughmen and gentry respectively. Garstin sighed. He could not see Sherren's face but he knew from the set of his shoulders that his expression was disapproving. The pagan associations of the effigy were a sore trial to the serious-minded. You must wink, sir, wink, he said to Sherren silently. And here, he thought, looking back to the carriages which were drawing up to the gate, we have an illustration of the wisdom of that policy. Here it is best to wink with both eyes and see nothing.

The Vauchurch party was being helped down from the carriages. There was a wave of slight movement amongst the farm-men as they saw Garstin go forward to greet the dignitaries, a stiffening of backs, a placing of hands on the coarse coats of their horses, touches to gain confidence under the guise of giving it.

Charlotte and Quinn had stepped out of the brougham. Frank, Olivia and Holland, carrying sal-volatile in case her mistress should need to be revived, emerged from the landaulet. Deep mourning was being worn by both family and maid. The widow was so densely veiled that no feature could be discerned beneath the silk.

Garstin led the procession back along the headland towards the line of ploughs. Charlotte followed on Quinn's arm, the children walked a little behind, neither addressing the adults nor being noticed by them. Holland was at the rear, keeping her distance with the discreet readiness of the personal servant. Olivia's face was not covered and Sherren, observing from his post beside the table, saw that it was as haunted as ever but that it contained some new fire that differed subtly from its old intensities. Frank was close at her side and, for the first time, Sherren discerned a similarity between brother and sister.

'Mrs Margrave,' Garstin had reached the teams, 'Mr Holman. With your permission?'

Charlotte nodded, her veil swaying, and Garstin slid effortlessly from country gentleman to officiating clergyman.

Olivia did not listen to the prayers nor join in the singing of the hymns. There was no place in her heart for a forgiving deity. Her gods were older. She stared at the ridges of the winter field and saw the corn spring, die and spring again in the cycle of seasons that had always called for blood to be spilt upon the earth. The King was dead. Another must come into his own.

The longing for Margrave filled her mind with the wild, vertiginous despair that racks the bereaved when the first, merciful numbness has fled. I will keep Frank true to you, Papa, she thought. I have already begun to teach him where evil lies.

She let hatred of Quinn drive out her misery as she watched

him standing with her mother. He had been staying at Vauchurch since the deaths, occupying the same tower-room he had used for these five years. Charlotte had told the mourners at the funeral that she relied upon her husband's cousin to take charge of what was needful in this time of sadness and shock; she had no strength alone. It was an acceptable explanation. No one would question the desire of a widow to lean upon a male relation, but this widow had been a wife who had never been weak and whose loss was opportune.

Nothing had been said by the guests, as they drifted from solemnity to benevolence over the port and raised-pies of the funeral feast; nothing openly. Enough prudence had always been exercised by Charlotte and Quinn for them to be able to appear publicly without being cut. Their liaison was, of course, known but, not having been flaunted, it had stayed just within the limits of what could be overlooked. Although no announcement had been made – how could it so soon? – Olivia did not doubt that the adulterers would marry and Quinn would govern Vauchurch until Frank had grown to be a man. She had seen Quinn take on the role of master, assuming it easily as he stood amongst the carnage on Christmas Eve. His resemblance to Margrave, that she had recognised and spurned, was more apparent in the days that followed when servants and equals alike deferred to his word and, in her bitterness, deep within her troubled spirit, she understood why her mother loved him.

Dark crags of cloud were forming in the cold sky, moving from the west in monumental grandeur. There would be rain by evening, drumming the last pristine whiteness from the land. Let it fall upon grave and vault, pouring its libations for burials where tears had been unshed. There would be vengeance yet.

The last plough had been blessed. All eyes were upon the team chosen for the honour of drawing the furrow. The horseman whispered to the great Shires and went to the shafts of the plough. Garstin lifted the Corn King and held it to be taken for the offering. Frank tensed on the brink of motion.

Quinn stepped forward and took the corn. He raised it to the threatening skies and laid it before the blade of the plough. The horses set their shoulders to the harness, their heavy hooves thudded on the soil, the blade cut and the corn returned to the earth whence it came.

★　★　★

177

Charlotte had lain her bonnet on her bed. Its trailing veil was assertively black against the white linen but she did not find that or the heavy, dull crape of her gown dreary. She wanted everything about her black. It had become a joyous colour, the representation of release from bondage, and she believed she could not have too much of admiring it. There had been exultation in her every thought since she had seen Margrave dead. She no longer lived in the same state of consciousness that had been unquestioned before. The world was full of glory.

'It's done, ma'am.'

Holland stood back from arranging her mistress's hair and examined her handiwork. The thick braid that crowned Charlotte's handsome face was wound with pearls and her chignon confined by a black velvet net studded with jet. The effect was opulent and stately, entirely suitable for reminding the clergymen, who were to share the early Plough Monday dinner, that she was their superior.

Not that there had been a need to remind anyone that her rank put her above criticism. The progress of the past fortnight had been smooth and, oddly for a time that encompassed violence, betrayal and deceit, an inquest and interment, uneventful. No alarms and suspicions had disturbed the flow of her widowhood. There was Olivia, it was true, but she had been silenced by threats it would be no trial to carry out. And what harm could one strange girl do? Quinn had shown Celia that his lady was not to be insulted. He had given his love death as a gift.

She held out her hands before her, running the tip of a forefinger over her mourning rings. Quinn had sent Celia to her judgement but these slender, capable hands had had the killing of Margrave. She was a murderess and it was a voluptuous knowledge; she revelled in it with the sensuous appreciation of a cat slowly licking cream from its sleek fur.

Standing up in a rustle of skirts, she surveyed her magnificence in the cheval-glass.

'You're very fine, ma'am,' Holland said.

'I believe I am.' Charlotte turned this way and that, the folds of her gown writhing about her. 'And part of it is your doing.'

Holland bent to gather the discarded cloak and bonnet. She had the acceptance that she had wanted from Charlotte and as much of closeness as she thought it possible that so proud a mistress could give a maid. Her ambition was fulfilled and she found herself living in fear. Her caustic nature was no protection against an awe that had no name. Dread of certainty make her meek. Folding the cloak, she put it on a shelf in the wardrobe and set the bonnet in its box, rolling the ribbons into coils.

'Is there anything else?' she asked.

'No. Come back to unhook me when the guests are gone.'

When she was alone Charlotte looked again at her reflection gleaming darkly in the glass. From long habit, she locked her door, remembering that in a few months this would not be necessary.

The staircase to the tower-room was narrow. She raised the front of her gown with both hands but the width of her skirts made the rough surface of the crape rasp against the enclosing walls. It was not a climb for a woman but she set her feet firmly in the concavities of the ancient steps, confident in all that she did.

Quinn was standing at the window in his shirt-sleeves, smoking. As he heard her enter, he laid his cigar on the stone sill and crossed the room, walking once around her, looking her up and down.

'Well?' she asked, amused.

'Everything becomes you,' he said. 'When you're my widow I shall demand just this same air of elegance but the grief – ah! the grief must tear your heart.'

'Am I not your widow now?'

'Indeed you are and in a much more agreeable manner.' He lifted her chin and kissed her. The ash of his cigar tilted, parted and fell, hitting the floor in a soft puff of white-grey flakes.

'You'll set us a-fire,' she said.

'That is my intention.'

The scent of smouldering tobacco was hard and dry in the room. She liked its masculine connotations. Sitting on the bed, she stroked the length of the frock-coat that he had thrown there. The black that was a joy to her was here in plenty, in the clothes showing in the open chest, in the neck-cloth draped across the chair, around the edges of the envelopes waiting on his writing-desk. Mourning suited him; she would have him wear no other.

'How I wish those clergymen were gone,' she said.

'Do you, love?' He sat beside her and put his arm about her waist. 'So do I. We've had too little solitude since my unfortunate cousin chose to come home. But now he's gone and she's gone, and they will go. The duties are over and all that remains is for you

179

to find me indispensable in your sorrow and thus become my wife.'

She sighed, contented.

'I've been of prime importance to Vauchurch today, I think,' he said. 'I've put the corn beneath the plough. The grain will swell and flourish. There will be a new harvest.'

'We must all be grateful to you.'

'It makes me dwell on beginnings and continuations. We've had deaths. Let us have birth.'

'What's this?' She turned her head to him and he touched his lips to her brow.

'I believe,' he said, 'that it's no longer necessary for me to emulate Onan and spill my seed upon the ground. We have our liberty. We could have an heir.'

'An heir? Frank will inherit – there's no help for it.'

He hesitated for an instant. 'I've property of my own to leave,' he said.

'Good God!' She rose and went to the window, striking his cigar from the sill. 'Have I not been hounded enough for a son?'

'Ah, Lotta, Lotta.' He came to her side and took her hands in his. 'Would I persuade you to anything that isn't your own desire? This must be of your choosing or it's no wish of mine.'

'I've grown old.'

'No, you're young yet. Young, strong and splendid. And loved, so very much loved. I've shown how much I love you and what I'll do to keep you from harm.'

'So you have.' She looked out over the bleak hills, where scudding rain corrupted the last white ruins of frost. 'Can you do more? I think, after all, there are ghosts walking.'

The library had been stripped of its sparse and mouldering shelving in the late 1760s and re-clothed from floor to ceiling with bookcases that were supposed to be in the Stawberry Hill vein. The carpenter, possibly affected by the general atmosphere of the house, was not a lighthearted man and, although the Gothic arches and fanciful ornamentation had conscientiously been provided, no trace of frivolity was to be seen.

Olivia had learnt early in her career of solitary reading that if she was not to have her nose brushing the page, some form of artificial light was necessary throughout most of the day. She had been harangued many a time for leaving a burning candle perched perilously on the edge of a shelf and had countered the scoldings with deep and scowling silence.

The window was imposing but it was more stone latticework than glass and that glass was in the purples, emeralds and rubies that had turned so many of the rooms at Vauchurch into a Pre-Raphaelite heaven long before the Brotherhood had donned their smocks. Its colours were muted as dusk fell. The lamp glowing on the circular table, where periodicals and bound collections of local views were placed in neat, ignored piles, did not shed its alluring, yellow light as far as the window and, the evening being overcast, no alleviation of the gloom came from outside.

Olivia, almost invisible in her dark clothes, sat perfectly still on the folding steps in the far corner. She was sheltered by a vast lectern on which a depiction of the Margrave estates under Henry VIII was preserved beneath a roll of baize. It was an excellent position for lying in wait.

She knew the curate's habits. He had been shown to a bedroom where he could change for dinner and, being reluctant either to linger there as if vanity prolonged his dressing or to enter the drawing room before he must, he would hide himself in the library. It was a fitting habitat for one in his position. No one would complain of his being there nor accost him for conversation.

The heat of the fire did not penetrate to her concealment. Her feet and hands were stiff with cold but she did not flex them, fearing that any glimpse of movement as he entered would drive him away. She was aware that he was not at ease in Vauchurch and intended to increase his discomfort. Her mother and Quinn must be punished. Responsibility for justice had fallen upon her and she had accepted it gladly. A drop of poison to infect a mind here, another there and gradually the world would draw away from the accused ones; ostracism would declare their guilt.

Since she had heard Sherren defy the ordinance of the church by reading over Celia's grave, her opinion of him had risen. His covert disapproval of Charlotte and Quinn, his pity for a fallen woman and the tender conscience that he wore upon his sleeve made him ideal to begin her campaign. He would not believe her insinuations and yet would lie awake, tormented by a creeping conviction.

Her judgement had been right. Sherren entered the library, glanced round to be sure it was empty and, not seeing her, crossed to take a copy of the previous Thursday's *Times* from the table.

181

Instead of seating himself humbly on a straight-backed chair in the pool of lamplight, however, he removed himself to the fireplace and sat in an armchair. Much to her interest, he did not seem to walk with quite the degree of self-effacement that was his usual custom.

Resting the broadsheet on his knee, he gazed at the advertisements on the front page without seeing them. Hunger was making him curious about what was for dinner and he was wondering whether this novel ability to sit within a nest of vipers and think of beef-steaks showed that he was being infected by Garstin's insensitivity or whether he was becoming less intimidated by wealth and rank.

A sense of being observed, rather than the hearing of a sound, made him lower the paper and look up. With a sudden surge of disquiet, he saw Olivia slithering towards him, weaving through the cabinets, canterburies and free-standing bookcases, with her penetrating eyes fixed on his. Firmly, he quelled his alarm, reminding himself that she was only a fourteen-year-old girl in the throes of bereavement. He remembered with shame how he had avoided her after she had snubbed his naive efforts to provide her with spiritual guidance. She drew closer, settling onto the edge of the chair opposite his and, despite his resolute thoughts, he could not help feeling that if he were a Roman, he would begin to tell his beads at her approach.

'Mr Sherren,' she said, 'you read the Order of the Burial of the Dead over Miss Eliot even though the prayer-book specifies it is not for those who have laid violent hands upon themselves.'

'I did.'

Her cold fingers were clasped in her lap. She was sitting inflexibly upright, not touching the back of the chair. It was one of her peculiarities that her demeanour was invariably both prim and fervent. Had she been wearing a mask, no one could have appeared more demure.

'Are you a botanist, sir?'

'I can't claim such a title. I have some slight knowledge.'

'This library has been a home within a home to me,' she said. 'A home within a house. It's provided me with more than a slight knowledge on a variety of subjects. I'm aware that there are common plants – plants to be found in garden and conservatory – that can bring death with a bloody flux. As my father died. Plants which, when burnt, leave no certainty of their use behind.'

'Quite so.'

'I believe you need feel no guilt for having read the burial service.'

'My dear Miss Margrave, what can you . . .' He faltered. She held him with her remorseless stare and he was conscious of horror creeping over him as if he were being pressed down into icy waters.

'My brother is very young, sir,' she said.

It was no longer possible to gain a spurious security from the glow of fire and lamp. Darkness seeped in from the hidden corners of the room, whispering of a greater darkness beyond.

'Very young,' he said.

'You are conscious of the evil at large in Vauchurch.'

Her words were not a question. He saw again the desolation that had been in Celia's soul.

'I think it has no place for the innocent,' he said.

It amused Quinn to keep up the pretence that his relations with Charlotte were virtuous. He was careful never to be found in her bedchamber and though the staircase that linked her room with his was not secret, he had not let himself be seen using it. Now that he was soon to gain the respectable title of husband, he toyed with the idea that they should transfer themselves to Margrave's sanctum, but decided against it despite tradition and its undeniable grandeur assigning it to the master of the house. It was not that he had qualms about usurping his victim's bed – that would, he thought with a shark-like smile, be a precious piece of affectation – but that loving memories bound him to where they had luxuriated in their seclusion.

The clergymen had outstayed their welcome. Garstin had grown loquacious over the port. Plainly believing that Quinn would now be abandoning the pose of quiet country gentleman to assume the mantle of lord of the manor, he had delivered himself of a searching and censorious account of local politics that the object of his lesson had listened to with admirably concealed contempt. The curate, who Quinn had previously looked upon as an empty suit of clothing, liable to crumple to the floor should anyone shout 'Bo!' had surprisingly achieved a physical presence and sat fingering the nutcrackers with a troubled countenance. Their company was tedious and Sherren, on their return to the drawing room, had murmured some earnest remark to Charlotte that

Quinn had not heard but that made her stare abruptly at the young man and find he did not drop his gaze.

Walking slowly through the labyrinthine passages late that night, after recovering from his civilities in the smoking-room, Quinn mused on what the curate could have said to startle his hostess, then set the riddle aside; it would only have been some impertinence asked in a blundering attempt to give religious comfort to a widow.

Silence filled the house. Servants and family were in their beds. Charlotte would be waiting for him, drowsing against lace pillows or meditatively brushing the mass of her dark hair with smooth strokes from brow to waist. It occurred to him that when she was his wife, he would take less exercise since it would no longer be necessary to climb by this circuitous route to his tower before descending to her arms.

As it was, he walked with the pride of ownership, confident that life was good if you forced it to be so. He had not shared the elated excitement that had stirred Charlotte since the murders; his was the proud satisfaction of one who casts down a false king and ascends the throne himself. It did not matter whether he was a true son of this house. His blood was Margrave and Vauchurch was his domain. He had avenged the frail shadow who was his mother and the man who had owned the name of father. The banishment and humiliation of his youth had been repaid in full. There was power in taking what was his by right of superior subtlety and cunning; a fierce triumph that ran through his veins, investing his slightest action with arrogance. Margrave was crushed beneath his heel and Celia – ah, Celia – there is a voluptuous sweetness in destroying the weak.

He had reached the turn in the corridor where the bedroom candlesticks were placed. Only one remained on the table. Lighting it from the lamp, he went on, protecting the flame with his hand as a draught made it waver and lean to melt the wax.

His attention being distracted, he was almost upon Olivia before he noticed her. She came towards him, spectral against the darkness in her white robe. Her lack of a light was, in his opinion, merely her playing the role of a creature of the night. It must, he thought, be a disappointment to her that he had never been unsettled by the queer ways that were her indulgence.

'What are you doing wandering the house at this hour?' he asked.

'I've been reading to Frank.'

'He's too old to want cosseting.'

'He's only a boy and is grieving for his father.' She tried to keep her voice cool but anger crept in. To her annoyance, she saw that Quinn was entertained by her show of feeling.

'Then he may comfort himself for he'll soon have another. Could you come to call me "Papa", Olivia?' He could not resist teasing her. The helplessness she suffered in the face of her knowledge interested him. She could do no harm but surely one of her disposition would attempt some devilry. Her absurd devotion to Margrave would not let her rest.

She tried to go past him but he caught her by the loose sleeve of her robe.

'Your mamma and I haven't given you our thanks,' he said. 'Remiss of us.'

She stood looking further down the passage and did not speak.

'Too modest to ask what our gratitude is for?' He held his candle nearer to watch her expression. 'For repeating the sorrowful Miss Eliot's words concerning her imminent and very final departure and her need for forgiveness. The jury found them most affecting.'

'I find lingering in corridors affecting. It begins to chill me through.'

'Excellent, my dear. It will be sport to have you as my daughter.' He brandished the edge of her sleeve at her playfully. 'But you haven't wished me joy of my wedding and it is a joyful matter. The Holmans will be masters of Vauchurch for generations to come. Or should I change my name to Margrave? Would it be fitting, do you think? The bloodline would be pure. Your father and I were so closely related.'

Charlotte rode out across the plateau behind Vauchurch. Her groom followed at a few yards' distance. She had always liked to ride. The illusory sensation of freedom combined with the simple pleasure of motion had endeared it to her at a time when her life was all restriction. She had no patience with those who claimed they liked to show their dexterity by subduing a rebellious horse. It was a waste of effort and skill to be in a continual state of struggle. The easy dominance of a willing and mettlesome mount was a surer sign of horsemanship in her eyes.

This morning she was doing what she had done in January for

the past five years. She was beginning to make her round of the Margrave farms, checking that her tenants were not extending their Christmas idleness. At this season, when there was little to do in the fields, the men should have been set to fencing, repairing gear and cleaning the stackyards. With their experience of Charlotte as landlord, it was not to be expected that any of the farmers would be caught seated comfortably at the fireside and she intended to keep them in a constant state of looking over their shoulders for her.

If she were not a widow, she would be waiting at home, dull and useless, her talents wasted in the long tedium of her days, while Margrave or his land-agent carried out this task. The relief that she was still in control of the estate made her relish her business more and she raised her face to draw in the scent of winter as it turned towards spring.

There was a mildly boisterous wind blowing, enough to toss the supple branches of elder without stirring weighty limbs of beech. In the two days since Plough Monday, the last frost had melted and run away to fill the ditches. To see brown and green where all had been white was a novelty that had not yet lost its interest. She watched two blue-tits contending for a withered bunch of hawthorn berries, their claws clutching the prancing twigs as they eyed the dangling fruit with quick, sharp angles of their heads.

She was glad to be out of doors occupied with managing the farms. The exhilaration that had buoyed her spirits since the deaths had ebbed a little, leaving her with a need for another stimulus. She was perfectly aware of what had lowered her elation and she was seeking a distraction that was enough to furnish a release from the necessarily claustrophobic and intense atmosphere that had pervaded Vauchurch this last fortnight while giving her the opportunity for reflection. This ride combined activity with the contemplative solitude of one who does not regard her groom as a companion.

Her mare walked at an eager, balanced pace and Charlotte sat at ease in the saddle, rocking with the horn that gripped her leg, her skirts swaying against the iron-grey flank. She was brooding upon Quinn and the dark reach of his ambition. Her adoration of him had never lessened. His love satisfied the ravenous emotional hunger that had been born of Margrave's starvation of her affections. Her fierce passions responded to his pride and the cruelty in his nature, valuing his tenderness the more because it touched no one but herself. She had accepted Celia's disposal as the savage gift it was. His shameless, calculating barbarity had kindled in her the consuming, intoxicating bloodlust of a maenad and she laughed at the memory of how she had disguised her joy as the wildness of first grief.

A doe stepped out of a thicket of spindle-trees and gorse at the edge of the plateau. It gazed at the riders with wide, damson eyes, lifting a foreleg in readiness for flight. Its gentle hesitation reminded Charlotte of Kate. Sorrow and the old rage welled up in her with such force that she bent forward in pain, laying a hand on the mare's warm neck for comfort. One child had been sacrificed to men's arrogance; she would not lose another. She could cherish a panther that stalked at her side, bending its velvet head for her caress, but she would not trust it amongst her doves. She had seen Quinn seize the Corn King, heedless of Frank's right; she knew of his lack of conscience and his hatred of Margraves. She had no faith in her son's safety.

And, strangely, dangerously, this was a concern that was not hers alone. As she had sat in the drawing room on the evening the clergymen dined at Vauchurch, the curate had approached her, bending close to her ear in the pretence of urging her to a piece of crystallised fruit. He had whispered that it would be as well if Frank could make a long stay with relations. An excellent scheme, he had said, to the benefit of all and he had neither explained his remarks nor been intimidated by her stare.

Was this the beginning of discovery? Or was a suppressed sense of sin causing her to see accusations of guilt where none existed? An earnest young man might consider it desirable for a bereaved boy to have a change of scene. There might be no meaning in his urging that was not innocent.

The track curved around the thicket to begin its descent to the valley. Her mind was occupied and the sudden rise of a black-clad figure in her path startled her. The mare threw up her head and danced sideways. In calming her horse, Charlotte recovered herself and looked with disfavour at Olivia. It did not please her to see her daughter in mourning, as it pleased her to see crape upon others, since it was the girl's habitual wear. She felt with repugnance that a raven had settled to bar her way.

'Mind where you're going,' she said. 'You made Vashti jink.'

'I intended her to stop. Mamma, I wish to speak to you,' Olivia nodded towards the groom who was almost upon them, 'privately.'

It was Charlotte's instinct to ignore Olivia's request. She was vexed by having been alarmed and was not accustomed to taking her daughter's desires into account but she was also unused to having those desires laid upon her; in these exceptional times, perhaps it would be as well to attend to anything out of the ordinary.

She turned in her saddle. 'John,' she pointed with her whip, 'wait beyond the copse until I call.'

When the groom was out of sight, she raised her eyebrows imperiously. 'Well?' she demanded.

'Are you going to dismount?' Olivia asked, unperturbed.

'I see no necessity for it.'

'As you prefer.'

Charlotte had imagined that the simple act of looking down on the sombre girl would give her dominance but she found it was not so. Olivia stood with the authoritative composure of a Jesuit. She who knew what her mother was should have been in fear yet her singular independence and severity seemed to have increased, fusing into an audacious confidence. Charlotte searched the cold, white face that had once suckled at her breast and saw one who would go coolly to the stake, despising her persecutors.

'You should have lived amongst the Puritans,' she said. 'You're hardly suited to modern life.'

'A curious observation from you, Mamma.'

They stared at one another.

'I waylaid you here,' Olivia continued, 'instead of seeking you in the house because I wanted to talk without interruption from your paramour.'

'Who will be your papa.'

'Who will never be my papa though he marries you ten times over. Nor will you ever provoke me by calling him such.' She held her hands apart, palms open towards Charlotte, as if inviting her mother to mark her lack of response.

'Being free from interruption,' Charlotte shifted her grasp on her whip, 'what do you have to say?'

'Mr Holman has stepped into Frank's proper place. He will not want to give it up again. We both know what means he's prepared to use to achieve his ends.'

The mare stretched forward her neck, shaking her head in a jangle of bit and chain. Charlotte collected her with one smooth movement and did not take her eyes from Olivia's.

'How like me you are,' she said. 'Not a changeling, after all.'

'Insult me as you will but attend to my words. Are you aware that Frank's bosom companion is Philip Rencombe?'

'I am. Though you consider me a poor mother, I read the letters his schoolmasters send.'

'I have written to Mr Rencombe. While he's only your second cousin, he has the family pride and, as you know, does not approve of your closeness with Great-uncle's bastard.'

Charlotte gathered her reins. 'I'm attending to your words as you direct,' she said, 'but wonder whether you're merely choosing them for your amusement.'

'I told our kinsman I was sorely troubled that Papa's death and the continued absence at Knapp mean that Frank has no guardian to stand between him and Mr Holman. He's as concerned as I and has offered to open his home to Frank when the boys are not at school.' Olivia moved closer to the mare and laid a hand on its bridle. 'For all our sakes, Mamma, and most particularly for Frank's, I urge you to accept his offer.'

The moon, that had shone on Vauchurch without alleviating its darkness, had waned. No light would show the way. Olivia carried a lantern beneath her cloak. She did not need its illumination to follow the winding path to the chapel nor did she want to attract notice from the house. The way to Margrave's burial-place was already so engrained upon her heart that she could walk it blindfold.

The wind stirred the laurels at her side, rustling the slender branches, causing black to slide over black, giving an impression of movement caught from the corner of the eye, movement that could not be discerned when looked at directly.

Frank held the edge of her cloak, keeping to her heels with steps that he forced to be firm. He trusted her to know where to tread. Tomorrow, he would leave this world of betrayal and deceit, of faces that hid death behind their smiles. School-hall would receive him with its regimented life of antique languages and idealised skirmishing on wintry games-fields. The tedium of its days beckoned him like a loving mamma and he longed to be enfolded by it yet he was a Margrave and the lure of standing apart, marked by the secret of what had been done by night, had a perverse fascination.

They were going to the vault for Frank to bid his father farewell. Charlotte had summoned him to her boudoir and told him that he would not return to Vauchurch until he was a man. She gave no explanation and he asked for none. It was balm to the grieving, haunted boy to learn that he was to be Rencombe's charge and he shook the hand, that he knew to have killed, without shrinking from her touch.

The chapel was before them, its bulk sensed more than seen. Olivia led Frank to the grove of yews and opened her lantern. An owl swooped down upon the glimmer of flame, its wings hushing the air. It loomed and was gone.

They stood together, silent and still. The night-wind filtered through the yews, trailing fingers of cold across the pensive mourners. The lantern's glow fell upon the pillared arch and iron-sheathed door that led down to past generations of Margraves. Sorrows and passions had beaten within breasts that were dust on lead-lined shelves.

Olivia put her hand on Frank's shoulder.

'Remember,' she said. 'Hold fast to what our mother has done. Remember – and she will learn to fear her children.'

PART THREE

A Doubtful Ease

1869

Chapter Fourteen

At Knapp, sunlight filled the valley with the pale gold of September. It had a tranquil, liquid quality as if the scene were being viewed contentedly through a glass of hock. A late stand of oats was being reaped. There was a flurry as a pair of rabbits bolted from their hiding-place amongst the grain and the younger harvesters gave chase, calling unheeded directions as they tried to dash their hats over the fleeing beasts. Two sets of hind-paws vanished through the hedge and the men resumed their scythes, mopping their necks with kerchieves and laughing good-naturedly at the disparaging banter of the older men.

The gamekeeper, his gun under his arm and his old pointer at his heel, watched the reapers as he made his way along the path beside the stream, thinking already of the seed he would want for the pheasant chicks next spring. He had been walking the woods, considering which coverts should be beaten, and was returning to his cottage for a bite of bread and cheese. From the lawn beyond the ha-ha, he could hear the desultory clack of mallets as Hermione and the vicarage children played an erratic game of croquet that had been the ruin of a clump of Michaelmas daisies, planted, the elder boy said, just where anyone's ball might go.

Crossing the stream by the stepping-stones, the keeper climbed the slope towards his home. He had lived in the squat house, with its matted thatch and small, deeply-set windows, since he was born, as had his father and grandfather before him, so that any name it might have had was forgotten and it was known only as 'up Braddon's'. He opened the gate in the fence of stout ash-poles, cut from the copse that rose above his roof, and his dog slipped through into the garden. An edging of lavender and pot-herbs lined the cinder-path, giving an impression of ornament to the approach but the rest of the enclosure was purely functional in its collection of outbuildings, vegetable beds and poultry-runs.

Braddon was a man alert to the duties of his work. He applied thought to every detail in the field, never drifting into doing as his forebears had done unless he was convinced their ways brought the best results, yet he had changed nothing in house or garden in all the years they had been his, accepting that they were as they were and hardly seeming to notice either as he dug his early potatoes or sat in the kitchen oiling his guns. 'There now, Grip,' he said as they reached his porch with its dry, twisted stems of honeysuckle.

Given his release, the dog drank noisily from a basin beside the bench and threw himself down with a grunt to bask in the mellow sun.

Leaving the door open, Braddon went into the kitchen, hanging his gun on the oak beam that crossed the ceiling and his hat, a sloughed snakeskin inside its crown to ward off headache, on a nail by the dresser. The house was empty but the brick floor was ruddy and damp from recent scrubbing and the loaf on the table was warm. A slice of cold bacon, one of blue-veined cheese and an onion were waiting by the bread together with a covered tankard of sharp cider.

He washed his hands at the pump in the scullery and sat down to cut the soft crust. His wife had died long since. It was his daughter who saw to his needs and added to their income with button-making and the curing and stitching of the furs that were his perquisite. A mound of tawny cat-pelts lay in a basket on the settle ready to be sewn into a carriage-rug.

When he had finished eating, he broke a new cake of tobacco and took his filled pipe out to the bench. His dog raised his head and, finding that his master had only come to join him in wallowing in warmth, lay down again with a single thump of his tail. Braddon scratched his old companion behind the ear and drew on his pipe, holding the stem between his teeth and making a series of sucking grimaces that coaxed the fine shreds of tobacco to glow. It was his rule not to smoke until evening but today he had cause for celebration.

The inner pocket of his velveteen jacket contained a note that was his share of a packet of letters that had arrived at Knapp that morning. The gardener's lad had been dispatched to seek him out and ask him to step into the housekeeper's room at his convenience. Once there, he was given the news. The master and mistress were returning. Forston had sent instructions for the readying of house and estate to receive them and his desires for

194

the season's sport were set forth in lines that were more welcome to Braddon than a billet-doux.

Leaning back comfortably, the keeper surveyed the valley, the roofs and chimneys of Knapp and the wooded hills, well satisfied with life. The shooting had been leased to gentlemen without enough land of their own and though Forston had stipulated that Braddon must not be replaced by men of their choosing, it had not been the same as bringing on the birds for the squire. There had been years when October had gone by without a pheasant shot. The hunt had not gathered in the courtyard since the master had followed his errant wife to India. His skills had been unnoticed.

He wondered what changes there would be in the Forstons after so long in heathen parts. Miss Hermione had been a child when her mother had bolted with Eliot and the brothers had crossed the world in pursuit. Now she was a grown woman, Margrave and his trollop were dead – a queer business – and his widow married to a man who could not swear who his father was. And Mrs Forston coming back to be curtseyed to as if she had never been an adulteress. If his daughter behaved like the gentry, he would take a stick to her.

It was of no consequence. Let them act as they pleased. An estate must have a master. He was too close to nature not to know the scream of a fox in heat and the dark spurt of blood as white teeth severed a spine. Fecundity and death were the essence of his world and he had guarded them as a true and faithful servant.

The water plashing softly from the fountain in the centre of the courtyard fell into the marble bowl with soothing monotony. It was, thought Forston as he emerged from the cool, dim rooms strewn with crates, very like his wife – beautiful, ornamental and the unthinking provider of sensuous comfort. Lighting a cigar, he leant against a pillar and shut his eyes, letting the constant purl give him the illusion of an English stream rippling between fern-draped banks, around moss-grown stones, under canopies of green, green woods. He had a hunger for rain and a world that was green, brown and green again.

'Green,' he said lovingly and looked with amused disdain at the unsatisfactory grey sheen on the felucca palms that arched at the corners of the tiled paths. Not that he had been unhappy here. It was curious that one who had been content with life at Knapp should have found the East so compelling. Remaining first in

India and then Alexandria had been his choice and he had profited by it both financially and . . . he hardly knew how to define the change there had been in his character. He had never had a low opinion of himself; even when Eliot had stolen his wife, anger had left no opening for the degradation supposed to be suffered by a cuckold, but the pursuit of Eleanor had wakened a bold and vengeful spirit in his breast that was more primitive than Margrave's and entirely satisfying.

He moved to a stone bench supported by two scowling representations of Anubis and sat down with his legs stretched out. Half of the courtyard was still in shade and he gazed out of its depths to where heat was wavering against the thick walls of the house with their bleached frescoes of vines and darting birds. As he watched, the vicious Egyptian sun struck the fountain and the tumbling jet of water was suddenly alive with a flashing brilliance that sent dancing points of light onto porcelain jars of water-lilies and the balcony opposite his seat where Eleanor kept her aviary of cooing, murmuring doves.

The solid, all-encompassing quality of the heat here and in India had always intrigued him. It was like a heathen god, merciless, conscienceless, taking life from the unwary with the crushing progression of a Juggernaut. He crossed his legs lazily and smiled. Why pretend to himself that he could not say how his transformation had come about? He knew perfectly well and it was at one with his fascination with the remorseless sun. Eliot's seduction of Eleanor had begun the metamorphosis. Lying in his hotel room in London on the night after the guilty pair had bolted, his new self had come into being. Sleepless and racked by images of their coupling, he had shed the superficial adherence to civilisation that had made him the milder of the brothers. Margrave had wanted to destroy Eliot's fortune; he had wanted blood.

And he had achieved his end. He had hunted Eliot, prepared to be hanged. Throughout the long journey East, as he sat on deck staring at the restless sea as if his vigilance could draw the horizon closer, he had grown into a state of mind that was at once serene and violent. It was the cool assurance of a tiger which has stalked its prey and has only to spring. He did not confide his intentions to his brother and Margrave, used to being the more aggressive of the two, noticed a change but was too secure in his arrogance to see how deep it was. There were moments when Forston marvelled at his own determination to kill. Just as he had not realised the strength of his love for Eleanor until she had left, so he had had no inkling that adultery would sweep all moderation, all tolerance from him, leaving him in the image of the Margraves who had built Vauchurch on foundations of battle and treachery. He knew that in this effete century what he was to do would be called murder; it did not deter him.

No warfare was ever more timely for one of its participants than was the Mutiny for Forston. Riding at the head of native guards, whose families had been loyal to his family for generations, he found his true place in the world. He should have been a warrior. Margrave was competent and pitiless with a gun but Forston was more than this; he took pleasure in killing. The jarring thrust and soft slide of a sabre as it entered bone and flesh excited and satisfied him as nothing else had ever done. Savagery was his element and he revelled in carnage that was sanctioned by the official desire for revenge. His men admired his malevolence and he laughed at his brother's surprised discovery of how the balance between them had changed.

By the evening that they had reached the house on the Jumla, with its fretted screens and silk awnings, where Eliot and Eleanor were sheltering behind barred gates, he believed Margrave understood what was to happen but nothing was said. The one remaining male servant, an elderly syce with no taste for terror, had opened the compound, garrulous with welcome at the sight of British gentlemen and their force.

The change in Eliot's eyes as he saw Forston enter the salon would remain with his pursuer for ever. Relief, uncertainty, realisation, fury. It pleased Forston that his quarry showed fight. He had come prepared for cowardice that must be dispatched as he would shoot a dog that quailed at the sound of gunfire; he found boxes of cartridges stacked amidst sofas and chiffoniers and an enemy armed and ready.

Eliot fired the first shot. It was wide and he did not have the chance to fire another. No man amongst the guards blamed Forston for killing his wife's seducer – their only puzzlement was that Eleanor did not suffer the same fate – and Eliot had begun the attack. To Forston and his company, it seemed that justice had been done and Margrave swallowed his uneasiness to tell himself that it was so.

Eleanor was glad to be rescued. She had no conception of the scale of the rebellion nor the danger she was in but she was disturbed by the reduction of her comfort and the irritating attempts of Eliot and the frightened maids to waken her to what was going on. She had grown bored with her life as a pampered but fallen woman and was eager to return to the ease and status of Mrs Forston. Her husband's new ruthlessness and ardency were alluring and, it could not be denied, it was deliciously romantic to have him kill for her. She resumed her place at his side without a suggestion of shame and Forston, amazed afresh at his devotion to this brainless creature, reloaded and joined Margrave in planning their perilous flight to the north.

They reached safety with none of the hysterics both brothers had expected from their prize. They travelled by night, relying upon their numbers and obvious weapons to discourage ambush. What skirmishes there were served only to pique Eleanor. She was unable to connect the bodies on the road with the living people they had been and could complain of the stench of a corpse as if the death had occurred to annoy her. To do her credit, she endured nightmares in later months which she refused to describe but her shallowness protected her during their journey and unlike many of the more courageous women, no lasting misery haunted her.

Forston's atavism did not desert him. Leaving Eleanor well protected, he and Margrave rode with the soldiers who were reasserting British might and his intoxication with the fray did not fade. When the Mutiny had been subdued and its perpetrators were themselves only stains upon the parched earth, he had no desire to return to an England that seemed too tame. Eleanor was at home wherever there was luxury and neither had any yearning for the daughter they had always ignored. The Margrave commerce flowed in a seamless circle from the West to the East and back; it was as easy to oversee from one point on its route as another and so the Forstons remained in India, then Alexandria. It was a good life and Forston was, as the French say, comfortable in his skin. Days of fierce skies and the deep shade of shuttered rooms passed in contentment until gradually the call of autumnal rain and the cold crimson of a winter dusk grew unendurably beguiling. He began to ride through the odorous streets in stuffy carriages longing for the moist November scent of beech leaves; he watched crocodiles motionless upon sandbanks and remembered the play of a trout on his line. The siren-song was irresistible; he succumbed to its beckoning and now packing-cases littered his house and tickets for the passage home lay securely in his pocket-book.

The indolent rustle of silk that signalled his wife made him look up. Eleanor had come out onto the balcony and was running a ringed finger along the slender bars of the aviary. She was dressed for visiting in a gown the colour of violet leaves that he had ordered for her when the yearning for an English wood had been strong in his heart. He liked the fluid fall of the skirt as she faced him and the frivolous hint of a bustle when she turned. Her ability to delight the eye had increased over the years. The suggestion of prettiness that had tempered her perfection when young had been refined into a pure, elegant beauty. If a pearl had become a woman, it would have been Eleanor. Forston watched her kissing the air to her birds and wondered affectionately whether anything was occurring in that lovely head.

She took a small gold case from her watch-pocket and opened it to look at the dial. Frowning a little, she closed it again and gazed about her vaguely. Coming to the rails, she peered down into the courtyard and seeing her husband lounging in the shade, dangled her watch at him, letting it swing on its chain that returned the fountain's brilliance in a thin line of startling light.

'Gerard!' she called.

'I hear you.'

He stood up, leaving the stub of his cigar on the stone seat and crossed the garden to enter the house on the far side. They were to sleep at an hotel that night, before boarding ship the next day, and Eleanor was about to pay the last of the farewell visits she had been making for a fortnight. Before she left she was to indulge in a parting gesture that had taken her fancy and that required his presence in case graceful benevolence proved insufficient for her purpose.

She was to release her doves.

'If they're not to be my chicks, let them go free,' she had said, quite unconscious of the arrogance of her words.

Forston did not consider that they were birds who were fitted for liberty. They had lived a pampered life within their cage, protected from the sun by a rampant growth of passion-flowers over their arched roof, and cosseted with the best of seed and water. When they were let out, they rarely made more than a brief circling flight across the house-tops, electing instead to sit in white rows along the eaves, squabbling cheerfully or cooing in slumberous felicity. Independence would be the death of them.

Better by far to donate them to one of the many friends who could accommodate what were, after all, playthings – but Eleanor, whose imagination did not often stir into vitality, saw herself as the spirit of freedom and was not to be persuaded otherwise.

Climbing the stairs, he passed through her empty boudoir and onto the balcony. She turned to him, her hand on the aviary's lock.

'I'm late,' she said. 'I must be at the Taplows' on the hour.'

'Then let's set to. You must have your final kettledrum with the ladies and tantalise them with thoughts of home as you take your tea.'

She opened the door and stood aside for him to enter the cage. As he stepped in, he paused and drew her to him, clasping her waist and bending to nuzzle her neck.

'Ah,' he said, 'you smell of violets – clothed in their leaves and scented with their flowers. Do you remember the dell behind Vauchurch where the dog-violets bloom so early?'

'I remember that Charlotte thought them finer than ours – how she wanted first place in everything. Forston, I can't keep the horses standing in the square in this heat.'

He let her go and went under the canopy of passion-flowers where the doves were a cluster of lilies amongst the curling tendrils of the vines. They showed no sign of wishing to leave their cool shelter and he lifted the two nearest and carried them out.

'Here,' he said, holding them towards her, 'unloose their shackles. End their servitude.'

Backing away with renewed rustling, she put her hands behind her back. 'No, they might soil my gown. You do it.'

Forston went to the edge of the balcony. The soporific birds had begun to suspect they were not simply to be admired and were staring at their captor with wide, expressionless eyes. He threw them suddenly upwards and their wings beat like a snow-flurry as they righted themselves in the air and climbed towards a sky whose azure was more piercing for their bright presence.

'Adieu, my darlings,' Eleanor cried, lost for a moment in a beauty that was not her own.

Forston returned to the cage and repeated the liberation. As the fifth pair rose to follow the flock, Forston saw that Eleanor had grown bored. She had not troubled to watch the flight and was wearing the puzzled frown that meant life was not exactly as she wished it to be.

'Why don't you go to pay your calls?' he asked. 'I can attend to these last few alone.'

'Could you? I really am late.'

'Of course I could.'

She gave him the smile that was so captivating to those who needed no sincerity to make them victims. He shoo-ed her and she was gone in a swirl of silk.

'That bustle,' he said to the four remaining doves, 'is ridiculous and charming.'

The bird nearest to him set its head on one side questioningly.

'You don't think so?' he said. 'You feel it's more saucy? Follow me, lads? Well, perhaps you're right.'

When the aviary was empty, he sat on a wicker chair in its shade, remembering the years that this house had been their home – years of energetic success in trade, of cheerful social pleasures and the deep, enduring peace of his resurrected marriage. England would not be quite as he wanted it. He would have liked to have shared his wine at the first dinner at Knapp with his brother, exchanging news and taking up their comrade-ship where it had been left off, but Margrave was gone and the bastard was master at Vauchurch until Frank came of age. Perhaps Quinn's position would sour their homecoming. No, it could not. Frank would reach his majority in November and Vauchurch would be in the possession of the true blood again. He was glad he and Eleanor would be there for the celebrations. If the boy – the man – could not have his father toast his health on that day he should have his uncle.

And Hermione would also be there. He had a curiosity to see his daughter despite a suspicion that she would cause him annoyance. She had been a docile child – hardly, to one of his mind, noticeable at all – and he felt no loss at having missed her progress towards adulthood. So many British children died in India that it was usual to send them back to their native climate to preserve their health, and the custom was enough to dispel any guilt he might have suffered. He had known that she was safe in her solitude at Knapp and had never been concerned that she might be lonely. It was only when she was twenty-one that a qualm had prompted him to act on her behalf. She had not been presented at court nor moved in society that would display her to potential husbands of her own rank and fortune. However little real interest he had in her welfare, it was unfair to hamper her

201

chances of a match by keeping her cloistered.

After discussing the matter with Eleanor, who had not been eager to have her age revealed by the appearance of a mature daughter, he had invited Hermione to join them in Egypt. Politely and firmly, she had declined to do so. He had written again, urging her to overcome any shyness or fear of travel that was making her shrink from her opportunity. With civility and immovable determination, she had refused.

It had not pleased him. He could have ordered her to come in the name of duty to her parents but he had no confidence that she would obey. Her actions showed that she had a mind of her own. Perhaps, in his absence, she had been influenced by Charlotte and learnt an unsuitable and unfeminine independence of thought. She had no money to call hers. He could have tried to force her into submission to his generosity by closing Knapp, leaving her homeless and destitute, but he did not want to take extreme measures. Let her be an old maid if she wished.

It occurred to him, as he tipped his chair back against the wall to watch the doves gathering along the edge of the roof, that if he had played the tyrant and Hermione had found herself deciding between poverty and obedience, she would have taken a third course and thrown herself upon the mercy of her aunt. There was no doubt in his mind that Charlotte would have welcomed her in those circumstances. How that woman loved to be provoking. Did she lead Quinn the same dance she had led Margrave? She had certainly not waited long to begin. Only three months before casting off widow's weeds was not decent. They must have been lovers. At least, Leo, he thought, you put her in her place before you died, brandishing your concubine before her. That humiliation must rankle.

The old anger was rising. Of all the men Charlotte could have summoned to her bed, it must be Quinn; of all the men to have free run of Vauchurch, it must be Quinn. The childhood home of the legitimate brothers was given into the power of the byblow; it was a pollution, an abomination. And Frank lived elsewhere but soon he would come into his own.

A dove landed softly beside Forston. It was time for seed to be scattered and one after another the birds left the roof and drifted down to the balcony. He put his hand towards the first and it hopped onto his finger, its claws pricking his skin, a susurration of hope and complaint in its gaping beak.

'You won't be fed here,' he said 'now you're not one of us. Don't you know what happens to those who claim property that's not theirs by right?'

Raising his free hand, he stroked the milk-white head and, with the pressure of his thumb, he snapped its neck.

They left their horses at the foot of the rise and climbed the promontory on foot. There was mist in the valley and they moved in a glimmering haze lit to opalescence by the earliest glint of a hidden sun. The route they had chosen was steep but they were young men, strong and agile, and they did not labour as they walked.

This was a private visit. They would arrive at the house, mounted and in state, later in the day but Frank wished to return to Vauchurch for quiet reflection beside his father's tomb before he was encumbered by the need to be courteous to his mother and Quinn; they moved with a discretion that verged on secrecy.

So many years had passed since he had been here that Frank had felt unsure that he would find the way. His fears were unfounded. Even with the path veiled by cool mists, it was as familiar to him as if he were a boy again. He noticed how fruitful the land was. The hedgerows, heavy with dew, were a storehouse that would soon be raided to make the jellies and cordials that had been his delight when he would sit on the settle in the great kitchen with his boots dangling above the flagstoned floor. Sloes awaited the first frost to make them tender, blackberries, gleaming and laced with spiders' web, were thick on arching briars, crab-apples, disappointing to the taste until their curd dripped through its muslin sieve, weighed down slender branches whose leaves were turning an autumnal red, rose-hips glowed like discarded rubies.

Such a harvest brought a swell of pride to his breast. These meadows, woods and hills, this house and its earth fortress were his. He had come back to be Margrave of Vauchurch. By winter, he would have command of his estates and there would be no doubt who was master.

Olivia had taught him well. There was neither love nor forgiveness for his mother in his heart. The horror that had come upon him while he stood in the candlelight before Margrave's corpse, listening to his sister's low-voiced vehemence as she told him what had been done, had never eased. He had drawn it to the frozen centre of his soul where it lay untouched by the warm affections of friends or the innocent pastimes of his youth. The shadow had lain on him and he had cherished it.

His nature was benevolent and warm but there was a strangeness in him that made him embrace the dark passions that were his inheritance. The hatred that Olivia had sown had rooted deep within his spirit, enticing him to revel in being set apart from his fellows by the sins that were upon his mother's head. There was to be no mercy. He did not deceive himself that Charlotte and Quinn could be brought to book for their deeds. Their chastening would lie in being cast out from Vauchurch, banished in retribution as he had been banished for his safety. He mourned the loss of his years on these heights but his sister's self-sacrificing love had preserved him and he had returned in vengeance.

They passed beneath a Spanish chestnut, whose spiked seedcases piled in bristling profusion on the ground, and reached the wild hollow where the child, Olivia, had concealed her journal in a decaying oak. The spindle-trees were yellowing and the windcarved hawthorns were ablaze with scarlet berries. The fruits of the hawthorn were scarlet, the bryony, the guelder, the bittersweet were crimson. He stared at the scarlet, the crimson, red upon red, and the blood Vauchurch had seen pulsed in his veins.

'We're above the mist. What a view it gives.'

His companion's words roused him and he turned to look out towards the sea. The mist was a step below them. It filled the valley with a shining vapour illuminated by a glow that seemed to come not from the sunrise but from some shimmering source of light within its depths. The summits of distant hills could be discerned as vague shapes in its opacity and trees near where the watchers stood loomed wraithlike to the eye but all else was lost in a pearl-like gauze spread to the horizon.

'We might be beyond the clouds,' Philip said.

'It is another world.'

Frank moved back to his friend and the two gazed at the encroaching dawn side by side. The pair were as familiar with each other, their lives as intimately connected, as if they were brothers. Their attachment had been born in their most youthful schooldays, when fondness could be shown only by splashing each other as they leapt into puddles or offering the best of the conkers they found with an air of indifference. It had flourished on learning that Frank was to take refuge at the Rencombes' elm-shaded manor in Warwickshire until he should come into his property.

Mr Rencombe was not a sentimental man. He made no secret of his conviction that Charlotte, his second cousin, had disgraced herself in her husband's absence and that her connection with Quinn was both shameful and dangerous. The solemnising of the lovers' relationship did nothing to lessen his disapproval. He had his own suspicions about the convenience of Margrave's death and though he did not voice them when the boys spoke to him in hints, he did not scruple to reply in hints that confirmed their fears and their acceptance that the matter must not be bruited abroad.

With such a harrowing skeleton in his cupboard and such a propensity for embracing it, Frank might have been expected to grow into a sombre man. The normality of his life at a school where the violent excesses of many contemporary establishments were replaced by an amicable, if monotonous, fraternity was both steadying and cheering. He was neither roasted in a basket nor subjected to strenuous evangelism nor introduced to the carnal and illegal activities favoured by the Ancient Greeks whose conjugations caused him so much distress. Between terms, he and Philip rode their fat, shaggy ponies and then their sleek hunters, shot, fished, wrote execrable poetry, punted on the shallow, rush-fringed lake and talked of what they would do when Vauchurch was theirs – for they were never to be separated. They went up to Oxford together and acquitted themselves respectably but without the distinction they could have attained had either needed to enter a profession. And while this devotion prospered, an unceasing stream of goodwill flowed towards them from the lonely, warped pen of Olivia and the astute and humorous pen of Hermione.

The quantity of care lavished upon Frank saved him from himself. Philip recognised the melancholy within his friend and the magnetism that the sinister had for him. Diverting him from darkness had not been a stern task but that, Philip was aware, might change when they entered Vauchurch. The house and its history had become a part of Philip, as it was of Frank, yet he had never been within fifty miles of it nor encountered one of its inhabitants. He anticipated their welcome with a lively interest tempered by trepidation. Social intercourse held no anxieties for him yet there was an awkwardness here that could not be denied.

He had not, to his knowledge, been introduced to murderers before. Would shaking their hands cause a galvanic impulse to seize his arm? He thought not. Much of the world was wicked and looked as harmless as a grocer.

He turned to stare up at the massive walls and chimneys that could be seen dimly in the half-light, towering above the ramparts at the top of the slope.

'Perhaps we should go on,' he suggested. 'Before people are astir.'

They climbed again, wending their way through tall grasses, following the base of the lower embankment until they could duck beneath an elder to join the path to the chapel. Theirs had not been the most dignified approach for an heir to enter his kingdom but a gravity settled upon them both as they walked, changing the nature of their quietness. Frank had come here last at night, a boy hiding his fear from the sister he had not seen since. Memories of those final, tormented weeks at Vauchurch kept him silent as the slate-grey dawn showed him the laurels that guarded the chapel-yard. They uncovered their heads before they reached the grove of yews that sheltered the vault. The sacred ground brought the profane act that laid Margrave in his tomb clearly to their minds. Evil had been done and was unpunished.

There were roses lying at the threshold of the vault; drooping heads of Souvenir de la Malmaison. Frank remembered that the bush in the corner of the flower-garden had always had a late flush of blooms. Dewdrops clung to pale petals giving them a life they could no longer truly claim.

Frank knelt before the iron door. Philip hung back. Slow moments passed. A hush was on the grove. Frank's lips formed, 'Amen,' and a soft footfall was heard between the yews.

A young woman in mourning stood holding a sheaf of bronze chrysanthemums. Her white face was tense and severe but it seemed to Philip, who observed her with interest, that this was its habitual state. She watched Frank rise with a dazed puzzlement in her eyes as if she were trying to recapture a dream that was eluding her.

'Olivia?' Frank said.

Her brow creased. She glanced down at her burden and, in raising her head once more, she caught sight of the pearl that was fastened to Frank's watch-chain. Putting her hand to her throat, she drew out a thin silver chain and gazed at its ornament, the companion to the pearl.

'I gave you one of my earrings for a keepsake,' she said, 'as Papa had given them to me. Oh, Frank, are you come home?'

'I am.'

He strode towards her as ardent as a lover. Philip lifted the damp, autumn-scented flowers from her arms and Frank grasped her hands.

'Dearest sister,' he said, his voice tender for the suffering her pallor betrayed, 'your solitude has ended. The boy that I was lies in ashes; I'm here as Margrave to set all to rights.'

Chapter Fifteen

The fire in the smaller dining room at the Bull had been lit early that morning, as had all the fires in its public rooms, and the ground and first floors of the inn were, if anything, a little too warm. It was market-day in Bridport and a press of trenchermen, calling for the hearty refreshment buying and selling requires, flowed through the hospitable portals from noon until night.

The door into the said small dining room was now locked. Its table had been stripped and relaid an hour before, and a *Reserved* notice placed prominently in the centre of its starched, white linen but this had not prevented two bag-men, deep in a discussion of trade prospects – with particular reference to striped cottons and wrought-iron furniture – from seating themselves at the cloth and banging their knife-handles for service. Having ejected the travellers with civil apologies and a passable pretence at enjoying their humour, the harassed landlord had turned and pocketed the key and stationed the pot-boy at the street entrance to look out for the magistrates who had ordered their cutlets for half-past three.

The JPs arrived five minutes before their time and, having all ridden from the courtroom, delivered their mounts to the ostler and entered from the coach-yard. A brisk rattle of the locked door brought the landlady, stouter than when she had welcomed the melancholy Miss Eliot but no less accommodating, hurrying through the thronged, convivial passageway to their aid. The key was found, the room opened and an agreeable brown steam was soon issuing from beneath the lids of a selection of tureens.

Dispensing justice invariably had a stimulating effect on the appetite and a substantial late luncheon was always provided for whichever magistrates had been presiding that day. As well as the cutlets, there were beef-steaks with fried potatoes and onion sauce, gravy soup, buttered cabbage, stuffed marrow, a stewed ox-cheek, boiled currant pudding and lemon dumplings.

'You couldn't say it was a dainty meal,' Sir Joseph Cobb observed, tucking his napkin under the top button of his waistcoat, 'but, damn me, it makes a man feel whole again. I come to be as hollow as a husk by the seventh case of poaching. Ready to give the rascals an extra thirty days for the ghost of their rabbit-pie.'

Charles Lucas spread the tails of his frock-coat and sat down to his plate. 'If it were just rabbits,' he said, 'but the number of deer the keepers can't account for would turn a glutton off his feed. There's many a cottage with a right royal dinner in its bake-oven, do what we will.'

Quinn came from the window, where he had been scrutinising a stall of saplings and joined them at the table. He did not find the company of either invigorating, but since Margrave's death, he had been prepared to cultivate the society of such men in order to be firmly of their clan. Suspicions flourish around an outsider but it is difficult for the unimaginative to accept that one who regularly dines and hunts with them can be a villain. No voice from his own class had ever spoken openly of murder and his marriage had stifled much of the scandal about his previous association with Charlotte. The events of a decade before were an old tale. He had easily achieved a state in which he was secure from insult, and yet there remained a disquiet in those who knew him, derived from an uncertainty that his strength of will would always be used for good. The nature of his unflinching confidence seemed to indicate a capacity for wickedness that he did not choose to exercise.

It was rare for anyone to cross him. His presence on the Bench was feared both by more lenient magistrates and by those who awaited judgement.

'Well, gentlemen,' he said, leaning back in his chair to let Mrs Wakeley ladle his soup, 'I believe we caused some discouragement today.'

They laughed complacently.

'Aye, so we did,' Sir Joseph said. 'Ma'am, we will each take a pint of sherry.'

The bottles were brought and the lady departed to oversee the communal table in the large dining room where song had begun to break out.

'I hear Knapp is being burnished up and down,' Lucas said to Quinn. 'They say the Forstons are to return from the Orient.'

'For once, what they say is correct. Or partially so. They come from Egypt.'

'Such a time away. No doubt you'll be glad to see your cousin – your brother-in-law . . .' Lucas became aware that Sir Joseph was regarding him with malicious amusement. 'Glad after such a time,' he finished lamely.

'My wife will be pleased to see her sister,' Quinn said.

'By Gad, so will we all!' Sir Joseph exclaimed. 'An enchantress. A Venus. An ornament to the county until – but there! You'll not take it amiss, Holman, if I say it's a misfortune for the young blades that Miss Forston doesn't have her mother's face. But,' he added with asperity, 'young men are not what they were neither.'

Quinn refilled his glass. He was entertained by his companions' blunderings. Now that he was master of Vauchurch, he felt no anger at the thought of meeting Forston and, indeed, had never felt the embarrassment and awkwardness that was plainly expected of him. And Eleanor was just a lovely fool; her daughter a nonentity.

Lucas helped himself to the ox-cheek. He was inclined to stand upon his dignity and an irritable need to repay Sir Joseph for noticing his faux-pas prompted him to make that gentleman uncomfortable by drawing attention to the mentioning of the notorious Mrs Forston. It could not be done, however, without risking antagonising Quinn. What a set those Margraves – and, he cast a glance to his left, *demi*-Margraves – were for adultery. There was that shocking business of Leo Margrave's doxy committing felo-de-se within the very walls of Vauchurch.

His weak fancy ranged over the sordid happenings of years ago, exciting him, and his mind drifted away from the slight he felt he had received. It would be wrong to sour a profitable day. He had not attended this court to sit on the Bench but to be sure that one Joshua Collins, a firewood-seller on the Lucas estate, should be sufficiently persuaded that the hedgerows and spinneys were the property of the landowner and not a useful source of merchandise. A month with hard labour had been duly awarded to the reprobate and Lucas was prepared to regard the world with benevolence. 'Are we to see a jamboree shortly, Holman?' he asked. 'Feasting and merrymaking?'

'I've no idea. To what do you refer?'

'Why, your stepson's coming-of-age.' Lucas lifted a slice of marrow onto his plate. 'I hear he's come home. No doubt you're intending quite a celebration.'

'We do have plans.'

'The old must give way to the young, eh?' Sir Joseph shovelled salt onto his steaks with the flat of his knife. 'This'll put your nose out of joint, Holman. The princeling will want to be master of his own.'

'He'll have nothing to complain of in my management of the lands.'

'Oh, no. No indeed. An ungrateful wretch if he had. And you've a pretty property to your name close by. Or will you and Mrs Holman stay at Vauchurch?'

'That may be necessary.' A shadow of care passed across Quinn's face. 'Frank is not as strong as we could wish. The mild Midland air that was supposed to be so sustaining . . . His mother doesn't feel content to leave him. And,' he said more firmly, 'there's many a delicate lad who grows to be a vigorous man. We must have faith.'

'My dear sir,' Sir Joseph was a younger son who had gained his title through the death of a cherished brother and he never travelled without a miniature of the lost playfellow, 'I had no notion. My bailiff saw Margrave riding with his companion and said he was a fine-standing gentleman – though slighter than his father.'

'It's often the way. The surface is not the substance. We do not talk of it.'

Silence settled on the table. In the corridor there was a rise of jovial conversation as a corn-factor and three farmers forsook business to vie with each other in retelling how the maltster had bought a stolen horse from a gypsy and found it danced the tarantella whenever it caught the strains of a hurdy-gurdy.

'I'm told you're thinking of laying down a few acres of orchard on the Home Farm,' Lucas said. 'Seeing you looking at those John-apple-trees reminded me.' He recollected himself. 'But that's at Vauchurch. I daresay the heir will have ideas of his own.'

'Oh,' Quinn said, letting drops of angostura bitters fall into his sherry one by one, 'I believe he'll rest quietly with mine.'

The years had passed slowly in the old nursery. There had been very little change there since the children had played Snappentongs on that distant day before sin had been replaced by evil.

Olivia had never been one for dolls and childish toys nor for the bows and muslin frills of maidenhood. No infantile trinkets, no feminine gewgaws had encumbered this room; its spartan simplicity had remained.

She had contemplated claiming the Green Chamber. The few moments she had spent in it with Celia Eliot had become sanctified in her starved heart as the nearest she had approached to the tenderness of adults. In her memory, she had often stood in the firelight before the woman who shared her yearning, receiving the quivering drops of pearls and diamonds chosen by a loving papa, holding them in hands chilled by the ice that clasped Vauchurch. She had no dread of sleeping next to the scene of murder and suicide. Rumours of haunting did not disturb her. She would have embraced her father's shade; she honoured Celia for her devotion. It was the proximity to Charlotte and Quinn that prevented her making the move. They had not taken Margrave's apartments but Olivia could feel their taunting presence too keenly through the empty rooms with their connecting doors for her to be easy in her choice.

There was nowhere else that she preferred to the nursery. She could dream as well in its familiar walls as in any others. Still, she grew older and understood that she must have territory that was more personal than the drawing rooms and library yet less intimate than a bedroom. She annexed the large closet beside the nursery, where the upper-nursemaid had slept, turning it into a private sitting room before Charlotte had learnt what she was about. Her mother was glad of any occupation that would keep her louring face out of sight and did not object. The room was furnished with Gothic pieces filched from half-forgotten corners of the house. It was compact and well-heated by a small hearth with a hob for a kettle; it was, after its severe fashion, snug.

While Quinn was eating cutlets with the magistrates, Olivia and Frank sat at her round, plush-clothed table, drinking fragrant cups of Gunpowder tea. Philip, whose delicacy directed him to amuse himself elsewhere while brother and sister talked alone, was walking through a copse with the under-keeper, discussing the progress of the pheasants that season. The late afternoon sun was slanting down in watery brightness on both the walkers and the tea-drinkers, who were stationed between the crackling sea-coals and the window.

It pained Frank to see how obsession and solitude had marked

Olivia, and he was gentle towards her, warming her with his affection and loyalty. He realised how little he had considered what her life had been like, drifting from day to bleak day in a house where she was silently mocked for her knowledge and helplessness. She had become a fanatic, dedicating herself to hatred and remembrance, leaving Vauchurch for no society except the occasional visit to Hermione. Throughout the decade, her cousin had urged her to leave this scene of misery and guilt to make her home at Knapp, believing rightly that Charlotte would welcome the arrangement, but Olivia would have none of it. Her stricken spirit was adamant that her duty lay in being a constant thorn in the flesh of the wrongdoers and so she stayed, her bitterness fierce and vital and her lonely peculiarity setting her more and more apart from the world.

For all his own love of shadows, Frank had been too surrounded by friendship to have learnt despair. He was confident that he could rescue Olivia from sorrow. Talking to her of the approaching time when he could banish their mother and Quinn and he and she could live together in happy companionship, brought colour to her pale cheeks and a softer light to her piercing eyes. 'You must take her from her prison,' Philip had said, as they sat over their cigars late on their first night at Vauchurch, and they had formed plans to coax her into the normal pleasures of her age and class. Balls and sketching-parties were spoken of, tours of the Italian lakes and the services of Parisian dressmakers, who would lead her away from black. They were indignant and compassionate and, in their innocence, had no notion of the strange and stubborn passion of a zealot.

'Another cup?' Olivia asked, lifting the delicate pot that had rarely been called upon to provide for two.

'I will. I've such a thirst that I could drink from the spout.'

Olivia busied herself with the ritual of tea, milk and sugar, slop-basin, measuring-spoon and the pouring of boiling water from the singing kettle onto fresh leaves. She was as close to contentment as she had ever been and she laughed to be revealed as a domestic angel.

'This is only your third day here,' she said, setting the cup before Frank, 'yet I feel as comfortable as if we had never been separated.'

'We won't be parted again.' Frank watched complacently as she put another maid-of-honour on his plate. 'But, serious now, Livy,

I've had the easier path to walk. These years have been hard for you – harder because I couldn't come to temper what you endured. All that you suffered was for me – for my safety – and I thank you for it.'

'I'm repaid a thousandfold to see you grown to such a man.'

'Grown to return as your protector.'

Secure within the fortress of her obsessions, Olivia could feel touched that he saw her as vulnerable.

'Were you ever afraid?' he asked.

'Afraid?' She was puzzled. 'Of what?'

'That what was done to Papa and might have been done to me would be your own fate?'

She gazed out of the window, over the dizzying drop to where a distant wood, glorious in its autumnal change, was dappled amber in the glowing afternoon.

'Do you know,' she said, 'I don't believe I ever was. At first, I tried to raise suspicions against them and I thought it kept me secure. They knew what I was about and must have been aware that my death would have served my purpose, not theirs. But my attempts were ineffectual. I planted seeds of doubt here and there – no more than that. I was just an odd little girl, then an odd young woman, not to be taken seriously. A danger to no one. "An original" is the kindest thing people say of me.' She tore the corner off a pastry. 'And, of course, there was always Mamma's threat to have me put in an asylum if I was troublesome. It wouldn't have been hard to find a doctor to condemn me.'

'Oh, Livy, a sad, sad life.'

'Not at all.' She smiled maliciously. 'I've been the bane of this house. The spectre that has prevented them ever being perfectly content in their unholy possession of the lands. The constant reminder that what should have been our father's will one day be yours. There have been occasions when Quinn has enjoyed trying to provoke me, parading their freedom from punishment, the advantages their crime has . . .'

Frank leant forward, interrupting. 'He has admitted murder?' he asked.

'No, my dear, he's far too clever for that. What he says is oblique. I never rose to his jeers. I was cool and firm. It disappointed him. He appears to take little notice of me but he and I understand each other and he has never been as much at his ease in his position as he intended.' She crumbled the fraction of pastry that she held. 'And I've been the guardian of the tomb, keeping the neglect it would have had at bay.'

'A faithful priestess,' Frank said and broke off to look towards the door.

Philip was holding it open for Charlotte. She came into the room and he followed. A cold hostility emanated from the possessors of the tea-table.

'I found Mr Rencombe bewildered by the complications of our ways,' Charlotte said. 'He was at a loss to find the refreshment that waited for him here.'

Frank stood up and indicated the spare place that had been set for the wanderer's return. Philip hesitated.

'I believe Mrs Holman wishes to join us,' he said. 'I can take the window-seat.'

'That will be unnecessary.' Frank advanced a step towards his mother. 'Let us have no pretence of family intimacy, madam. Until I come of age, we must sit together at dinner and be civil to one another before the servants, but there need be no private conversation. After that day, I will not vex you by asking you to cross the threshold of what was once your home. I know what you and your husband are and I will not have you at Vauchurch.'

They lay together in the bed that had known the sweet, lascivious satisfactions of their adultery and the victorious arrogance of their wedding night. Their faces were older than when Frank had been sent to sanctuary but no less handsome, alert or calculating. Conscience had not worked its way out from within, blighting their confidence and luxurious gratifications, etching their sordid history in lines of remorse and fear. Charlotte's dark hair spread across the white pillow as richly as when Margrave had first run possessive hands through its scented waves; Quinn watched her with the same proud love that had fully corrupted his already decadent spirit.

Their years had held few troubles since their conquest of Vauchurch. In vanquishing Margrave and acting as proprietors of the estate, they had done nothing which caused them to feel guilt. They had defeated an enemy who threatened to hold Charlotte in servitude, and it was proper for the successful to enjoy the fruits of their daring. Olivia had been a burden but she had proved to be a serpent whose venom was not fatal and they were used to her.

216

The decade had slipped by in the vainglory of an ownership that was not truly theirs and now the heir had come to humble them. Quinn was wealthy and Charlotte's otherwise neglectful father had ensured that the settlement at her marriage to Margrave had provided a generous widow's jointure. Poverty or, indeed, any reduction of their material comforts did not await them when Frank became master of his inheritance. Financially, they were free to go where they chose and purchase lands that would give them the status they believed to be theirs by right but, emotionally, they were bound to the house that had seen Quinn's birth and banishment, Charlotte's struggle against subjection and their triumphant revenge against the family that had tried to stifle them.

Quinn reached out to the dish on his bedside cabinet and tore a cluster of purple, hot-house grapes from the bunch that lolled there.

'Will you have one?' he asked, dangling them in the air.

Charlotte opened her mouth and he lowered the bursting ripeness into her parted lips. The bloom on its dark skin was like moonlight in winter. She bit into the flesh and a drop of rosy juice ran down her chin. Leaning over for her lace handkerchief, she pressed it to her face and replaced it by her watch-stand.

'These are delicious,' she said, 'but the pips make them a trial.'

'It's the nature of life.'

'Where are yours?' she asked, as he held up the half-stripped stem.

'Already disposed of.'

'I didn't notice.'

'Sleight of hand. Such an attribute. I shall become a conjuror when we're thrown upon the parish.'

Charlotte did not reply. There had been much silence between them since Frank had written to say that he was returning to Vauchurch. It was a silence made up of knowing too well what was in the other's mind and on Quinn's part, it was simply a matter of waiting for Charlotte to agree to his unspoken proposition.

He did not intend to leave Vauchurch. His domain was not to be meekly handed over to a boy. No son had been born to them to make him jealous for the rank of his descendants and he had had enough awareness of himself to realise, after a few months of disappointments, that he had no interest in a real child. The flesh-and-blood presence of the infant he had briefly craved, with its

217

tedious antics and achievements and its train of nursemaids and schoolmasters, was not alluring. He had left bastards behind him in his younger days and had felt no tug on his heart nor qualms at the sale of those he had got upon his slaves. The urge for an heir had only been to emphasise that the Margrave property was his to command and, once that was plain, he had laughed at his foolishness, casting posterity from his thoughts. The far future did not concern him but his lifetime did. He had no scruples over what must be done to keep their lands but Charlotte, for all her lack of sentimentality, was a mother and he would not hurry her in her slow, undoubted turning towards his decision.

Charlotte let her eyes follow the play of firelight on the brocade bed-curtains. As the flames darted, their glow made folds of the silk shine and grow dull, shine and grow dull. Though she was still, she could not rest. Anger and humiliation coursed through her as fiercely as when Frank had insulted her. She could not remember having been so dumbfounded and it did not soothe the violence of her feelings to realise that, for an instant before she could gather herself, she had let her shock show. Olivia had flushed with the enjoyment of it. This was how the son she had preserved repaid her. The ruddy light flickered over the room, drawing answering gleams from glass and silver, polished wood and gold, reddening the whiteness of the pillow where she lay.

'It grows colder,' she said.

'Frost has brought changes before.'

Quinn raised himself on one elbow and drank from the glass of hock and seltzer that stood beside the depleted grapes. There was a trace of grey at his temples but the hair above the collar of his nightshirt was as full and black as it had ever been. Charlotte ran the tip of her finger through it as he leant away from her. When he settled back, he took the hand that had caressed him and kissed it.

'You've never been one who had to be shielded from troubles,' he said, 'but sometimes there are problems that it would be better I dealt with alone.'

The silence that held so much menace in its unspoken words was with them again. Charlotte felt herself quiver under its heavy insistence. Her pulse beat in a firm, determined measure.

'You compliment me on my strength,' she said. 'I also have my weakness. I've never been generous enough to be interested in the welfare of strangers.'

★　★　★

218

The perfect confidence that existed between Olivia and Hermione came, unknown to the latter, to a sudden end on Frank's return to Vauchurch. Olivia's joy on discovering that all her hopes of her brother had been well-founded made her selfish. His unwavering condemnation of their mother and Quinn, his reverence for their father and his tenderness towards herself were exactly what she had prayed for – though to what dark gods those prayers had been directed it would be difficult to say – and she did not wish to share his affection with her cousin nor to have his harsh passions softened by Hermione's persuasions.

She was aware that Hermione was saddened by her dedication to hatred of the living and adoration of the dead. Although the two girls had quickly become united in the belief that Charlotte and Quinn were, in truth, murderers, Hermione had adopted the view that as the crime could not be proven, it would only add to the sinners' triumph to see useless desire for retribution burning within those their violence had harmed. It was not that Hermione believed, as Mr Garstin had believed for lesser guilts, that corruption should be winked at if it was indulged in discreetly, but that the yearning for revenge rubbed a gall upon the soul of those tormented by it; she, herself, had judged her parents and quietly set them aside as unworthy of her concern. And it was a source of perpetual bewildered pain for Olivia to have realised some years previously that Hermione did not respect Margrave as a pattern of virtue.

Before this revelation, it had never occurred to the doting daughter that any but the depraved could think that her beloved father had faults. The distress she had felt caused her to shy away from her one firm friend throughout a lonely, perplexing summer until she was coaxed back into their usual correspondence by the constant flow of loving letters from Knapp and her decision that Hermione's opinion was influenced by Forston's failings.

So it was that Olivia hugged the news of Frank's arrival to her happy bosom, writing of how she looked forward to the day of his majority without mentioning that the hero of the celebrations was already at her side. Knapp was just far enough away from Vauchurch for the estates to be within different circles of gossip and it might take many weeks for intelligence from one to be carried into the other.

As Hermione and Ward walked along the corridor towards Forston's bedroom one blustery morning in late October, when scurries of beech-leaves were being blown in scatterings of iron-veined copper across the flagstoned terrace, they were oblivious to Frank's presence in his ancestral home. Their thoughts were occupied with Forston and Eleanor, who were due to return at the end of the week. The house had been scoured, sluiced and beeswaxed from rafter to cellar and gave the distinct impression of being on its best behaviour for the edification of guests.

Hermione opened the door to the bedroom and they went in. The blankets and embroidered coverlet that had been stored in the cedarwood chest had been put back in their proper place and the scent of the aromatic wood was heavy in the air.

'Should we open a window?' Hermione asked.

Ward sat gingerly on a hard chair. For the past five years, she had been slightly troubled by arthritis and she found the onset of winter made her want to take the weight off her knees. 'It would let the dust in,' she said.

'Yes. I suppose we could leave the door ajar – that might help.'

'It's a clean enough smell,' Ward cupped her hands protectively over her aching joints, 'and, like as not, the master's used to all manner of outlandish perfumes – incense and myrrh.'

'I daresay he is.' Hermione watched her with concern. 'Do you want to go and lie down?'

Ward stood up stiffly. 'No,' she said, 'I'm better moving. It's only the change of weather.'

'Tell the kitchen to make you a warm compress.' Hermione reached out and gave her companion's hand a gentle squeeze. 'I can't have you ill with Mamma and Papa home, Wardy. Who would fuss over me?'

'I would, my honey, from my sickbed. But I'm not going to be laid up. I walk a few steps and, see, I prance like a jack-rabbit.'

She paced up and down the rug to set her chick's mind at rest. Though her legs were grumbling, it was the unwelcome prospect of Eleanor and Forston at Knapp that made her tired enough to hanker for chairs and comforts. She did not want their quiet life in this slow, contented household to change but, with the master and mistress in residence, change would be inevitable. Where there had been harmony and cheerfulness, benevolence and soft words of appreciation, there would be fretfulness and self-centred petulance, bustle and arrogant demands. She had caught herself using the endearments she kept for occasional use during the intimacy of late-night hair-brushing or when acting as nurse because she knew she would not dare be so informal in the Forstons' hearing. Nor did she look forward to meeting Eleanor again, knowing that this wanton woman would face her deserted maid without shame, oblivious to the hurt and fear she had caused. The expectation of being regarded as a cipher once more brought a cold gust of insecurity into her settled world. An anxious jealousy intruded repeatedly on her thoughts and a dozen times a day, she assured herself that she was loved.

Hermione was regarding the alleged jack-rabbit when they became aware of an uncertain presence on the threshold of the room. One of the new footmen, hired to satisfy the needs of an enlarged family, was hesitating in the doorway, unable to decide whether he should enter such territory. Hermione took the letter he was carrying on a silver tray and went to the window to unseal it.

In the grey-blue light of the windblown day, the tears that came to her eyes shone like opals as they slid to her cheeks.

'What is it?' Ward asked, sharply.

'It's from Frank – from Vauchurch. Frank is home.'

'Then what's the matter? Why are you sad?'

'Sad?' Hermione said. 'Oh, Ward, is there such a thing as sadness in the world?'

As Olivia walked across the plateau the wind caught at the loose sleeves of her mantle and tried to pull the dried heads of Queen Anne's Lace from her gloved hands. She paid no attention to the buffeting nor to the chill edge of winter in the brisk air. The sky was in billowing movement. A churning mass of whites and variegated greys coiled in the heavens, making the swaying trees and bending grasses on the solid earth seem peaceful and anchored in comparison.

Beneath the turmoil of the clouds, the small black figure pursued her determined way in an unusually sanguine frame of mind. She was dreaming happily of the future and gradually, with the rusty uncertainty of one who has been long occupied by greater matters, deciding to buy herself a dog. In the childhood when her character was being forged into its distinctive shape, she had loved a terrier pup that she believed to have been drowned on Charlotte's orders. Part of her young heart had been broken by its death and she was not one to let such a wound heal. To have given her affection to another pet would have been to let her mother think the killing had been trivial. It could not be done but now the time of the singing of birds was come and the voice of the turtle was heard in the land; she was free to love where she chose.

Her good humour extended to Hermione. Frank had told her three days before that he had written to their cousin, apologising for being too distracted to do so earlier and inviting her most particularly to attend the approaching celebrations. Olivia prided herself upon having received this news without the possessive anger she had expected. Instead of a surge of jealousy, she had grown calm in the anticipated pleasure of being at Frank's right hand as he took his just position as master of Vauchurch. Forston and Eleanor were to reach England this very afternoon. Hermione would be too busy with their arrival to drive over to visit before the coming-of-age and, on that day, it was appropriate that Frank should be shared with the world.

The seed-heads were becoming a nuisance. She intended to make a pen and ink sketch of them and, having brought them from beyond the summer-house, was reluctant to abandon them to the wind. Clasping them to her breast, where they were gripped by the thick velvet of her mantle, she walked more quickly.

Far out over the bay, the sun broke through a chance rent in the clouds and shone in a steel line of brightness on the sea. Olivia watched it until its brilliance was withdrawn and the agitated waves were again slate and indigo.

The sound of a sharp crack drew her attention back to what was ahead. A blue and white striped marquee had been erected on the parkland before the walls of the flower-garden. Its gaiety was incongruous against the sombre rise of Vauchurch and made her smile. The gentry were to be dined and entertained on the great day in the house while the farmers and chief tradesmen were treated to beef and pudding under canvas. An ox was to be roasted over a bonfire for the satisfaction of the labourers, who were not considered to need a roof over their rejoicing. Sunday clothes were to be worn; favours and sovereigns were to be distributed. Such sports as the weather allowed were to be played – running and leaping matches, archery and wrestling for a pig – and in the evening, there would be dancing in the ballroom and the tent. And there would be speeches and congratulations; all underlining the glory and power that were Frank's and thus the fall of Charlotte and Quinn, whose trunks were being packed for their departure.

At this moment, the marquee was struggling to make an escape. It had been well pegged down but still edges were flapping and the section that could be folded back to form the entrance had flown loose with the crack that had attracted Olivia's notice. She changed direction slightly to go to make the necessary repairs.

The wind was pressing the heavy cloth of the door flatly against the side of the tent. Olivia grasped its corner and dragged it back into place. It was surprisingly heavy and bucked against her strenuous pulling so that she found she must step inside the marquee and stand on the rebellious canvas while she tied the strings that held it shut. She left a low gap that she could slip out of if she stooped but before she attempted it, she stood catching her breath and mooring her hat tightly against her dishevelled hair.

She was holding one long pin in her teeth and using both hands to adjust the set of the hat when the voice spoke.

'Do you admire nothing living?' it said.

She turned, drawing the pin from her mouth, feeling startled and foolish. Quinn was advancing from the far end of the tent. He was dressed for driving in a full-skirted great-coat and seemed absurdly self-assured for one who was about to be ejected from his home by an accusatory stepson.

'Must it always be grave-flowers?' he asked as he drew close to Olivia and touched the seed-heads she had laid on the grass with the toe of his boot. 'Always the withered blossom, the alluring scent of decay?'

Olivia had regained her composure. The happiness that had entered her enclosed life was bringing back the fervent boldness that had ebbed into tired obsession during the lonely years. She looked at her questioner with the confident hatred that had fired her as a child.

'Are you on your way to your house?' she said. 'To see that all's in readiness? It's usual to take your wife to your own establishment when she's a bride but better late than never.'

He raised an eyebrow. 'I came from my house,' he said, 'a minute's walk from this. Your mamma and I are going into the valley to attend to final arrangements. And while the chaise is brought round, I thought I'd make sure the work here had been done. We don't want accidents. Not for such an historic day.'

223

His tone roused her suspicions. There was nothing in it that would make a stranger wary but it reminded her of another winter and its bitterness ran an icy nail down her spine.

'Picture the scene.' He gestured at the empty interior. 'Will there be merriment? Tears of – joy?'

'The chaise will be waiting.' She gathered her stiff bouquet from the ground. 'You must lock the view in your memory whilst you go down. As Margrave will not have you on his land, you'll have no more opportunities.'

'You were ever a tiresome creature – hanging on the coat-tails of the dead.'

'Who will mourn *you*,' she said, 'as my dead have been mourned?'

Her contempt riled him. He believed that he had endured her perverse veneration of a worthless man with patience but the waste of so fierce a nature in blind infatuation was an offensive folly. If she had only opened her eyes, she would have respected her mother.

'And you call him Margrave?' he said. 'The dearly beloved Frank. But he is not Margrave yet.'

The wind found the loose corner of the door. It forced its boisterous way in filling the wide space with movement. The cage of Olivia's gown belled to one side, Quinn rocked on his heels and shifted to stand more firmly. As abruptly as it had come, the squall died, leaving a silence intensified by the sudden calm.

The peace was external. It did not exist in the breast of either of the two who faced each other. Quinn was alive with the predatory anticipation that had carried him towards the killing of Margrave and Celia. Frank's reign would not be toasted by gin-heated farmers beneath this straining roof. A soporific in the decanter in the smoking-room, where Frank and Philip sat late each night over their cigars, would slide them into sleep as they lounged. A lamp would overturn, the oil spill, the fire spread with vicious speed. The alarm would be raised too late and the anxieties he had voiced over the habits of the young men would, alas, be proved true. There had been deaths by fire at Vauchurch before; he did not care to break with tradition.

Olivia's white face blanched further as she stared at him. The blood seeped back from her skin, giving her piercing eyes a startling emphasis. She could not hide her realisation of what she recognised in Quinn.

'You will not harm him,' she said. 'I'll have you sent from here today.'

He stepped closer and took her chin between his finger and thumb as if she were a child again.

'You have no right,' he said. 'No power.'

She threw up her hand to knock his away and the pin she still held drew a gash across the pallor of her cheek. Twisting from him, she wrenched at the strings she had tied and ran out into the cold that swirled over the plateau.

Frank and Philip were riding. They had told her their intended route. If they had not changed their minds, they would soon be following the path she had taken. Dropping the hat-pin and flowers, she pressed her handkerchief to her bleeding face and hurried across the rough grass to warn Frank of the danger that lay in wait.

She could not endure another loss; she felt the madness Charlotte had used to taunt her to be very near, hovering at her shoulder, beckoning her to be enfolded in its ragged wings. There was temptation in such a surrender. She spurned her weakness, straightening from the half-crouch in which she cradled her wound and walking with renewed purpose.

The sound of hooves reached her before she saw the riders. The summer-house was behind her. She was almost at the thicket where she had accosted her mother to demand Frank be sent to the safety of their Cousin Rencombe.

'Frank!' she called, and her cry was the brittle wail of a keening woman.

The speed of the hoofbeats increased. Her heart was in time with their drumming. The riders appeared, vigorous and earnest against the tumultuous sky.

'Frank!' she called again, and there was courage and hope in the use of his name. His vitality was a talisman against the evil that held this place. He reined in his horse and jumped down from its back. She saw the dark imperiousness of their father in his face and was glad.

'What has happened?' he said.

'Quinn—'

He grasped her by the wrist. Her wound had gaped as she ran and blood was smeared in bright swathes across her cheek and neck.

'He did this to you?' he demanded. The grim rage that drove all sympathy from his voice was balm to her.

'I've spoken to him,' she said. 'He will not have you inherit. He will do with you as he did with Margrave.'

His grip tightened on her arm.

'Oh, God preserve us.' She put her hand on his. 'It is so. It is so.'

He looked up at Philip. 'Attend to my sister,' he said.

He remounted and set his horse to a gallop. He had ridden this summit with Kate, throwing up turf as the reaching strides of the gelding were throwing it now. His father had been living then; a man powerful in his pride. Then Quinn had come. And with him, death and disloyalty, the horror of truth told by one child to another. He saw the sweat on his horse's flanks; he saw the red on white of Olivia's face.

The lion-gate was before him and he was through it. The garden with its incongruous propriety fled past. He was in the stable-yard and grooms rushed out, holding twists of hay and pieces of harness, alarmed from their industry by the clangour of his impetuous arrival.

'Where is Holman?'

'Just gone out in the chaise, sir.'

Out of the yard, the house to the right and the ancient rise of the fortress to the left. Out onto the drive that wound down the precipitous slope, the horse slipping on the steep road.

The chaise was below him. Quinn and Charlotte had turned on the high seat, wondering at the violence of such a rapid descent. He was upon them. The mare that pulled the chaise stepped sideways as Frank's hunter loomed above her. She leant against the outer shaft, her eyes wide. Charlotte clutched the edge of the chaise. Quinn was speaking soothingly to the mare.

'Damn you, sir.' Frank bent and grasped Quinn's whip. 'You have injured my sister.'

'What?'

There was amused contempt in the word. Frank heeled his horse closer. He would wrench the whip from Quinn's hand and strike him as Olivia had been struck. The gelding surged against the swaying carriage.

'Get back, you fool!' Quinn was trying to pull the mare's head from the drop, trying to prevent her shying away from Frank's heavy mount. 'You'll have us over.'

Two wheels had climbed the narrow verge and were bumping over the white stones that warned of the fall. Frank did not give

226

way. The weight of his hunter was against the body of the chaise. Lips shrinking from her exposed teeth, the mare screamed. The chaise tipped, balanced and was gone. The splintering of wood and the drag of flesh on rock lasted for a moment, no more, and then there was only the wind and the lament from the house above.

Chapter Sixteen

The sun that glittered on the curling waves and gleamed on the brass ornaments of the vessel poured enough heat onto the deck to warn that the more fragile Europeans would need to cluster beneath awnings before noon. Two ladies in white muslin had already opened their parasols as they strolled back and forth and the fringed silk, hiding their faces, gave them a curiously dehumanised appearance, as if they were columns of pure light. At the rail, a Greek Orthodox priest was holding up his small, wriggling nieces, balancing one on each hip like the panniers of the overburdened donkeys that laboured on the bleached and stony tracks of Attica. Sleek and grinning dolphins were surging through the azure waters, diving and resurfacing with a joyous ease that delighted the girls, making them reach out their plump arms and struggle in their uncle's clasp until he was forced to let them slide down his robe to the planking. A hot scent of cinnamon, honey and rosewater was drifting along the gangway from the kitchen.

Philip dipped his pen, secured the lid of his travelling ink-well and wrote:

7th April, 1870
At sea

Dear Miss Forston,
I would begin by assuring you that my constitution is more than equal to the motion of the ship, were I not aware that impatience for news of our friend would have your fond eyes flitting across my estimable script in search of the beloved name. Tender as I am towards your affectionate anxieties, I will not delay in telling you that the invalid continues his slow, and now sure, progress to recovery. I do believe that I could say with confidence that the physical battle had been

won, if it were not that the enduring spiritual prostration manifests itself in a lethargy indistinguishable from bodily weakness. Do not be alarmed, I beg, for his well-being has increased to such a degree these last weeks that I have perfect faith in restoring him to you as he was before the tragic events of last autumn brought about his disorder.

Resting his pen in a groove on the portable writing-desk that had crossed the Continent with him, Philip paused to consider his wording. Any deviation from the truth, however generously meant, would not only be unkind in the end but, with Hermione, pointless. The staunch and unsisterly love that she had unleashed upon Frank, as he lay raving with brain fever after the accident had killed his mother and stepfather, would not be shaken by knowing of an increased sombreness. She was, he reflected wryly, of the tribe of Margrave and even more used than he to dealing with their vagaries.

He looked over to where Frank was lounging in a squat-legged basket-chair, his legs crossed on a neatly coiled pile of rope. Frank was dressed in deep mourning. His one concession to the demands of the Mediterranean, a broad-brimmed straw hat with a trailing black scarf in place of its band, was pulled down over his face. He was thinner than he had been when they arrived at Vauchurch but the painful gauntness of an invalid had been vanquished and his appearance was of one who had been ill in the past and now was almost in health.

The frivolity that animated Philip's correspondence was invariably as much to cheer himself as its recipients. In the first month after the deaths, he had feared for Frank's life. It was an alarm with an element of nightmare in its two-pronged threat for, until the inquest, it was possible that Frank would be held to account for the incident and, should he ever rise from his sickbed, it would be to answer in court for the deliberate slaying of the Holmans. As he had sat through long nights, pressing cool wet cloths to his companion's brow, harrowed alike by the thrashings of delirium and the unnatural stillness of the sleep that fuelled the madness, he had reached moments of despair in which he was tempted to pray that Frank should be allowed to depart so blighted a life. Hermione would have none of such folly. She had entered the house as the coming of summer, soothing, strengthening, removing Olivia, with her maenad frenzy of triumph, from Frank's chamber, forcing her reluctant father to take charge of legal and funeral arrangements; she and her maid had assumed command of all at Vauchurch and when her patient had regained his wits, he had opened his haunted eyes upon love that had waited throughout the years.

Perhaps the jury were truly convinced that the chaise had fallen because the mare had shied, perhaps the suspicions Olivia had sown caused a lack of sympathy for Charlotte and Quinn, perhaps the violence of Frank's grief made him seem innocent. A verdict of Accidental Death was brought in and the building of a wall advised.

The law was kinder to Frank than he was to himself. He was overcome by horror and remorse for what he had done. There was none of his forebears' ruthlessness in his nature and his vengeance brought him only suffering. He was unable to say whether it had been his design to send the chaise over the edge but he embraced the guilt with a will. Opinion supported him. Though the deaths were accepted as mishaps, old histories of the Margraves were resurrected and the evil reputation of the family grew. Heads were shaken; calls were not made to enquire after his convalescence; he was shunned. It was decided that he should try a warmer climate for his health.

Philip continued to write:

We came aboard at Piraeus with no difficulty but some vociferous excitement over our luggage. When the whirlwind had settled and our helpers were beaten back by handfuls of small coins, we found ourselves still in possession of all our belongings. Thus we are singled out from the luckless Mrs Davenport. We have encountered her several times on our journey from Calais and at each meeting she has been a portmanteau the poorer. She goes to her husband, who is attached to the Consulate in Syria, and one can only hope that she will have a shirt to her back when she joins him.

Our only loss has been my cherished shaving-brush, left in a balcony-room overlooking Lake Lucerne. It is, even now, pursuing us by means of the postal service if the major-domo at the hotel is to be believed.

Europe is behind us and it would be claiming a sang-froid that is not rightly mine to say that my heart does not beat more quickly at the prospect of setting foot in the Holy

Land. A tear would dew the cheek of my old Scripture master if he could know that his thankless labours to teach me chapter and verse had resulted in this laudable excess of feeling.

We are, like Jonah, to be cast ashore at Jaffa – our choice being decided by seasoned explorers informing us that at this entry a judicious bribe will remove us from quarantine within a day. Should we rashly disembark at Beirut, we will be prodded with poles until we enter a confinement where we are at the mercy of extortionate chefs for almost a week. Life, my dear Miss Forston, is trying enough in all conscience without prodding, as the Mrs Davenports of this world will tell you.

From this indignity, we pass on, certified as uncontagious, to Jerusalem and so towards the East. Shall I hazard a speculation on my talents with a camel? I think not.

The dragoman leading his party of guards through the valley of Jordan knew that the barren lands ahead would be more to the taste of one of the two travellers who had hired him. He was rarely in sympathy with the foreigners he escorted from picturesque ruin to striking oasis, despising their enthusiasm for drawing materials and dead Romans. They were an excellent source for increasing his wealth, especially when he organised a profitable ambush along the way, but he had little interest in those he protected on their journeys. The strangers came and went and were replaced by others.

There was a difference in this pair. They were young and must be of high position in their own country for they had the assurance that wealth gives to any man, regardless of race, yet one carried with him a shadow that darkened his days, enclosing him in silence, and the other watched his cousin with the care of a willing guardian. This was a pilgrimage. God had touched Margrave with a darkness of the soul and, though the stricken traveller was only a Christian, he had come to renew his spirit in the wastes where there is nothing between a man and the Infinite.

And so it had not surprised the guide that Frank had ridden like a creature of stone through the sweet luxuriance of the Plain of Sharon, with its myriad orange-trees and swathes of roses, nor that he stayed in Jerusalem only to follow the Way of the Cross, nor that his austerity was unseduced by the verdant invitation of the Jordan Valley. The wilderness where his Christ had fasted and been tempted by the Devil was before them and there, amongst the desolation of its arid hills, he would begin to find salvation.

Philip was intrigued by the Bedouin way of life. The tribesmen were fierce, courageous and active, it was true but, though he did not say so, he considered the code of honour prevailing in the desert, with its treacheries, its raids for gain disguised as noble strategy, its feuds and changing allegiances, to be strikingly similar to the commercial enterprises of past generations of Margraves.

There was much to be said for it, he thought as he made his way up the slope towards Frank. Screaming war-cries as you gallop fine Arab mares down upon caravans of silks and spices had more of a flourish to it than sitting before a ledger but was it enough to fulfil one's needs? A good English bathtub full of good English rain was growing consumingly beguiling.

He reached Frank, who moved a little further along the boulder on which he sat to let his friend join him. Their feet were lost amongst tangles of camomile. Frank's brown face was less tormented than it had been when they came ashore at Jaffa. The long ride, often monotonous, often exhausting, had subdued his guilt as the rocking of a cradle subdues a raging infant. He had forgiven neither himself nor those he had killed, but he had begun to see beyond his past. The hardships of the journey, the crushing heat of the days, the sudden cold that could drop from the glittering night-sky, splitting rock with its force, distracted his mind. There had been an evening at Tiberias when he had torn a flower from an oleander bush and flung it into the quiet waters of Lake Galilee, weeping as he sank to kneel by the lapping waves, but his passion had eased and Philip was confident that he would soon be whole.

They sat in amicable silence as the sun rose. In the hollow where they had camped, tents were being folded and packs stowed. The smell of thick, strong coffee hung in the still air.

'The road to Damascus,' Frank said. 'And do your ideas remain fixed on making your toilette?'

'They do.' Philip examined his hands. 'At present, my cologne is eau de roast lamb.'

'You fool no one. You're not such a Philistine that you can look on this and be unmoved.'

'Would that I were. I could have stayed at home.'

233

From their seat on the heights of Salhiyeh, they saw dawn cover the orchards and palaces of Damascus. Light touched the maze of waterways that ran from the great river, a shining lattice of pools and culverts enclosed by city walls that had seen St Paul lowered to safety in a basket. Minarets rose above fertile gardens and fountains playing in marble bowls were tantalising points of brilliance.

They were near their journey's end. Here they would exchange their horses for camels and cross the harshest of deserts to Palmyra and the ruins of Zenobia's capital. And then they would turn back towards the world whose barbarians were as versed in cruelty as ever the first builders of these sites had been. Philip, remembering ruthless queens, thought of the lovely Eleanor Forston, who had come reluctantly in her daughter's wake to pay a duty visit to her ailing nephew, and the havoc her immorality had caused. Frank dreamt of Hermione.

The sun had risen fully as they rode over the wooden bridge to the city-gates and on into the winding, cluttered streets that had been enticing from a distance. The shade from the overhanging houses was welcome but the filth, the press of staring crowds in the narrow alleys and the constant clamour of the hawkers were wearing after the silence of their travels. Disappointment and unease affected them both but neither spoke of it, each privately telling himself that it was only fatigue and the contrast between the peacefulness of isolation and the hurry of the swarm that caused the disquiet.

Their dragoman took them to a hotel in the European quarter. They visited a public bath-house and, pummelled and oiled, returned to their rooms to eat.

'We should go out,' Frank said as he sprawled on the divan, spooning the last, tart granules of lemon ice from his dish. 'You've had your bathe. You've no excuse for reclusiveness now.'

'When did I shrink from society?' Philip was stretched at full length on a pile of tasselled cushions, listening to the murmur of voices in the courtyard, and drawing the moist smoke of dark, rich tobacco through the mouthpiece of his hookah. 'But, yes. When we've come this far it will not do to turn into harem ladies. We must rouse ourselves.'

When evening was falling, releasing the town from the severity of the afternoon heat, they left the shelter of the hotel and went, unattended, to wander past cafés where robed men played intricate board games, beside jasmine-draped mud-brick walls, beneath mulberry trees hung with coloured lanterns, through souks and byways. The strangeness of the bustle of a multitude had a hypnotic effect so that they walked like yokels gaping at London, gazing about them without comment or recognition, losing their concentration and direction. They did not pay heed to where they were and they did not notice the men who followed them.

Chapter Seventeen

Though there seemed no reason for it, the espalier pear had come adrift from its moorings overnight. Mrs Lambourne, carefully pegging it back into position, puzzled over its escape and then, all at once, realised what had happened. The boy she was trying to train as a gardener had let his enthusiasm run away with him and, instead of confining his attention to the roots, had watered the spreading branches from the top until the surface of the wall had dissolved away as it did during the rare, heavy downpours that left Damascus – the 'Pearl of the Desert' – wallowing forlornly in mud.

There was no likelihood of such an event this morning. The sky was the loveliest of blues and the air was already as dry as tinder. In the pure sunlight, the undersides of the tender young rose-leaves glowed like garnets in their first red-black flush. A rustling behind a hibiscus told her where her pair of gazelles, with their slender, tip-toe legs and languishing eyes, were grazing.

Having secured the pear-tree to her satisfaction, she walked down the tiled path to the small pavilion where a jug of sheep's milk was waiting on her writing-table. It was a drink she would not have considered before she came to the East but, after fourteen years in this place, she would find the morning incomplete without it. Pouring herself a glass, she sat on the edge of a raised pool and touched the froth of the milk with the point of her tongue. The jug had been waiting in a thick-walled, windowless pantry until the milk-seller came crying his wares and its contents were far enough from being warm to be called cold, which was as much as she could hope for without ice.

Stroking a lily-pad with her free hand, she gently pressed its rim downwards, submerging one side, so that when she released it, globes of water were left upon the leaf, shining like the clear, glass marbles she had played with as a child. She tilted the pad, making the drops run into each other before releasing them back into the pond.

Her face was calm as she amused herself. A French artist had asked to paint her in just such a pose but she had not trusted him to keep the painting private and had refused. More ardent requests that had been urged on her from time to time had also been declined. Although only in her thirties, she had come to the city as a widow and intended to remain in that state. Her income was small but adequate and allowed her to pursue the retiring, devout and scholarly life she enjoyed.

The history of her residence in the city made the quietness of her existence something to be treasured. This was her second house; the second garden she had tended. Ten years before, she had been living in the Christian quarter when a rumour spread that the blood of a murdered Muslim had been used to draw a cross on a mosque wall. She thought that hell had taken possession of the earth. A mob invaded the streets, butchering Christians right and left; women were raped amongst the taunting crowds, young girls captured and sold to Turkish harems; arson destroyed what the looters had left.

Her early years had shown her the wickedness of man. She had not lingered to see whether the insanity would pass. At the first sign of barbarism, she had fled to the British Consulate and from there, disguised as an Arab, had escaped to the protection of the Emir's palace. The horror that she witnessed in those days and in the weeks that followed the suppression of the riot – the unburied dead rotting amongst the ruins, the mutilated corpses dragged from their Christian graves, the destitute with no roof to shelter them – made her look outwards again and remember that others had suffered betrayal as well as she. Her distress did not make her vilify Islam, for her misery had been at the hands of those who professed her own faith, and she recognised cruelty as universal, but she embraced more closely the religion she had always loved and the sincerity of her beliefs could be judged by the kindness of her deeds.

The sun had risen high enough to have reached the pomegranate bush and was lighting the loose petals of its fragile flowers to a dazzling crimson. She spent so many hours reading and writing in her pavilion that she could measure the passing of the day by the changing shadows as accurately as if the whole garden were one luxuriant dial.

The hurry of bare feet on the path roused her from her reverie. Her maid was hastening towards the pool, concern upon her young face. Mrs Lambourne stood up. She had bought Pascua shortly after the massacre when the girl was a lively nine-year-old, who was proving too minx-like for her master. He did not have the heart to beat her into docility but had no objection to selling her to rid himself of trouble. Her new mistress had freed her and offered wages, startling her into a protectiveness for a grown woman who was foolish with her money. Her appearance was North African and she had a vague recollection of a long, baffling journey when she was carried by someone she thought was her mother but she had nowhere and no one to go back to and she had settled contentedly into a cheerful and unsuccessful attempt to have dominance in the household.

The only fear that could make her wake sweating in the night was bringing her precipitously along a path designed for sauntering. A cat darted from its bed in a clump of poppies as she brushed past and she snatched her loose robe out of its way to arrive panting before her mistress.

'Ma'am,' she said in the accented English she had learnt without effort. 'Oh, ma'am . . .'

Mrs Lambourne was alarmed. Pascua revelled in becoming excited over trifles and could conduct extended and intricate altercations with any number of tradesmen but it was unlike her to be genuinely agitated.

'Sit down,' she said. 'Collect yourself.'

Instead, the girl seized one of Mrs Lambourne's hands in both of hers and clasped it tightly. 'I heard from the spice-seller,' she said. 'Two Englishmen have defiled a mosque.'

Mrs Lambourne felt a coldness in her breast. It was probably only a rumour but she had known what rumour could do.

'Where?'

'Here. Here! In the city.'

'And how did the spice-man have the news?'

'His sister is married to a guard where they're held.'

'Have you spoken to anyone else who knew? No? Then be sure you say nothing in your turn.'

Hope was asserting its strengthening presence. A decade was too short an interval for the executions after the massacre to have been forgotten. No one would wish for such another blood-letting. There had been none of the sporadic tit-for-tat killings that had

239

led up to the last conflagration. It was likely that this was a matter of greed. Innocents had been duped into a compromising situation and were to be menaced into paying dearly for their liberty.

'Now, my dear,' Mrs Lambourne said, 'nothing violent need come of this. I'll write a note which you must take to the Consulate. I know the Consul is away but you must see that his staff understand its importance. You will tell me where the gentlemen are imprisoned and I'll go to visit them.'

'I'll go with you.'

'You will not. You know I've often attended prisoners and come to no harm.'

For discretion's sake, she covered herself in a hooded cloak and gauze veil before leaving the house. Although she believed the captivity to be a vehicle for extracting heavy bribes, it was possible that, even if severe violence did not break out again, there would be insults and assaults. It was prudent to hide her European dress.

She was encouraged by the everyday aspect of the streets. There were no knots of men talking heatedly as they stared at neighbours who had suddenly grown horns, no shops were unexpectedly shuttered and barred, doors stood open. The atmosphere was that of a city going about its business and, in the anonymity of concealing garments, she prayed inwardly that it would continue to be so.

Turkish guards were lolling at the gates of the gaol. They had an air of pomaded self-importance that worried her but she approached them without hesitation. Begging them to accept the repayment of money she had borrowed from their wives, she asked to be conducted to their commander. The men made no difficulty about her request. One led her across the compound, through an ante-room to a bench beside the Governor's door. She knew what to expect. The soldier would knock and enter the office, reappearing to announce his regret that his master was occupied but would endeavour to spare her a moment. An interval would follow in which she could almost hear the Governor calculating how long she must be left to be reminded that she was a humble supplicant. She despised the love of power and the use of authority to belittle others. Her contempt allowed her to wait without loss of dignity, meditating upon what depths the wearisome creature's avarice would reach today.

An audience with the prisoners proved expensive, though not as much as she had anticipated. She was obliged to empty her purse but did not have to disclose the wallet she had hidden in her gown. The Governor was prepared to be generous, according to his lights. His dealings with Mrs Lambourne had shown her to be a virtuous and charitable lady, who would pay for the favours she asked with proper delicacy. Being an Englishwoman, she would, of course, have a greater interest in her countrymen than in those of the other races she had succoured and, he was gratified to see, had come with enough gold to cover the raised price.

She walked behind a gaoler down dim passages lit by small, barred apertures in the ceiling. The rank smell that she could never quite define – of unwashed bodies sweltering in humid, unwashed cells and some strange stench like the carcass of a rotting sheep – made her draw her cloak over her veiled nose and mouth. She was aware that to enter this place was to risk disease; it could not be helped.

Their way took them into a region that was new to her. A door was unlocked and they descended steps that dropped steeply below ground-level. The coolness was welcome to a visitor. She could not decide whether the relief from the extreme heat of day would compensate the imprisoned for the bitter cold that would be suffered here at night. It might preserve them from fever.

Another lock was turned and the gaoler drew back a door for her to enter. She stepped into the cell and felt a moment of claustrophobia as she was shut in. The room was darker than the corridor. A thin rectangle of window, covered by a grating, was set high in the far wall but it was even with the surface of the compound and sand had blown against its ironwork, blocking much of what light could slide in. As her eyes adjusted, she heard two men rising to their feet and was amused that, after her experiences, she could still be reassured by Englishmen's politeness towards women.

'Good morning, gentlemen,' she said and sensed at once a relaxation in her listeners as they heard their native tongue.

'Good morning,' said one young voice and the other, moving nearer, asked, 'Ma'am, may I offer you this stool?'

They were interrupted by the gaoler. He came in without a word, laid an earthenware oil-lamp, no bigger than a duck's egg, on the floor, and again left the three alone.

The tiny flame wavered and grew straight but barely added to the light in the cell. However, she had become used to the dusk and found that she could distinguish men and furniture in the gloom and then make out the features on the strained, exhausted faces. She seated herself gracefully on the stool as if she were in a drawing room and the prisoners made use of the pallet that had been their bed during the sleepless night.

'My name is Mrs Lambourne,' she said. 'Perhaps you'll think it presumptuous of me to be interfering in your affairs but, though I've lived in Damascus for many years, I retain a fellow feeling for my countrymen. If you would allow me to offer you assistance? It may be that I'm more privy to the ways of the city than you are yourselves.'

'All help would be most gratefully received, Mrs Lambourne. We're plainly not fit to be abroad without our nursemaids. Such foolishness to end like this.' The young man was attempting to speak gaily. The unsuccessful effort to disguise his anxiety touched her. His companion appeared to be less apprehensive but it seemed only because a greater sorrow held him aloof from his surroundings.

'May I ask your names, sirs?' she said.

'Ah, forgive me, yes. Mine is Rencombe. This is my kinsman, Mr Frank Margrave.'

'Margrave?' Her question was a whisper. She put her hand to her throat. 'Of Vauchurch?'

'Indeed.' Frank was surprised by his notoriety. 'Are you acquainted with my family, Mrs Lambourne?'

'I have heard the name. But the Governor of this benighted place is contrary – my time here may be short. If you would be good enough to tell me what led you to this pass, I can alert the Consulate. My maid is already making the first overtures to the British authorities.'

Philip looked up to the narrow shaft of light penetrating the window and back to the composed, intrepid woman who could sit in confinement, veiled and robed, talking with perfect tranquillity of turnkeys, Consuls and her familiarity with the Margraves. An irrational confidence in their release replaced the fears of the dark hours but was unable to banish the embarrassment he felt for their naivety.

'The tale is that you defiled a mosque,' she said. 'I daresay it's been exaggerated in the telling.'

'We can hardly say.' Philip glanced at Frank, who showed no sign of joining in the explanation. 'If we did, and we are *told* we did – it was why we were arrested – it wasn't intentional. We arrived yesterday, Mrs Lambourne, tired from our journey and my cousin

242

not yet recovered from an illness. In the evening we went out to view the sights. We wandered the streets, became lost, dazed by the complications of the city, the – the sheer busy foreignness of it all . . .' He regarded her queryingly and she nodded. 'Eventually, we did pause at the entrance to a mosque. We were hemmed in. There seemed such a crowd, a jostling. And we were pressed by the throng. Pushed backwards a step into the mosque. And then it was all commotion and shouting. We were dragged here.'

'You went inside the mosque wearing shoes?'

'A step, no more, and against our will. They say we have polluted a holy place.'

She was silent, considering their situation. The sound of ragged marching crossed the compound and drifted into lackadaisical conversation before dying away.

'I won't keep from you,' she said, 'the possibility that this could get out of hand. The cry could go up that you are defilers of the faith. But I believe that you've been played upon – that you were recognised as inexperienced travellers without protection and followed with the purpose of discovering you in an activity that could justify incarceration. A little diplomatic to-ing and fro-ing and a heavy bribe, and you should have your freedom. Then I advise you leave Damascus as soon as you may.'

She saw both men shift their position slightly as relief and hope eased their tension. Footsteps passed overhead but did not descend the stairs.

'Mr Margrave,' she said, 'perhaps you will indulge me with news of your family. It's a great while since I was in England and I've lost touch with many of my circle.'

Frank's face tightened.

'I see you're in mourning,' she said gently. 'Are your mother and father well?'

He sat farther forward on the pallet and clasped his hands on his knees. 'I'm afraid, ma'am,' he said, 'I can only give you regret in return for your kindness. My father died some years since and,' he touched his black neck-cloth, 'my mother recently.'

'My dear sir. Such grief. I remember an occasion when Mrs Margrave tried to save me from myself. How different life would have been if I had listened. And Olivia?'

'She – is in good health.'

'There were two girls, I recall.'

'There's been much sadness in my family, Mrs Lambourne.

243

My elder sister drowned fifteen years ago.'

'Drowned!' She straightened as if she would rise to her feet. 'I have never heard she drowned.'

'She was travelling to India as a bride. One day out from Suez, her ship was struck by a sudden storm. It sank with all hands.'

'*All?* There were no survivors? No one was rescued?'

'No one. I'm sorry to distress you.'

'You say she was a bride. Did her husband share her fate?'

'He did. All perished. Everyone aboard.' He turned to Philip. 'Is there water left in that pitcher? Mrs Lambourne, a little water?'

Philip reached down for the jug that held the last of their ration. She unhooked her veil to drink. Her hands shook as she lifted the vessel to her suddenly parched mouth. If her trembling had been from fear, she would have despised herself but it was not. She was, she had learnt, her mother's daughter.

She set the jug on the floor.

'Does the mist still fill the valley beneath Vauchurch?' she said. 'Is the fountain by the summer-house still broken? Frank, dear brother, you have shown me that there *is* justice in the world.'

Before she closed her shutters on the night, Kate stood at her bedroom window and looked out on the moonwashed fantasy that was her garden. There was no colour but grey in its trees and shrubs. Streaks of silver wavered on the rippling surface of the rill that ran from pool to pool. The warm, sweet scent of blossom lingered in the cooling air. Beyond the high walls, roofs shining with quiet light flowed in uneven layers towards the minaret, whose muezzin would wake her with his wailing praise of God.

This was her home and she had been, after a fashion, happy here. This evening she had been restless, burdened by the unsettling realisation that she need no longer make herself content with secrecy and the insecure safeguard of a desolate land. She had so much of importance to dwell upon yet she found her thoughts flitting in undisciplined riot from one memory to the next, and the longing to put out her hand and feel the cold stone of Vauchurch was like a physical hunger that could not be assuaged. For all her wretchedness as a girl, she was a Margrave and the call of their bleak eminence was strong.

Fastening the carved wooden shutter, she climbed into her muslin-curtained bed, sitting upright against the pillows. The glow from the filigree brass lamp fell softly on the room that had been a refuge within a refuge. In her thin white nightgown with her hair falling down about her shoulders she seemed as young as when her father had sold her to Unsworth to advance his desire for vengeance and trade. Her eyes gave her away. There was no youth in them. Tonight, the gentleness and pity that was the major part of her had been set aside. Had Charlotte been able to see her daughter's face, she would have recognised the depths of resentment, scorn and rage that had dictated her own path.

Throughout the day she had been racked by ecstasy. It reared up like a tidal-wave, thrusting other emotions into its depths, engulfing her in pure joy. True to the essential goodness of her nature, she had tried to attribute it to the reunion with Frank but honesty prevented her believing it. Her bliss was more primitive. She was in rapture because Bryce Unsworth was dead.

She had been taught to hate on her wedding night. It had not been a difficult lesson. For eighteen years, no harsh sentiment had invaded her mind. Her only condemnatory judgements had been of her own dissatisfactions. And then she had been sacrificed, handed by the cruelty of one man to the cruelty of another. She had faced the treachery of her father and the corruption of her husband and, beneath a surface of continuing meekness, she had shed her power to excuse evil. Often since then, she had mourned for the girl she had been but, if she were not to have the life she had hoped to be given, it was better that she had changed. Her heart, full of love and trust, had hardened. It kept its compassion and generosity, and its iron shell protected her, granting an independence her mother had never achieved.

Shutting her eyes, she pictured Bryce struggling for breath as the Arabian sea closed over his head. It did not trouble her that she had been in hiding unnecessarily for so long; her gladness was too complete for regret. Widowhood was enough. The time of her concealment now felt short; the time of her marriage long.

Bryce had taunted her as they had driven away from the church. He had never been interested in her love. All he had coveted was her body, obedience and a closer connection with her father yet, discovering at the altar that she had been deceived into expecting to marry his nephew, witnessing her reluctance to accept her fate, he had grown angry and his anger must always have a victim. Too innocent to understand that inflicting humiliation and pain is a pleasure to a vicious man, she had sat in shock on the carriage-seat, her bouquet clutched in her quivering hands, as he mocked her for her preference. As cold as snow, she had listened to him whisper that he would make her rue her mother's interruption to the service, and had longed for the day to end, longed for the night. When night had come, she had longed for the day.

She remembered his nails. They were tapered and ridged like almonds. There was a scar on the tender flesh of her inner thigh from his use of them.

When the first dawn of her married life broke through the blinds of their opulent, impersonal hotel room, loathing had begun her transformation. He did not notice. They boarded ship and, as England faded from her sight, she silently left her maiden mildness on its shores. There was no outward sign of rebellion as they strolled the deck through the Bay of Biscay, as they passed the Rock, as they paused in Malta and he took her to the Catacombs, maliciously playful in his reminders that youthful bloom must come to dust.

Her face became hollow. Matrons, who had watched her and taken the measure of Bryce, shook their heads and despised the parents who had delivered her to such a husband. They landed at Alexandria and took the steam-barge up the Mahmoudieh Canal to Cairo. Reaching the beginning of the East appealed to Bryce. While Arabs with flaming torches ran beside them to another hotel, as much a private hell for her as the last, he resumed the opium-taking that he had discarded since the wedding. In the hot night, while she sat as far from him as she could, sleepless, aching and nauseous, she listened to the grunting breaths of his rest and looked for an escape.

Religious scruples did not mar her plans. She was convinced that vows taken amidst lies and tyranny were worthless. Her God was the Good Shepherd and would not forsake her because she fled from wolves.

For those who did not wish to sail the length of Africa and back, it was necessary to cross the desert to Suez before taking ship again. Awkward, four-horse vans plied to and fro at a bruising pace, stopping briefly at caravanserais for fresh animals to be exchanged for those whipped to exhaustion. Before Bryce had woken in Cairo, Kate had despatched a chambermaid to buy her an enveloping covering with veil that would shield her from the stinging sand on the journey. She joked about it prettily to the other occupants of the van and they were amused by her combination of childlike eccentricity and practical sense.

246

At Suez, the prospect of having no other chance of liberty before India strengthened her resolve. They were shown to their cabin and Bryce, tired by the jarring they had endured, lay down to refresh himself for the evening. She said that she would go on deck where she would not wake him and he sneered at what he believed was an infantile enthusiasm for seeing the ship leave port. His eyes lost focus as he derided her. Weariness and his drops gave her release from observance. Wrapping herself in her Egyptian robe, she emptied his pocket-book and purse, placed what jewels she had not sewn into the lining of her gown in her bosom and walked quietly down the gangplank amongst the press of porters hurrying to load the last of the baggage.

The vans were leaving at once, bearing the passengers who had disembarked from her ship that morning. She bought a seat amongst a group of British officers and jolted, unspeaking and afraid, throughout the night-long ride as they reminisced happily of the Old Country and planned their autumn's slaughter of wildlife.

From Cairo, she returned to Alexandria and from there made her way to Jerusalem. At every moment, she expected to find herself snared and dragged back into bondage. She had no legal right to be apart from her husband and Bryce, she knew, would want revenge for her desertion.

In Jerusalem, the courage of desperation that had upheld her failed. Terror of Bryce and her solitary condition overtook her and she lay in the room she had rented at the far end of a noisy side-street, weak and feverish with fear. She was very young and used to submitting her will to others; she had always been provided with the means to live and her future had required no speculation. For three weeks she kept within her refuge, sending out the landlord's daughter to buy her necessities. Then, one morning when the sun had an amber sheen that had drawn her to sit at the painted lattice of her window, she had found herself saying to the empty room: 'If I had that stall over there, I'd put a board across the front to stop the oranges rolling off. And I wouldn't leave my grandmother to tend it – she dozes and boys snatch the fruit. I'd watch it myself and shout my wares.'

Both the thought and its decisiveness startled her. Though the idea was repellent, it seemed that the enterprising spirit of the Margraves was surfacing in her. She pondered on what this implied and concluded that energy and resolve did not have to mean greed and malice. Roused from her debilitating dread, she began to take stock of her advantages. She was accomplished after the fashion of her class; she could speak German, French and Italian, sew, draw and paint, play the piano and sing, write a fair hand and be soothing at a sickbed. It would surely be possible to sustain herself by selling these talents. Lessons could be given on any of these subjects or, indeed, she could teach English. A place as a governess could be considered but that seemed to hold more threat of being discovered with visitors to such a household who might recognise her and the requirement of references. Living alone would give her greater anonymity.

The prospect of supporting herself was simultaneously encouraging and daunting. There was an excitement in the notion of earning her own bread, yet she had been brought up as a lady and could not help but feel uneasy at becoming a working woman. Pride had to be put away for the sake of practicality and she began her career by attempting to replenish her funds. Venturing into a jeweller's shop, she sold one of her rings. Its worth had been a mystery to her but, after the transaction in which doubts of ownership were used to intimidate her, she was certain she had been robbed.

Angry and afraid, she took a bracelet into another establishment and here she found she had fallen amongst honest men. Mr Isaacs, looking over his gold-rimmed spectacles at her pale, resolute face and examining the bangle with hands clothed in fingerless black mittens, saw and pitied persecuted innocence. As a youth, he had lived with an uncle in Marseilles and was fluent in French. Kate did not tell him her true position but she confided that she was in difficulties and wished to live quietly upon what she could make from her learning and the sale of her possessions. She trusted him enough to reveal all the ornaments she had carried from her jewel-box and was astonished to learn their value. Margrave and Bryce had used her person to flaunt their wealth, and the sum their ostentation could fetch would preserve her gentility. The gems, in strictness, belonged to her husband but she had no qualms over disposing of his property.

Isaacs believed her to be fleeing a rich seducer and, having handsome daughters of his own, was ready to do what he could to protect her virtue. He gave her an excellent price and one of his sons invested her money so that she was able to live in prudent comfort without seeking pupils.

This was more security than she had hoped for but still she was not free from anxiety. Too many Europeans visited Jerusalem for her peace of mind. Before the year was out, she chose to move deeper into obscurity by taking up residence in Damascus. Apart from the terror of the massacre, she had been content there. She had lived a nun-like existence that suited her. Sometimes she pined for the loving husband and children she had imagined would be hers but she filled the days with other interests and did not waste her spirit in grief nor did she ever want to be touched by a man again. She missed Olivia and Frank, often wondering how they had fared, and she revered the mother she had thought had not cared for her but who, as deceived as she, had tried to save her at the very steps of the altar.

How strange that she was to embrace her family once more and because of such circumstances. Slipping off the bed, she went to the cabinet where she kept the likenesses of the three she loved. Ornate, silver frames enclosed two small sketches that she had drawn at Vauchurch the month before she was taken to be married. In one, Olivia stood on the crest of the outer rampart, staring seawards with her piercing gaze; in the other, Charlotte sat with regal ease on a bay mare while Frank held the bridle of his pony. She did not need to look at the portraits – they were engraved upon her heart – but she handled them tenderly and almost with awe, as if their subjects had come back from the dead. During the intervals of her ecstasy over widowhood, she felt a deep happiness at having her brother and sister returned to her life. She could not say that she had suffered sharp sorrow on hearing of Charlotte's death, for her mother had been lost for so long. The length and nature of her separation from them all allowed her the rare satisfaction of joy untroubled by regret.

It did, however, reinforce what she had always known. Family, for good or ill, had an importance that reached far beyond a name. She was, and ever would be, a Margrave. Others should have a brighter Fate. Setting down the sketches, she rang for her maid.

Night had fallen and, in the darkness of the cell, cold rose from the depths of the earth with persistent stealth. It wound about the limbs of the still figures, back to back on the pallet, sheathing them in the numbing chill that makes movement seem a distant memory. Frank, having fallen into an exhausted sleep, woke abruptly from a dream of Vauchurch and believed himself to be within its glacial walls. His pulse beat with feverish haste as his disordered mind struggled towards the events of the day and he orientated himself.

He could see nothing. Lying with his eyes open to the perfect blackness of his surroundings, listening to Philip's breathing, he thought of Kate and what her story signified. They had been visited by an official from the Consulate that afternoon. He was a Mr Marshall, a young man verging on middle-age, whose painful conceit that it was proper, in his position, to cultivate dandified languor, conflicted with his natural tendency towards neat efficiency. This strife was echoed in the disunion between his wish to show the cool power of British diplomacy in effecting their release and his fear that the situation would get out of control. As matters were, it appeared that Kate had been right and they were being held to ransom. A bribe would secure their freedom and they would return to England, with Kate as much at liberty as they.

It was his sister's experience on which he dwelt as he lay, aware that he would not sleep again. She had told the tale of her past, letting silence and the expression of her unveiled face relate what she did not choose to put into words. In his boyish innocence, long ago, he had not questioned whether she wanted to marry Unsworth. Girls had no desires; they simply grew older and became wives. And when Olivia had taken him to their father's corpse and revealed that the world was not what it seemed, he had never extended his knowledge of its violence to the loss of the sister drowned years before.

But now he was a man, well able to recognise cruelty, and Kate was not an ideal from his childhood; she was a flesh-and-blood woman of intelligence and love, of endurance and hatred. What she was could only be a continuation of what she had been. A different life might have developed her talents to different degrees but she had survived because of what had already been there. Margrave was astute and calculating. He would have understood the enormity of handing such a girl to a rake; he would have weighed his daughter's misery against the advantage to himself and found her wretchedness worthwhile. The father he had believed to be heroic had sacrificed Kate for gain; the mother he had believed to be callous had tried to protect her. The darkness was heavy and gave him no relief.

Philip shifted to lie on his back. 'I'm not asleep either,' he said.

'I thought you were.' Frank turned towards him. 'I thought the vermin in this foul straw and I kept vigil alone.'

Philip sighed. 'The East is a disappointment,' he said. 'I was given to understand that its couches were equipped with houris and all I have are bed-bugs and you.'

'But I present a moral conundrum. So much more of a diversion.'

'I believe I'd prefer to contemplate it under English skies.'

They thought of their freedom with longing.

'You must tell Mrs Unsworth . . .' Philip began.

'I'm sure she'd prefer you used her Christian name. Religion has, after all, brought her strength.'

'Very well. You must tell Kate more of how your parents died. You must do it before she accompanies us.'

'Yes.' Frank closed his eyes. In his shock and gladness at the reunion with his sister, he had not burdened her with the truth of either death.

Philip clasped his arms about himself. 'The cold is oppressive,' he said.

'Is it?' Frank was perplexed. 'I find I've grown accustomed to it.'

The aromatic smoke of incense rose from the perforated lid of a silver canister and eddied about the framed self-portrait of Kate that Pascua had tearfully asked to keep as the two women packed what belongings Kate was to take to England. There had been a little weeping by both and in each case happiness and anticipation had mingled with the sadness of their parting.

On hearing the astonishing news that her mistress had been reclaimed by her brother and would go back to her family home, Pascua, never one to be excited in silence, had shrieked and wailed, begging to be taken to Vauchurch, proclaiming that she wished never to be separated from Kate even if it meant living in a land of snow and foolish clothing. Smiling, Kate had whispered a young man's name and sudden confusion overtook the girl, who burst into lamentations of a different nature.

Kate did not torment her. She had been aware of the interest a carpenter had been showing in her maid – his female relations were so often in her kitchen that she could not have helped it – and approved of the match. A marriage had been arranged to take

251

place a fortnight after Kate's departure and she had given the proud, laughing bride the house with most of its contents as a dowry. Three chattering aunts of the bridegroom were to move in as chaperones until the wedding had come.

Kate had been gone only one day and already there had been changes. Bright swathes of silk had been draped over demure chairs and a garish rug was spread on the tiles. The room was full of cheerful noise. A celebratory gathering was in garrulous progress. Women in decorated robes were on every seat and squatting where no sofa or cushion was to be had. As they talked and sang, ate from the bowls of sweetmeats and exclaimed at Pascua's good fortune, they clapped their hands in time for the girls who were dancing and swinging their long hair in jubilation. In the garden, kohl-eyed children played a complicated game with pebbles and flower-heads, skipping along paths that had known only quietness.

The women sang, the children played and in the desert, the Margraves set their faces towards the West.

Chapter Eighteen

It was rare for Eleanor to put other people's concerns before her own and her eagerness to see Hermione married was no exception to her general rule. This did not prevent her upholding an affectation of acting only for her sweet child's good.

Her attitude towards her daughter had wavered this way and that since she and Forston had set foot on English soil to be greeted with the news that Charlotte and Quinn were dead. She had already been viewing Hermione as an incumbrance, likely to detract from her splendour by emphasising her age and, obscurely, she blamed the girl for the trouble that banished the easy round of hospitality that was to have been their homecoming. Hermione was the representative at Knapp of the family members who were causing such difficulties and, for the first day, Eleanor had relieved her agitation by visiting a series of barbed remarks and petty criticisms upon the head of one she believed to be too placid and uninteresting, too *plain*, to retaliate.

On the second morning, when Hermione had received an overwrought message from Olivia telling of Frank's collapse, Eleanor was left in no doubt that she was dealing with a woman, not a girl, and one who was used to independence. She had not thought it proper that Hermione should take charge of Frank's nursing in that high-handed manner. It was both headstrong and a reflection upon the reluctance of the elder Forstons to become involved in this fresh scandal. Then, when she had felt obliged to pay a duty call on her nephew, she, having never been astute in anything except dress and romance, had recognised the reason for Hermione's ministrations to Frank and a determination to end what she termed a 'squalid liaison' replaced her previous irritations.

She ordered Hermione home and was given a composed refusal. Taken aback by having a wish flouted, she insisted upon obedience. Hermione had enquired whether her journey to India had been all that she desired and the contempt in the eyes that she had always thought to be mild drove Eleanor to return to Knapp, declaring that she washed her hands of such a hussy.

On a cold, bright afternoon in early March, with a crackling fire burning to dispel the cutting draughts that eddied by the window-seats, Eleanor sat in the Small Drawing Room, contemplating her approval of her daughter's prospective happiness and really coming quite close to sincerity. She was feeling heartily pleased with life. While still in the East, she had wondered whether she would find Knapp dark and oppressive after the luxurious establishments she had enjoyed in warmer lands. Her fears had been unfounded. The charm of the ancient building had asserted itself at once and was present with particular grace in this room in conditions that combined the best of winter and spring. The leaf-green damask of the sofa and chairs and the rose-pink of the curtains were not quite as vibrant as they had been, it was true, but the sun was shining with promising gaiety through glass that had been frosted at dawn and the cheerful flames were giving warmth and compan-ionship. There was to be a ball that evening at which the courtship might reach a conclusion. All was right with the world.

She crossed her neatly-shod feet on a low, velvet stool and gazed contentedly at the white kid of her Louis heels. The deep black she had worn for her sister had been set aside after a month and she had appeared resplendent in white and the becoming shades of dove and lilac that were half-mourning. 'I was so long in the Orient,' she would explain with a poignant air, leaving her listeners bewildered. It seemed to her that there was no problem that could not be solved if people would only accept her lead.

Forston came into the room, bringing a gust of outdoor air and two spaniels, whose bedraggled ears showed that they had been questing beside the stream. The dogs slumped in front of the fire and Forston took the wing-chair beside the hearth. He prodded the bronze rumps in a friendly fashion with the toe of his boot and their docked tails quivered.

'Shall I ring for tea?' Eleanor asked.

'I sent for it as I was coming through.' He held out his hands towards the heat. 'It's still bitter out there. Not,' he turned to her with a smile, 'that it affects the young. I met a certain person riding up the drive and invited him in but when he heard Hermione was in the wood, he felt that a walk was what he required.'

The look of complacency that was Eleanor's most usual expression deepened.

'Then perhaps tonight will answer,' she said. 'If he can't keep away even when they're to be dancing tonight . . .'

'He's brought her a bouquet for the ball. Hot-house flowers.'

'Ah, he does everything that he should. We can only pray that she appreciates his attentions.'

Forston shrugged. 'She's a girl, isn't she?' he said.

'I'm afraid she has no understanding of good manners, no polish. She's inclined to be a little coarse-minded.'

They were interrupted by the arrival of the tea-trays and were silent as silver and bone-china, anchovy toast and maids-of-honour were arranged on a table between them. Eleanor used the interval to lapse into her familiar irritated disapproval of her daughter. Another woman, in these circumstances, might have suffered outrage, indignation or despondency over Hermione's poor judgement, but Eleanor could not summon such strong emotions on someone else's account. Her annoyance was as far as she could advance towards sympathy, and it was born out of regard for Charlotte.

In her own shallow style, she had loved her sister.

Charlotte's death was not the wrench it would have been if their parting had not already been so long but, nevertheless, it was a grave disappointment. And a cause for anger. Both Forston and Eleanor knew their family well and they believed the killing to have been deliberate. Neither wanted to increase the tarnish on the Margrave name by seeing Frank hang for his deeds, but they wished to shun him as much as was compatible with preserving the public illusion of unity. To their variety of conscience, evil swept under the carpet was innocence restored yet they had been too close to Charlotte to be easy with Frank. They had observed Hermione's attachment to the invalid with repugnance. Even the temptation of gaining the Margrave wealth for their child could not reconcile them to Frank thus inheriting theirs. The intentions of the young pair had not been divulged to their elders, who hoped that their nephew's absence would cool Hermione's heart. In their eyes, she was without passion and, given time, could be steered into a more suitable marriage.

Their patience appeared to be bearing fruit. A commercial acquaintance of Forston's – one Enoch Bayley of Manchester – having made himself remarkably and enviably rich in the cotton trade had been overcome by the desire to turn his son into a gentleman. The unfortunate infant had been christened Thaddeus and, directly he was breeched, afflicted with tutors and, his head awash with irregular verbs, despatched to a public school that allowed the offspring of manufacturers to sidle in amongst the landowners if Papa's substance was startling enough.

The youthful Bayley had held his own. He was not an inherently ignoble boy but he grew to have the brutishness and arrogance of both his worlds, covered by a veneer of the urbanity Eleanor admired. His father saw his supercilious confidence and felt that his money was well spent.

Bayley did not oversee his father's mills. He had been bred as an heir and an ornament and lived a life of opulent leisure. In the New Year, he had come down to the west to join a house-party near Dorchester. His host was an old school-fellow, who had married three months before and loudly recommended the condition. The gregarious new wife was enjoying her transformation into the mistress of an establishment and spread her cheerfulness to all corners of her house, making the days pass very comfortably for her guests. Bayley had intended to stay for a fortnight's shooting but, pressed to extend his visit, did so willingly and began to think what an admirable notion wedlock was.

The first time he dined at Knapp, Hermione was staying at Vauchurch. On the second, she was present at her parents' table and he found her and her prospects pleasing. If she had been penniless, he would not have considered her, but knowing that her fortune and connections would add to his own status and gratify his father, he set himself to pursue her. Forston and Eleanor were well acquainted with the solidity of his financial background and had heard rumours that Enoch's donations to political funds and carefully chosen public works were likely to lead to a peerage. They encouraged the young man's suit.

When the door had closed behind the maids, Eleanor held her cup poised in her tapered, white hand and sighed. 'Hot-house flowers,' she said plaintively. 'She simply doesn't deserve him.'

Forston was tossing pieces of anchovy toast to the attentive spaniels.

'Not every woman is born to be loved, my dear,' he said.

It could not be denied that winter still held the valley in its grip, but in the glade where Hermione sat on a fallen log, sorting through a lapful of snowdrops, there was a valiant declaration of the spring to come. The furled leaves of cuckoo pint were thrusting through the leaf mould, the chestnut-tinged catkins of an alder dangled from twigs whose sap was rising, tightly budded violets crouched in the shelter of oak-roots, a blackthorn was opening its froth of snowy petals on spiked branches bare of any green.

Hermione laid the snowdrops carefully into the basket by her feet and beat her hands together. She was wearing thin gloves to help her pick the fragile flowers and the cold was making her fingers throb. The sound attracted Ward, who had been roving amongst the points of bluebell spears that were just showing above the ground. She came back to the log, a colourful figure pinned into a vast shawl of predominantly scarlet tartan.

'There are three celandines out,' she said. 'Three little blossoms as brave as can be.'

'I love to see them when they're lining all the paths,' Hermione said. 'I love the way they gleam in the sunlight.'

'Have you collected enough snowdrops now, do you think?'

'Yes.' Hermione looked down at the basket. 'I believe so. These will serve for a wreath and a spray at my waist.'

'Don't you want a garland across your skirt?'

'No. A posy and those in my hair are plenty for my kind of appearance. I don't set myself up for a beauty.'

'You'll be beautiful to someone there,' Ward said archly. 'The only one with eyes to see, in my opinion.'

Hermione gave an open, unashamed laugh that would have caused her mother to accuse her of vulgarity.

'I will,' she said. 'Oh, Wardy, how I long to be with him.'

'I know, my dear, and we'll have you decked like a queen but, mind, you mustn't go breaking your heart if he isn't there. Travel's an uncertain business. He might not arrive in time.'

Hermione reached into her watch-pocket and drew out a tightly folded note. She could have recited its contents with the accuracy of a diligent child repeating her catechism but she smoothed it to read again.

'He says that he and Kate should reach Vauchurch in the early afternoon and will begin for Combehayes directly the greetings are over.'

'Such an awkward journey all in one day,' Ward said, with a smile. 'One day and one reason.'

A cole-tit was gripping the dry, twisted stem of a honeysuckle

257

that writhed around a wild cherry, its small beak darting at the streaked bark. Hermione watched it with a blush on her joyful face. She was suffused by the happy anticipation of her reunion with Frank. They had not announced their betrothal – they would not trouble themselves to ask Forston's permission – because Frank could not endure leaving her to be persecuted by her parents while he sought his health abroad. Indeed, she would be hard-pressed to say when their engagement had begun. It seemed that they had passed from the first, turbulent weeks of severe illness when no coherent words were understood to their future married life being a settled matter without any formal question and acceptance. She had loved him since they were children, never expecting him to see her as anything other than an older cousin, but the long separation when he was being protected from Quinn had taken away the restraints of familiarity. In his vulnerable condition, he had seen her with the clarity Eleanor and Forston lacked and what he valued, he loved. She awaited him with the certainty that his affection had not changed. The shadows that had darkened his world would bring difficulties through the years, she was sure, but she was, as she had always been, unafraid of the Margraves and their passions. Her strength would be his deliverance.

'And, of course,' Ward said, 'there'll be one more person there who'll think you lovely.'

Hermione turned away from the industrious bird. 'No,' she said, 'he finds Papa's wealth lovely and so is prepared to forgive me for not having Mamma's particular attractions.'

'Have you told the master and mistress that Mr Frank is to come?'

'No, nor do I intend to. Let them have the agreeable surprise of encountering their relations unexpectedly.'

At the edge of the trees, a pheasant flew up with a clatter of wings. Ward looked towards the sound and drew back a step.

'Oh, Lord, miss,' she whispered. 'It's himself.'

'Being?'

'That Mr Bayley. I glimpsed him coming through the gate. He has an armful of hyacinths and lilac.'

'Do you think he saw you?'

'No, he was busy with the latch.'

Hermione lifted her basket and stood up. 'Come,' she said. 'We'll make our escape. I've other concerns today.'

She held out her hand and, in perfect understanding, they fled towards the heart of the wood, where the season was more advanced and more flowers bloomed.

In the gallery above the Great Hall at Combehayes Manor, the orchestra was playing with the confident energy that follows the slightly forced élan of the first dance. They had warmed to their task and were no longer reading their much-rehearsed music as they sent a sprightly melody down into the midst of the swirling throng of ball-gowns and tail-coats. The heat from the hundreds of candles in chandeliers and sconces was rising upwards with suffocating force, bringing with it the scent of the floral tributes from conservatories and glass-houses all over the county that were adorning ringlets, skirts and shoulders, be-ringed hands and buttonholes. From his seat by the balustrade, the cellist gazed absently at the dancers weaving through their measure and the older pleasure-seekers lining the walls in companionable clusters, and thought how wise his brother had been to open a market-garden.

Before they had reached the end of their piece, the musicians were disturbed to hear a faltering in the rhythm of the feet below and a murmur that surged the length of the ballroom like the high wave of a spring-tide. Playing determinedly on, they craned to see what had occurred.

Four guests had entered through the ancient iron-studded door and were having their cloaks taken as Dr and Mrs Carmody, the owners of Combehayes, came forward to greet them. One of the men and one of the women were in mourning and these two were the objects of the intrigued glances and shocked comments that were disrupting the cheerful flow of the evening. It was plain that scandal had descended on the house and, from the manner in which those nearest to the arrivals had turned their backs or moved away, it might be that the entertainment would be brought to an abrupt close. The newcomers were being judged and condemned.

Censure did not appear to affect the four, however. They regarded the frowning crowd with equanimity and amused arrogance, returning stares with a boldness that made their accusers waver in their silent denunciation.

Carmody approached them with admiration. He was no stranger to notoriety himself, having married two heiresses from the same family; the first when she was already dying and the second when he was hardly out of black for the first. His own experience had taught him what it was to suffer the criticism of those who did not know the truth behind an action and he was inclined to sympathise with those who had lost their virtue.

'Mrs Lambourne,' he said, bowing. 'Miss Margrave. Mr Margrave. Mr Rencombe. I'm gratified that you were able to reach us after your journey. May I introduce my wife?'

Selena Carmody had been teased by her husband on her last birthday that, now that she was forty, she would instantly become plump and staid but she had found she had neither lost her delight in mischief nor her tendency to find their conventional acquaintances tiresome. The Margraves and their questionable past were fascinating. Carmody had put it to her that she was prepared to leave their guests' innocence undecided if they proved to be piquant company and her denial was unconvincing.

Kate received her welcome with no loss of self-assurance. She had wondered whether confronting her old world would bring back the diffidence that had been her state of mind when she had lived amongst these grieved-for hills. It pleased her that she was sure she could snap her fingers in any censorious face. She did not choose to be intimidated; she would not vex herself by answering enquiries about her name; her spirit was consumed by watching over those she loved.

Her meeting with Olivia had caused her the utmost pain. She had seen at once the degree of lonely suffering that had warped the ardent, wounded nature into the strange complexity that Frank and Philip had warned her to expect. Her own tribulation, with its opportunities for active struggle and purposeful change, had seemed trivial in comparison to the monotonous torment that had made Olivia what she was. Perhaps, she thought, I overestimate her misery. We have been only three hours together. She smiles as she takes Mrs Carmody's hand. She is unembarrassed to wear a white gown when her brother and I are in mourning. A form of happiness is in her eyes. Let it soften and remain.

It was Olivia's doing that they were gathered in this place. An invitation had been sent to Vauchurch and Olivia, eager to parade Frank and Kate, had, to the initial consternation of the Carmodys, accepted on behalf of them all. It was a defiant brandishing of her pride in what she believed Frank had done and so was a matter of anguish on her sister's part. The desolate tale of the deaths of Margrave and Celia, Charlotte and Quinn had been recounted to Kate before she had left Damascus. Sorrow for the waste of the goodness that resides in every soul, goodness thrown away for the sake of avarice, lust and violence had engulfed her but she had remembered the impetuous, amiable boy Frank had been and gave no credence to his guilt. Her fear was that he would embrace the darkness that Margraves could rarely resist. Philip had told her how, since their early youth, Frank had been enthralled by the malevolence within Vauchurch and, during their slow return, she had witnessed his attraction to the sombre melancholy of acknowledged sin. As they stood, each making polite remarks to their hostess, the centre of a bewitched, appalled, almost lecherous attention, she saw him bask in it, revelling in the role of one who causes dread by his misdeeds. If he became wedded to his bleak preference, he would be lost.

Philip was taking his turn in being presented to Mrs Carmody. To Kate's relief, Frank, released momentarily from conversation, scrutinised the dancers with a brief expression of eager hopefulness. He must be searching for Hermione. She surveyed the hall in an attempt to pick out the young woman who had still been a child at their last meeting, interested to learn how the lover's description would match the reality. A face of extraordinary beauty arrested her. The vision was watching the Margrave party in the intervals of lifting her comely head to make comments to the man at her side.

'A glass of punch, Mrs Lambourne?'

'Thank you,' she smiled at Carmody. 'I will but, first, I believe I spy more of my relations. If you'll excuse me . . .'

'I'll have your wine brought to you.'

Kate moved between the outer line of dancers and the chaperones, wall-flowers, fathers and tongue-tied, left-footed men who were grouped against the oak-panelling. The rhythm of the steps that had hesitated at her arrival had regained its steadiness but she felt herself followed by stares and the hushed impertinent use of her maiden name.

She could not help but marvel at her aunt. The loveliness that had brought destruction down upon them all was, if anything, more radiant than it was when she had been sold to Unsworth to facilitate the chase for the faithless wife. She did not doubt that the delicate form was as empty of inner grace as it had ever been.

'Aunt Eleanor,' she said. 'I see you've returned from your travels as I have.'

Eleanor resented the implication. The news of Kate's apparent resurrection had obscurely unnerved her. Though she had forgiven herself with ease for her marital disloyalty, she was severe upon the girl who had fled her husband, considering that it encouraged an independence of thought on the part of daughters that could disturb the even tenor of their parents' days. She had no desire to have Hermione's wishes thrust annoyingly into her notice nor to listen to the complaints of a niece who had, after all, been provided with a very rich man.

Forston saw Eleanor's irritation and, to avoid public argument, spoke before she could reply. 'I trust you're well?' he asked.

'I am well,' Kate said. 'Better than could be expected. But, really, Uncle, I don't think you should use the word "trust" in my hearing. It reminds me of the past.'

Forston flushed. His part in arranging Kate's marriage was the one unsavoury action of his callous life that could brush against his conscience like the settling of frost, chilling him into a restive dissatisfaction with himself. It was not her supposed drowning that made him fretful, for a storm was accident or Fate and had meant the end of her trials; it was his willingness to deliver a lamb into the jaws of a wolf. He had sat in Unsworth's study, knowing him to be a libertine, and set forth the terms of the contract as if the gentle girl had been the cargo of an East Indiaman, aware as he did so of the depravity she would have to endure. His heart had not yet been hardened, his corruption had not been complete and the tenderness his wrongdoing had left in his memory had never quite healed.

A drawnout note from the gallery marked the end of the quadrille. Carmody, intending to avoid the obvious ostracising of the Margraves that could occur if they found themselves standing in grim isolation with the multitude crushed into the farthest side of the hall, signalled to the musicians to continue. A waltz struck up and the majority of the breathless, perspiring dancers put a hand to their throats, laughed, exclaimed and swung back onto the floor where they were joined by several couples from the onlookers, who had felt the years leaving them as they were infected by the gaiety of the lilting refrains.

Forston, having it borne upon him that the lamb he had sacrificed had returned with a distinct resemblance to Charlotte and anxious to avoid unpleasantness, offered Eleanor his arm and they were swept into the circling swarm. Kate observed their escape with contempt and accepted the silver cup of punch that a footman had brought her. Philip and Frank were approaching and she waited for them to reach her as the steam from cinnamon, nutmeg and brandy, claret and lemon rose in a pungent cloud from the cup.

'We are,' Philip said, coming to her side, 'as we anticipated, causing something of a spectacle. Are you ignoring it manfully?'

'I'm ashamed to say I'm playing up to it. I've just said "Boo!" to my uncle and aunt.'

Frank had been glowering at the dancers and now turned to his sister. 'Have you seen Hermione?' he asked. 'She must be here.'

'I don't know what she looks like.'

'I told you. She's perfection.'

'Yes, my dear. Shall we stroll here and there seeking her? And where's Olivia?'

Frank gazed around vaguely.

'She went in pursuit of soda-water,' Philip said. 'She seems quite at home.'

'Then we will make our progress through the adoring multitude in search of our cousin. Come, no bashful looks.'

The alcove beside the stairs had been decked by a table laden with refreshments and delicacies to invigorate those guests who could not last until supper without sustenance. Having found a soda-syphon and filled a glass, Olivia was eating preserved cherries and frightening nervous young men. Her reclusive life had not made her shy and she saw no reason why she should not converse freely with those others who were browsing amongst the sweet-meats and potted shrimps that covered the linen cloth. The uncompromising nature of her views on the abilities of the dancers, their choice of finery and their incivility towards her family soon had her standing unconcernedly alone. She refilled her dish with candied fruit and, after emptying her glass, noticed that Bayley was helping himself to a ham sandwich as the manservant behind the table was pouring him more champagne.

'Mr Bayley,' she said. 'Good evening. Aren't you waltzing?'

Alarmed that she might be hankering for a partner, he said firmly that he had no intention to dance. He had met Olivia at Knapp, when Hermione had enticed her over to admire a litter of puppies, and found himself inadvertently backing away, almost oversetting a bowl of port-wine jelly that was melting in the increasing heat of the room. It was clear that he had already had more wine than was advisable and Olivia, comparing him to Frank, scorned his vanity in aspiring to the hand of one destined to be a Margrave.

'Have you been introduced to my brother?' she asked. 'Or my sister? She has returned from the dead.'

'So I've heard. Your family leads an eventful existence, Miss Margrave.'

'We do and it's like to continue. You didn't answer me, Mr Bayley. Have you encountered my brother?'

'I have not.' He drained the glass that had been filled for him and passed it back to be replenished.

'Then perhaps we should go in pursuit of him. He wishes to explain to you that you must not think of my cousin. He will marry her himself. It's quite an agreed thing.'

Bayley's face, reddened by wine, blanched then returned to its raddled hue. He despised eccentricity of conduct and any forthrightness that did not accord with his own opinions.

'Is it?' he said spitefully. 'Is it? We'll see who wins. We'll see who's stronger.'

Olivia leant her head to one side enquiringly. 'Are you being threatening?' she asked. 'Is that wise? Surely you know why Frank's arrival caused such a – what shall I say? – *discreet commotion*? My uncle must have told you his history?'

Bayley snatched his glass from the outstretched arm of the footman and turned on his heel. He paused on the edge of the dance-floor, glaring this way and that and, catching sight of Eleanor and Forston, strode into the midst of the whirl to intercept them.

'I must speak to you,' he said.

'Then come out of the dance.'

Forston was displeased to be the focus of interested eyes again. He led Eleanor and Bayley to an unoccupied space by the wall.

'Well, sir?' he demanded.

'I've been talking to your niece. Miss Olivia. It was disturbing.'

'You've met her before. Did you expect sense?'

'She warned me off Miss Forston. Apparently, there's an understanding between her and Margrave.'

Eleanor gave an exasperated sigh and fanned herself.

'Nothing of the kind,' Forston said, 'but . . .' he stopped to consider, 'it would be best to have an end to delay. Am I right to suspect that you were planning to make Hermione an offer tonight?'

'I was, but I didn't anticipate the rest of your family making an entrance.'

'Your tone is discourteous, Mr Bayley,' Eleanor said.

'I beg your pardon, Mrs Forston. I'm considerably agitated.'

She bowed in acceptance and Forston, weighing Bayley's level of intoxication against the danger of Hermione meeting Frank before she was betrothed, decided that he was still acceptably near sobriety.

'I urge you to speak to my daughter immediately,' he said, 'before there can be interference. I suggest you go to the conservatory. It's too early for many others to be there and if you don't have solitude, you must take her onto the terrace. I'll bring her to you.'

Leaving the suitor to find his own way to the trysting-place, Forston mounted the wide stairs and followed the passage to the library. The door was ajar and he could hear the low laughter of friends who are at ease together coming from the lamp-lit interior as he approached.

Hermione was perching on the edge of a pedestal table, listening to her host's elder daughter give a vivacious account of the routing of a stout colonel, who had thought to woo her during a disastrously muddy fox-hunt three weeks last Tuesday. Mahala Carmody had the observation of her godmother, the artist Philobeth Alleyn, coupled with the wicked humour of her namesake, her father's first wife, and had almost been able to distract Hermione from her fervent anticipation of her lover's arrival.

On seeing her father Hermione rose, believing herself to be about to be accused of concealing the imminence of the Margraves.

'Mr Forston,' Mahala said, perfectly aware of his disapproval of Frank, 'I hope you've come to ask me to waltz.'

'Don't try to persuade me that your card isn't full,' he said, 'for you'll be a deceiver. My dear,' he turned to Hermione, 'may I have a private word?'

'Let me leave you to yourselves.' Mahala gathered up the bouquet she had laid on a canterbury and, giving her companion the merest hint of a wink, she went lightly towards the dance.

Mahala's lilies reminded Forston of his vexation on having

265

Hermione enter the carriage for the ball ornamented with humble snowdrops instead of the forced flowers that Bayley had left at the house after a fruitless search for his quarry in the woods. Remembering that coaxing would further his ends more satisfactorily than issuing orders, he endeavoured to remain benevolent.

'My dear,' he repeated, 'I know you to have a kind heart and a sensible head. I'm here on an errand that requires you to make use of both. To your great advantage, your mamma and I think.'

Hermione was watching him intently. 'And the errand is?' she said.

'Mr Bayley wishes to speak to you. He's pacing the conservatory, a victim of his honourable and avid feelings.'

'Is he, indeed, poor soul?' She spoke blandly. Papa has heard that Frank has come home, she thought. He relies upon me pledging myself to this Manchester man before the news reaches me. I have suffered Bayley's attentions with politeness and so must be halfway to the altar. Mamma is always foolish but Papa should be able to tell when a deal will not be closed. Very well, let us have this over.

'I won't make him linger,' she said.

They walked back towards the stairs. The waltz had changed into a polka and a rapid, spinning gaiety hid the floor with streaming gowns.

'There's no need to accompany me,' she said, as they reached the last step. 'I'm not one to run away.'

She went alone through the supper room, the morning room and so into the fern-scented conservatory. Lanterns of blue, crimson and amber glass had been placed beside the wrought-iron and wicker chairs, that were paired amongst the arching foliage, and their gem-like light glimmered on the fountain that plashed before the double-doors onto the terrace.

Bayley had been staring out into the night, trying to force his fuddled mind to clear. He heard the soft shush of her skirts on the stone floor and faced her. With a pang, he saw she neither carried nor wore any flowers of his. He did not love her but he believed he did. Some attribute of hers that he could not name made him feel comfortable and praiseworthy as if he were greater in her company than alone. Until this evening, he had assumed that when he, with all that he had to offer, made his proposal, she would accept. He no longer had faith that her dear, clever eyes would look on him

266

kindly and he dared not lose her. His needs had always been supplied, his whims pandered to; he did not know how to submit to disappointment.

'I am come, Mr Bayley,' she said.

Her composure riled him. This tribe of Margraves had an assurance that should not sit with their ill-repute. She was a plain girl who should have been flattered by his interest. Nervousness fed his irritation.

'You wished to talk to me,' she prompted, pitying his awkwardness.

In the ballroom, Frank was making his way around the edge of the polka. He had seen Hermione descending the stairs but had been too distant from her to be noticed amongst the throng. She had passed into another room, walking purposefully as though she must discharge a duty. He pursued her.

Advancing along the hectic dancers, he sensed that the atmosphere had changed. The moment for spurning him had slipped by without being grasped. Music, playfulness and high spirits had overtaken the assembly and a sudden return to severity would only seem false. Acceptance would follow and his sins be forgotten. He was glad for Hermione's sake.

She was not amongst the supper-tables. A glow from an open door led him into the empty morning room. The jaunty lift of the polka was quieter and he thought he heard a raised voice in the conservatory beyond. The frond of a palm obscured his view as he entered the hothouse. He heard Hermione speak.

'Let me go, sir,' she said. 'Why lengthen this? I have only to call out.'

Frank stepped forward. Startled, Bayley turned towards him. He had Hermione's wrist clasped in his hand and his sharp movement jerked her arm.

'No need to call,' Frank said. His eyes, fierce within the austerity of his face, were fixed on Bayley's. 'Do as she bids you. Let her go.'

Bayley stared, transfixed.

'I am Margrave,' Frank said levelly. 'You will know of me.'

Bayley was used to the casual cruelties imposed by his class on those beneath them but he had no experience of the deliberate visiting of extreme violence by one of his peers on another. This man bore with him the shadow that was Vauchurch and the bleak barbarity of the desert; he wore mourning for those he had killed.

Margrave was young in years and old in evil. Dread made Bayley tighten his grip on Hermione's wrist.

'I don't think he means to hurt me,' Hermione said, 'but then, I've grown tired of those who don't mean to hurt me and do so just the same.'

'He will stop now.'

Bayley looked at each. They spoke calmly as if nothing untoward were occurring. The Margraves were not of his world. He wanted the frivolous geniality of the ballroom. His fingers opened slowly and Hermione drew her hand free, nursing the weal where he had ground her bangle into her flesh.

She watched Frank. He was creating fear by the power of his reputation and he found it entrancing. The three stood in silence. The dusk lit by points of ruby, sapphire and golden brilliance gathered about them. Footsteps crossed the stone. Forston, warned that Frank had gone this way, had come to prevent the thwarting of his plans. Eleanor followed in his wake.

'Mr Bayley,' Forston said. 'May I propose my congratulations?'

'Ah,' Frank raised his eyebrows. 'This was an offer. A curious means of procedure, I have to say, Mr Bayley. And all while under a misapprehension. Miss Forston has already given her word to me.'

'You have no right—' Forston began.

'No right?' Frank spoke with unconcealed contempt. 'There's been little in our family that was right but there was always one amongst us who knew what path the heart should take. She will be mistress of Vauchurch and perhaps we'll have virtue enough to learn from her.' He took Hermione's hand gently in his own. 'Can you be ready this day week?' he asked.

'I can, my love,' she said.

Epilogue

Kate sat on the carriage-seat opposite Philip and Frank. They were almost at the church. The wedding would soon begin. Hermione, confident and loving, and Olivia, glorious in her joy, would be driving down the sheltered, violet-lined lane from Knapp, white-satin ribbons on the coachman's whip. There was no shade of Kate's bridal-ride in this journey, but tenderness for her brother's tentative relinquishing of guilt made her guard him as she would a fragile child, anxious that grief would not touch him again.

The landau drew up at the gate. As they walked down the path, they saw the wild daffodils, that fluttered in delicate abundance on the turf, gleam in the strengthening sun. Philip led Kate to her pew and took his place as groomsman at Frank's side.

Frank waited with a yearning that was a pain within his breast. In this last moment, he believed she would not come; she would realise he did not deserve her; Vauchurch would be abandoned to its ghosts.

There were horses on the road, steps on the path. The guests rose. He turned and Hermione walked towards him, bringing the bright warmth of spring.

The Kindly Ones

In Greek myth, the Furies, who wreaked vengeance on wrong-doers, were also known as 'the Kindly Ones'.

Characters from the Oresteia and their equivalents in the novel

Agamemnon	–	Leopold Margrave
Clytemnestra	–	Charlotte Margrave
Orestes	–	Frank Margrave
Iphigenia	–	Kate Margrave
Electra	–	Olivia Margrave
Helen	–	Eleanor Forston
Menelaus	–	Gerard Forston
Hermione	–	Hermione Forston
Paris	–	Paul Eliot
Cassandra	–	Celia Eliot
Aegisthus	–	Quinn Holman
Pylades	–	Philip Rencombe
Atreus	–	Henry Margrave
Thyestes	–	Jack Margrave
Pelopia	–	Maria Margrave, née Holman

Place names

Mycenae	–	Vauchurch
Sparta	–	Knapp
Tauris	–	Damascus

The imprisonment of Frank Margrave and Philip Rencombe after being discovered as disguised Christians wearing shoes in a mosque is based upon the punishment of Henry Anson and John Fox Strangways in 1828. Kate Margrave's escape to Damascus was inspired by the life of Jane Digby.

The unfolding events in Greek myth, matched by the corresponding actions in the novel

GREECE

Paris, a prince of Troy, arrives in Sparta. He falls in love with Helen, wife of the Spartan ruler, Menelaus. While Menelaus is away, Paris flees with Helen.

Menelaus and Agamemnon gather an army to pursue Paris and Helen to Troy and take her back by force.

Agamemnon's fleet is becalmed by Artemis, who demands the sacrifice of his daughter, Iphigenia. She, his son, Orestes, and wife, Clytemnestra, are sent for on the pretence that Iphigenia is to be married to Achilles.

DORSET
1855

Paul Eliot, a wealthy merchant from British India, goes to Knapp in Dorset to stay with a fellow merchant, Gerard Forston. He becomes enamoured of Forston's wife, Eleanor. While Forston is away on business, Eliot and Eleanor flee.

Forston and his more powerful brother, Leopold Margrave, go to London to apprehend the guilty pair. Finding themselves unsuccessful, they determine to take revenge by sailing to India where they intend to crush the Eliots' business empire and retrieve Eleanor.

Margrave wants to improve his strength by an alliance with a rich, elderly, debauched nabob, Bryce Unsworth. The nabob demands to marry Margrave's elder daughter, Kate. Margrave agrees and sends for Kate, allowing her to believe she is to marry Unsworth's nephew. Margrave plays upon her dutiful nature by insisting the marriage is necessary to save the family from the shame of bankruptcy.

Clytemnestra discovers the plan to sacrifice her daughter and tries to prevent it. Agamemnon insists upon death and Iphigenia agrees for the sake of her father's expedition. She is led to the sacrificial altar. Artemis spirits her away. Clytemnestra departs in bitterness against her husband.

It is only at the altar that Kate and Charlotte discover Margrave's deception. Charlotte, in fury against him, objects but he is insistent and Kate sacrifices herself for the sake of the family. She is married and sails with Unsworth for India, ahead of Margrave and Forston. News of the ship sinking with no survivors reaches Charlotte.

1860

Clytemnestra has never forgiven Agamemnon for the sacrifice of their daughter. While the army is at Troy, she has taken her husband's cousin, Aegisthus, for her lover.

Charlotte has never forgiven Margrave for Kate's marriage and drowning. He and Forston are still in India. They have survived the Mutiny and are increasing their possessions and trade in its wake. Charlotte has taken her unscrupulous cousin, Quinn Holman, as her lover.

Agamemnon returns in triumph from Troy with Paris's sister, Cassandra, as his slave. Clytemnestra welcomes him with false joy and tells him a feast to celebrate his victory over the dead Paris is being prepared.

Margrave returns to Vauchurch. He has been rendered more cruel by the violence of his experiences in India. He brings with him Eliot's sister, Celia, who has been compelled to become his mistress after the ruin of her family. Eliot, denied shelter by Margrave and Forston whilst fleeing from mutineers, has been killed in the uprising. Eleanor has been taken back by Forston and the pair are returning to England and their neglected daughter, Hermione. Charlotte pretends to welcome Margrave.

Agamemnon enters his house across a crimson carpet. Cassandra, prophetically seeing blood, cries out but is thought to be crazed by grief.

Agamemnon had asked for a bath. While he is bathing, Clytemnestra nets him by throwing a mantle about his head and Aegisthus murders him with an axe. Cassandra laments him and is killed by the queen.

Clytemnestra and Aegisthus are married and take control of the kingdom.

Clytemnestra has never loved her two younger children, Electra and Orestes. Electra realises that Aegisthus intends to kill Orestes before he is old enough to avenge Agamemnon. She charges a faithful servant to flee with Orestes. They are given refuge by Strophius, King of Phocis. Orestes and Strophius's son, Pylades, become inseparable friends. Electra is left to watch over her father's tomb.

Celia recognises the danger to Margrave from his wife and Quinn. She is torn between her own hatred of him and the wish to prevent harm.

Margrave asks for a bath and a fire in the bathroom as he is no longer used to the British climate. Charlotte and Quinn put oleander on the fire and Margrave is poisoned by the fumes. Quinn murders Celia. The two bodies are found together, giving rise to a scandal that supports the appearance of accident.

Charlotte and Quinn marry. Quinn is resentful that the estate will pass to Margrave's young son, Frank, when he reaches his majority.

Olivia Margrave does not trust her mother and stepfather and is conscious of the benefit there would be to Quinn if Frank did not reach twenty-one. She persuades an old family friend, Rencombe, whose son, Philip, has become Frank's bosom friend at boarding-school, to invite Frank to spend the holidays at their home. Charlotte, who wishes to be rid of Frank's presence but cannot bring herself to destroy her own child, agrees to the separation. Olivia nurses an obsessive love for her father.

When they reach manhood, Orestes and Pylades return to Mycenae for revenge, bearing an urn they say contains Orestes's ashes. They spend the night at Agamemnon's tomb, conducting rites for the dead. At dawn, Electra finds them there and breaks down at the news of her brother's supposed death. Orestes then knows her and reveals himself.

Shortly before his majority, Frank, who has been told by Olivia of her belief that Margrave's death was murder, and Philip return to Vauchurch. Frank has revealed his bitterness towards his mother to Philip but not his intention of taking revenge. Before they have gone to the house, they meet Olivia at their father's graveside. She does not recognise Frank at first and then is ecstatic at his arrival.

The men go to the palace and are welcomed for bringing the message that Orestes is dead. They kill Clytemnestra and Aegisthus.

They go to the house and are given a hypocritical welcome. After so long an absence, Charlotte has lost her desire to protect Frank. She and Quinn want to prevent him coming into his inheritance. Returning to his home rouses old resentments and disappointments in Frank. He is half-mad with hatred of Charlotte and Quinn. Whilst riding beside their open carriage on the precipitous road to Vauchurch, he crowds his horse against theirs in a fury during an argument. The carriage overturns and falls down the steep slope. Charlotte and Quinn are killed.

Orestes is overcome by horror and remorse at his mother's grave. He raves madly or lies like a dead man, tended by Electra and Pylades. No one

Frank is overcome by horror and remorse. He does not know whether he truly intended to do harm. Falling ill, he raves madly or lies like a dead man, tended else will eat with him or sleep under the same roof. Some elders of the city want him stoned to death to avert the anger of the gods but most vote for banishment. He is cast out of Mycenae.

Orestes reproaches Apollo for spurring him on to murder. Apollo tells him to go into the wilderness, then to steal the image of Artemis from the temple at Tauris before being called before a council of the gods that might absolve him of his crime.

Iphigenia had been taken to Tauris to be priestess of Artemis. Orestes and Pylades, claiming to be shipwrecked sailors, are brought before her after being found lurking round the temple. It is her duty to sacrifice them but, learning who they are and what has happened in her family, she determines to save them.

Iphigenia has Orestes and Pylades taken to prison where she steals in at night to plan their escape. She tells the King that the captives are so stained

by Olivia and Philip. The deaths are accepted as an accident yet there is suspicion and he is shunned. He is advised to go to a warmer climate for his health.

Frank travels to the eastern Mediterranean, hoping to derive stoicism from the classical sites and salvation and forgiveness in the Holy Land.

Kate did not drown when the ship foundered. She had loathed her husband and his depraved habits. Unable to face living as his wife, she had fled ashore just as their ship was to set sail on the Red Sea, leaving Unsworth dead drunk. He never knew that she had left and she did not know of the sinking. She believes that he is still alive and so could claim her if her whereabouts were revealed. The sale of her jewels lets her live in modest comfort in Damascus, under an assumed name. The desert appeals to her religious sense.

Frank and Philip are imprisoned in Damascus after being discovered wearing shoes in a mosque. Kate hears of the plight of two English gentlemen with guilt that they would pollute the temple if they are not ritually cleansed in the sea. She takes them to the shore where all three flee by ship.

and visits them. Their relationship is revealed. She learns of the deaths of her husband and parents and Frank's part in the latter. She returns with him to Dorset.

They take the image of Artemis to Athens where Orestes pleads for mercy before the gods. The votes cast are equal on each side until Athene votes for pardon. The Furies sink howling into the earth. Orestes returns to Mycenae and is welcomed. He marries Hermione, daughter of Menelaus and Helen, after winning her in mortal combat from the son of Achilles to whom she was betrothed.

Frank is unsure whether the suspicion against him will cause him to be shunned. They go to a ball to test the waters. At first, acceptance and disapproval are equal but acceptance triumphs. Forston has been trying to force an unwanted marriage on Hermione but she will have none of it. She has grown into a strong and loving young woman, capable of dispelling the violence that hangs over the family. Frank and Hermione marry.

Principal sources

The Oresteian Trilogy by Aeschylus (525–c. 426BC)
Classic Myths and Legends by A.R. Hope Moncrieff